Exclusive

A. O'Connor

POOLBEG

PRAISE FOR *THIS MODEL LIFE*

"Could A. O'Connor be the new Patricia Scanlan? This debut novel is an entertaining blend of high gloss and Dublin grit" – *Image*

"Read this debut novel because they'll all be talking about it" *Herald*

"You should invest in some more copies of this first novel, as there's the possibility that it may become a collector's item" – *Ireland On Sunday*

"A. O'Connor's pot-boiler . . . is certain to be a hit around the swimming pool this summer" – *Sunday Independent*

"I would recommend this book. There was a lot of substance to the story and interesting observations on how fickle the world of glamour and business can be" – *Woman's Way*

"Quite the little page-turner – if you're looking for that plane-read to distract you on your journey – this might just be it" – *Bibliofemme*

"It is definitely a book to bring on holiday, and it has a cast of characters that will keep you guessing to the very last page" – *Irish Emigrant*

"Features-driven moneyed people going to openings and launches" – *Social & Personal*

About the Author

A graduate of NUI Maynooth and Trinity College Dublin, the author has worked in marketing for several years and lives in Dublin and Meath.

A. O'Connor's novel *This Model Life* was published by Poolbeg in 2005.

Published 2006
by Poolbeg Press Ltd
123 Grange Hill, Baldoyle
Dublin 13, Ireland
E-mail: poolbeg@poolbeg.com

© A. O'Connor 2006

The moral right of the author has been asserted.

Typesetting, layout, design © Poolbeg Press Ltd.

13 5 7 9 10 8 6 4 2

A catalogue record for this book is available from the British Library.

ISBN 1-84223-239-8
ISBN 978-1-84223-239-2

Typeset by Type Design in Palatino 9.5/13pt
Printed by Litografia Rosés, S.A, Spain

www.poolbeg.com

Acknowledgements

A big thank-you to the staff at Poolbeg: Kieran, David, Lynda, Niamh and Connor. Paula Campbell, who's had an amazing and very busy year but still manages to be at the end of an email. Gaye Shortland, who makes the whole editorial process a pleasure, and whose guidance and attention to detail is much appreciated. Thanks to all the booksellers for their support. A big thank-you to my family including Monica, Con and Adam. Deirdre Heavey at RTÉ. Janice Scanlon for her input. Thank you Orla, Sue and Justin. And thank you to Gina.

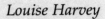

Louise Harvey

CHAPTER 1

Kathryn Foy had told the security men on the door to be extra vigilant that night. She knew Affidavit were playing at The Point, and they always tended to come into Exclusive after playing a gig. She knew this was an open secret and lots of their fans would be trying every trick in the book to get into the club.

The club was established as the most exclusive in Dublin. It strictly catered to the in-crowd and was members only. She had been manager there for five years, and it was under her expert guidance that it had become *The* Place, and stayed being *The* Place. There were a lot of pretenders to the throne, but none could overtake Exclusive. Everyone knew or pretended to know Kathryn, and she was constantly being tempted away to manage other clubs.

Kathryn liked to be at the door herself for part of every night. Now she took up position as a group of young women, all glammed up, walked up the steps to the large open double Georgian doors.

"Sorry, girls, members only," she said.

"It's okay. I'm a friend of Kathryn's," said the tall girl at the front confidently, as she tried to walk past her.

Smiling to herself, Kathryn stood her ground and asked, "Really, where do you know her from?"

The girl looked annoyed. "We were in school together," she said haughtily.

Kathryn wondered if she should take that as a compliment – she guessed the girl to be twenty, which would make her ten years younger than she was herself. "Sorry, as I said, members only."

"You had better get out of my way and let me in, or I'll report you!" The girl was becoming angry.

Kathryn had people getting angry with her on a nightly basis. It didn't bother her in the least, and she knew she had three well-trained security men behind her if any situation started to get ugly.

"That's Kathryn Foy herself!" hissed one of the friends. "I've seen her photo in *Hi Life* magazine!"

Embarrassment mixed in with the girl's anger.

"Nice try." Kathryn smiled coldly.

The girl gave Kathryn a filthy look and the group trooped back down the steps and walked off. As they got to the bottom of the street, the tall girl turned around and shouted: "It's true what everyone says about you! You *are* a bitch!"

Kathryn turned around and raised her eyes to heaven to the security men, who all started to laugh.

Her mobile rang and, seeing Cathal Fitzgerald's number come up, she went into the reception area to answer.

"Cathal, how did tonight go?"

"Great, thanks. We're thinking of coming over."

"No problem at all, I have a table reserved for you."

"Thanks, Kathryn!" He hung up.

Kathryn took out her walkie-talkie and radioed up to a hostess. "Affidavit will be here shortly – make sure their table in the members' lounge is cordoned off and get some champagne ready to open when they arrive."

She walked back out to the front door. "Pierre, Affidavit will have their own security with them, but I want you to stay with them as well – make sure nobody annoys them."

"Sure, Kathryn."

*   *   *

The Point theatre was packed to capacity. The crowd had been worked up to a crescendo of excitement and their wild applause could be heard backstage where the four band-members of Affidavit were making their way to the dressing-rooms as the production team clapped. It was the last night of a two-month gruelling tour that had taken them to some of the biggest stadiums around Europe.

Cathal emptied a bottle of water over his head to cool down. "Your voice was on top form tonight," he said to his cousin James, the lead singer.

"I'm not so sure – it's strained after all the concerts."

"The crowd was roaring so much nobody cared what we sounded like!" laughed Cathal.

Matt, their chief security guard, came up to them. "Lads, some of the staff here would like you to sign some stuff for them."

Cathal watched as James, Seán and Rob promptly disappeared into their dressing-rooms. He too was longing to have a shower and take off for a night's hard partying but . . . "Er, sure, no problem," he said, aware the staff would delay him for a good twenty minutes.

Nevertheless he bounded over to them, took a pen and started to sign their souvenirs.

While he chatted and signed, his mobile rang. He flipped it open.

"Cathal, how'd it go?" It was Sylvia Henderson, their manager.

"Great! Just signing some stuff here for the fans!" Even after nine years together as a band including five at the top, he still always tried to impress their record bosses.

"You can give me a full report tomorrow. You and the guys are off out on the town now, I suppose?"

He could hear the note of warning in her voice. "Well, yeah, it is the end of the tour . . ."

"I'm not saying you don't deserve it. I'm just saying take it easy, okay? Try and stay out of trouble. And no pics!"

"Okay, talk to you tomorrow." Cathal flipped his phone closed.

James came out of his dressing-room with his fiancée, Donna. "Are you not even showered yet?" he shouted over at Cathal.

"Thanks, folks, see you again!" Cathal said to the staff and headed towards his dressing-room.

Seán emerged from his dressing-room, looking irritated. "Oh, for God's sake, get a move on, Cathal! It's getting late."

"Why don't *you* go talk to the fans *and* talk to Sylvia at the same time while I have my shower for a change!" Cathal snapped as he walked past.

"Get off your pedestal, Cathal!" said Seán. "You should hear yourself! The fans, the fans, the fans!"

James came over to them quickly, well aware of the antagonism that was brewing between Cathal and Seán and not wanting to see it bubble to the surface. "Can we argue later and get a move on?" he urged.

Cathal went in and slammed the dressing-room door behind him. It annoyed him that the others never really made an effort for the people who had put them where they were. He was well aware that compared to the others he wasn't as talented. James was a great singer, Seán a brilliant drummer and Rob a gifted guitarist and great songwriter. Okay, but he more than made up for that with sheer hard work as most of the organisation was left to him. He was the one who had to sort out the problems and set the agenda. Not that he minded – in fact he loved doing it. He was thirty-three and as enthusiastic about the band as ever. But Seán's comments were beginning to really annoy him.

"Right, there's a large group of fans outside the back," said Matt, "so we're going to quickly make our way through it to the two waiting cars."

"That means no stopping to sign autographs, Cathal!" warned Seán.

"Cathal, James and Donna, you come with me in the front car," ordered Matt. "Seán and Rob, you can go in the back with the other security. Where are we going to?"

Cathal looked at the others. "So Exclusive's okay with everyone? I already spoke to Kathryn Foy and she's expecting us." Everyone nodded. He called to the production team: "We're going to Exclusive! Just show your production passes to Kathryn Foy when you get there. Phone me if you've any problems getting in!" He turned to the others and smiled. "Right, let's go."

*   *   *

"Why do you let Seán get to you?" James asked Cathal, as they sat in the back of the Mercedes while it swept through the Dublin night streets. James was holding Donna's hand, which proudly showed off an enormous diamond on an engagement ring.

"You should just ignore him," urged Donna.

Cathal liked Donna a lot. She was a model whom James had met while they were shooting a video for the third album three years ago. James had fallen head over heels with her and they had been inseparable ever since.

"I do ignore him," Cathal responded.

"No, you let him get to you tonight," said James.

"Seán Kelly doesn't bother me in the least. I couldn't give a damn about him, or anybody else for that matter," Cathal defended himself.

* * *

Tony O'Brien finished off the last of his pint in Cocoon. He'd had a very difficult day at the office and had hit the pub straight after with a gang from work. He looked at his watch. It was after midnight on a Friday night and he didn't feel like going home yet.

"Anyone fancy going on to a club?" asked Tony.

They all readily agreed.

"Better just check it with the missus." He reached into his pocket for his mobile and headed outside to make the call, as his workmates jeered at him, singing the old 80's song: *"Don't Want To Be Under Your Thumb Forever!"*

"Fuck off!" he shouted, laughing he went out into the street.

He dialled home and waited for the ringing tone to be answered.

"Hello?"

"Hi, Nic, what you up to?"

"Just trying to catch up with one of my patients' file. I have to have it completed by Monday." Nicole was a psychotherapist with her own practice.

"I'm sorry I didn't phone you earlier – it's been a really difficult day."

"Did you get many sales?"

"I nearly lost a big client – they had a cheaper offer from another magazine. I've never done such a hard sell in my life. I was on my knees begging them down the phone not to leave us, while all the other ad staff were gathered around me egging me on. I even started singing "Don't Give Up On Us, Baby" down the phone to their marketing manager!"

"Really?" Nicole started laughing. "Poor you! It worked though?"

"For now. I promised to bring them out for dinner next week as part of the bargain. I *hate* advertising sales!"

"I know, I know," she soothed. "Where are you now?"

"Outside Cocoon. We were going to go on to a club, if that's all right?"

"Of course. Just don't wake me up coming home!"

"Course I won't," he said and blew a kiss down the phone.

When he joined his friends, they were still singing the same song. "Right, lads, it's on for Disneyland!" he said, smiling brightly.

Tony worked for *Irish Property*, a trade magazine aimed at developers, and had been working in the advertising department for a year. He had applied to write articles for them lots of times, but they had declined. He was thirty-four and it was eleven years since he had graduated with

7

a degree in journalism. He had drifted through a range of media jobs, never getting the real journalism career he craved. He had been with Nicole for five years. They had met through mutual friends at a house party. It was love at first sight and they quickly moved in together. He had drifted into doing some promotion work, which had led him into advertising sales. Some people are natural sales people, Tony definitely was not. He felt it soul-destroying to be in a job he found so unrewarding. Every so often he would manage to get a temporary job as a journalist with some publication on a month's contract. But nothing permanent ever materialised. So he was continually sending his CV off to any job in journalism that came up.

Grafton Street was packed with socialisers. Tony loved the buzz of Dublin on a Friday night.

"Where to?" asked Malcolm, as they walked towards Stephen's Green.

"Will we try Exclusive?" suggested Tony.

Malcolm laughed. "Let's not waste our time. We'll never get in there."

"You forget, I am a member of the National Union of Journalists, and I have my member card to prove it. One flash of that at the door, and we'll be shown straight into the members' lounge!"

"Yeah, sure. Like Kathryn Foy is going to fall for that!" said Malcolm.

"Well, look, if we don't try we won't know, okay?"

As they walked along Stephen's Green to Exclusive, Tony began to feel nervous. He knew how hard it was, in fact, to get into the place and now he realised he had set himself up to look stupid in front of his colleagues.

As they approached the steps to the front entrance of Exclusive he noticed his friends were falling back into single file behind him. Obviously, all the talking was going to be left to him. He saw Kathryn Foy standing at the top of the steps, flanked by two security. She was slim and tall, with blonde hair, and was wearing a black trouser suit. He couldn't remember if she had been a model or not, but she certainly looked good enough to be one. He had seen her photo in magazines a lot, and occasionally saw her walking around Grafton Street. She had a reputation for being very cold and businesslike. As he climbed the steps, he hid his nerves.

"Good evening, gentlemen, can I help you?" Kathryn fixed Tony with a steely stare.

Tony produced his NUJ card and flashed it at her. "Just out for a couple of drinks!" Kathryn knew most of the journalists in town, and she didn't recognise this one. "We're full tonight, guys – maybe come back another time?"

Tony felt humiliation sweep him as he heard Malcolm snigger behind him. "But I work at RTÉ, and these –" he pointed to his workmates, "are a team over from the BBC doing a documentary."

Kathryn raised her eyes to heaven, confident the story was untrue. At that moment her phone rang and she saw it was Cathal Fitzgerald's number.

"Hi, Cathal, where are you?"

"Just coming around the Green now – can you make sure the coast is clear for us?"

"No problem, see you in a moment."

She saw a few possible Affidavit fans hanging around and quickly looked around for any potential dangers.

"So I really think, in the interest of good relations between your club and the BBC . . ." Tony was droning on.

She didn't want these four guys in the way

complaining while Affidavit arrived and, worse, blocking their smooth entry into Exclusive. She gave them a quick look over and decided they seemed like professionals. "All right, guys, you can go in tonight. But ring ahead in future. Now, get in quickly and please don't block up the reception area."

Smiling brightly, Tony led his party in.

As the two black Mercedes pulled up outside Exclusive, Kathryn was waiting on the footpath with two security. Very quickly, the cars doors opened and the band stepped out with their security. There was some excitement and calls from some of the passers-by on the street.

"Hi, guys, just follow me through," said Kathryn.

She quickly walked up the steps. The entourage followed her. As soon as everyone was inside, Exclusive's security closed the front doors of the club.

"I heard the concert went great," complimented Kathryn.

"To be honest, we're just exhausted after the tour, and glad it's over," said Cathal.

"I can imagine. Donna, you look really well." She had known Donna for years as she used to come to the club as a model before she hooked up with James Fitzgerald.

"Thanks," Donna smiled.

"Is my wife here yet?" asked Rob.

"Yes, Heidi is upstairs at the table I've reserved for you," said Kathryn. "Will we head up?"

At the top of the stairs, a security man opened the door and they entered the club. The place was packed, the music pumping loudly. An Affidavit song was playing, as Kathryn had organised in advance. With the help of security she had previously positioned, she cut through the crowd, leading them into the members' lounge.

This was why Cathal loved Exclusive. Not only was the club spectacular and opulent, dripping in luxury, but Kathryn Foy knew what they needed and made sure they got it. Nobody bothered them in Exclusive.

The members' lounge was large and much more sedate than outside in the main crowd. They headed over to the main table that had been reserved for them, where Heidi had been sitting talking to a hostess. Champagne was immediately opened and glasses handed around.

"If you need anything at all, just give me a shout," said Kathryn, and then she headed back to the front door.

*   *   *

Lana Curtis sat speaking on her mobile in the back of a cab. "I should be there shortly. I was delayed. There was some concert on in The Point."

"Well, we're in the members' lounge, darling, so see you shortly," said her friend Patricia.

Lana took out a cigarette and went to light it.

"No smoking in the cab," objected the driver.

She sighed, placing the cigarette back into the packet.

"You're on for a big night out?" he asked.

"Something like that," she said, keeping her eyes fixed firmly on the view outside.

The cab pulled up outside Exclusive. Lana handed the driver a twenty and stepped out.

Kathryn spotted Lana immediately. It was hard to miss her, wearing a short white mini-skirted dress, and a long fake-fur white coat. Her dead-straight glossy chestnut hair hung in a thick gleaming curtain to one side, all but concealing one of her beautiful green eyes. As she came up the steps, Kathryn wondered how much the diamond necklace she was wearing would be worth. Lana Curtis was on the A list at Exclusive and everywhere else. It wasn't because of anything she had done, but because of who her father was. Barry Curtis was one of the country's richest men. He was also the major shareholder at Exclusive.

As always with Lana, Kathryn felt uncomfortable. It was certainly nothing to do with Lana's father. Kathryn had met all types at Exclusive, and that kind of thing didn't impress her at all. But it was very hard to make the usual small talk with Lana. She seemed uninterested. Kathryn knew Lana was thirty-one, but she had the eyes of someone older.

"Anyone interesting in tonight?" asked Lana, as she took off her coat and handed it to the receptionist.

"Affidavit is here – they just finished their tour at The Point," answered Kathryn.

Judging by Lana's uninterested expression, Kathryn wouldn't have been surprised if Lana hadn't a clue who Affidavit were. Lana had the best of both worlds. Despite her father's wealth and fame, only those in certain circles would know who she was. She had a very low profile, and seemed to like it that way. This enabled her to go about her business uninterrupted. Which was just as well, because Kathryn had seen her worse for wear on many occasions.

Upstairs Lana walked through the club, surveying the crowd, all the usual faces. The security man at the members' lounge door nodded to her, and she walked past him without acknowledgment.

"Lana!" Patricia shouted over to her and waved.

She walked over, smiling, and kissed everyone at the table on the cheek. She had been friends with this crowd since school.

"When did you get back from London?" asked Patricia.

"Only this morning. I had a great time. The usual places, you know."

"Did you stay with Susan?"

"For most of the time." She beckoned to a hostess. "Could I have a double whiskey, please? Neat."

*   *   *

"I tell you, top totty here, or what?" said Tony.

They'd managed to get a table in the main club area and were taking in the whole scene.

"You played a blinder down there at the door with Foy," complimented Malcolm. "Didn't think you were going to pull it off for a minute."

"How could you ever have doubted my abilities? I think I'm going to start coming here on a regular basis."

"Right, Tony. Did you hear what she said? Ring ahead next time. In other words, tonight is a once-off."

"I told you, I'm a member of NUJ – I can get in anywhere."

"Sure, Tony." Malcolm smiled sarcastically and, as he watched Tony head to the bar, he turned to the others and said, "Just because he got a lucky strike tonight it's gone straight to his head. You know what Tony's like. He's going to be *big!*"

*   *   *

The Affidavit party all clinked their beer bottles together.

"To a job well done!" shouted Cathal. He'd had a couple of drinks, and was feeling relaxed and ready to enjoy himself.

Rob waited anxiously as he listened to his wife talking on her mobile to their childminder. They'd had their first child six months ago.

"Well?" he asked as she hung up.

"He's fine, sleeping away." Heidi smiled and drank from her bottle.

Cathal winked over to Donna. "It'll be your turn next."

"Oh, please God, not for a while!" pleaded James.

"Right, everyone," said Cathal, "I want to propose a toast!"

Seán looked at Cathal developing into his usual life-and-soul-of-the-party persona.

"To the next concert!" cried Cathal. "And the concert after that and the concert after that!"

Most of the production team had arrived in and they all cheered and clinked their beer bottles together again. Except for Seán, who had slunk off to the bar.

* * *

"It's the group Affidavit who are making all the noise, incidentally," explained Patricia, as she caught Lana looking curiously over at them. "I like some of their stuff. Although looking at their antics tonight, they seem to be real big-heads, no class!"

Lana shrugged her shoulders as she ordered another drink.

* * *

"Cathal, remember me – Joanne Bailey? I interviewed you the other day."

14

Cathal studied the dark-haired beauty in front of him, and tried to recall her. "Yeah, sure! You work for MTV."

"That's right," answered Joanne, a little annoyed he hadn't remembered her straight off. "You're out celebrating the finish of the tour?"

"Ten out of ten for observation!"

Joanne wondered if he was worth the effort. Still, she thought, it wouldn't harm her career to be linked to him. "I just loved your last album," she said, moving closer.

*　　*　　*

"Look, I know he's your cousin and everything, but don't you agree with what I'm saying?" Seán was sitting next to James at the table, practically talking into James' ear, making sure no one else could overhear the conversation.

"I take your point but . . ." James felt uncomfortable.

"I just would like to know who decided to appoint Cathal the boss? Because in his own mind, he thinks he is, you know."

"But look, he's great at dealing with the record companies."

"I'm not saying he's not good at that side of things. But let's be honest here, he's no great musical talent. I mean tonight, I had to play the drums with extra oomph to drown out his shit guitar playing."

James didn't like this rivalry that was developing between Cathal and Seán one little bit. They had come along way, and had success beyond their dreams. He didn't want to see this animosity jeopardising things.

"Will we move out into the main club?" asked Cathal loudly.

"It's too packed out there, we won't get a table," objected Seán.

"No probs, Kathryn will organise it for us." Cathal whipped out his mobile.

* * *

As Kathryn quickly climbed the steps, she was irritated. Cathal had rung her looking for a table in the main club. She would never understand people. Everybody in Dublin wanted to be in the members' lounge in Exclusive. And yet, Affidavit, who had the best table in town, wanted to be out in the club with everyone else. She quickly surveyed the crowd, and saw that the guys who'd pretended to be from the BBC were occupying a great table overlooking the dance floor. She beckoned a security guard to follow her over to them.

"Hi, guys, are you enjoying the evening?" she asked.

"Really great, thanks," smiled Tony, impressed that the manager had come over to ask after them.

"I'm going to have to ask you to move from this table, I'm afraid."

"Move? Why?" demanded Tony.

"It was reserved."

"No, it wasn't. There was no reserved sign on it," objected Tony.

Kathryn sighed to herself – she had sensed this one would be trouble. "Look, it's no big deal. I just would like you to move."

"Not till you tell us why," Tony stuck to his guns.

"Okay, I'll tell you why. Affidavit need a table, and they are going to get *this* table."

"That's outrageous!" Tony's voice rose. "Just because

16

somebody famous wants our table, you're expecting us to move?"

"I'm not expecting you, I'm telling you." Kathryn was becoming more irritated by the minute – irritated with this jerk for not going, and irritated with Cathal for expecting to move tables at this late stage of the night.

"Well, we aren't moving." Tony sat back, folded his arms, and looked across at a nervous Malcolm.

"Look, don't be stupid. You chanced your arm and got in here. Now just quietly move and enjoy the rest of the night."

"Forget it. We're customers too. We paid like everyone else"

"Okay," Kathryn sighed. "I'm asking you to leave the club."

"What? You can't do that!"

"Right now. Come on, guys. Up and out!" Kathryn insisted.

Two security men moved in front of her, and one grabbed Tony's arm, pulling him up.

"Get your hands off me!" Tony shouted.

The security man let go. "Okay, get up so."

"We can do this the nice way or the not-so-nice way," Kathryn said.

"If this gorilla puts his hands on me once more, I'm calling the Guards."

Kathryn took out her mobile "No, I'm calling the Guards to get you out of here." She started dialling.

"Come on, Tony. Let's go – please!" Malcolm was upset. "Think about Nicole."

Tony thought for a bit before saying, "Okay, we'll go. Wouldn't stay in this madhouse, anyway." He grabbed his jacket and walked to the door, followed by the others.

Kathryn followed them with the security. "Give them their money back," she ordered the cashier when they reached the reception.

Tony turned around and faced Kathryn. "Forget it." He gave her a filthy look and left.

Kathryn was annoyed with herself as she made her way into the members' lounge. She shouldn't have let those guys in. Her instinct had told her so at the start. In her business, you always had to go by instinct. She was running an exclusive venue for a certain set – once you started diluting that set, the game was lost.

"Cathal, I have that table for you." she said, smiling.

"Great, thanks Kathryn. Come on, everybody!"

He headed into the main club, most of the team following him. Only Seán and a couple of others elected to stay in the members' lounge.

Kathryn showed them to their new table and sent over some drinks. Then she went and stood at the bar, observing them. She had been ruthless, she knew, but she had to be. There were too many venues anxious to steal away Exclusive's status. Affidavit would have a terrific night; they would tell everybody about it. It would be all over the press tomorrow that they had been there. You couldn't buy that kind of public relations.

Cathal seemed to be having quite a few drinks and was kissing the TV presenter Joanne Bailey. She wouldn't last long, Kathryn was confident. They never lasted long with Cathal Fitzgerald. She remembered when Affidavit had first started coming to Exclusive, five or six years previously. They had seemed very young and naive then – apart from Cathal, who seemed wary of people. She had watched them grow big over the years. She liked their music but was surprised at how successful they had

18

become. MPI records had got behind them and pushed them to the top.

As she watched Cathal, she reflected that here was a guy with little talent who had just been in the right place at the right time. Just because he'd been lucky, he had tables organised for him in a second, and TV presenters throwing themselves at him. She wondered where the justice in it was. But in her job she had seen them come and seen them go. One minute people were flying high, then they were finished with no future.

*   *   *

Tony walked down the street where he lived. It was an older street in Ranelagh – very small Victorian terraces. He felt dejected and annoyed. He had said goodbye to Malcolm and the others in Grafton Street and grabbed a taxi home.

He opened the little gate, sat down on the little front wall and looked up at the house. They rented it. They couldn't even afford to buy a house in today's Dublin house market, because his career was so shaky. It was Nicole's therapy practice that really kept them going. He fumbled in his pockets and, groaning loudly, realised he had forgotten his keys. Looking at his watch, he saw it was nearly 2.30. There was nothing for it but to wake up Nicole.

He rang the doorbell and half-shouted up "Nic!", trying not to wake the neighbours.

Luckily Nicole was a light sleeper, and a light came on in the window upstairs. The curtain was drawn over and she opened the window.

"I forgot my keys!" he apologised.

"Oh, Tony!" she snapped.

Twenty seconds later she was at the front door, opening it. Seeing he was upset, she became concerned. "What's wrong?"

"I need a hug," he said, stepping into the doorway and into her arms.

* * *

Cathal and Joanne were dancing closely on the dance floor.

"You always like to party so much?" she whispered into his ear.

"Only after a big tour," he answered. "I work hard and deserve to have some fun."

"I'm not saying you don't ! But it's getting late. Are you going to invite me back to your place?"

"Looks like you've already invited yourself."

* * *

Lana took her coat out from the cloakroom.

"Do you want me to get you a taxi, Lana?" asked Kathryn.

"No, thanks, I'm fine." She managed a smile, then walked out the front door and down the steps.

Patricia and the others were still partying inside, but she needed to get out. She walked down Grafton Street, her coat fastened, her hands in her pockets. As ever there was much joviality on the streets, people falling out of clubs and late-night bars, laughing, joking. They were heading to late-night restaurants and diners, or wine bars that stayed open till morning. She took a turn off Grafton Street and continued her journey. It was something she often did, walk around late at night. It allowed her to think straight. Or sometimes she would just walk and not think at all. This was an aimless walk with no destination. On lampposts everywhere her father's face smiled down, inviting people to vote for him.

Barry Curtis had decided his next achievement in life was going to be politics. The elections were a long way off, and nobody else had their posters up yet, but Barry Curtis was always ahead of the pack. Barry had fought his way from humble beginnings to become one of the country's richest men. His business interests were extensive and included Construction, Retail and Hotels. Not only was he one of the most recognised people in his native country but he was also famous in the UK, where a lot of his business interests lay, and was known throughout Europe. He was connected to everybody worth knowing. But he was known as much for his generosity as his money. He had a hugely altruistic nature, and tried to use his money and power to fund-raise as much as possible. When he had expressed a desire to enter politics, one of the major parties quickly accepted him as a candidate, and it was expected he would be a very popular choice.

Lana's high-heeled shoes clicked along the cobblestones of a deserted street. She looked at her watch, and realised she had been walking for two hours. Sighing, she stopped and sat down on the kerb. She lit a cigarette and stared up at one of her father's posters.

* * *

"To The Westbury?" Matt, who was driving, asked.

"Yeah," answered Cathal.

Matt observed Cathal and Joanne through the rear-

view mirror. Cathal looked as if he had drunk too much –
luckily there had been no photographers outside
Exclusive.

"Why are you staying at The Westbury anyway?"
asked Joanne. "Don't you have a home in Dublin?"

"Yeah, but we always stay in The Westbury when we
do a concert in Dublin."

The car pulled up outside the hotel, and they got out.
Joanne pushed his dishevelled hair into place. Then she
put her arm around him and headed to the front entrance.

"Cathal!" a voice called behind them, and as Cathal
turned a flash went off.

"For God's sake, a bloody photographer!" said Cathal.

"Oh, never mind!" soothed Joanne, hoping her make-
up looked all right.

*   *   *

Nicole passed Tony a cup of tea, and sat down beside
him on the sofa.

"It was so infuriating," he said. "There I was, feeling
really great after managing to keep that contract at work,
and celebrating in Exclusive with all the in-people. And
then Foy comes over and says we have to move to allow
Affidavit to take our table!"

Nicole pushed her auburn hair back from her forehead
"You know how those places work – they are so vacuous
and false."

"But why should we move for a bunch of no-talent,
ugly fuckers?"

"Well, er, they're not actually. But, you're right, Tony.
She had no right to ask you to."

"It just was a big reminder of how unsuccessful I am."

"Don't put yourself down —"

"I'm telling it like it is! Here I am, at thirty-four years old, in a job I hate, with just a few articles published and going nowhere. We can't even afford to buy our own place. And why can't we afford to? Because of me. You're doing great with your practice, but it's me that's holding us back. You'd be better off without me, Nic."

Nicole put her tea down quickly and put her arms around him. "Tony, you know how much I love you. I don't care what we have as long as we are together."

"Well, I care."

"Tony, come on. Snap out of this! You're usually upbeat and enthusiastic."

"What's the point? I just want the break, Nic. I want it so much."

*   *   *

Cathal pulled a bottle of champagne from the fridge and opened it.

"It's a fantastic suite!" Joanne kicked off her shoes and lay down on the couch.

"Should be with the amount it costs." He sat down on the edge of the couch and poured two glasses of champagne.

"So, tell me about yourself, Cathal," she urged.

"I told you about us, when you interviewed us."

"Not 'us' – *you*. I don't want a press interview for Affidavit, I want to know about you."

"Like what do you want to know?" he laughed. "I come from Castletown. My father's a civil servant, my mum's a housewife. I've got a brother, Sam, who's an engineer, and a younger sister, Mags, who's a nursery teacher. Sam's engaged –"

"Hold on." She put a finger to his lips. "This is sounding like a press release from MPI's public relations department. I want to know the real you."

"Why?" He looked perplexed.

"Because I like you."

"And why do you like me ?"

"I just do."

"You like me because I'm in Affidavit. You like me because I'm supposed to be rich and famous, end of story. Let's be honest here, you're not interested in me, Cathal Fitzgerald, you're interested in me being a supposed star. So, you want to hear the press releases – anything else might disappoint you." He spoke quickly and honestly, looking her straight in the eye.

Startled, Joanne lay back in the couch. "What has you so cynical?"

"Life, sweetheart," he chinked his glass against hers, "life!"

* * *

Kathryn walked through the club, turning off the lights, while a security man stood by. She was always the last to leave and to lock up. And she worked five, sometimes six nights a week. It had been a very successful night, though Affidavit's presence had been very demanding. She looked at the grand piano in the members' lounge and contemplated telling the security man to head off home so she could spend five minutes on it. But no, it was very late as Cathal Fitzgerald and his new lady friend had held on to the very last and delayed closing time.

She and the security man made their way to the back entrance, set the alarm, locked the back door and made their way down the fire escape to the underground carpark. The city streets were almost empty as she drove home in her Volkswagen Golf convertible and the sun was just beginning to lighten the morning sky. It didn't take her long to get home which was a two-bedroomed apartment in the south city centre. An old warehouse had been turned into a small development, and Kathryn lived on the top floor. She let herself in. It was six o'clock. She tried to make as little noise as possible.

It was obvious from the interior that the building was a converted warehouse. The ceiling of the living room was thirty feet high, with two huge windows, one over the other. A stairs led up to a balcony which circled the living area. One of the bedrooms led off from the living area, and another from the balcony upstairs. She went into the kitchen, which was pristinely new, and fixed herself a sandwich. In the bathroom, she removed her make-up and filled herself a hot bath. She stepped into the sunken bath and relaxed and soaked for half an hour, allowing the night's activities to drift away.

Towelling herself dry, she crept into the main bedroom where Simeon was fast asleep. At thirty-six, he was five years older than she. From the ashtray, she could see he had been smoking hash, and so realised he was out for the count and she needn't have been so careful being quiet. She looked through their CD collection, found one of Simeon's early recordings and put it on low. God, how she loved his music! She climbed into the bed, putting her arm around him, but sleep refused to come easily.

CHAPTER 2

Cathal, eyes still closed, reached over from his bed and groped for his ringing mobile.

"Yeah?" he answered, realising his head was thumping.

"Congratulations!" It was Sylvia Henderson. "There's a lovely picture of you on the front page of today's *Sun*, entering the hotel with some TV presenter."

Cathal pulled himself up in the bed and leaned against the headboard. Hearing the shower in the ensuite, he assumed Joanne was in there.

"When I say you look an absolute mess in the photo, I am in no way exaggerating. I thought I told you no pics in the papers today?"

"I had a few drinks to celebrate finishing the tour – so what?"

"You know what really pisses me off? That everyone worked to put together this great tour and all the papers should be giving great reviews. But instead they are concentrating on your sex life!"

"Okay, okay, Sylvia! Look my head is killing me – can we talk about this later?" He got out of bed and pulled a bathrobe around him.

"All right. Give me a call and we'll discuss this week's itinerary." She knew when not to push him too far.

Cathal put down the mobile and dialled down to reception. "Could you send me up some black coffee? Oh, and a copy of *The Sun*."

"Of course, sir. Also if I could inform you that Mr James Fitzgerald left a message to ask you to join him and the others in the restaurant when you are ready."

"Thanks." Cathal hung up.

The shower turned off and Joanne emerged from the bathroom with a towel around her, smiling brightly. "Hi there, and how are you this morning?"

"Could be better. Could be a lot better." He walked out into the sitting room and sat down on the couch.

She followed him and, leaning down, kissed his forehead. "Well, I couldn't be better."

There was a knock on the door and she went over to open it.

"Coffee, madam," said the waiter as he wheeled the trolley in.

Ignoring him, Joanne went into the bedroom to change.

"Will I pour, sir?"

"If you wouldn't mind." Cathal smiled appreciatively.

After the waiter had gone, Cathal went over to the trolley and picked up the paper. "Oh, shit!" he said, realising Sylvia had been right. He looked a mess. Beside him, Joanne was immaculately groomed, smiling brightly for the camera.

"Are we in that?" asked Joanne, now fully dressed.

"Unfortunately." He passed her the paper. "I'm going to shower."

Joanne scrutinised herself in the photo and was very

28

pleased. Hearing Cathal safely in the shower, she took out her mobile. "Hi, it's me. Thanks a million – I'm really happy with the photo! Not sure yet. I'm playing it by ear, but I'll give you plenty of advance if there's another photo opportunity."

Cathal felt much better after the shower. He slipped into a black T-shirt and jeans. He planned to do some shopping that day so he put a baseball hat on as well. Unless there was a big event like last night's concert, which attracted the die-hard fans from around the country, Affidavit could go about their business without too much interruption. Sure, they got lots of second looks and occasional eagle-eyed autograph hunters, but a simple baseball cap was usually sufficient disguise.

"You know, I really enjoyed last night," said Joanne, "and I'd love to see you again. So, I've taken your number and I'll call you real soon, okay?" She put her arms around him and kissed him.

"Yeah, fine. But I don't know how long I'm going to be in Dublin, to be honest with you. I might have to go to London soon . . ."

"You forget I interviewed you two days ago. You're going to be here for a while. You have to shoot a video, then it's into the studio for recording a new album, remember? So we'll have plenty of time. Speaking of time, I'm late for an appointment." Smiling, she took his hand and they left the suite.

*   *   *

James, Rob, Seán and Donna were having breakfast in the hotel restaurant.

Donna was looking at the photo in *The Sun*. "He looks

wasted."

"You know Cathal. Never knows when to stop," said Rob. "He certainly won't like that photo."

"Speak of the devil," said Donna, nodding over to where Cathal was coming in.

Everyone glared at him as he sauntered over.

"All right, all right!" Cathal pulled up a chair and joined them. "I've already had Sylvia on the phone, so I can do without any smart comments from you lot."

"Poor Cathal! Feeling a little delicate this morning, are we?" said James.

"I'm fine."

"She's very attractive," commented Donna, looking at the photo in the paper.

"If you like that type," said Seán.

"Enough about me!" snapped Cathal. "Let's go over our schedule."

But just then his mobile bleeped. It was a text message. He opened it up and read: *"Actually, what are you doing tonight? Joanne. X"*

*　　*　　*

In the recreation room at Mountjoy Prison, Stephen Rourke balanced the pool-stick carefully, eying the white ball carefully. With one sudden movement he slammed the ball, which in turn sent the black ball spinning into the corner hole of the pool table.

"Game!" he said, dropping the pool-stick on the table.

He sauntered over to where a few of the other inmates were watching some music show.

He sat down and suddenly his interest was caught by the front page of a newspaper. He picked it up and looked closely at the photo of Cathal Fitzgerald. It was unbelieveable that this was the same Cathal he used to know. Like a different person almost. As ever, when he saw Cathal on TV or in a magazine, he felt his anger boil. It was an anger that seemed to consume him as he thought how their lives had taken such diverse paths. How he had rotted away in prison for years while watching Cathal Fitzgerald climb to fame and riches. And it had all been Cathal's fault.

*   *   *

Nicole loved sleeping in on a Saturday morning. The light streamed through their bedroom window and she stretched luxuriously and yawned. Finally she got up and went downstairs, to find Tony sprawled out on the sofa watching some kid's Saturday morning music show.

"Are you in a better mood this morning?" She sat down beside him, stroking his hair.

"Yeah. Sorry I was in a bit of a state last night. I was just pissed off with everything."

"That's all right. That's what I'm here for. Anyway, it's the thing I like most about you."

"What is?"

"You're the most open person I've ever met. There's never any play-acting or messing with you. You wear your heart on your sleeve -- when you're happy you show it, when you're upset you show that too. I wouldn't have you any other way."

"Wouldn't you like me to be mysterious? You know, the strong and silent type?"

"I'd hate it! I'm a therapist, remember. I spend my whole life trying to unravel people's lives and their minds. With you everything is upfront. Don't ever change."

31

"I wish I could! Then maybe I'd have some high-flying career in journalism, instead of being stuck where I am."

"Send a few more CV's out today and see what happens,"

She got up, went into the kitchen and poured herself a bowl of cornflakes. She could see from the empty packet of doughnuts that Tony had already had his breakfast. Tony had shiny black hair and a handsome face, and she thought being somewhat overweight kind of suited his build. She always was careful not to fall into his bad eating ways though. She too enjoyed her food a lot, and so it would be easy for her to balloon if she wasn't careful. As it was, she had a slim trim figure and she liked the way she looked. Her features weren't standard pretty, but were arresting, especially her keen blue eyes which looked even more vivid against her bright auburn hair.

Even though she dearly wished Tony got a break in journalism soon, because she knew how much it meant to him, she was very happy with their lives. She loved the little house they rented which suited their needs perfectly. Downstairs was just one big sitting-room that led into the kitchen in the back. Upstairs was their bedroom, and a smaller second bedroom which they used as a study. The rent was exorbitant, but then Victorian cottages in that area were very sought after. Of course, she wished they could afford to buy their own place, but she hoped that would come in time. Although, as Tony had pointed out last night, at thirty-four neither of them was getting any younger. But they had each other, that was the main thing.

"My family or yours for lunch this Sunday?" she called.

* * *

32

It was twelve midday by the time Kathryn woke up.

"Simeon!" she called, coming into the main room.

Realising he wasn't there, she looked around for a note but couldn't find one. She tried phoning him, but his mobile was turned off. She sighed. She hadn't actually spoken to him since Tuesday. That was one of the bad things about her job – the hours she worked often played havoc with her personal life. She scraped her hair back into a pony-tail and, realising she was late for lunch with her sister, dashed down to her car. It was such a lovely day that she decided to pull back the top. She drove out of the tree-shaded carpark into the city streets.

She parked near Baggot Street and walked towards Grafton Street. Dressed in designer jeans, a simple top and high sandals, her over-sized sunglasses resting on her head, she cut a striking figure.

Her phone rang. It would be the first of many calls concerning the club that day. Because she had to be at Exclusive during the night, but also had to be contactable during the day, she was on call nearly twenty-four hours a day. It was one of the things she sometimes hated about her job.

Her sister Kelly was already seated in the patio outside The Bailey with her nine-year-old daughter Sara.

"Sorry I'm late," apologised Kathryn as she kissed them both and sat down.

"Had a late one last night?" asked Kelly.

"Every time Affidavit are in, it's a late one."

"Affidavit were in Exclusive last night?" Sara's face lit up. She was a fan.

"Sure, they were in with us." Kathryn looked at her niece, who was dressed up in designer clothes, just like her mum. In fact, she was the image of her mother.

There were only two years between Kelly and Kathryn. As she studied her elder sister in the sunshine, she marvelled at how good she looked. But her look was very manicured and cosmetic. She had blonde hair, which was perfectly groomed, her make-up was perfect and her jewellery expensive. There were only the two of them in their family, and in spite of their very different personalities, they had done everything together growing up, and had always been very close.

When they were in their early twenties, they had partied like mad around Dublin and had become well known on the social circuit. Kelly had worked at a top hairdresser's and Kathryn at a trendy nightclub doing promotions, quickly working her way up to assistant manager. Kelly had met her husband, Jim, around the same time Kathryn started going out with Simeon. Kelly and Jim had married quickly and she had given up work to settle down as a wife and mother. Jim was in the carpet business, had now opened his fifth store and they lived in considerable comfort in Castleknock.

"They took Mammy's photo for *Hi Life* magazine and it's going to be in next week's edition," said Sara.

"What at?" Kathryn asked Kelly.

"Just at a do at the Dublin Chamber of Commerce. They probably won't even print it. Don't worry, I'm not about to steal your crown as the style icon of our family."

Kathryn laughed. "Oh sure! How's Jim anyway?"

"Working till nine tonight. Him and his goddamned shops! I've told him he's very lucky to have such an understanding wife as me."

"He's working all those hours to keep you in your bling jewellery!"

"It's not bling! How dare you! It's Cartier actually!"

She fiddled with her bracelet. "How's Simeon? I haven't seen him for ages?" She managed to keep her tone light.

"Simeon's great! He's been really busy recently because he's got in with this new record producer and he's shown him some of his stuff."

"Excellent! His old music or is it some new?"

"Er . . . a bit of both, really."

"Let's hope it works out for him. His old stuff was . . ." she smiled but somehow her face turned sad, "well, he was in his own league."

Kathryn nodded and her eyes were sad too "I know . . ." She became upbeat. "But his new songs are, I think, even better."

"Well, let's hope it works out this time. Listen, why don't the two of you come over tomorrow evening? Mum and Dad are going to be there."

"Sorry, I can't – I'm working tomorrow night."

"God, Kathryn, going into work on a Sunday night! I don't know how you do it!"

"I buzz on it. You know I love it."

I know you love it, thought Kelly, but I also know it's just as well because you've got no choice either.

* * *

Cathal surveyed the display of watches laid out in front of him in Weir's jewellers. He loved the Gucci, but it was just so expensive. He could tell the middle-aged sales assistant hadn't a clue who he was and was suspicious of this jeans-clad, baseball-capped customer. He held up the Gucci one more time.

"Yep, this is the one."

"Certainly. Will that be cash or credit card?"

"I'm going to slap it on the Visa." He took out his wallet.

"I'll just gift wrap it for you." The assistant went to take the watch.

"No need, I'll just put it on now." He strapped it on his wrist.

The sales assistant shot the security man a nervous look and he in turn moved gently to the front door.

Cathal caught the action out of the corner of his eye. "Don't worry. I'm not going to take off without paying." He slammed his Visa card down on counter, resigned to seeing the familiar stunned look on the assistant's face when she recognised his name.

"I wasn't for a moment – "

"Yeah, whatever. Just do the deed, please."

Walking back to the hotel, he spotted Kathryn Foy eating outside The Bailey. He went over to her.

"Enjoying your lunch?"

Kathryn looked up and for a moment didn't know him. Then, as Sara gasped, she recognised him and asked, smiling: "How's your head today?"

"A bit sore earlier but fine now. Just wanted to say thanks for looking after us last night."

"My pleasure."

He turned and looked at Kelly and Sara. "We always have a great time in Exclusive."

"It's a good spot all right." Kelly smiled broadly.

"Cathal, this is my sister Kelly, and my niece, Sara."

Sara whispered into Kelly's ear.

"Oh, Sara!" Kelly was irritated, but Sara pulled her sleeve. "Oh, all right then. Sorry, Cathal, would it be too much trouble to give my demanding daughter an autograph?"

"I'll do better than that." He whipped off his baseball cap, took out a pen and scribbled his name across the cap, before placing it on Sara's head.

"Thanks, Cathal." Kathryn was impressed,

"See you next time I'm in Exclusive." He waved and then disappeared into the crowd of shoppers.

"Wasn't that a lovely thing to do?" said Kelly.

"It was actually," agreed Kathryn.

"I always thought he came across very big-headed."

"Well, I guess he is but he's always polite . . . as long as he's getting what he wants. I've seen him tear strips off people a couple of times when they upset him. Anyway, I'd better make a move. There was some hassle with a delivery to the club and I want to pop in to make sure it arrived okay." She reached over to get the bill. "I'll just go and pay this."

"Don't worry, it's already taken care of. I paid for it on my way to the loo."

"Kelly !" Kathryn was genuinely annoyed. "You're always paying for lunch. I wouldn't mind but it's me who's working, not you."

"Don't worry, Jim can afford it with all the carpet he sells."

"That's not the point, Kelly – you should let me pay as well."

"Look, you've got enough expenses in your life, working every hour God sends, a big mortgage and only one wage coming in."

Kathryn felt herself become angry "You see, this is what annoys me. You insisting on paying isn't you being generous, it's an attempt to make me feel you've done better than me . . . an attack on Simeon!"

"That's not true!"

"Yes, it is. Poor Kathryn with only one wage coming in! I know what you're getting at, or at least trying to get at!"

"Look, I have no idea what your domestic arrangements are"

Kathryn stood up, grabbing her handbag. "No, you don't." She turned and walked off.

* * *

Cathal packed up his things at The Westbury and got the hotel to call him a cab to take him home. He was looking forward to having a few days to unwind and relax by himself. The tour had been hard-going and there were people around all the time.

Home was on the top floor of a new twelve-storey apartment block. He tapped in the code and the glass front doors of the building opened. The foyer was all white tiles and mirrors. The lift took him to the top floor. There were two penthouses and his was the front one with views over the river. The apartment had three bedrooms and a huge living room with floor-to-ceiling windows that looked out on a spacious patio. The patio ran right around the apartment with another door leading out from the main bedroom.

He threw his bags into the bedroom, went into the kitchen and poured himself a glass of water. This apartment was his dream home. It had cost him a fortune. He had tied up a huge amount of his earnings in it.

His phone rang. It had been buzzing most of the day and he had ignored the calls, assuming it would be journalists asking him about Joanne Bailey. Now he recognised the number of Kitty Mulcahy, a journalist from *The Star*, and he decided to take it. She was a trusted contact.

"Hi, Kitty."

"So what is it between you and the TV girl?"

"Nothing. I know Joanne through work. We met up in Exclusive last night and had a few drinks, that' s all."

"Well, the photo in *The Sun* sees you going into The Westbury with her."

"The tour was over, and everyone from Affidavit was out having a good time. Joanne was with the Affidavit party as well, and that's the end of it."

"Can I quote you as saying that?"

"Er . . . yeah."

"Okay. If anything develops and another journalist prints it before me, I'll kill you."

"Look, you're the only journo I'm making any comment to."

"Thanks, Cathal, talk to you later."

He hoped Joanne would stick to the same story if the press contacted her. He didn't really need any hassle at the moment. He checked quickly through his messages. There was one from his parents, one from his sister and one from his brother, all saying they had seen the photo in the paper. He knew they would be bubbling with curiosity as to who Joanne was and whether it was serious.

He headed over to his bar and opened a can of beer. He sat down at the bar and stared at was himself in the mirror. He thirty-three, and in control of his life. He had everything he'd ever wanted. There had been so many times during the struggle when he didn't think he would make it. But he had. He would never be back to where he was before.

His mobile rang again and he answered it.

"Cathal, it's Joanne here. I'm going in to Exclusive tonight and just wondered if you were heading in?"

"No, I don't think so. I'm still wrecked after last night."

"Why don't you give me your address and I'll come over and make you feel better."

"Thanks, but I'm heading straight to sleep now."

"Well, I'm going to text you my numbers. Call me during the week and we'll meet up."

"Okay, you do that."

* * *

Nicole left the building, glancing up at her name plate on the wall: *Nicole Donnelly*. It had been a tiring afternoon with a couple of her more troubled clients. She walked the ten minutes home.

Letting herself into the house, she picked up the mail and divided it into three piles, one for her, one for Tony and one for bills. She heard the door open, and Tony came in. He looked tired and stressed.

"I don't want to even talk about today," he said, kissing her.

"Bad, eh?"

"To say the least." He tore open his letters and, crumpling them up one after another, threw them in the fire grate. "More fucking rejections. Not even an interview this time." He went over to her and enfolded her in a hug. "Anyway, how was your day?"

"Not bad." Nicole had a policy of leaving work behind her once she left the office. She loved what she did, but she was aware that being a therapist meant it was too dangerous to ever get emotionally involved in any of her cases. So she mentally shut herself off when she left the office. There was also the issue of client confidentiality, which meant she wouldn't discuss anything, even with Tony.

"What do you want to do tonight?" he asked. "Go out for a meal? There's that new restaurant opened on the main street."

"We shouldn't really." She nodded over to the bills. "It's that time of the month again."

Tony pulled a face. "When is it not?"

"You know what I'd love? I'd love if we could order a Chinese – there's a good film on a little later on and we could curl up on the sofa, watching it and stuffing our faces. How does that sound?"

"It sounds perfect to me." He hugged her tightly. "What did I do to deserve you? You are this great person and have so much going for you, and yet you believe in me."

"I'll always believe in you." She kissed him, wishing he could get the break with his job. Then their happiness would be complete.

*   *   *

Club business had taken up most of Kathryn's afternoon and early evening. It was eight o'clock by the time she got home and nine before she was ready to leave again. She usually tried to be at work for ten.

There still had been no word from Simeon. She locked up the apartment behind her and tried phoning him again, only to find his phone was still off. She decided to leave a message. "Hi, it's me. Just wondering where you are." Her voice was soft and low.

She drove through the city streets. After all these years it still struck her as unusual to be going to work when everyone else was heading out to enjoy themselves. She worried about Simeon and hoped he would be back by the time she got home. She had checked their balance in the bank that evening and was surprised how much money they had gone through recently. She supposed Kelly was only trying to be nice paying for the lunch that day and regretted having lost her temper like that. But she knew there was always an unspoken agenda against Simeon with Kelly.

CHAPTER 3

Lana loved her house. It was a three-storey-over-basement in Lower Leeson Street. It was really too big for her to live there on her own, but she was used to space. As an only child, she had lots of it when she was growing up. She walked up the staircase to the second floor. Her bedroom had wooden floors and a wrought-iron bed. Combing her gleaming chestnut hair, she examined herself in the full-length mirror. She was slim and tall, her face strikingly good-looking with a fine bone-structure. She peered closely into her green eyes in the mirror and studied her face carefully. She looked well for thirty-one.

Going into her dressing-room, she slipped off her silk dressing-gown and began to choose an outfit. What would she do today? Patricia was down the country playing golf. She wished she had gone too, but there had been a party last night in Donnybrook that she hadn't wanted to miss. She vaguely remembered getting home at four in the morning. She decided she would pay her father a visit. With that in mind, she picked out a pale green suit with a figure-hugging jacket.

*   *   *

"I can cut that by ten per cent but that's as far as I can go," Tony haggled on the phone with a customer, trying to negotiate selling advertising space. "For that price you're getting a quarter page black and white . . . okay, fifteen per cent discount and that's my final offer . . . perfect, I'm going to fax you a booking form, which you need to fill out and refax to me. Talk to you later." Tony slammed down the phone and sighed with relief. He looked around the office he shared with Malcolm and two other guys, all of them busy haggling on the phone as well.

His mobile rang and he answered it. "Tony O'Brien speaking."

"Tony, this is Vivienne from *Hi Life* magazine – you sent your CV in to us recently for a position we advertised."

"Oh, hi, yes, could you hold a minute, please?" Tony jumped up from his desk and went out into the corridor for privacy. "Sorry about that."

"We would like to invite you in for an interview. Say, Friday morning at eleven o'clock?"

"Eh . . . perfect," answered Tony, wondering how he could organise the time off work.

"We'll see you then," Vivienne said and the phone went dead.

Hi Life magazine. He could barely remember the advert in the paper, but he remembered sending his CV off to them all right. He had thought he hadn't the right experience for them and so hadn't paid much attention to it.

"Yes !" he quietly roared to himself and punched the air.

*   *   *

As Lana drove her Mercedes past her old school, she allowed her memory to drift back to her schooldays. Being an only child, she had loved meeting all the new people and forming lots of friendships. It was a mixed school for the children of the wealthy. She remembered the wild parties. Her friends from school were all still her circle. They understood each other and where they were from. After school she had spent some time in London living with an aunt and sampling the delights of that city. She still wasn't sure what she wanted to do, but some of her friends were heading to the South of France and so she joined them. She used the South of France as a base to tour Europe, and the months went by quickly. She was twenty-four when she returned to Dublin. She had missed home and it was great catching up with everyone. And then life drifted on for her. She was always being invited somewhere and always had somewhere to go.

She drove quickly through the countryside outside Malahide till she came to the gate lodge of Kildara, her father's official home. She drove up the winding driveway to the huge mock-Tudor dormer manor, set in twenty acres of perfectly manicured gardens. She climbed out of her car and walked up the steps, opened the wooden door and stepped into the huge circular marble hallway, complete with staircase winding up the circular wall.

"Hello!" she called.

There was no response and so she headed towards her father's office which was situated downstairs at the back of the house – a large room which had numerous patio windows offering excellent views of the gardens.

Sure enough, there he was. Barry Curtis was dressed in a T-shirt and track-suit bottoms and was on an exercise bike, cycling away at a leisurely pace. He was fixated on a large screen that hung from the ceiling. Also in the room were Barry's head of Public Relations, Eddie Haughey, a secretary and an immaculately groomed woman in her mid-forties, who Lana had been introduced to before as Gloria Reagan. Lana didn't make her presence known immediately but stood at the door observing.

On the screen was footage of Bill Clinton greeting a group of dignitaries.

"Now, watch how Clinton is shaking their hands," said Gloria. "He is clasping their hand firmly with his right hand, and then he is bringing his left hand up and holding them firmly just above the elbow." She raised the remote control, freeze-framing the image on screen. "By doing this Clinton is reinforcing the fact that he is in control, he is the dominant one, he is the one with the power. But he is also reassuring each person that they are important to him and making them feel special."

"And the eye contact ?" asked Barry.

She zoomed to a close-up on Clinton's face. "His eye contact lasts a split second longer than it has to. Again this makes the person he is greeting think they are getting special attention."

Lana coughed loudly, causing everyone to turn around.

"Hello, darling!" Her father smiled broadly without pausing in his cycling and beckoned her over to him. "You didn't say you were going to drop by!"

She walked over and he gave her a hug.

"You know Eddie and Cáit?" said Barry.

Lana nodded to both of them.

"I can't remember if you've met Gloria before?"

"Yes, we've met a couple of times." Gloria smiled and, standing up, approached Lana and shook her hand.

Lana half-expected her to do it Clintonesque style and

grab her arm as well, but she didn't.

Gloria, a lecturer in Sociology specialising in Behaviourism at UCD, was becoming a permanent fixture at Kildara. Barry had met her at a function and, being very impressed with her, had invited her to join his political campaign. From what Lana could see, Gloria was nearly taking control of the campaign at this stage.

"Take a seat, honey," advised Barry. "You might find this interesting. Carry on, Gloria."

Gloria pressed a button on the remote and began to talk through a variety of politicians' body language. Barry was glued to the screen.

Forgotten, Lana sat down on the antique couch.

"It's amazing to think that such small details are so important," said Barry.

"Every small detail is subconsciously being absorbed by the public," said Gloria, flicking back her platinum-blonde hair.

The phone rang on Barry's desk and Cáit answered it. "Yes, could you hold on for one second and I'll check for you." She put the phone on mute. "It's Jack – there's a problem in London."

Barry nodded and she passed the phone over to him. "Hi, Jack, what's going on? . . . Uh huh, and why's that? . . . I understand your concern but what are we going to do about that? . . . Well, that's a good suggestion. Let's try that and see how it works. Good man – bye." Barry gave back the phone and indicated to Gloria to continue her show.

Lana smiled to herself. Her father had dealt with Jack as he dealt with all aspects of life. He had done nothing to help solve Jack's problem, but listened and then fired the problem back at him for him to solve. Her father hired only the best staff and let them get on with the job, gently coaching whenever he was pressurised to. It was a policy that had enabled him to amass a fortune. As Gloria continued her floorshow, Lana knew Gloria must be the best at what she did to be in that room that day.

There was a knock at the door and a suited man entered.

"Hi, what's up?" Barry's tone was as ever relaxed.

"I've got a journalist outside who says he's got an appointment to interview you about the election."

Barry looked at Eddie, a little confused. "We're not scheduled for any interview this afternoon, are we?"

"Certainly not." Eddie looked hassled.

"I wonder how we're going to get rid of him without upsetting anybody?" asked Barry.

"I'm going to take care of it right now." Eddie jumped up and walked swiftly out of the room.

"I was wondering if you had made those arrangements for photos of you and your wife to be taken yet, Barry?" asked Gloria. "I feel it is so important to give the whole view of the man to the people."

Lana looked at her father and loudly said "What!"

"You know I'm still working on getting a date for that one, Gloria."

"A date!" scoffed Lana.

"Could we finish this later, Gloria, if that's not a problem?" Barry smiled kindly at her.

"Of course. I've got a lecture soon anyway, so I should be making tracks." Gloria stood up and gathered her papers. "I'll see you later, Barry." She nodded to Lana and left with Cáit who closed the door after them

"Isn't she something?" Barry asked, continuing to cycle. "You know, she was the youngest lecturer ever in the Sociology Department in UCD."

"She's obviously been lecturing for a long time then,"

said Lana, knowing sarcasm was lost on, or ignored, by her father. Then, her face incredulous, she asked: "You're having a photograph taken with Mum?"

"I haven't said yes or anything." Barry stopped cycling and came and sat beside Lana. At nearly fifty-five, he was a tall and handsome man with silvery hair.

"For obvious reasons," said Lana.

"So, what've you been up to? Out partying?"

She sighed. "Yeah."

"Have you spoken to your mother recently?"

"Have you?" Lana shot back.

The phone rang on Barry's desk and he sauntered over to answer it. "Yeah . . . hi there, Frank . . . uh huh, that could be trouble all right . . . what would you do if you were in my situation on that one? . . . Really?"

Lana stood up to go.

"Hold on a second, Frank," Barry covered his mouthpiece. "Are you off, honey ? Give me a call, later . . ."

Lana nodded and headed to the door.

"Hey! You never said what you thought of my election posters!" he called after her.

"Smashing," she sighed.

He smiled and returned to his phone conversation. "You know, that's a really good plan you've come up with there, Frank. Let me know how it goes."

*　　*　　*

Nicole had gathered as many past issues of *Hi Life* magazine from the reception at work as she could find and brought them home. That evening she and Tony sat on the floor in front of the fire, scanning through them.

"It's very glossy," commented Tony, staring at a full-page photo of the Beckhams.

"Well, it's a celebrity lifestyle magazine – it's meant to be glossy," said Nicole.

"There's no actual journalism in it. All the interviews are just tailored to making the celebs look good."

"It's a feel-good magazine, like *Hello* or *OK,* presenting a glamorous perfect lifestyle to its readers. It's designed to make people emulate their lifestyle . . . your mother reads it all the time."

"I wouldn't exactly be covering the cutting edge of world affairs."

"I know. Would you be okay doing this kind of stuff? I know your heart is more into serious journalism."

"At this stage, I'd interview the President's poodle as long as I got away from the job I'm in now!"

Nicole looked worried "Don't get your hopes up too high. You don't have much experience in this kind of stuff. I don't want to see you disappointed."

* * *

Kathryn had heard a rumour that she was going to be shortlisted for Ireland's Social Personality of the Year Award hosted by *Hi Life* magazine, so had spent the day updating her wardrobe. As she pulled into the carpark, she didn't even want to think what next month's Visa bill would be like. It was her night off and she was looking forward to just chilling in the apartment. She was desperately worried about Simeon. She hadn't seen him in days. She knew he had been back to the apartment, but his phone had been off and he had ignored the notes she had left him asking him to call.

As she let herself into her apartment, she heard music

playing.

"Simeon!" she called loudly and excitedly, throwing the shopping bags on the floor and running into the kitchen.

Finding him cooking, she paused for a moment to check what mood he was in. But seeing he was smiling broadly she ran to him and he enveloped her in his arms. Simeon was tall and thin, with hair that was shoulder-length. He looked every one of his thirty-six years. His face was weathered – a face that had received a lot of life's hard knocks.

"Where were you?" she asked, holding him tightly.

"Joe's rented a studio and was recording some of his stuff and he wanted me to be there to give my opinion."

"But your phone's been off."

He looked down at her and pulled a face. "Er, dah! I said I was in a studio. I don't think Joe would've appreciated my mobile's ringing as part of his soundtrack, do you?"

"I was worried sick."

"But you knew I'd been back and forth to here. And you've been working every night, so I just made sure I'd be here on your night off."

"You piss me off sometimes." She playfully punched him.

"As you can see, dinner is nearly ready, so take a seat and I'll serve up." He kissed her forehead and she took a couple of plates and cutlery and sat at the table.

"So what was Joe's music like?" she asked.

"Not bad at all." He scooped out the stew he had cooked from the pot onto their plates. "I tell you what," he sat down and smiled at her, "it was great being back in a studio."

"Did it stir you in a creative way at all?"

"Yeah . . . yeah, it did. Kind of got me back into the swing of things a little . . . you never know, I might try writing some songs again."

She leaned over and clasped his hand "Oh, I hope so!" He looked happier than she had seen him for a while. Although it was always up and down with him. "Thanks for being here on my night off,"

"How's work been for you this week?"

"Busy as ever."

"Joe mentioned he might like to go in to Exclusive with a couple of people from the record industry on Saturday night."

"Sure – if I'm not at the door, just get him to tell one of the guys to call me. I'll look after him."

"Great."

Kathryn's phone rang and she saw it was Kelly ringing. "Hi," she said coolly. They hadn't spoken since their falling out the previous Saturday.

"I was just wondering if you wanted to meet up for lunch on Saturday?" said Kelly.

"I'm not sure," answered Kathryn.

"Sara would love to see you . . . and I insist you pay!"

Kathryn smiled. "In that case, okay."

*   *   *

Simeon stroked Kathryn's hair as they lay in bed. It was dark outside, and somewhere in the distance an ambulance wailed.

"I really was worried about you," she said softly. "Every night I'd come and pray you were here."

"You know I can take care of myself – you don't ever have to worry about me."

"Isn't that what we're supposed to do – worry about each other?" She felt completely happy and content in his arms.

CHAPTER 4

"Damn it, it's just not working!" shouted Sylvia Henderson, causing everyone to jump. They were in the process of filming the video for the last song to be released from Affidavit's album. Sylvia knew that now after the tour the market was right to have a big hit with the song. They were in studios in the south city centre.

Everyone sighed. It had been a long day and Sylvia had made it longer with her continual interruptions.

"What exactly isn't right?" asked James.

"The backdrop, your expressions, I don't know – the whole fucking thing!"

"But we're doing it exactly as you said!" said Cathal.

"Well, then we're going to have to start again from scratch with a different concept. Because this is shit."

Cathal spotted the RTÉ crew coming into the studios to do an interview. "I think this might be a good time to do the TV interview," he suggested, "and let us all get a break from filming."

Sylvia sighed. "Okay."

Cathal walked over to the programme's director. "Who's doing the interview?"

Joanne Bailey stepped out from behind the camera and, smiling broadly, said, "I am. Hello, everybody!"

Seán burst out laughing, enjoying Cathal's obvious discomfort.

"Joanne!" said Cathal. "But you interviewed us a couple of weeks ago for MTV!"

"That was just a gig I got – this programme is my regular job." She gestured to the band to sit down opposite her. "Will we begin?"

"Go ahead," said James, sitting down and trying not to smile at Cathal's irritated face.

"Okay, starting in five. Go for it, Joanne!" said the director.

Joanne smiled to the camera. "Affidavit has just completed their tour of Europe. Today they are filming the video for their next release and we have joined them on the set for a chat." She turned to the band. "You must be exhausted after your tour. Have you managed to have any time off?"

Seán who usually was surly with people, as ever became alive when a TV camera focused on him. "Yeah, it was pretty tough going all right. But we loved every last minute. Nothing quite brings you to the fans the same way a concert does."

"Rob, it must have been extra difficult for you being away from your newborn baby?"

"Yeah, I missed him all right, but we've been catching up a lot recently."

"Has it been making the rest of you feeling broody? James, have you and Donna planned any kids yet?"

"No," James laughed and pretended to wipe his brow. "We have to get the wedding under way first. We'll concentrate on kids later."

"What about you, Cathal, are you feeling broody at all ?" She looked him straight in the face.

"Er, not yet, anyway." His eyes met her challenging gaze.

"When you see Rob with a baby and James getting married, it doesn't make you want to put your wild days behind you and settle down?"

"I didn't realise I was having wild days." He laughed nervously.

"Well, you certainly have a reputation for being a bit of a party animal. Would you not like something a little deeper in your life?"

"I think I've got a good balanced attitude to life."

"How?" She stared at him directly.

"How?" He felt himself go redder.

"How is your life balanced?"

Cathal shifted uncomfortably.

James jumped in to his cousin's defence. "Cathal's very busy with the band at the moment and takes care of a lot of the business decisions and arrangements for us. If the rest of us pulled our weight a bit more on that front, Cathal might have some more free time!" James was trying to inject some humour.

"I see!" snapped Joanne, noticing the director giving her a warning look to lay off that line of questioning. "James, you've really stepped up your charity work over the past year. Do you want to tell us a bit about that?"

"Yeah, it's something that both myself and Donna take very seriously. We're delighted to be involved in helping the underprivileged – people who are not as lucky as we are."

"As lucky as you are? Do you see your success as luck or something more? If Affidavit hadn't become successful, where do you think life would have taken you?"

"Well, I was in college with Rob studying engineering at the time we started the band, but I really wasn't enjoying my studies. I think I would have kept trying to sing somewhere, somehow."

"Rob?" asked Joanne.

"I'd have stuck with the engineering course and I suppose I'd be designing bridges somewhere, but probably would have been concentrating on song-writing in my spare time, banging off music to record companies all the time."

"And Seán?"

"Well, I always wanted to work in the entertainment field, and I love doing television, so I would have pursued a career maybe in TV or journalism. Doing your job, Joanne!"

"And what about you, Cathal? Where would you be now, if Affidavit hadn't happened?" She stared at him.

Cathal had been thrown by Joanne's previous line of questioning, and now his mind went blank. He had a flashback to his life before Affidavit. He stared intensely at the camera focusing on him. "I don't know," he said.

*   *   *

"What the hell was all that about?" Cathal snapped.

"What was what about?" Joanna was coolly filing her papers into her briefcase.

"Trying to make me feel embarrassed, asking me personal questions after what happened between us last week."

"I don't know what you're talking about. I was merely wearing my journalist's hat."

"Journalist's hat! You're doing a crummy music show, hardly Pulitzer-prize-winning stuff!"

"If I may point out, you're not exactly The Beatles yourselves!" She closed her briefcase and turned, looking him in the eyes. "You never called. You told me you would call and you didn't."

"We've been very busy with shooting this video and everything."

"I don't care. I'm not some silly groupie who hangs around for you at the back of concerts. I am Joanne Bailey, a respected television presenter."

"What's your problem? We had a good time and neither of us was looking for anything else."

"Oh, so simple to move on, isn't it? Well, I've had my photo in the paper with you. I have been linked with you."

"I can't help that. I was as furious about that photo as you were."

Sylvia shouted over, "C'mon, let's try and shoot this fucking video!"

"Look, I have to go," said Cathal. "See you around."

"I'll be in Exclusive later – we can talk about it there."

"We might be shooting here all night."

"Then phone me and we'll meet up this week," she insisted.

"I'd better get back." Cathal turned and walked over to the set.

She watched as he started talking to Sylvia about the video.

Seán sidled up beside her and said, "You're wasting your time, you know."

"Sorry?" She was startled.

"You won't get him to change his ways."

"I'm not with you?"

"Cathal is Cathal. Lives life on the run, on the road. Never will settle down. But if you want to have a night out in Exclusive, I'd be very willing to take you." He shrugged and smiled.

"I think I've had enough of rock bands for now."

*   *   *

Tony stood nervously outside the gleaming glass building that housed the offices of *Hi Life* magazine, puffing on a cigarette. He looked at his watch. The interview was for eleven. It was now seven minutes to the hour. He was never sure when the right time to walk into an office for an interview was. Was it ten minutes before? Five minutes? Or exactly on time? He threw the cigarette on the pavement and stamped it out, drew himself up to his full height and walked to the door.

He pressed the intercom and when it was answered he said, "Hi, Tony O'Brien here for an interview at eleven."

He heard the buzzer sound and pushed open the door. Inside was a large foyer with cream-tiled floors, white walls and two receptionists.

"Tony O'Brien, I have an appointment with Ralph Conway."

"Upstairs, the first door on the right."

He climbed the wide staircase winding upwards. At the top of the stairs was an open-plan office, again with cream tiles on the floor. On the white walls hung framed front covers of former editions of *Hi Life*. Two glamorous blondes, in their thirties Tony guessed, sat at two desks. One was busy talking on the phone.

"Tony?" asked one of the women, smiling.

"Yes." He smiled back, hiding his nerves.

"I'm Vivienne. We talked on the phone. Take a seat." She nodded over to one of the couches that lined the walls.

He sat, glancing around, struck with how bright everything was. On the coffee table beside him were about twenty copies of the latest edition of *Hi Life* meticulously arranged. He studied all the front covers on the walls, which featured everyone from international celebs like Madonna to VIPs on the Irish social scene.

He listened in to Vivienne's telephone conversation.

"Yes, well, Tuesday is out of the question, Ralph is attending a charity lunch that day . . . No, I'm not sure what time it finishes at . . . Wednesday, no, he's in London that day for a meeting at A2Z . . . That's fine, I'll check it with Ralph and give you a call back shortly." She replaced the receiver and began typing at her computer. Then her phone rang. She picked up and listened without comment. "Ralph will see you now, Tony, if you want to follow me."

Tony grabbed his folder, stood up and followed her.

Vivienne knocked on a door, then holding it open nodded at Tony to go in. He stepped inside and she closed the door behind him.

He was immediately struck by the size of the office, how big it was. The colour scheme was rich reds and purples, and on the walls hung more covers of *Hi Life*. There was a big boardroom table in the centre and a couple of sofas and a coffee table to the right. At the other end of the room, behind a gigantic desk, sat a man in his late forties, in a designer suit.

As Tony got to the desk, Ralph Conway stood up to shake his hand. He saw Ralph's eye take in every inch of him, assessing him before he even opened his mouth. Ralph was not a physically good-looking man, but he had presence.

"Thank you for meeting me," said Tony.

Ralph nodded to the seat and Tony sat down, facing him across the desk.

"You've been writing quite a while, but really only in a freelance mode, nothing permanent," said Ralph, looking down at Tony's CV.

Tony found himself sitting towards the edge of his seat. "Yes, I've had a lot of experience in different places, as you can see from the articles I enclosed with my application. I've had a few articles published by *The Herald*, and a lot of stuff printed in the provincial papers." While Tony continued to speak about his career, he felt Ralph's eyes inspecting his suit and drifting down to look at his hands. He guessed appearance was very important to this man. When he felt he had been talking non-stop for ages about his writing skills and experience, he made himself stop speaking.

"To be a staff writer on *Hi Life* writing skills are, of course, important attributes," said Ralph, "but even more important is your personality. How you get on with people. We deal with very rich and famous people here every week. People open their lives up to us and we in return present their lives to the public. So, there's a great deal of trust going on there, do you understand me?"

"Of course, when stars open their homes and lives to you, you have to treat them with a great deal of respect." Tony felt the sweat break out on his forehead.

"I've had staff writers in the past who got ahead of themselves, who stopped treating the people we cover with that respect. When that's gone there's nothing left. Each person we cover in *Hi Life* is a star to us and they get the star treatment. What kind of personality do you need to be able to give that attention?"

"Er . . . a very tolerant personality. It needs the kind of person who wants to understand what makes these people tick."

Ralph hit the table with the palm of his hand. "Damned right it does! When we are doing a special on somebody, we don't just go, take a few photos, ask a few questions and bingo, go to print! We get to know that person, we practically live with that person for a while, getting to know them and getting them to trust us before we do the story. Now we can't do that with every story in every issue, but I'm talking about the big stories, the ones that get printed in the *Hi Life* magazines Europe-wide."

Tony had done his homework on *Hi Life*. The magazine was owned by the London-based A2Z publishing company, owned by the Harton family. They printed the UK edition. They then franchised it to other countries around Europe. Ralph Conway owned the franchise in Ireland. This enabled the Irish edition to have a dynamic mix of features from the UK and local features. Tony realised that most of the UK newspapers ran the same set-up with their Irish editions. It was a formula that proved to be very successful. And with the amount of celebrities coming out of Ireland over the past few years, the Irish edition had scored a few international hits, syndicating their stories to the other editions of *Hi Life*.

"And the stars that we cover, they become our friends as well. When they open their homes to us, they are doing it as friends."

"Of course, there has to be a trust there." Tony nodded in agreement.

"Who do you know?"

"Know?"

"In a social sense. On the social circuit, who do you

know? What are your connections?"

Damn, thought Tony, as he wracked his brains and thought of all the people he might have come into contact with. "Well, having worked in the media for a long time, I know a lot of the editors of the papers and magazines."

Ralph looked unimpressed. "Where do you socialise?"

"Café en Seine, Cocoon, The Westbury for drinks. Lillie's, Renard's, Exclusive for clubs."

"You go to Exclusive regularly?"

"Yes, I was there only the Friday before last."

"You know Kathryn Foy?"

"Of course. I had a big chat with her that night." Tony hoped he was coming across as convincing.

"Kathryn's a great woman. She runs the best place in town, and can organise any party. She's an old friend of us here at *Hi Life* . . . Are you married?"

"No, but I've been with my partner for a good few years."

"What does she do?"

"She's a psychotherapist." Tony watched as Ralph looked impressed and sat up straight. "She's in her own practice," he added for good measure.

"We provide a service to the people. *Hi Life* is so much more than just a magazine. It's a little bit of magic that comes into people's lives. But you have to be hungry for it. Very hungry. You need to be able to put it before everything else. Do you understand?"

"Yes. I certainly would like the opportunity to do that."

*   *   *

"How did it go?" asked Nicole. Tony had rung her as soon as the interview was over.

"I'm not sure. Okay, I guess. I think he liked me."

"Conway? What's he like?"

"Kind of frightening. He was very polite and everything, but there's something about him that's intimidating. And then after the interview they got me to do this psychological test."

"What kind of test?" Nicole sounded concerned.

"This really long questionnaire I had to fill out. Things like: what would you rather do – a) a parachute jump, b) scuba diving or c) visit the zoo? So I haven't a clue how I did on that one."

Nicole was curious. "What did you answer for that one?"

"What I wanted to put was visit the zoo, because it sounded like the safest and easiest option. But I put down parachuting because I thought it the most impressive answer."

"You were probably right. And did it seem like a nice place to work?"

"I don't know. I suppose. If I got it the job, it would certainly be the break I've been looking for. They deal with so many celebrities."

"And would you be able to deal with all the egos and the bullshit that would go with a job like that?"

"Sure I would."

CHAPTER 5

Lana opened her eyes and felt her head thump. She glanced around the room, wondering where she was, before realising she was at Patricia's. She tried to remember the previous night but it all seemed very vague. She remembered being in Exclusive and dancing a lot. She couldn't remember leaving, but she vaguely recalled walking around the city centre streets for what seemed like ages. Then she must have got a taxi back to Patricia's, but she couldn't remember getting there. Just another night of walking around aimlessly, she thought. She ran her hands through her hair and climbed out of the bed.

"Patricia!" Lana called, coming out of the bedroom and onto the landing. Patricia lived in an architecturally designed house in Dalkey with her fiancé, Henry McGrane, who was a consultant doctor.

"Down on the patio – join me for some lunch!" Patricia called.

"Lunch? What time is it?" said Lana, descending the stairs.

"It's one o'clock, darling," said Patricia, who was having a salad on the patio. "I was just about to call you for a bit of grub."

Lana sat down at the table and Patricia began to dish salad out onto her plate. The sun was sparkling down on the clear water of the swimming pool.

"My head is killing me," said Lana, as she poured herself some water.

"I think we all indulged a little too much last night."

"Why did I come back to yours?"

"I don't know! You left Exclusive earlier than we did, so I rang you to make sure you got home all right. You didn't answer but you turned up here in a taxi later."

Lana angry with herself for having blacked out. It was one thing wandering the streets when she was alert, quite another when she wasn't.

"Oh, look at the time, I'd better dash! We're shooting a commercial at three." Patricia worked for an advertising company but she had cut down her hours considerably since becoming engaged to Henry. "Stay here for the day, if you like. Chill out by the pool; it's a lovely day for it."

"Thanks, I might as well."

"See you later." Patricia kissed Lana's cheek, and walked into the house, calling back: "And don't forget about the party we're having here on Saturday night, okay?"

"Of course I'll be here."

Lana got up and sauntered over to a sun lounge, and lay out on it, still wearing her Versace.

*　　*　　*

Tony walked home from work, smoking a cigarette. All he could think about was the job at *Hi Life*. He'd had a really bad day and now he so desperately wanted that job.

He prayed he would get it. He had been secretly a bit dubious about it before he went in for the interview. It really wasn't the kind of journalism he aspired to. And he believed Conway had a bad reputation as a hard man to work for. But he could cope with all that. He knew this was a golden opportunity to get where he wanted. And now he realised he had been too nervous during the interview and had probably come across as a bit edgy. Damn, he had probably blown it! He knew he hadn't the right experience for it and his only chance had been to exude confidence and capability and he was sure he hadn't done that.

He let himself into the house.

"Guess what?" said an excited Nicole as he came in. "Vivienne from *Hi Life* left a message on the answering machine . . . they want to see you for a second interview!"

"Really! Oh, thank God! I thought I'd fucked it up!" Tony was overcome with relief. He sat down on the couch and buried his face in his hands.

"Tony?" Nicole asked, full of concern. She sat beside him, placing her hand on his arm. "Are you okay?"

He looked up at her, and his face was upset.

"What's wrong?" she urged. "This is great news. They want to see you again."

"I don't know. It's stupid, isn't it? I just feel so far I've let everybody down. You, myself. I just want to get a break. Is that so much to ask? I want it so much and I try so hard to get it."

"I know you do!" She enveloped him in a hug.

"I kinda feel that this is one of those chances you get in life and if you don't take them, or try hard enough to get them, then they pass you by. And then you've missed the boat. I feel this chance with *Hi Life* is like my last chance to make it."

*   *   *

"I'm afraid Ralph is out of the country from the day after tomorrow, and he'll be gone for a couple of weeks. He wanted to see all the candidates that have been shortlisted tomorrow. Is there no way you can get time off work?" asked Vivienne, when Tony rang the following morning to arrange the second interview.

Tony glanced at his angry-looking sales manager. "I finish work here at five – any chance I could come after that?"

"Could you hold a minute and I'll check for you," Vivienne put him on hold.

Tony said a quick prayer this would be all right.

"That's fine. Ralph will stay a little later tomorrow evening to meet you. We'll see you at five fifteen."

*   *   *

After parking his Land Cruiser in the underground apartment, Cathal nipped around the corner to the Spar shop to get some milk and other essentials. The middle-aged man who ran the shop, Hakaam, as ever chatted to him for a few minutes, before Cathal headed back to his apartment.

He threw the keys on the ornate table inside the door, and after throwing the bags of shopping on the kitchen counter, threw himself on the couch and stretched out to think. They had spent the day shooting the video, and nobody, particularly Sylvia, was happy with the results they were getting. It would be the last song released from that album – to Cathal's relief, as nothing to do with that album had gone smoothly.

Affidavit were due to start recording a new album soon and were already beginning to search for material. Even though they had all worked very hard on the tour, Cathal realised they hadn't been as focused recently as they used to be. He remembered when they were starting off, how they used to tour the country in a beat-up old van playing any gig they could get. They had really slummed it, but they had such good times as well. Then when they had signed their first contract, they had put their heart and soul into it as well. And as they got bigger and bigger they had put in more work. But recently there had been distractions. First of all Rob had married Heidi, who was totally supportive of Affidavit – she was certainly no Yoko Ono. But now the baby had arrived on the scene, and he had obviously been preoccupied with that. Also James had fallen for Donna, and there was all this talk of wedding plans now which James seemed to be more interested in than the music. Not to mention all this excellent but time-consuming charity work James was involved in. Then there was Seán. Cathal and Seán went through their up and downs. Over the years they had been at times really good mates and hung out with each other all the time. But then there were times they couldn't stand each other. Seán seemed to be resentful of the managerial role Cathal assumed in the band. But there was something else going on in Seán's mind at the moment that Cathal couldn't figure out.

Cathal believed it was time the band became more focused and regrouped. They needed to shake up their music somewhat and start experimenting with new tracks and sounds. They needed to play with their image a little more. And most importantly they needed to aim for much bigger success. Sure they had success outside Europe, but they were nowhere in U2's league. He believed they had the talent and ability to achieve much more than they had and all they needed to do was keep focused and fresh. And he was going to be the driving force behind it.

His mobile rang.

"Hello?"

"Hi, Cathal, it's Joanne."

He hadn't thought he would hear from her again after their little spat. "Yes, Joanne?"

"I just wanted to apologise for being a little aggressive during the interview. I'm sorry if I upset you." Her voice was soft and sweet and he was taken aback.

"That's all right . . . I'm sorry for not ringing you when I said I would."

"Friends?"

"Sure, why not?"

"What have you been up to?"

"Are you wearing your journalist's hat when you ask that question?"

She laughed lightly "No, I'm asking as a friend."

"Just been shooting that stupid video again. Hasn't been going as well as might have been expected."

"You're probably knackered, are you?"

"I'm not too bad."

"Fancy meeting in Exclusive tonight?"

*   *   *

Kathryn put the phone down in her office and smiled to herself. Simeon had just been on, letting her know that he was at Joe's studio and probably would stay there the whole night and so not to worry when she got home and found him gone. He had been brilliant all week. When she had got home from work in the early hours of the morning, he had been waiting up for her, and it was great spending that time together. The work he had been doing for Joe had really made a difference to him and she prayed it would ignite his creative talent again. When Simeon was being creative nobody could match him. God, if he could get that back, she knew everything would be good in their lives. The only reason things went bad was because of Simeon's frustration with himself for not being able to fulfil his potential. She remembered meeting him first. She was the promotions girl for a nightclub in Dublin. She and Kelly were just becoming known around town and getting invited to lots of parties and events. Their good looks made them very popular on the party scene. Kathryn had always been mesmerised by music and that was the reason she went to work in a nightclub. A record producer used to come into the club regularly and she befriended him and he invited her to attend a music studio where a couple of artists were recording. She jumped at the chance. She clearly remembered the day she and Kelly trotted into the studio and sat quietly looking on. Simeon was recording one of his songs. Kathryn had never seen or heard anyone like him before. She was entranced by his looks, his coolness and his music. As he sang his song she sat besotted with him, the exquisiteness of his music almost too much to bear and she had to wipe away a tear. She sat there for hours listening, not understanding what effect this man and his music was having on her.

When Simeon came over to speak to her and Kelly after, she could barely speak and had to let her sister do all the talking. They all went out that night and she sat on the periphery of the group listening to his every word. He was well known on the Dublin music scene and recognised as a big star of the future. He had been giving small concerts for years and the big record labels were showing a lot of interest in him. When he asked her out at the end of the evening she could hardly say the word yes. She was used to all the guys she met bringing her to expensive restaurants, but Simeon brought her back to the empty studio, got fish and chips from the takeaway next door and they sat on the floor talking and eating. He told her money wasn't his motivator. He had been offered contracts by the record labels but refused to sign them. He was aware how big his talent was and his main mission was to protect it and not let it be bastardised by record companies. When he signed a contract he would have complete control and take his pick. Then he played his music to her and sang to her, and again it stirred something so deep inside her. Then he kissed her and they had become intimate. She never really felt worthy of his love back then. They moved in together and her own career in nightclubs started progressing up the ladder. But she knew her career must always play second fiddle to Simeon's. However, as he wasn't earning any money at the time, she needed to be good at her job as it was she who was paying the bills till he made it to the big time. And everything was fine: they lived their lives working and around his music. She used to go to the studios often just sitting and listening, fascinated by the whole process and by Simeon's talent that seemed to get better with each contract he turned down. Then one day he came home looking unwell and had gone to bed. He hardly got out of the bed for four days and she was worried sick about him. Once he got out of bed, he just hung around the house for days, barely speaking and not wanting to go to the studio. After a couple of months he went to the studio to record something. He spent an hour there and then rushed home to bed again. He hadn't been able to play or create music ever since then. It was as if that wonderful light inside him that created brilliant music had somehow been switched off.

Kathryn shook off her troubled thoughts. She could hear the music thumping from the club. She got up and locked her door behind her, then walked down the corridor and opened the fire-exit door that led into the main club. It looked like it was going to be a busy night for a Thursday. It was only just after eleven and the club was fairly full already.

She made her way downstairs to the front door

Upstairs, George Scanlon, a photographer with *The Sun*, was scouring the club looking for Joanne Bailey.

Suddenly she appeared at his elbow. "Any trouble getting in?" she murmured.

"No, I did like you said and got in before Kathryn took up her post at the door – just flashed the membership card at the security." Joanne had borrowed a membership card for him – at a price. He glanced about nervously. "I'd better keep well out of her sight now. If I know her, she'd have me arrested for fraud!"

"Relax, George!"

"Well, where is he?"

"He's not here yet."

"For fuck's sake, Joanne, I'm after dragging my ass in from home to get this shot – don't tell me he's not turning up!"

"He'll be here. Anyway, George, lighten up. Get a drink. You might even enjoy yourself." She waltzed off back to her crowd.

* * *

Cathal jumped out of the taxi and bounded up the steps to the front door.

"Hi, Cathal, I didn't realise you were coming in tonight," Kathryn smiled.

"I didn't myself up to a couple of hours ago. Is Joanne Bailey here, by any chance?"

"Yes, she's up in the members' lounge."

"Better head up so," smirked Cathal.

"Oh, and Cathal!" Kathryn called after him. "Thanks for giving Sara your cap."

"Don't mention it!"

Kathryn turned and wondered what the story between Cathal and Joanne was. They were obviously seeing each other. Joanne seemed to be the glamorous type Cathal always went for. She had known Joanne on the social circuit for a few years, and wondered if Cathal knew what he was playing with when dealing with her.

Joanne was delighted and relieved when she spotted Cathal. She gave a quick look over to George to check he was paying attention.

Cathal came over to her table.

"Hi, good to see you!" she said, standing up and kissing him on the cheek. "This is Cathal, everybody!" she said to her crew. "And, Cathal, this is everybody!" She took his hand and drew him to sit beside her. She poured him a glass of wine.

"Thanks," he said, taking it.

"You look a little stressed."

"This video we're shooting is proving a nightmare. Everyone knows it could be better, but we're already over budget on it so we'll have to wrap it up."

"Why isn't it working out?"

"That's what I'm trying to figure out. People seem to be distracted. And I think the director has lost touch – we only use him because we've always used him in the past. There are a lot of people on the Affidavit team that we probably need to review – that's strictly between ourselves, incidentally."

"Don't worry – I've left my journalist's hat at home tonight!" She refilled his glass.

* * *

Much later they were on the dance floor, dancing intimately and kissing. Joanne held Cathal close and, looking over his shoulder, spotted George still in attendance.

"Hey, let's go back to my place," said Cathal.

"No way!" said Joanne. "It's too early – I want to dance some more!"

"But I want to have sex with you *now*," he mumbled, kissing her neck.

She laughed. "Well, you can't."

"I must!"

She laughed again. "Come on, then," she whispered into his ear.

She took him by the hand and led him through the crowd to the back of the club, where there was a fire-exit door. Turning, she smiled mischievously at him before pushing the bar of the fire exit open and and slipping through to the corridor outside.

"Eh – what are we doing out here?" he asked, but he was smiling as she led him along the corridor and down the steps to a lower landing.

He could still hear the music thumping from the club as she stopped and began to kiss him passionately while opening his shirt and pushing it off his shoulders.

"You can't be serious!" he said, but he was laughing as he began to undo her top.

"Well, you insisted! Anyway, I like fun and I like risk, Cathal – don't you?" She kissed his neck while his hands roamed over her and then found the zip of her skirt.

"I wouldn't be here if I didn't," he said as her skirt dropped to the concrete floor.

As Joanne felt her bare back being pushed up against the cold wall behind her, she glanced up to make sure George was on the landing above, camera in hand.

*　　*　　*

"I just don't want them to grab a photo of us like last time." Cathal explained to Kathryn. He and Joanne were at the reception of Exclusive.

"I completely understand," agreed Kathryn. "I've been at the door all night and haven't seen any press, but you never know – somebody in the club might have alerted one of the papers. So I've ordered two taxis, the first one for you and the second for Joanne – she can leave ten minutes later in the second one."

"Thanks, Kathryn," smiled Cathal.

Kathryn wondered why anybody would be bothered looking at a photograph of the talentless one from a band and a second-rate TV presenter. But she knew that in fact there was a huge number of people who would want to see just such a photo. That was what living in a celebrity-obsessed age was all about. Real talent got lost along the

76

way and was replaced by something that sold newspapers.

"Here's your cab, now," said Kathryn, seeing Cathal scribble down an address and hand it to Joanne.

"See you in twenty minutes," said Cathal to Joanne. "Thanks, Kathryn, for everything." And then he quickly made his way to the taxi.

"Do you mind if I wait here beside you until my cab arrives?" asked Joanne.

"Of course not."

"He's really great, isn't he?"

"I've always liked Cathal. He and the other guys started coming here early on in their careers and they never got big-headed like a lot of the stars we get here."

Joanne, interested by Kathryn's air of familiarity with Cathal, looked her quickly up and down. "Are you friends with him?"

"No, friendly, but not friends with him."

Joanne smiled in a secure fashion, "There's so much interest in Affidavit, it's amazing. Since I had my photo in the paper with him a couple of weeks back, my phone hasn't stopped hopping with people looking for me to do work or give interviews."

"That's . . . good." Kathryn shrugged.

"I've even had *Hi Life* on wanting to do a full feature on me. But what I'd really like is to get the feature in the UK edition as well and start getting established over there. I've done a couple of interviews for MTV and I'd love to do that permanently. I've only got a small window of opportunity to make it big, and if I miss it . . . well!"

Kathryn nodded, wondering why the woman was sharing her career aspirations with her and also being slightly concerned about her thought processes.

"Anyway, here's your cab," she said, showing Joanne

to the door.

*　　*　　*

"Wow, this place is gorgeous," said Joanne, looking around Cathal's apartment.

"Thanks." Cathal took out a bottle of vodka from the fridge and brought it over to the coffee table with two glasses. "It cost me a hell of a lot – more than I could afford really."

"Come off it!" She was opening drawers in the kitchen, looking through them. "You must be worth millions!"

"Ha!" he snorted. "I wish I was. We only started making serious money the past couple of years and I ploughed a lot of money into this place and a house I bought for my family at home."

"That was good of you." She joined him on the couch and took the drink he had poured for her.

"They're a good family," he replied.

"Yeah, but still a lot of people in your position would have just fucked off and not given their family anything."

"Would they?" He looked unsure. "They've been so good and supportive of me through the years, you wouldn't believe it . . . I wasn't exactly a model child."

"Who was? You should have seen me as a teenager." She picked up the crystal ashtray. "Is that a Louise Kennedy?"

*　　*　　*

Kathryn did a final check around the club and made sure everything was secure. She looked at her watch. It was four in the morning and everyone had left. A security guard was waiting for her.

"Everything seems fine, Jake. I've a bit of paperwork to do, so you head off home."

"Okay," Jake nodded and left.

She collected some papers from her office and made her way to the grand piano in the members' lounge. Since Simeon had said he would be home every night, she hadn't had any time to play that week at all, and so was grateful for the opportunity to spend some time on it now. She sat down at the piano and spread her papers out. Her fingers began to tap on the piano keys gently as she scrutinised the music sheet in front of her.

*   *   *

Cathal looked at the bottle of vodka that they had practically consumed. And emptied the rest of it out into their glasses. Out through the patio windows he could see the night was still pitch black.

Joanne, as drunk as himself, was dancing on the white sofas to an old Affidavit song.

"I think this is my favourite of your songs of all time," she said, getting down off the sofa and curling up in his arms.

"That was our first hit in the UK. You should have seen us when Sylvia rang us up and told us. We were giving some radio interview at the time and we just started jumping up and screaming and shouting all over the place."

"I can imagine . . . so what now for Cathal Fitzgerald? Where to next?"

"Just keep the band going and try and stay at the top for as long as possible."

"And do you want to settle down at some stage?"

"Yeah, sure, at some stage. She'd have to be very understanding to put up my work schedule at the moment. And then it's hard to know when you meet somebody if they are interested in you or because of who you are and what you can do for them."

"I can understand your concerns." She stroked his arm. "There are a lot of vultures out there."

CHAPTER 6

Lana and Patricia came out of Brown Thomas, laden down with shopping bags, and headed into an expensive boutique.

"I want something really nice for Saturday's party," said Patricia, as she riffled through the clothes. "What are you wearing yourself?"

"I haven't decided yet – probably pick up something between this and then."

Patricia pulled out a satin oyster-coloured dress. "What do you think of this?" She held it against her.

"Gorgeous, try it on," advised Lana.

Patricia disappeared into the changing room.

"For you," Lana confirmed when her friend emerged a minute later.

Patricia thought so too and shortly after they made their way to the till.

"Who's going to be at the party anyway?" asked Lana.

Patricia handed over her credit card. "The usual crew, also a few people involved in the photo shoot I've been working on."

The sales assistant put the credit card through the

machine and then handed Patricia the print-out. "Now, Elaine, if you could just sign this for me," she smiled.

"Elaine?" Lana turned to Patricia, confused.

"Yes?" Patricia shot Lana a warning look as she signed the receipt.

"Er . . . is Greg Archer going to be at the party?" Lana could feel herself blush.

"Should be, he's invited anyway." Patricia handed the receipt back to the sales assistant who quickly checked the signature and then handed the credit card back to Patricia. "I'm hungry," said Patricia as they left the store. "Time for lunch."

Lana waited until they were safely down the street before speaking. "What was that all about? Why did she call you Elaine?"

Patricia looked mischievous. "Why do you think?" She reached into her purse, took out the credit card and held it out for Lana to read.

Lana saw the name Elaine McGrane printed on the card.

"Elaine McGrane?" Lana was completely confused. "Henry's sister?"

"Yes."

"But why did she give you her credit card?"

"She didn't. I nicked it from her drawer when I was over at her house yesterday!" Patricia giggled like a naughty schoolgirl.

"Nicked it?"

"Well, borrowed it, really. I'll replace it this evening, so there's no harm done."

"Let me get this straight. You've forged her signature to get that dress?"

"Yes."

"But what will happen when she finds out?"

"She won't find out. My wonderful fiancé has three sisters, spoilt bitches every one of them. They go through money like water and I know for a fact they never check their credit-card bills. So what's a little added on here and there? They never notice."

"They never notice? You mean you've done this before?"

"Yes, it's my new hobby."

"But it's a crime! If you get caught!"

"I won't get caught."

"But you can afford to buy this stuff yourself, can't you?"

"Of course I can. But that's not the point. I get a real kick out of doing it. When I'm at the till and signing their signatures, I get an adrenaline boost."

Lana was full of concern.

"You should try it. You'd enjoy it. Come on, let's go to lunch . . ." Patricia flashed the credit card. "It's on Elaine!"

* * *

As soon as the clock hit five, Tony jumped up and raced out of the building. He ran out onto Baggot Street and after about five minutes finally managed to flag down a taxi. The traffic was atrocious and it was six o'clock before he reached *Hi Life*. The main lights in the foyer were off and there didn't seem to be anyone about. He pressed the buzzer.

"Yes?" It was Ralph's voice.

Tony got a fright on hearing him answering. "Hi, it's Tony O'Brien, here for the interview."

A second later another buzzer sounded and he pushed

the door open. He knew how bad it looked being so late and had an overriding urge to run away. But he continued up the steps, through the empty reception and down the corridor to Ralph's door. The building seemed eerie at that time of the evening.

He knocked gently and heard Ralph call, "Come in!"

Red-faced, he sported what he hoped was a suitably embarrassed look and said: "I'm so sorry for being so late. There were road works and the taxi –"

"That's fine, sit down," Ralph said abruptly.

Tony did as he was told, reminded how intimidating Ralph could be.

"You scored very high on the test you did here," said Ralph.

"Did I?" smiled Tony. "That's good, I –"

"I do have my doubts about your lack of experience in pure journalism, particularly in this field of celebrity journalism." Ralph reached into his drawer and pulled out some photographs of different stars and spread them out on his desk facing Tony.

"I want you to look at these photos and tell me which ones you think are best."

*   *   *

"I got it!" shouted Tony running through the door.

Nicole screamed and jumped into his arms.

"I fucking got it!" he yelled.

"Fantastic! What happened?"

"I met him after work and he gave me some kind of test judging photos, then started asking about my opinions on stars and how I'd deal with situations. I start in two weeks. I can't wait to give in my notice. This is it, Nic. We're on our way!"

*   *   *

Tony stirred in his sleep. He started whimpering and thrashing around.

Nicole woke up and switched on the light beside him.

"Tony!" she called softly and with a start Tony woke up.

"Sorry, I was having such a bad dream."

"What was it about?"

"I was in the offices at *Hi Life*, and there were these people there and Ralph. But it all seemed sinister and not right. And then this woman came up to me – I don't know who she was – and pleaded with me not to take the job. She said if I took the job I wouldn't leave there alive . . ."

"It's all right." She stroked his hair. "It's just a dream caused by the stress you've been feeling over getting this job. Now that you've got the job, your subconscious is scared that you'll fail at it, causing a negative dream about it."

He giggled.

"What's funny?" she asked.

"You are! I love it when the psychologist in you takes over and manages to rationalise everything."

"Well, it's true what I'm saying. Relax. You're not going to fail at this job; you're going to be a big success. Think positive."

"You're right. I will be a success; I'll do whatever it takes to make sure I am."

CHAPTER 7

Cathal pulled his Land Cruiser into the gravel drive of James' home on the south side of the city and jumped out. James and Donna's home was a lovely old ivy-clad house set in two acres of beautiful gardens. He rang the doorbell and Donna, barefoot and dressed in jeans and a black T-shirt, answered.

"Hiya!" She kissed him on the cheek and he followed her inside.

The house had been slightly dilapidated when James bought it. They had lovingly restored it, and had hired the best interior designer in the country to furnish it to its now brilliant modern standard.

In the lounge James was sitting on the couch, a bottle of beer in his hand. "Hi, Cathal!"

"Hiya, mate!" said Cathal, sitting beside him.

"I hope you brought your overnight bag with you," Donna called as she went through to the kitchen. "The party's only up the road, so it would be pointless your going back into the city!"

"Yeah, it's in the Jeep," called Cathal.

"And you have to stay for Sunday lunch tomorrow as

well – Donna insists," laughed James.

Donna came padding out of the kitchen with a beer and gave it to Cathal.

"Whose party is it tonight, anyway?" asked Cathal.

"It's this girl, Patricia, who works for the advertising company that has been throwing lots of work my way," said Donna, joining them on the couch. "She's been on a good few of the photo shoots with me. She's a bit affected, but very nice though. She's seems to know everybody so the party should be good."

"We deserve to enjoy ourselves now that fucking video is finished." James sat back and drained his bottle of beer.

"I've been giving the band a lot of thought, and I was thinking of calling a meeting next week at Sylvia's office," Cathal said.

"Yeah, how so?"

"Well, we're due to start recording the new album shortly and I think we really need to sharpen up our act, especially if we're going to get really big in the States."

James raised his eyes to heaven. "Here we go – you're on your America trip again!"

"There's no reason why we couldn't make it in America as big as here, if we put in the time and effort and work really hard at it." Cathal was becoming angry as James looked bored with the conversation.

"Look, Cathal, if it ain't broken don't fix it, that's always been my motto. And we have great lives." He put his arm around Donna. "Why are you always thinking things will go wrong?"

"Because they do if you don't watch everything and make sure things are going the right way!"

"You're a control freak!" accused James.

"Look, enough already!" Donna intervened. "You can

talk about this next week. What I'm more interested in is what's happening between you and Joanne Bailey, Cathal. James told me you saw her on Thursday again!"

"Oh, here we go." Cathal flopped back in the couch. "I see someone more than once and you're all ringing the wedding bells!"

"You'd make such a cute couple," said Donna.

"Being part of a cute couple might not be what I'm looking for." He looked at the two of them. They were a media dream. James with his looks and Donna with her doll-like features, and tumble of golden blonde hair. All that, topped with James trying to save the world with his charity work. It was no wonder the celebrity magazines were always after them.

"And she's on TV," continued Donna. "She's in the business, so she'd understand the pressure of your work,"

"Look, I hardly know her yet, so I don't know what she's like."

"She could be the one for you!" said Donna.

"Look, Donna, can I just say that firstly not everybody is looking for that mushy love you and James have and secondly – be totally honest with me here – do you really think the two of you will be together happily ever after?"

Donna took James' hand quickly. "Of course – we wouldn't be getting married if we didn't."

"I know you're in love now, but do you expect you'll always feel the exact same way about each other."

"Sure we do," James nodded.

"Well, I really hope you do. But in my experience people are just out for what they can get and then they're off, and if they stay it's out of fear or because they need security or something like that."

"You're so goddamned cynical!" snapped Donna.

Cathal got up. "Anyway, I'll fetch my bag from the Jeep."

Donna waited until he had left the room. "He can say nasty stuff sometimes. I mean I love him and everything, but . . ."

James stroked her hand "You have to be a bit understanding with him, love. You have to take the rough with the smooth sometimes. He's fucked up so many times, I suppose it's left him a bit bitter." He allowed himself a grin. "And twisted."

*   *   *

Donna rang the doorbell. Loud music was blaring from inside the house. Through the clear glass front door they could see the party was in full swing even though it was still only eleven.

"Hi!" said Patricia, in her new oyster-coloured dress, opening the door and kissing Donna. "Thanks so much for coming! Come on in!"

"This is my partner, James, and this is Cathal."

"Hi. I love your music," she said, shaking their hands. She passed the compliment in a relaxed ungushing fashion, with the ease of somebody who was never in awe. "There's drink all over the place, so help yourselves – food is laid out by the pool."

Patricia touched Donna's flat stomach. "Unless carbohydrates are still off the menu, Donna!" she laughed.

"No, I think I'll indulge tonight."

"Good, and there's lots of people from my ad agency and your model agency here, so . . . mingle!"

People were dancing around the swimming pool. Cathal and James looked on as they drank their beers.

"I think I'll take a look around" said Cathal and he sauntered into the house which at this stage was packed. He observed a couple go to a door and open it, and immediately was struck by the strong whiff of marijuana escaping from the room. Curiosity led him over to the door, and he opened it and let himself in. The room was in darkness, apart from candles lit around and Cathal quickly closed the door behind him.

He counted nine people seated around in a circle passing joints. He discreetly sat down and observed them. He was immediately struck by a girl with heavy straight hair which gleamed chestnut in the candlelight and a strikingly beautiful face. She was smoking a joint to herself and seemed to be spaced out. There was something about her that he couldn't make out, something mysterious and it drew him to her.

The man beside him offered Cathal his joint. He took the joint and glanced at it for a second before taking a drag and passing it on. Drugs had surrounded Affidavit from the moment they entered the music industry. They were easily on offer and constantly pushed at them. They had all experimented a bit. James was always too much of a goody-two-shoes to bother. In fact, one of the charities he was involved in highlighted the hazards of drugs. Cathal wondered whether he himself would have become a major user, if he hadn't had earlier experiences with the drugs world. He thought back to when he worked for a nightclub, long before he was famous. He remembered being in Stephen Rourke's office, the cocaine lined up on his desk and Stephen holding out a twenty-pound note for him to snort next. He remembered approaching the desk and taking the note.

He quickly got rid of the image and concentrated on

observing the girl who had intrigued him. She suddenly got up and exited the room. He waited a minute and then discreetly slipped out as well.

Out in the foyer he saw her reach under a beautifully ornate telephone table and pull out a bottle of vodka and a glass; he watched as she poured herself three glasses, knocking them back in quick succession. Then she sashayed out to the swimming pool.

He went out and found James and Donna. He saw the girl was dancing with the crowd, but she seemed to be in a world of her own.

"Who's that?" he asked and nodded over to the girl.

Donna followed his gaze and said, "That's bad news."

"What do you mean?"

"Her name's Lana Curtis, and she's exactly what I said she is: bad news. She's on the party circuit and anytime I've met her she's been either extremely aloof or just out of it. Her father is some big shot."

Cathal continued staring at her.

"I think Cathal's interested in her," smirked James.

"Oh, Cathal stay away from her!" advised Donna.

Cathal watched as Lana suddenly stopped dancing, and walked over to a man who was leaning against a wall having a cigarette. She began talking to him, and after a couple of minutes they were kissing intently. Cathal, surprised by this, couldn't keep his eyes off her. After minutes of passionate kissing, she pulled away and walked into the house, leaving the man looking confused.

"I'm going to take a walk inside," said Cathal, heading indoors.

He watched as the girl climbed up the stairs, then followed her.

He saw her disappearing into a bedroom, closing the

door after her. He wondered what she was up to. A voice inside him told him to walk away but he found himself knocking on the bedroom door. When there was no answer after many knocks, he turned the handle. It was unlocked. He gently opened the door.

Inside, Lana Curtis was seated on the edge of the bed with a mirror on her lap, snorting cocaine from it through a twenty-euro note.

She looked up and said "Either come in or get out, but whatever you do, close the fucking door!"

Cathal, taken aback, thought for a second, then quickly entered, closing the door after him. He glanced around the opulent bedroom. He sat down on the bed beside her.

She put down the mirror, reached over for his can of beer and drank from it.

"Do I know you?" she asked.

"I'm Cathal," he said, realising she hadn't a clue who he was.

"That's nice. Nice but boring." She suddenly fell back onto the bed and started laughing hysterically.

"Are you okay?" he asked. He stared at her and then asked, "Why is a beautiful girl like you ruining her life?"

She stopped laughing and stared back at him. "I'm bored now. Bored with this party and bored with you." She abruptly jumped up and strode out of the bedroom.

He watched from the top of the stairs as she descended, then reached under the telephone table, grabbed the hidden bottle of vodka and walked out the front door.

He raced down the stairs and out after her. She had walked down the driveway and onto the street. "Hey, wait up! Where are you going?"

"For a walk and then home."

"But you can't just walk around in that state!"

"I'm actually very good at just walking around in this state. It's my hobby."

"Wait, I'll call you a taxi."

"Look, just fuck off back to the party!" She swung around but lost her grip on the vodka bottle and it smashed on the ground. She stared down at it in horror. "Look what you've made me do!" Suddenly she was upset.

"Look, my friends live nearby – come back to the house and clean up."

"Go away, I'm not interested in you."

"I'm not talking about that. But you're in a state – you can't just walk around like that."

"Is there drink back there?" she asked, wiping away a tear.

*   *   *

Cathal let them into James' house with the key they had given him. Lana found the alcohol like a radar and fixed herself a strong drink.

"Do you always drink so much?" he asked.

"Do you have a problem with that?" she shot back.

"No, but I think you do."

Lana took a seat opposite him "It makes me feel good."

"And do drugs make you feel good too?"

"Actually, when I want them, yes they do."

"What's your name?" he asked.

She stopped swirling the gin around in her glass and eyed him suspiciously. He looked vaguely familiar and she wondered where she had seen him before. Was he an acquaintance of her father's? He'd seen her do cocaine in the bedroom back at the party . . .

94

"Is it relevant?" she asked.

"Well, you know my name, it's only manners to give me yours."

"Do I know your name?"

"Yes, I told you back at the party. Cathal. Cathal Fitzgerald."

Over the years he had become an expert at playing the fame game. He could spot the instant recognition when people realised who he was. But he could see this girl genuinely hadn't a clue. Judging from her accent and style, maybe she only listened to classical music? The people at the party had seemed pretty highbrow. He suddenly felt relaxed and intrigued at being in the company of a woman for whom he was just a normal guy. It was like going back in years to before fame.

She observed him intently and decided he seemed harmless enough. If he did know her father, and said anything back, he wouldn't believe him. She reached into her purse and took out her stash of cocaine.

"Do you have to do that here?" He was filled with concern.

Lana got up. "If it makes you uncomfortable, I'll leave."

"No, wait!" He gestured for her to keep her seat. "It's fine. It's just – it's not my house, and my friends don't really dig that scene."

"That's their problem." She toyed with her bag of coke. They eyed each other up suspiciously.

"Are you a friend of Patricia's?" Lana asked.

"Who?"

"The girl whose party it was."

"No, a friend of a friend."

"Do you work in advertising like Patricia?"

"I'm in the music industry."

"What, like a DJ or something?"

"Yeah, something like that. I play music."

"It's kind of irregular work, isn't it?"

Cathal couldn't help smiling to himself – he was enjoying this. "I suppose it is. Like recently I had big gig travelling abroad and that took up a lot of time, but now things are at a bit of a slower pace."

"Is there much money to be made in that line of business?"

"I get by . . . What about you? What do you do for a living?"

She leaned slowly forward "What do I do?" she repeated and sighed, then sat back into the couch. She felt sleepy and her eyes began to close.

He couldn't take his eyes off her as she slept. She seemed beautifully relaxed, unlike earlier. After a while he went over and nudged her awake.

"Yes . . . what?" she asked sleepily.

"There's a spare bedroom upstairs if you want to sleep there?"

She seemed quite out of it so he helped her get up and took her up the stairs. He put her in the bed, turned off the light and closed the door.

CHAPTER 8

The light streaming through the window woke her. She stretched out lazily and looked around, totally unaware of where she was. She began to recall the previous night. Patricia's party, leaving, coming back to the house with some guy. They had talked for a while and then she must have crashed out. She got up, slipped into her shoes and grabbed her purse.

She left the room and walked down the corridor. She observed the house had a lot of money spent furnishing it, but she remembered the saying – you can't buy class. Not an antique in sight. She came down the stairs and heard some talking in the sitting room. She crouched down at the banister and looked through the open doors of the room. She recognised the Cathal guy from last night talking to another man and a pretty young woman.

"Why did you bring her back here?" snapped the woman.

"I had to. She was a total mess," Cathal said defensively.

"Exactly, she's a lost cause. She's trouble, as I told you last night at the party. She's not good for you."

"Oh, relax!"

"I'm not relaxed!" said the young woman, picking up the bag of cocaine that Lana had left on the couch "You allowed her to bring coke in our home, Cathal!"

"What if the press found out about it?" said the other guy. "What would my fucking anti-drugs charity say?"

"The point is, Cathal," said the woman, dropping the bag of coke down on the coffee table in disgust, "that girl is not someone anyone sane wants to hang around with. She's dangerous and she brings people down who are associated with her. And I don't want to be associated with somebody like that, and neither should you!"

Lana entered the sitting room, smiling. "Good morning, everybody. Isn't it a lovely morning? Just thought I'd pop in to say goodbye before I left." She savoured the look of surprise on their faces. She walked over to the coffee table and reclaimed her coke before turning and leaving, slamming the front door behind her.

She walked down the drive and onto the street. She thought she was somewhere in Dalkey but hadn't a clue where.

"Wait!" Cathal came racing after her.

She waited.

"Look, I'm really sorry about that," he said.

"That's no problem at all," she said, smiling boldly, but he could see she was upset. "If you assholes want to talk about someone, I would have thought you would have the manners to make sure the person wasn't around." She continued walking at a quick pace, with him walking alongside her.

"They didn't mean it."

"Oh, yes, they did."

"Will you slow down and talk to me?" he pleaded.

"Why? I don't know you."

"We talked a lot last night, remember?"

She remembered him being kind. "Can I remind you it was you who insisted I came back to the house last night. Tell your friends that."

"I know. I was just concerned about you taking off into the night like that."

With relief, she saw a taxi come down the street and flagged it down.

Cathal took out a pen from his pocket and jotted down his number. He held out the paper to her. "You seem to have some problems – if you want someone to talk to, give me a call."

The car pulled up beside her and she opened the back door. She ignored the offered paper and said, "I don't need help, I'm fine. If you want to help someone, go join the Samaritans."

He pushed his number into her pocket as she sat in.

The taxi pulled off, and she took out the paper and ripped it up.

*   *   *

Tony and Nicole usually went to either of their parents' houses for Sunday lunch but, more often than not, they tended to go over to Tony's family. She had three siblings whereas Tony was an only child and so there was always some emotional blackmail used by his parents to see them more. That Sunday they fitted in both sets of parents to tell them Tony's good news. Everyone was delighted.

Tony's parents were thrilled and made such a fuss of him. She got on very well with them. But sometimes she couldn't help herself from feeling a little jealous. Almost as if they were pulling Tony away from her in their love for him. And then she was furious with herself for having such stupid thoughts.

*   *   *

Lana turned off the piping hot water that was sprinkling down from the shower. She stepped out and took up one of the towels the housekeeper had folded immaculately on the bath and wrapped it around her. She walked out of the Clive Christian bathroom into her bedroom and then she went downstairs and curled up on the sofa in the sitting room . She felt terrible from the night before. But she felt even worse after overhearing that conversation that morning. She couldn't believe they had described her in those terms. Those people had no class; you could see that from what they had done to the interior of that lovely old house. And they seemed to be quite deluded thinking the press would give a damn about them – who were they anyway? She remembered their comments about her – trouble, dangerous, a total mess, lost cause, not wanting to be associated with her. How dare they! Didn't they know who she was? The trouble was, they did know who she was and that was the image they had of her. Was that really the impression she made on people?

The phone rang beside her and she answered it.

"Hi, where did you get to last night?" It was Patricia.

"I went back to a house with some guy."

"Really? You were up to no good then."

"Are you kidding me? Nothing happened between us."

"You must be losing your touch."

"I didn't want anything to happen, actually."

100

"Who was he anyway?"

"I haven't a clue. Can't even remember his name."

"Anyway, just checking you got home okay."

"I did, eventually. There's a party on at Jonathan's on Tuesday night, if you're around?"

"Sure. Talk to you tomorrow." Patricia hung up.

Lana took the remote control and flicked through the channels until she saw her father on the screen. She sat up with interest. Barry Curtis was making his way through a loud crowd, shaking hands and smiling.

"It's very early days until the election but Barry Curtis has already started on the election campaign today," said the voiceover. "He was out and about meeting the people in Dublin and receiving a warm welcome."

Lana watched as her father interacted with a couple of locals who were sharing a joke with him and clapping him on the back. As Barry continued to mix through the crowd, Lana spotted Gloria walking beside him, directing him.

"We caught up with Barry Curtis for a few words about the campaign."

The camera cut to Barry, away from the crowd.

"Is it not very early to start campaigning for an election which could be some months off yet?" the journalist asked.

"I don't think it's too early to be out on the streets and listening to people and their concerns, Jim." Barry as ever was coming across as earnest but good-natured. "And that's all I'm doing now, listening to what the people are saying."

"There are rumours circulating that, if you are elected, your career is to be fast-tracked. That the Taoiseach has already earmarked you for a ministerial role?"

"I've no knowledge of those rumours and I couldn't comment."

"What would you say to critics who say your career would be fast-tracked due to your friendship with the Taoiseach and your vast economic clout?"

"Well, Jim, I think in an election critics will be saying all sorts, so I'm only going to stick to the issues at hand."

"You've always been a very public figure, but now that you are stepping into the political spotlight, how do your wife and family feel about this new move?"

Barry looked into the camera and smiled. "My family are fully supportive of me."

Gloria suddenly stepped into the camera's view. "I'm afraid we're going to have to leave now – our car is here."

"Thank you, Jim." Barry smiled broadly and started shaking hands with people behind him.

Lana switched off the television and rubbed her forehead. She wondered if her mother had seen it. Barry going on the political stage would intensify the spotlight on him much further. She wondered how he would explain the constant absence of his wife from events. When election night came and she wasn't there, how would he explain it? She knew her father didn't leave anything to chance, so what had he planned to explain her absence?

And she felt increasingly anxious over the constant presence of the controlling Gloria.

CHAPTER 9

Sylvia Henderson swung around her swivel-chair in her office in Dublin. She had just got off the phone for a major music show and had booked her new act, Insert, on it. She had great hopes for Insert, a group of young guys in their early twenties. They were talented, looked good and were not just hungry for success, they were starving for it. That's what she needed, that's all she needed and she would take care of the rest. She was thinking of marketing them as the new Affidavit – their style would be similar.

She remembered when she first met the guys in Affidavit. She had gone along to one of their gigs and they had begged and pleaded with her and got people who were friends of hers to beg and plead with her. She had listened to some demo tapes they had sent her and had been impressed so went along to the gig, and after much consideration felt strongly enough about them to offer to manage them. It was not a decision she took lightly, as she was inundated with people trying to get her to represent them every day. People knew that if Sylvia Henderson Productions were behind you, fame and fortune followed pretty quickly. She had discovered so many successful acts that she was now nearly as famous as the acts themselves. She was almost a household name. Having said that, she knew she was successful because she lived for her work. She'd had one brief, disastrous marriage along the way and resolved to remain single after that. Starting off as a receptionist in a recording studio twenty years before, she had moved on to taking bookings for bands. Then she had started managing some smaller acts. In the early nineties she set up her own management company and had launched some very successful acts at home and also in the U.K. By the time she found Affidavit, she was very much in with the giant MPI record company, and a nod from her in an act's direction could secure a contract.

Cathal had asked for a meeting that day and she was expecting the guys any minute.

Her secretary buzzed in to her and informed her they had arrived.

Cathal, as ever, was the first to walk in, followed by the others. She liked Cathal a lot. He was very bright, quickly came to understand the workings of the music industry and played the game the way Sylvia instructed him, ensuring Affidavit's success. Occasionally she worried about him, especially when she read in the papers that he gone wild on drink or had been dating some fame junkie.

"Right, it's off to London on Friday for everybody to do the promotion for the last single. I've got you booked on the usual suspects – breakfast shows, music shows, and the lot." Her face turned sour. "That video was so poor you're all going to have to be extra interesting to promote the song, okay?"

"Yeah, we'll be on top form," nodded Cathal.

"I've the whole schedule prepared for you and you can collect it from my secretary after this. Matt is organising the transport and as usual will be with you."

Matt was much more than just their head of security, he was also an excellent co-ordinator.

"Then, after a week of promotion, it's straight into the studio to work on the next album," said Sylvia.

"That's why I wanted to meet with everybody today," said Cathal. "I just think that the new album is a great opportunity to look at where we are, look at what we've achieved, and maybe plan where we want to go."

"What do you mean?" asked James.

"I think none of us has been putting in the work as much as we used to. Like some of the tracks on the last album were good, but they weren't great. And I just think that the first three albums were so good, we let ourselves down with the last one. We knew it would be a commercial success anyway, so we were lazy about it."

"I had a lot on with the new baby and everything," said Rob. "I found that last tour very hard, to be away for so long. I'm the first to admit I've got new responsibilities, more than I used to. I'm still dedicated to Affidavit, but I'm not prepared to put in the same hours on the next album as I used to do before."

"And, to be honest with you, I think Donna might object if I started living in the studio the way I used to," James said.

"Of course I'm not saying you have to put the band in front of your kid, Rob. And, James, I know Donna is going to take up much more time, but there still is no excuse to give our second-best. The fans deserve more."

"Always with the fans!" said Seán, raising his eyes.

"Yeah," snapped Cathal. "Our bread and butter, remember?"

Sylvia listened intently. There had obviously been little

issues developing in the band and she was grateful Cathal had called the meeting to see what was happening.

"Fans are fickle, Cathal," said Seán. "You seem to think they have this real relationship or something with us. Wake up – they don't."

"But they go out and spend their money on stuff we do, and it's like anything – whether you're a chef in a restaurant or a musician in a band – when somebody is paying for a service, you give them the best."

"Listen to you, with your degree in business studies!" jeered Seán. "Look, we're established now, we don't have to work every hour God sends to try and make money, and the money will roll in anyway. We need to just ride this gravy train for everything it's worth."

Cathal found himself becoming agitated. "Look, the bands that stay on top for the longest are the ones who give their very best always, like U2, and reinvent themselves regularly."

"Okay, Bono, calm down. Let's see all this great music you've been writing then for the next album." Seán smiled smugly.

"You know I don't write music," Cathal retorted.

"I think you mean you can't write as opposed to don't write," said Seán.

"This isn't getting us anywhere," Sylvia intervened. "Cathal is right, there's no point in doing an album if you don't give it your all. You might hold the fans for a while but they'll quickly drift off and once you've lost them you'll never find them again."

Seán shot Cathal a dirty look. Trust Sylvia always to side with him.

"Rob, you've been working on a lot of new music, haven't you?" she asked.

"Yeah, I have, and it is a bit different from stuff I've done in the past."

"Good. I want to hear it," pressed Sylvia.

"And me and James have been doing some writing together recently," said Rob. "Some of it's really good."

"Have you?" asked Cathal, surprised.

"Yeah," said Rob. "When we were touring, we got together and wrote some stuff."

James said nothing but looked at the floor.

"Right, as soon as you are finished promoting the single, let's start working and pulling ideas and songs together," suggested Sivlia. She filed her papers. "Seán, there's a BBC music show want a celebrity guest host this Saturday and they've asked for you."

"Really?" Seán said and Cathal noticed he was grinning broadly for the first time that afternoon. He loved doing presenting and was often asked to host as a guest.

*   *   *

Two hours later Sylvia switched off her computer, grabbed her handbag and rose from her desk. She checked herself in a mirror. She looked pretty good for fifty. She had sharp angular features, highlighted hair down to her shoulders and a slim athletic body, kept in shape by an hour in the gym every day. She left her office, walked down the corridor to the lift and pressed the button to call it.

The doors opened and Cathal stood there.

"You're still here?" she asked, stepping in.

"I had to go and check some things in Accounts – they wanted to see me."

"You sorted it out?" She had no doubt he would have.

He prided himself on keeping Affidavit's accountants and legal team on their toes. She glanced at her watch. She was due at a launch at nine, which she decided gave her plenty of time.

"Do you fancy going for a drink?" she asked.

They went to a little pub around the corner. Cathal went and brought back two pints of Carlsberg from the bar. It was nicely quiet but the people who were there looked over curiously at Cathal. The odd one whispered something to a friend. But nobody came up to him. That was the great thing about Dublin – it was so laid back. The only time the die-hard fans emerged en masse and there had to be security was when they were playing a concert.

"So what did you make of all that?" he asked her straight out. He was always honest and open with Sylvia.

"Well, it's as you said in there, enthusiasm has waned a little. I guess they've all just got new priorities in life."

"But if we could just get them to recapture that enthusiasm, we could achieve so much more." His face had an almost pleading expression.

"Cathal, please wipe that vulnerable look off your face. Firstly, it doesn't suit you and secondly it's bringing out the maternal instinct in me, a feeling I was never comfortable with but am certainly not comfortable with when it's someone your age!"

Cathal started laughing and took a pull of his pint. "No," he agreed. "Maternal isn't you."

"Glad to have it confirmed." She sipped from her own pint. "Having said that, in the absence of children, thank God, I suppose I do see my bands as my offspring in some way. I nurture them and bring them to their full potential."

"Well, you did with us – but I don't think the job is finished yet."

"I remember when I first took you on, you were all so fired up and ready to take on the world." She sipped her pint and then said abruptly, "What's the story with the television presenter? I guess she'll go the same way as the rest of them?"

"Please don't start lecturing me about that. I heard enough from James and Donna on the subject, trying to marry me off."

"I am the last person to ever advertise the virtue of marriage, I can assure you."

Cathal looked at her. He knew her extremely well, but she never talked about her private life. He was curious about her own long-extinct marriage and wondered if he dared ask. "Sounds like experience talking. Your own marriage wasn't a big success?"

"I'd be still married if it was, wouldn't I? No, my own marriage was a disaster. I was working as a receptionist in a record company in London at the time. I was very young and naive, although I should have guessed something was wrong when he gave me an engagement ring that looked like something that came free in a cornflakes packet. And my wedding day consisted of a trip on the No 19 bus to Wood Green Registry office and a meal at Madame Wan Tan Foos for afters. My parents were against the marriage so we did it in secret. They were really upset when I told them, as they had always pictured me in a white meringue walking down the aisle, not the black leather mini-skirt that I actually did wear." She drank deeply from her pint.

"Don't stop there – what happened?" It wasn't often you got behind Sylvia's tough facade.

"He was a communist, when being a communist was still vaguely trendy."

"I can't believe it!" Cathal said. The idea of Sylvia being

married to a communist was so ironic, as she was often accused of being the ultimate capitalist who used young people for financial benefit in the music industry and then casually discarded them when they had served their purpose.

"I shit thee not! His interpretation of being a communist was certainly conventional: sharing other people's wealth. He shared my wealth, or at least the little I was earning. I put up with his strident political views for two years, then one day I got bored. I was out working all day to pay for food and rent while he demonstrated at political marches and then came home to criticise *me* for being a capitalist ! I tell you, Cathal, I might have been slow learning my lesson, but when I did, I learnt it thoroughly and left him."

"Do you ever wonder where he is now?"

"I know where he is. He's is the past and that's all I need to know." She drank triumphantly from her drink.

"And there's been nobody serious ever since?"

"I'm too selfish and awkward for somebody to be around all the time. Don't you agree?"

"No, of course not!"

"So think on. You don't want to end up like me – old, bitter and alone!"

"I think I'd be very happy to end up with your qualities," he said earnestly.

"Cathal, I'm truly touched!" she mocked. "It's a rare day you'd give a compliment."

*   *   *

"I'm really not sure about this," said Lana, looking down at the credit card carrying the name of Imelda

McGrane.

"Go on! It'll be a laugh – you'll really get a buzz from it," urged Patricia.

"I don't know if I can pull it off."

"Look, of course you can. You've been practising the signature all morning and you have it off to a tee!"

"What if I don't hold my nerve at the counter?"

"Darling, you always hold your nerve! You've seen me doing it loads of times at this stage, so now it's your turn. Come on!" Patricia pushed the smoked-glass doors of the store open and walked in, followed by Lana. "I'll have the credit card back in Imelda's purse this evening and she'll never be any the wiser. Look at this gorgeous handbag! It would really suit you, don't you think?"

"Yes, I suppose." Lana took the handbag up and admired it, her heart racing.

"It's only two hundred euros – you should treat yourself!" Patricia said loudly.

"I don't know . . ."

"Oh, go on! You're worth it!"

"It is nice. You're right. I think I'll get it."

Lana approached the counter as adrenaline rushed through her body. She could feel her forehead perspiring and the whole thing was giving her a huge high.

The middle-aged sales assistant smiled as she took the handbag from Lana.

"You couldn't not take it, Imelda, at that price," said Patricia. "Well, it's a steal!"

Lana handed over the credit card. Her heart was pounding as she took the receipt from the woman and with a flourish signed it. The sales assistant glanced at the signatures and gave Lana her receipt.

"Thank you very much," said Lana, taking the

shopping bag from her.

She barely breathed as they walked out and then they were walking down the street.

"Congratulations!" Patricia said. "How do you feel?"

Lana stopped and caught her breath. "Fucking fantastic!"

* * *

Kathryn was putting on her make-up, standing at a mirror in her living room. It was Thursday evening and she had been invited to a launch before work. She wouldn't be able to stay long before she headed into work at ten. She was on every guest list in town, as all the PR's and Event Managers knew they had to keep in with her to gain access for themselves and their clients to Exclusive. Also, the party organisers liked her to be present because of her image, and she in turn realised it was important to have her photo regularly in the social pages for the sake of Exclusive's image.

A door slammed and she jumped.

"Simeon?" she called, going into the hall. She got a start when she saw him. He was pale and drawn, and not at all what he had been like recently. "Are you okay?" She went towards him, reaching out her hands.

"I'm fine!" he snapped and moved away into the living-room.

"Do you want me to fix something for you?"

He slumped down on the couch and stared into space.

"Simeon?"

"What?" his voice was barely audible.

"Can I get you anything?"

"No, I'm fine."

Her heart was jumping with apprehension. She moved closer to him and put her hands on his shoulders. "Did you do some recording today?"

He said nothing.

"I'll ring in to work and say I can't make it in tonight."

"No!" His voice was raised. "Go in to work I'm fine . . . I'm just tired, that's all."

She picked up her mobile "It doesn't matter. I'll call in sick."

"Don't!" he pleaded, his eyes caught up in a rage of anguish. "I need to be on my own tonight. Just leave me on my own . . . please."

CHAPTER 10

Cathal jumped out of bed and pulled on jeans and a T-shirt.

"Where are you going to?" Joanne asked.

"I'm hungry. I'm going down to the shop to get some Danishes. That okay for you for breakfast?"

"Sounds lovely. I would have thought you'd have minions to run around getting things like that for you." She yawned.

"This isn't LA. "

"What time's your flight to London?"

"Not till six this evening."

"Do you want me to drive you to the airport?"

"Er . . . no, it's okay. Matt is picking us all up. Right – I'll be back in a few minutes."

He turned and a few seconds later she heard the front door slam.

She got out of bed, put Cathal's dressing-gown on and smiled to herself. Cathal Fitzgerald wasn't so hard to control, in spite of his image. In fact, she was finding him putty in her hands. She had rung him the previous night and asked him to go out with her. He'd said he was too tired, so she had coolly informed him she would be over in ten minutes. He had opened the door looking slightly agitated and annoyed. She had thrown some drink down him and they were partying after thirty minutes.

Going out with Cathal Fitzgerald would really send her career into orbit and launch her in the lucrative U.K. market. Maybe she would even get a permanent job with MTV out of it. After all, look what going out with James Fitzgerald had done for Donna McCarthy's career. One minute she was just another Dublin model and now she was on billboards in London. Oh, Joanne knew the game and she knew exactly how to play it.

*   *   *

"Hiya, Haakeem," Cathal greeted, walking into the small Spar shop.

"Good morning, Cathal," Haakeem answered, looking very uncomfortable.

"What goodies have you in this morning?" Cathal sauntered over to the confectionery counter, selected a few Danishes and put them in a plastic bag. Then he grabbed a bottle of Diet Coke and two litres of milk and put them on the counter.

"You might want to look at a copy of today's *Mirror* as well," suggested Hakaam sheepishly.

"Why?" Cathal asked suspiciously, making his way over to the newspaper stand.

He reached down for a copy to be greeted on the front page by a photo of him and Joanne in the throes of passion against a wall.

"For fuck's sake!" Cathal shouted.

*   *   *

Cathal slammed the door as he came into the apartment. "Joanne!" he shouted.

"What?" she asked, concerned, coming out of the bathroom.

He threw the newspaper at her and she stared at the front page.

"Oh! What? How?" she cried.

He grabbed the newspaper back and looked at the write-up under the headline *EXCLUSIVE: Affidavit Star in Sex Tryst in Top Nightclub.*

"Just listen to this shit they've written! *'Cathal Fitzgerald has been photographed having sleazy sex at top nightclub Exclusive with TV presenter Joanne Bailey. Our exclusive photograph confirms the couple are an item and enjoy risky situations.'* I mean, how did they get this photo?"

Joanne sat down on the couch and put her hand to her forehead. "Such an intimate photo to be made public! I feel so . . . degraded!" She looked down at the huge photo. Although there was a lot of flesh on display, Cathal's back protected some of her modesty. And studying her face, she had to admit she looked damned good. "We were crazy to take such a risk, Cathal! But you were so . . . insistent . . . you wouldn't wait until we got back here to have sex . . ."

Cathal glared at her. "Are you saying that it's *my* fault?"

"No! Of course not! But that *is* why we went out through the fire escape in the first place!"

He had to admit she was right. "But that's beside the point!" he ranted. "I mean, you go to Exclusive because your privacy will be respected there! You go because you can do whatever the hell you want and nobody will bother you and it will remain inside the place. And then something like this happens!"

"It's just so embarrassing," Joanne moaned.

"This is all the fault of the club! I'm going to ring Kathryn Foy about this." He grabbed his mobile.

*   *   *

Kathryn sat in the kitchen. It was 10.30 in the morning and she was feeling pretty frantic. Simeon had been in such a strange mood when he came in last night. She had been worried sick all night and just wanted to get home to see how he was. When she had got home, the apartment was empty. That had been at three in the morning and she had been up pacing ever since. She had tried phoning him countless times but there was no response from his phone. What had happened? He had been amazingly upbeat recently and to go from that to the way he was last night, something must have happened. He had been helping Joe out in the recording studio and she remembered he said he was going to try and record something himself. She could only imagine it hadn't gone well.

Her mobile rang and she pounced on it. But she saw Cathal Fitzgerald's number come up. She wondered what on earth he would be ringing her for at that time in the morning. The only communication they had was when he rang up an hour before arriving into Exclusive looking for a table and VIP treatment.

She switched into professional mode. "Good morning, Cathal, how are you?"

"Really pissed off, actually." His voice was aggressive.

She was confused. "Really? How come?"

"Have you seen today's *Mirror*?"

"No, not yet."

"Well, there's a huge big photo of me shagging Joanne on the front and it was taken in Exclusive about a week ago."

Kathryn put her fingers to her head and started to massage her temple. That was very bad public relations for the club. The rich and famous came to Exclusive because they believed they could do what they wanted in privacy. Having a photo like that on a front page would unnerve a lot of their regulars. Having said that – what the hell were they shagging at the nightclub for? She really could do without this now, when she was so concerned about Simeon.

"How the hell did that happen, Kathryn?"

"What do you mean exactly – a photo of you shagging at the nightclub?"

"Some fucking photographer got into the club and photographed me and Joanne." He was becoming angrier.

She had only met him in good form before, and now she was realising his reputation was justified. "I'm as angry about this as you are –" she started.

"Good for you! But it's not a photo of you exposed on the front page, is it?"

"I understand your concerns –"

"No, you fucking don't! First of all, I'm going to get so much shit off Sylvia and MPI about this, and I hate this kind of thing!" He looked down at Joanne who was wiping a tear away. "I've Joanne here with me and she's crying over it."

Oh sure! thought Kathryn, publicity-mad Joanne "I've-only-got-a-small-window-of-opportunity-to-make-it-big" Bailey.

"Who took the photo?" Cathal demanded as if she were personally responsible.

"I don't know." She racked her brains. "It could have been anyone, a random punter –"

"I thought random punters didn't get into Exclusive? Only celebs and members. You used to run a tight ship but you're obviously letting things go in there and not operating as good a door policy as you used to. You've lost your grip on the place."

Joanne listened intently – she couldn't have imagined anyone speaking to the Kathryn Foy in that way.

Suddenly something snapped in Kathryn. Whatever was going on in her life she was always the ultimate professional and that was what made Exclusive what it was and she wasn't going to let Cathal Fitzgerald or anyone else say different.

"Where exactly was the photo taken?" she demanded.

"Out on the fire escape –"

"To be fair, what the hell were the two of you doing out there in the first place? Did you ever hear of the expression 'Get a room'?"

"What me and Joanne were doing was our business. If you can't protect your customers' privacy any more, if you can't give one hundred per cent then I'll go somewhere else in future, okay?"

"Get a life! So, go somewhere else! You're so ignorant, I don't want you back at Exclusive anyway." She hung up and fired the phone onto the couch.

"What did she say?" asked Joanne, nervous of his reaction, and even more nervous of his reaction if he ever found out she set the photo up.

"Nothing. Well, nothing in the way of a good excuse. That's the last time I go into that place, I tell you."

"Really? I mean, you like the place, so why should –"

"She didn't even apologise."

"I suppose it wasn't strictly her fault."

"She let some journo in there and they somehow took a photo. Some security guard should have seen it happen. Or the journo shouldn't have been allowed in the first place – however they found out we were in there."

"Just luck on their part, I suppose."

"Well, I'm not going in again, and I'm not having any more parties for the group or anything else in there again either."

*   *   *

Kathryn popped down to the shop to get *The Mirror*. Even though she burned with anger, five minutes after the conversation with Cathal she was regretting it. The photo looked seedy and certainly unflattering to both participants. Kathryn could understand why Cathal was upset. She shouldn't have lost her cool. She never lost her cool. It was all this business with Simeon that had put her on edge and so she had simply flown off the handle.

Cathal Fitzgerald was too big to talk to like that. He was too famous, too powerful and too connected. And when you were in the nightclub business you had to be aware of every little thing. People were very fickle and the most in-vogue place could very quickly get a bad reputation. That damned photo in the paper was bad enough and nobody would blame Cathal for knocking Exclusive after it. And from what she had heard this morning he was just hard and nasty enough to be vindictive about it. She would have to think of a way of getting around him.

*   *   *

Lana and Patricia were sitting over coffee after lunch. The great thing about Patricia's job was that she seemed to have complete control over her own hours and was always available to meet up.

"I saw your father last night on some talk show – he came across very well," said Patricia.

"Doesn't he always? Did he have a blonde woman standing in awe beside him ?"

"No – why?"

"Just that silly bitch Gloria seems to be everywhere he is."

"She's still on the scene?"

"Oh yes. Latest is, she's after taking an office at Kildara for the period of the election campaign."

"Really?"

"She seems to have appointed herself Campaign Director."

"Is she attractive?"

"Unfortunately, yes. In that groomed, platinum-blonde-hair-that-seems-to-be-set-like-concrete kind of way."

"Before I forget, what are you doing next Wednesday night?" asked Patricia.

"Nothing planned, as of yet," said Lana.

"Well, you do now. We're going to a party in London being held by MPI records."

"That sounds fun."

"I was hoping you were going to say that. I've already paid for the plane tickets! Courtesy of Imelda McGrane, of course." They both gave a little giggle. "Imelda should thank me really, as there was this deal that if you buy two tickets you get the other at half price, so I've saved her a few quid . . . I'd better get back to the office"

"Here, I'll pay for lunch." Lana reached for her purse.

"I wouldn't hear of it." Patricia reached into her handbag, took out a credit card and smiled wickedly.

Lana raised her eyes. "Which of the lovely McGrane girls is paying for us today?"

"None of them . . . Janice Harvey is."

"Who?"

"The executive in the next office to me at work."

Lana's eyes widened. "That's fairly risky."

"Relax, she's busy doing interviews all day. I just nipped into her office before lunch and borrowed her card. I'll have it back where I found it straight after lunch."

"But won't she –"

"She goes out to lunch practically every day, so she'll hardly remember if she was here today or not – and even if she does notice it – good! She'll spend ages trying to remember whether she was here or not and it'll cause her hassle!"

"You're certainly upping the stakes in this game." Lana felt a little uneasy.

*   *   *

Cathal was coming out of a book shop and heading towards Grafton Street when he spotted Lana striding down the other side of the street.

"Hey!" he called, but she either didn't hear him or ignored him. He raced across the street, dodging the traffic, quickly caught up with her and positioned himself in front of her.

"Hi there – remember me?" he asked smiling.

There was no look of recognition on her face, only a look of surprise that she had been obstructed. "Do I know you?" she asked.

"Yeah, we met at . . . eh . . ." he searched his memory for her friend's name, "Patricia's party!"

Recognition dawned. "Oh yes." She quickly walked around him and continued down the street.

Cathal looked after her. He was used to pushing people away who were always trying to get near him, and he found this situation very alien. He bounded after her. "You never called me!" he accused as he walked alongside her.

"Did I say I would?" she asked coldly.

"No, it's just – it would have been mannerly to."

"And you and your friends are so well mannered, from what I can remember."

"I'm really sorry about what you heard that morning. I –"

She stopped abruptly and looked at him in the face. "Why don't you go and say all this to someone who's interested. I have better things to do than listen. Now goodbye." She glided on down the street, leaving him open-mouthed looking after her.

*   *   *

Matt was driving the group to Dublin airport. Cathal was sitting up front beside him talking to Sylvia on his mobile.

"Don't worry, Sylvia. It should be fine. It's a tight schedule, but we'll be everywhere at the right time . . . okay, talk to you later."

"Oh, and Cathal, no repeat performances of today's front page, okay?" said Sylvia and she hung up.

Matt knew better than to mention the front page of *The Mirror* to Cathal, not wanting to be on the receiving end of a torrent of abuse.

Cathal sighed and looked out the window. What a day he'd had! After lambasting Kathryn Foy, he had phoned his parents to warn them not to go near any newsagent's, but he had been too late. His father had just been about to pick up the phone to give out to him. They were horrified – what would the neighbours think? Whatever he did in private was his own business, he was old enough to do whatever he pleased, but to advertise it on the front page of a national newspaper was irresponsible – in fact it was disgusting! Then Sylvia had been on, turning the air blue, explaining they were a serious band and this kind of uncontrolled PR was a disaster. Then, to top it all off, there was his encounter with Lana in the street which had left him feeling stupid. She'd been really pissed off over what Donna and James had said. Still, he had looked after her when she was out of it. She should be just a little bit grateful.

CHAPTER 11

The car from the television studio pulled up outside Cathal's duplex in a swish new London development. Affidavit spent so much time in London, Cathal had decided to buy a house there a couple of years ago. He was sick of living in hotel rooms – they had to spend enough time in them when they were on tour anyway. Also he had seen it as a good investment opportunity. He had spent ages going around the city viewing different properties. Finally he had come across a new development of townhouses and duplexes. He had been impressed with the complex's security and that had decided him. He had bought a townhouse.

Cathal climbed the steps to his front door, let himself in and headed straight for bed. They'd had to get up at 6 o'clock on Saturday morning, then straight over to the studios where they had performed the new song live on a Saturday morning show. That afternoon, they had recorded the song for an evening entertainment show. Then they had given some press interviews. Sylvia had flown over to be present during the interviews at the MPI offices, fearing Cathal's front-page photo would need expert handling. Sylvia had briefed all the journalists beforehand about what to talk about but she couldn't control all of them. One had refused to comply with her requests to avoid talking about the photo.

"Tell me, Cathal, are yourself and Joanne Bailey an item now?" the journalist had asked.

"I don't know what you mean by being an item. We've spent some time together, if that's what you mean."

"The photo in the paper indicates you are close, even though you've previously stated there was nothing happening between you."

"I do like to keep some parts of my life private,"

"But can't, obviously."

Cathal had become exasperated. "When media are scrutinising a relationship, it often doesn't have a chance to grow. I was just looking for some space that's all."

"So your relationship is growing with Joanne now?" the interviewer had persisted.

"I think Cathal has made it clear he doesn't want to talk about this," Sylvia interrupted, shooting the journalist a warning look.

"Oh, come on, Sylvia!" The journalist had become angry. "What's the point in having me here if I can't ask what I want?"

"Because it's his private business!" Sylvia was equally angry.

"I want to know what the story is with the Irish TV presenter."

Cathal decided to take control of the situation. "I have been seeing Joanne for a short while. I don't know where it's going to lead. I was very annoyed about the photo in the paper. We both were. Unfortunately that's the price you have to pay sometimes for leading the life we lead."

"Thank you!" snapped the journalist, giving Sylvia a triumphant look, "Now, I have my story. Cathal admits to a relationship with Joanne Bailey, and is also angry about intrusion into private life." The journalist stood up and flipped his notebook shut.

The press were uncontrollable, Sylvia knew that, but she knew how to play them. "You might have got your story this time," she said, "but I'm blacklisting you for future interviews."

The journalist looked disdainfully at her. "You make me sick, Sylvia. You think we're just here to publicise your acts," he glanced at Cathal and the other three guys, "and the way you want to. Well, I'm one journalist who won't be a vehicle for your publicity machine." And he marched off.

"See, I told you this would happen," stormed Sylvia after the journalist had left. "Now he's going to put a nasty spin on the story. We should have got a friendly journalist and you should have been honest about yourself and Joanne and got a nice slant to the story!"

"I can't believe this!" said Seán ironically. "We're supposed to be here discussing our new song and where we see the new album going and instead the press are more interested in who Cathal is fucking!"

"To be honest, I agree with Seán, Cathal." Rob looked angry. "Me and James have come up with some really good new songs for the new album – it's the kind of stuff that could take us into a new level of respect, but we're never going to be taken seriously if you allow your life to be tabloid fodder."

Cathal glanced over to James who was staring down at the floor. He took his expression to mean he agreed with the others.

"There's no point in you calling meetings at MPI and saying we're not being enthusiastic enough and then acting like a clown in front of the press," said Seán, who unlike the others was half-smiling and seemed to be enjoying this attack on Cathal.

"Seán's right, Cathal," said Sylvia. "You need to work on your personal life. I've warned you about this before."

Cathal felt the anger boil inside him. He couldn't stand when people ganged up on him. He looked at James again, who seemed to be staring deeper into the floor. His silence was as bad as their verbal attacks. Cathal jumped up, his face red.

"A fucking mistake! A fucking lousy mistake! I didn't want the fucking photo taken! I'm sorry if my antics have ruined your wonderful artistic credibility! In future I'll make sure all my PR is carefully stage-managed photos in *Hello* or *Hi Life* like the rest of you!" And he stormed off.

* * *

The next few days passed in a flurry – starting with breakfast shows in the morning and recording television shows for the rest of the day, all to plug the new song. There was a strained atmosphere after the bust-up on Saturday and Cathal stuck to being ultra-professional with them all.

On Tuesday afternoon, James came up to him and asked if he could stay over at Cathal's that night. Cathal recognised it as a peace-offering and agreed. They got on fine and talked about old times. But there was a part of Cathal that couldn't help feeling irritated. If only once James could do something wrong – upset the bosses, piss Sylvia off, agitate his family! Shout at Donna! Insult the press! Stop saving the world with his charity! Show himself to be as human and flawed as Cathal knew he himself was.

*　　*　　*

Lana and Patricia's flight to London on Wednesday was a mid-morning one. The two of them cut a striking presence as they walked through Heathrow, dressed up to the nines and wearing sunglasses. They hailed a taxi and were brought to Barry's house in Chelsea. His London home was a lovely old white manor-type house set up a small driveway. They knocked back a couple of drinks there, before calling a taxi to drop them off at Knightsbridge. Then it was lunch at the top-floor restaurant at Harvey Nichols, and a whirlwind tour through to the shops.

"It's too risky to play our hobby over here," Patricia had said sensibly. "I didn't bring anyone's credit card over with me. Harrods or any other London shop coming up on their bill would stand out too much."

"Good thinking," agreed Lana.

"Okay, let's hit a few more shops, then back to change at your father's. Then a drink in some bar on the Kings Road and onwards to the MPI party."

"Sounds good to me!"

*　　*　　*

Cathal was reading the interview in *The Star*, with the heading: "*Cathal Opens His Heart About TV Star.*" The article read "*Affidavit member Cathal Fitzgerald has finally come clean and admitted to being in a relationship with Irish TV*

131

*presenter Joanne Bailey. The two were photographed recently
enjoying an intimate moment in a Dublin nightclub. Cathal has
said they are enjoying being with each other and were waiting to
see what would happen. But in a swipe at rival newspapers who
have stalked the Affidavit star recently, Cathal has said it is hard
to maintain any relationship when it comes under media
scrutiny . . ."* Cathal threw the paper down in disgust. They
hadn't even mentioned the new song.

*   *   *

Joanne sat in the canteen at RTÉ reading Cathal's
interview with satisfaction. There it was in black and white
print that he and she were an item. The interview had
given her huge exposure. She was slightly annoyed with
Cathal for not having told her he was going to talk
publicly about them, but she could live with that. She had
tried phoning him a few times that day but his phone was
off. She started thinking of publicity ideas for the two of
them once Cathal got back from London.

*   *   *

Cathal surveyed the crowded function room in The
Selfridges Hotel and spotted Jack Better, Chief Executive
of MPI Records, arrive. Jack walked through the crowd
with a host of his dark-suited executives in attendance.
People smiled at him. Unlike Sylvia he kept a very low
profile, but everyone in the business knew how powerful
he was. When Affidavit had started out they had all been
totally intimidated by him and his team. It was only Sylvia
who'd protected them from being chewed up as industry
fodder during the first couple of years. But Cathal had

soon learnt to assert himself, not taking what Jack or his team said as gospel and speaking his mind when he felt he should. He knew a lot of the execs didn't like him as he challenged them and their ideas constantly. But as long as the sales kept coming, there was nothing they could do.

He observed Sylvia who was fussing around her new act, Insert, like a mother hen, busily introducing them to everybody and letting the assembled journalists interview them, as their music blared from loudspeakers around the room. He knew the MPI party was really being held for Insert, to introduce them to the press. He had met the five guys in the band and they seemed okay. Full of the usual mix of enthusiasm, terror and expectation.

His phone buzzed and he looked at it, seeing Joanne's number come up. He thought for a second before going out to a quiet corridor and answering it.

"Hi there," he said.

"According to *The Star* today I'm dating a member of Affidavit."

"I'm sorry about that. A journalist put me on the spot and they twisted what I said."

"A bit of notice would have been nice from you."

He guessed he should have rung her to warn her.

"This whole relationship is playing havoc with my life," Joanne said. "We're going to have to sit down and try and put some control on the press when you get back."

He glanced back into the room. There was a loud noise from the microphone as Sylvia tried to get the sound right on the stage. Then silence fell on the room as she began to speak.

"Okay, listen, Joanne, I'd better go. The speeches are starting. I'll call you tomorrow."

He slipped back into the function room.

"The press have always been so supportive of MPI," Sylvia was saying. "and especially the stars that I manage. So we decided to throw this little party by way of a thank-you. I'm sure you've spotted a few new faces amongst you this evening. A group of young men from Ireland who I'd like to join me on the stage . . ." She smiled brightly as she beckoned them up. "Ladies and gentlemen, let me introduce to you – Insert! And I'm proud to announce they have just signed with MPI. Remember them. They are going to be big!"

She stepped down from the stage as the crowd applauded. Music started and the band began to play.

At the table Patricia had reserved, she leaned closer to Lana and, speaking loudly over the music, said, "They're good, aren't they?"

Lana glanced without interest up at the stage. "If you like that kind of thing." She poured more vodka into her glass and gulped it back.

*   *   *

"Is everything fine with you fellas?" Jack Better asked, stopping by Affidavit's table.

"Everything's great," answered Cathal, smiling.

"I've been watching your promotion of the new song. Fingers crossed we make No 1 this weekend, hey?"

"That's why we're working flat out," said Cathal, smiling.

"Good, good . . ." The smile shifted uncomfortably for a second before he turned to one of his executives and said, "Send some more wine down to this table."

"Thanks, Jack!" James beamed.

Jack nodded to James. He had always liked James.

James always shut up and kept smiling, and that's what Jack liked in his acts. He wished he could say the same about Cathal. He smiled at Cathal and moved on, followed by his executives.

Cathal looked around the crowd and suddenly he saw Lana. He sat up straight and stared, to make sure it was her. She was with a group of people and one of them was Patricia who he remembered had hosted the party in Dublin.

Cathal nudged James. "There's that girl again. The one I brought back to your house."

James looked over. "Yeah, the mad one. You should stay away from her."

Cathal discreetly watched Lana, keeping count of the number of drinks she was knocking back.

Then suddenly she got up and walked towards him.

"Hi, do you remember me?" he said, smiling, as she reached his table.

She looked at him without interest. "Yeah, hi." She walked past him and into the toilets.

He went over to Patricia. "Hi there," he said, tapping her on the shoulder.

She turned around and stood up to kiss him on the cheek. "How are you? Is Donna here?"

"No but James is." He pulled up a seat, sat down beside her and started making small talk with her. He'd noticed Lana come out of the bathroom. She seemed much more spaced out than before and she headed onto the dance floor.

"I see your friend is here as well," he said.

"Lana? Yes, she loves parties."

"How long have you known her?"

"Oh, years. We went to school together. Why? Are you

interested?"

He pulled a face. "She seems nuts."

"She is nuts!" Patricia laughed, "Totally nuts – anything goes with her."

"Yeah, I saw that at your party." He looked serious.

Patricia gathered he had seen her take drugs. "Look, she's in total contact with her wild side."

They both observed as Lana started getting off with a guy on the dance floor.

"Don't you worry about her? That she might be overdoing it?"

"No, I don't," She raised her drink and took a sip."And I don't think anyone has the right to judge other people."

He looked at Lana kissing the man and she seemed out of it. "Why does she do it?"

"Why not?" Patricia countered.

* * *

"I think they are going to be fantastic!" Sylvia smiled proudly as Insert circulated the room. She was at a table with Jack Better.

"Well, you're usually right. I do hope so, considering the investment we're putting into them . . . I'm not so sure about the dark-haired guy, but I guess it's too late to push him out."

"Yes, it is! They come as a package. So leave them the fuck alone . . . I had to fight tooth and nail to keep Cathal in Affidavit when we signed them. You wanted him out."

"Hmmm, sometimes I wonder if I was correct. Lovely press he's been getting recently."

"There are always hiccups. But I'm not taking any

criticism on Affidavit – they've been a resounding success."

He raised his glass "I'm not arguing with you. Their success speaks for itself . . . however, reports are telling me the sales aren't going great on their latest song." He looked meaningfully at Sylvia, with her ash-blonde hair, and still slim figure. She was a very colourful character and totally dedicated to what she did. She received a lot of bad press, but she genuinely didn't give a damn.

*   *   *

Cathal studied Lana intently. She seemed dazed as usual. He waited for his opportunity and soon enough she went over to the bar. As she waited for service he approached her. "We keep bumping into each other," he said.

She turned and stared. "You again!"

He didn't know why he was drawn to her, but he was.

"Do you want something?" she asked blankly in a cold manner.

He became angry. This girl was impossible. "No," he said and walked away.

He rejoined James and the others.

"Donna's right. I don't know who she thinks she is," he said to James.

But he continued to watch her as she rejoined her table. The guy she had been kissing on the dance floor was sitting beside her and looking at her like an attentive puppy. Suddenly she got up from the table, left the guy mid-sentence and began to walk around the party. She spotted Cathal and came over to him.

"Do you want to get out of here?" she asked.

He looked at her, confused. "What do you mean?"

Turning to glance at her table and the man she had danced with, she said, "I'm bored . . . do you want to go or not?"

"Er . . . yes," he answered without even thinking. He watched as Lana walked towards the door without even saying goodbye to her friends. He stood up, still looking after her. "Eh, I'm off. I'll talk to you tomorrow," he said to James.

James did the impression of pulling the trigger of a gun to his head. Cathal put his hands in the air and followed Lana out.

* * *

"Taxi, Cathal?" the doorman asked, recognising him.

Cathal looked back at Lana who was taking her coat from the cloakroom.

"Do we want a taxi?" he asked.

"No," said Lana as she walked past the doorman and into the street.

"Where are we going to?" Cathal asked.

"Don't know," she answered.

He walked beside her in silence for a long while, not sure what to say. "We're just walking around aimlessly," he said after a long while.

"Just soaking up the atmosphere."

He looked around the dark empty streets she had led him to. "Not much of an atmosphere," He looked at her. "Why did you leave the party just like that, without saying goodbye to Patricia or any of your friends?"

"I told you. I was bored. There was a guy there I'd just met and he was coming across as very intense. He was boring me, so I needed to get out."

Bored. She seemed to use that word in a strange way, thought Cathal.

Every so often they would come across the back of a restaurant and some members of staff would be having a cigarette break out the back. She would stop and look at them for a while before moving on.

"What do you do?" he asked, trying to get her to talk.

"Do?"

"Besides going to parties and getting wasted?"

"Nothing much."

"Everyone does something."

"Well, I don't."

"Well, how do you live?"

"You're asking too many questions. If you want to go, just go."

"And leave you here walking empty streets?"

"You don't have to worry about me, I do it all the time."

They came to an empty park that was locked up.

"Give me a leg up," she said as she reached for the railings.

"You're going in there?" he asked incredulously.

She ignored him and started to pull herself up over the railings. He helped her up and she toppled over the railings to the other side. Cathal then hoisted himself up and pulled himself over.

"We're probably breaking and entering or something," he said but she was already walking through the trees into the centre of the park.

She found a piece of open tarmac in the centre of the park and sat down on the verge of it. She lit herself a cigarette and offered him one.

"No, I don't smoke any more."

"God, you really live the high life, don't you . . . what was your name again?"

"Cathal. What were you doing at that party?"

"Patricia invited me." She took out a small silver box, opened it and rolled up a twenty-pound note. "Do you want some?"

"No, and I don't think you should have any either. You've had enough shit for one night."

She started to inhale and seemed to melt into another world. He looked at her beautiful face in the moonlight. She started coughing slightly. She put down the silver box and then started to cough incessantly, sneezing as well.

"Are you okay?" Cathal asked, alarmed.

She started gasping for breath, shaking uncontrollably. Attempting to stand, she fell down and lay out flat on her stomach, gasping for breath.

Cathal stared at her, consumed with fear. What the hell was he doing in a park in the middle of the night with this crazy girl?

"You're having a fit," he shouted. "I'll call an ambulance."

He reached into his pocket and pulled out his mobile phone. He started to shake as he realised what it would look like: Cathal Fitzgerald in a park at night with a girl who seemed to have overdosed. The press would destroy him. All these years guarding his life, making sure what happened in the past never touched him. Having managed to narrowly escape destruction years ago and keep it away from the public eye, he was now going to be consumed in a similar scandal. He could run, he realised. Just run, get the hell out of there. But as he looked at the beautiful girl shaking on the ground, he knew he couldn't.

He started to dial the emergency number on his phone.

"Please!" she gasped. "Please don't call an ambulance!"

"I have to. You're very ill." But he paused.

"No," she pleaded. "It will destroy me if you call them."

He went and knelt beside her, stroking her back. "You're fine," he whispered. "Everything's going to be all right."

She felt him stroke her back over and over, saying soothing words, and suddenly she felt very safe and protected. Her breathing became easier and she wasn't gasping any more. Over what seemed to be an eternity she stopped shaking and relaxed. She lay in his arms, exhausted and frightened, and then her tears rolled down. She looked up into his face as she cried silently.

"What am I going to do?" she asked pleadingly.

*   *   *

The birds were singing and it was getting bright as Cathal led Lana down the street to his house. She was barely awake, with her arm around his shoulder. Cathal glanced down at his watch as they entered his duplex. It was just after six o'clock in the morning and he felt exhausted. He put her into the spare bedroom where she passed out immediately and then went to pour himself a strong drink.

*   *   *

She awoke later that morning and had that familiar feeling of not knowing where she was. Then she remembered the incident in the park and the guy called

141

Cathal who kept cropping up. She shuddered at the thought of the park. She got up, put her shoes on and grabbed her coat, hoping she could slip out without having to talk to anybody. She crept through the lounge towards the front door.

"You aren't going anywhere without having breakfast first," said a voice behind her. She turned to see Cathal in the kitchen area, cooking.

"I haven't time to stay . . . and I don't eat breakfast," she said, smelling the food.

"It won't take you five minutes to eat," he insisted, walking over to her. He took her hand and led her over to the breakfast bar.

"Look . . . Cathal . . . I really have to be going," she protested.

He sat her down at the bar and put a plate of bacon and eggs in front of her. "Ah! You remember my name! I think you at least owe me to eat my cooking."

"I don't owe you anything," she snapped, taking up a slice of bacon in her fingers and beginning to eat it.

"No, I guess you don't." He sat opposite her and poured her some coffee. Then he started eating his breakfast.

She drank some coffee and continued to eat.

"You gave me a bit of a fright last night," he said at last.

"Did I? Spare me the lecture, will you?"

He looked at her, amazed. He had never met anybody as thorny as her before. Except for himself maybe. "I wasn't going to lecture you. You asked me for my help last night."

"I probably wanted you to hail me a taxi or something." She pushed the plate aside "Thanks for the food, but I really can't eat any more." She got up to leave and walked towards the door.

Cathal stood up. "I really would like to see you again."

She turned and looked at him in amazement. How rude did she have to be to him? Even after seeing her in the state she was in last night, he still wanted to see her.

"Why?" she asked in exasperation.

"I don't know," he said honestly, surprising himself. "I just would."

"I don't know anything about you – and you probably don't know anything about me." She was testing him, wondering if he was after her father's money.

"Most people start off that way," he said, intrigued by this woman who seemed to be so articulate and intelligent but so self-destructive, intrigued at meeting somebody who not only did not want something from him but seemed to want to get away from him.

"What kind of thing are you suggesting?" she asked cautiously.

"I don't know, dinner or something." His mind was already busy. He didn't want to be seen out with her in case any photographer caught them. If she was a drug-dealer or something it could ruin his reputation. In fact every warning sign was screaming for him to run away from her. But he wanted to see her again.

She looked at him while she thought "Okay, maybe . . . but, I'd better warn you, if I get a call to go somewhere more interesting or just get bored in the middle of it, I'll just get up and leave."

He looked at her and smiled. "I don't doubt it for a minute."

CHAPTER 12

"I don't understand him any more," Mrs Reilly was saying, sitting on the other side of Nicole's table. "He seems to have lost all interest in me . . ."

"How is that making you feel about yourself?" queried Nicole.

"Well, it's a knock-on effect . . . he's lost interest in me and so I've lost interest in myself as well."

Nicole nodded. Mrs Reilly was a middle-aged housewife who had defined herself through her husband all her married life – of course she judged her own worth by how Mr Reilly saw her.

Her mobile started to bleep in her drawer, causing Mrs Reilly to look up startled.

"I'm so sorry, Mrs Reilly. Could you excuse me for just one minute?"

It was the morning Tony was due to start work and he was feeling very nervous. Nicole always made sure her mobile was off when she was in a session, but that morning she had left it on in her desk drawer, expecting he would ring her for support before going into *Hi Life*. She reached into the drawer, took the mobile and quickly walked out to the corridor.

"Tony?"

"Hi, Nic."

"Where are you?" she said, keeping her voice low.

"Down the street from *Hi Life* . . . I'm nervous about going in there."

"Don't worry. You'll be fine."

"I wish I had the confidence in myself you have. What do I know about celebrity mags, and writing what they want?"

"Listen to me," Nicole spoke firmly. "They wouldn't have chosen you if they didn't think you could do the job, would they?"

"I suppose."

"Just go in there, be yourself and work as hard as you can. All you can do is your best."

"Yeah, you're right. I'll head in so . . . Thanks, Nic, I don't know what I'd do without you."

"I'll see you this evening. Good luck."

* * *

Tony turned off his mobile, strode up to the front door and pressed the buzzer. He looked at himself in the glass of the door. He was wearing his best suit and looked good. God, but he needed to lose a few pounds! He really had to motivate himself.

"Yes?" called the voice on the other side of the intercom.

"Tony O'Brien here." The door buzzed and he let himself in. He climbed the stairs.

"Hi, again," said Vivienne, the bubbly glamorous girl who was Ralph's secretary. She had been sitting at the other desk last time, which was now empty. "Ralph's not in yet. Do you have an appointment to see him? You're not in his diary." She smiled, showing a dazzling set of teeth.

"Yes, well, no. I'm starting work here today."

"Oh, are you?" The girl looked surprised but her smile seemed to grow even bigger.

"Yes." Tony felt a little awkward and confused.

"What are you going to be doing here. In the advertising department?"

"God, no!" Tony didn't mean to sound disparaging, but he never wanted to see the inside of an advertising sales department again. "I'm going to be a staff writer."

"Oh!" Her smile faltered for a moment. "That's nice. You'll enjoy working here . . . it's exciting and Ralph is, you know, fine to work for."

Hearing someone come down the corridor, Vivienne quickly started to type a document.

The phone rang on her desk. "Good morning, *Hi Life* . . . Sure, I'll just put you through to the advertising department now." She pressed a button and put the call through.

Ralph came into the reception area. "Any messages?" he asked Vivienne. He didn't seem to be in a particularly good humour.

"Yes, I've had Sylvia Henderson on, wants you to give her a call. And also Margaux has been on and asked for you to call her back."

He turned to look at Tony. "Come into my office," he said.

Tony stood up and followed Ralph down the corridor to his office. He felt awkward that there was no small talk. Ralph put his oversized briefcase on his desk, opened it and started taking out forms.

"Sit down," he ordered and Tony obliged. "You won't be having your own office. That's your desk out there beside Vivienne's. You can work from there." He looked at Tony suspiciously and his attitude was very frosty. "We are about to have the annual competition, *Hi Life's* Personality of the Year. Who do you think we should nominate?"

"Personality?" Tony's head went blank.

"Yes, it's usually somebody who's a familiar face on the social scene – who do you think we should shortlist this year?"

"Er . . ."Tony tried his best to think, but nobody was coming into his head and he was aware that Ralph was looking at him with a look that bordered on contempt.

There was a knock on the door and Vivienne came in with some notes.

"Vivienne," said Ralph, "who do you think we should nominate for Best Personality this year?"

"Definitely the President. Mary McAlese is looking really well."

Ralph jotted down the name on a list he had taken out of his briefcase.

Damn, thought Tony, it was so obvious – why hadn't he thought of that ?

"You can go," Ralph said to Tony.

Tony stood up and followed Vivienne out. As he closed the door behind him, he heard Ralph begin a phone conversation in loud joyous tones. "Sylvia, how are you? You got back from London okay? Good, good . . ."

Tony went back to Vivienne and said, "This is my desk seemingly." He pointed to the empty desk.

"Make yourself at home!" Vivienne said as she answered the ringing phone.

*   *   *

"Will I get you a cup of tea?" Kathryn looked down at Simeon huddled on the bed.

"No . . . I'm fine," he said, speaking low and slow.

"Simeon, darling," she sat down on the bed and started to stroke his hair, "you haven't eaten anything for a couple of days . . . you can't survive like that . . ."

He ignored her, staring into the distance.

"I'm really worried about you," she whispered, tears in her eyes.

He had barely spoken or moved in a week. He just stayed in bed sleeping. She had tried everything to motivate him, but failed. Just like all the other times when he went like this, she knew deep down there was nothing she could do.

"Maybe I'll call a doctor —"

"Don't!" He raised his voice. "I don't want a doctor . . . just leave me the fuck alone!"

His words were enough to cause the threatening tears to spill down her cheeks. She wiped them away quickly, anxious he didn't see her upset. He had enough on his plate, without her causing him any further pain.

"Okay," she soothed, "I won't call a doctor . . . I'll let you sleep." She got up and walked quietly out of the room and closed the door behind her. She went and sat on the couch and hugged her knees close to her chest.

*   *   *

Tony looked at his watch. It was ten to five. He hadn't done anything all day. He had sat at his desk, trying to look busy with his computer but in reality doing nothing. Vivienne had seemed run off her feet, answering the phones and typing constantly. Ralph hadn't come out of his office. A few people had come in to see him and that had been that.

"It was horrible," said Tony as they were sitting down that night eating pizza.

"And nobody brought you around and introduced you to people or anything?" Nicole was incredulous.

"No, nothing. Nobody gave me anything to do or explained what I was supposed to do. They just left me sitting there at this desk."

"Well, maybe you should go in to Ralph and explain the situation tomorrow and just ask what you're supposed to be doing."

"No, it would make me look really stupid. And he's not the kind of person you just drop into for a chat, believe me. I don't know, maybe I'm supposed to automatically know what to do. Maybe I'm supposed to be ringing up and making appointments and doing interviews or something."

"Well, you can hardly start doing that without getting direction from the Publisher, can you?"

"I wouldn't have thought so."

"And Vivienne couldn't shed any light on things?"

"No, well, she was kind and everything, but she's just the secretary ."

"I'm sure it will be different tomorrow," Nicole reassured him.

It wasn't different the next day. Or the day after that. Tony sat at his desk, feeling increasingly disturbed as an array of people walked in and out for meetings with Ralph.

At lunchtime on the third day he met a very slim, fit-looking woman on the stairs. She was dressed in a designer tracksuit and he judged her to be in her forties.

"Hello!" she smiled. "You must be Tony?"

"Yeah, hi." He was relieved somebody was acknowledging him.

"I'm Diana Parker. I'm a contributor."

"Oh yes! You write the health and fitness column."

"Yes, 'Eaten Bread Is Soon Forgotten'. How are you finding it here?" Her eyes swept all over him, presumably checking out his weight.

"It's good. I'm enjoying it."

"That's good. Anyway, got to fly!" She jogged down the stairs and out the front door. Tony went back to sitting at his desk, reorganising an empty diary for the hundredth time.

*   *   *

"What did you do today?" asked Nicole.

"Nothing much. Just ran a couple of errands for Ralph."

"Very strange . . . Look, Tony, I really think you should take the bull by the horns and go in to Ralph and ask exactly what you should be doing."

"That's easy for you to say – you haven't met him and he's really intimidating."

"So what are you going to do? Just sit at your desk looking pretty and fetching his stamps for him?"

"Yes, if that's what it takes to get on in there, then that's what I'll bloody do!" Tony almost shouted and his face was red.

"I'm sorry," Nicole tried to soothe him, "I know you're

151

under a lot of pressure."

"I'm sorry too. I just feel so useless there."

"Of course you do. He's a bad manager who doesn't know how to manage."

"Still, Mum's right –"

Nicole was filled with concern. "What did she have to say?"

"I met her for lunch today and she said to just keep my head down and say nothing."

"Hardly a sensible approach to the problem, Tony."

"What options do I have?"

* * *

Cathal was watching Joanne who sat opposite him at a table for two in the Unicorn restaurant. Throughout the meal, she seemed to have one eye on him and one eye on everyone else in the restaurant. She talked loudly, laughed loudly, gestured loudly, and constantly flicked her hair back, ensuring they got attention from all the other diners.

She insisted on holding hands with him a lot, and there were constant interruptions from people who Joanne knew and were just coming over to say hello. If he didn't know better, he would have suspected she had pre-booked the restaurant for her friends. Since he had been forced to talk about their relationship, Joanne had taken this as a nod to open the floodgates. As they left the restaurant, two photographers were waiting and she draped herself across Cathal as she posed for them. It was clear to him that she was in her element.

Joanne's constant presence since he had returned from London ensured he hadn't had an opportunity to phone Lana. He continually replayed the night when they wandered around London and wondered how she was doing.

* * *

Sylvia looked at the four glum faces in her office as she put down the phone to Jack Better.

"Is he angry?" asked James.

"More disappointed than angry," she answered.

"Just reaching No 14 in the charts, which really sucks," said Seán.

"And sales are supposed to be even worse this week," Sylvia informed them.

James chewed some gum and looked out the window, feeling defeated.

Cathal tried to rally the troops. "Well, look, we still had a hugely successful album and the accompanying tour was equally successful. So it ended on a sour note, but that's life, isn't it?"

"At the end of a tour you should have great sales." Sylvia's eyes blazed. "I've already had the press on asking how come Affidavit's latest song did so dismally – are the fans deserting you – that kind of thing – were people not impressed by the tour?"

"Well, instead of us all just sitting here and moaning, let's try an analysis of what went wrong," urged Cathal.

"The song probably wasn't strong enough," said James.

"I don't agree with you," Sylvia said. "But I said all along it was a shit video. Videos are what sell songs, and that video was shit."

"Also all that rubbish appearing in the papers about Cathal and Joanne detracted from the song," said Seán.

"Go on, get the fucking dig in – again!" Cathal shot him a filthy look.

"Well, it's true!" said Seán. "That 'all publicity is good publicity' jargon is crap!"

"If I can get my point in," Cathal snapped. "It's what I said before – everyone's taking life easy, thinking we have it made. You can never rest no matter how much success you have. Personally I don't think this tour was as good as our previous ones and I think we're now seeing the result of that."

"Cathal's right," Sylvia agreed. "We start recording the new album in a week and everyone needs to knuckle down and give it their all."

* * *

Cathal came into his apartment, threw the keys on the coffee table and threw himself on the couch. What a disaster, he thought. The band had never had such a bad chart entry.

"Hello, darling," said Joanne, coming out of the bedroom.

Cathal jumped with fright, not expecting anyone to be there. He had left her in the apartment that morning but she was getting ready to leave then.

"What are you doing here? You were heading into RTÉ to do an interview."

"Yes, but it was cancelled . . . Wait until I tell you, I got a call from Ruth, the Social Diarist at *Hi Life*, and she told me that I could be nominated as Personality of the Year, can you believe that?" She was like a small kid in a sweetshop as she sat down beside him and put her arm around him. "If I won that –"

"Did she ask you anything about us?" Cathal was filled with concern.

"Just a few things, but nothing important."

Cathal thought for a minute. He had been putting it off but the time was definitely now, especially after the meeting that day. He didn't need this complication in his life at the moment. "Joanne, I've been meaning to talk to you about something – about us."

"Yes." Joanne's eyes widened. "I know. I want to talk about us too, and I think I know what you're going to say . . . I've been thinking the same thing myself."

"You have?" he said, surprised.

"Yes." She paused, savouring the moment. "A full-feature interview, including glossy photos at home – yours, of course – with *Hi Life* magazine!" She clasped her hands together. "Our first official interview together!"

"What?" Cathal almost roared. "No – not at all – in fact the opposite – I don't want to see you any more, Joanne!"

Joanne's smile fell as her eyes widened. She was heavily bronzed which disguised the fact that she had paled. "B-b-but why?" She could barely get the words out.

Cathal got up quickly and walked to the other side of the lounge. He knew she wouldn't go quietly. "No reason. I just don't want to go out with anybody right now."

"Are you –" Joanne gulped, "dumping me?"

"I'm afraid so, yes."

Tears started streaming down Joanne's face. "But we make such a great couple. The press are so interested in us!"

"I don't want the press to be interested in me – not in that way anyway."

She stood up angrily. "I will *not* be dismissed like the brainless little bimbos you have gone out with in the past!"

"What are you going to do about it? Claim squatter's rights?"

"You think you are so clever. Why don't you take a good look in the mirror and see yourself for what you are. A talentless guy who got a break, that's all, Cathal, that's all! But you know all this will pass one day, and what will you do then?"

"That's my problem."

"One big problem. You know, you're this guy who surrounds himself with a security system – the band, MPI, Sylvia, all your friends – they all have to form around you to protect you. And if they threaten you, they have to go!"

"Goodbye, Joanne."

She grabbed her handbag. "You haven't seen the last of me, I can assure you of that." She walked out the door and slammed it after her.

Cathal, feeling relieved she had gone, sat down on the couch. He also felt angry at what she had said. Angry but saddened.

CHAPTER 13

"Sorry, Lana, there's some mess-up with a photo shoot and I can't make lunch," said Patricia.

"That's no problem," answered Lana. She was driving through the city centre.

"Are you sure?"

"Of course."

"I'll meet you tomorrow, and we can go shopping." They both started laughing.

Since they had got back from London, they had been indulging their hobby with a passion, all courtesy of Patricia's family and work colleagues.

Lana turned off her phone, decided to take a drive up to Kildara to see her father and turned the car towards Malahide.

* * *

She got out of the car, walked up to the front door and let herself in.

"Hello, there!" said Gloria, who was walking across the hall.

Damn, she'd forgotten Wednesday was the day Gloria spent at Kildara! Lana cast an eye over Gloria's cool chic exterior – blonde bob, immaculate make-up, an exquisite beige suit.

"We haven't seen you for a while," Gloria continued.

We? Was she using the word in the royal context, or was she referring to herself and Barry, indicating Lana was an outsider?

"Yes, I've been busy," said Lana, refusing to let herself be intimidated by this super-confident woman.

"What?" Gloria allowed herself a small smile, a mocking smile. "With shopping and partying? I'm just going in to see your father – are you coming too?"

Lana nodded and followed Gloria towards her father's office.

"Hi, Barry, look who I found wandering around." Gloria went to Barry's desk and started opening files and looking through them.

"Here's my darling!" Barry got up from his desk and, approaching Lana, enveloped her in a big bear hug.

Lana felt unnerved as she saw Gloria slip into her father's seat and start writing some notes as if it were her desk. She knew Barry always encouraged familiarity with his management team, but Gloria was taking it to new extremes.

"Will you join us for lunch?" asked Barry.

Gloria looked up, displeasure showing on her face for a fleeting moment before being replaced with a smile. "Oh do, that would be so lovely!" Gloria looked at her watch.

"Although, Barry, if I can remind you, the Taoiseach is coming here at 2.30 for a meeting." She pulled a sympathetic face at Lana. "It would have to be a quick one."

"No, it's okay," said Lana. "I don't have time anyway."

"Lots of pressing engagements for you!" Gloria smiled in a condescending fashion.

"I just dropped by to say hello." She reached forward and kissed her father's cheek. "I'll phone you later."

"Okay, darling, I'll talk to you then."

Lana turned and walked out off the room. She burned with anger. That damned woman! With her Harvard education, and youngest lecturer ever at UCD, and amazing political observation skills . . . she was so goddamned worthwhile! She wanted to go in and mess up her perfect hair, or rip up her perfect suit. Anything to disrupt her perfect life. How dare she look down her nose at her? Suddenly a thought crossed Lana's mind. A daring, dangerous thought that was too good an opportunity to miss.

She quickly crossed the hall, went up the circular stairway and made her way down the hallway towards the room Gloria was using as an office. She looked down the well-lit marble hallway and then slipped into the room. The office was immaculate. Not for Gloria any files or papers thrown around the place. No, Gloria's office was as tidy as herself. Lana quickly went to the desk and sat down. She started opening the drawers. Everything was so perfectly in order she would have to be extra careful. In the third drawer she saw Gloria's wallet and took it out. Opening it up, she saw an array of credit cards.

"Visa, I think," she said, taking the card out and replacing the purse carefully.

She slipped out of the office and down the corridor to the stairs. She knew Gloria never left Kildara on a Wednesday until eight, workaholic that she was. And she would be very busy all afternoon tied up with Barry and the Taoiseach.

Lana was going to have some fun, and Gloria was going to be paying for it.

She knew Gloria wouldn't be like Patricia's future sisters-in-law or the people she worked with who barely checked their credit-card bills. She guessed Gloria would meticulously check her bill and have receipts for everything. But that was the point. She wanted Gloria to see a pair of 500 euro Gucci shoes turn up on her bill and have her perfect world thrown into confusion as she tried to find out how they got there. Smiling, she sat into her car and took off. She would have the Visa back in Gloria's purse within the hour.

*   *   *

"Look it's going to be great, I've already told Mum and Dad you're coming, and everyone's expecting you," Kelly said to Kathryn down the phone.

"Oh, Kelly, I wish you hadn't. I said if I got a chance I'd drop by for an hour, but it was only a maybe." Kathryn raised her eyes to heaven. Kelly always seemed to forget that Kathryn was not a lady of leisure – she would be working both Friday and Saturday nights and she just might not be in the mood to go to a barbeque in between.

Come off it, she then told herself. Why you don't want to go has nothing to do with work. It's Simeon, and the way he's been.

"Well, you can't let everyone down now!" Kelly pointed out. "So, we'll see you around three. Be sure to bring Simeon – how is he?"

"He's fine. I'd better run. Talk to you later." She hung up the phone.

Right, to work, she thought to herself. She needed to ring the breweries and get the orders of stock in. She also needed to sort out the work schedules for the next week. An Australian barman, one of her best, had gone back home without giving her any notice and leaving her in the lurch.

She opened her briefcase, taking her paperwork out. There was also the situation with Cathal Fitzgerald. The stubborn bastard hadn't been near the club since their falling out – nor any of his gang. She was so used to being the tough woman at work that she hated to pander to people's egos. But needs must. She picked up the phone, steadied herself, and dialled Cathal, hoping it wouldn't go through to message minder.

"Yeah?" said the irritated voice on the other end.

"Cathal, it's Kathryn Foy here."

"I can see that from the caller ID. What you want?" His voice was ice.

This wasn't the friendly, happy Cathal she usually dealt with. "Look, Cathal, I know –" she swallowed hard, "the hassle that photo caused you, and I really would like to apologise." True, she thought.

"What have you done about it?"

"I've fired the doorman who was on that night." Untrue, she thought.

There was a silence for a while.

"Cathal, we've known each other for a long while, and I'd hate for this to come between us." God, she made it sound as if they were best friends, instead of him being a customer who came into her nightclub. "I know you're busy, but if you want to meet up for a drink and try and sort this out?"

"Okay, where and when?"

"This afternoon at five – The Four Seasons?"

"Fine."

She put the phone down and sighed. One hour of grovelling to him should do it. She had thought Cathal was a bit different from the other celebrities at Exclusive, but he was just the same. She knew her reputation as a bitch to normal punters, but she just knew how to play the game. In a way she was the keeper of the game. Making sure that celebs and stars felt special and different from everyone else. Yes, one hour of pandering to Cathal should restore his fragile little ego.

The bedroom door opened and Simeon came out in his dressing-gown. He hadn't come out of the bedroom for so long she got a fright.

"Hi there," he said sheepishly, rubbing the back of his neck.

She quickly tried to guess how he was – she was an expert at it. "How are you feeling now?"

"A bit better," he looked down at the floor.

"Can I get you anything?"

"Just you," he whispered.

She got up and ran over to him, holding him in a hug.

* * *

Feeling confident and in control, Lana pushed open the glass door of the department store and walked towards the shoe department.

She browsed for a while, then tried on a few pairs.

"Do you need any help?" enquired the kindly looking middle-aged sales assistant, whose name badge said 'Jenny'.

"Yes, I like this one. Could I have the other one as well,

please?"

"Certainly!" Jenny disappeared, leaving Lana to check her text messages. A couple of parties on later. She could wear her new shoes to them, courtesy of Gloria.

Jenny returned and gave Lana the pair.

"They are lovely, aren't they?" said Lana as she admired them in the full-length mirror.

"Smashing, they really suit you."

"Bit pricey though." Lana pulled a face. She deserved an extra point for that one, she thought.

"I know," Jenny agreed, and managed to frown without losing her kindly smile.

"Oh, I'm going to get them anyway! I'll let the credit-card bill look after itself when it comes in next month!" And another bonus point to herself, she thought, as she managed to remove Jenny's frown and restore her full kindly expression.

She took the shoes off and handed them to the woman, then followed her to the counter.

"Credit card, I take it?" asked Jenny.

Lana smiled as she handed over the card. "I think so."

Jenny swiped the card and waited. "Nice weather today," she commented.

"Isn't it?" Lana smiled back, tapping her long fingernails on the counter as she waited.

"Sorry about this," apologised Jenny, still smiling. "Sometimes the system is overloaded with all the transactions going through."

"It's terrible really, isn't it? All the people who buy things on credit . . . and the interest they charge . . . it's just another case of Rip-Off Ireland!"

Jenny looked just a little concerned as paper began to be printed on the machine. "Could you hold on for just a second, please?" she said, still smiling kindly as she walked off down the store, the credit card and receipt in hand.

Lana stood wondering what the problem was. Surely Gloria wouldn't have over-stretched her credit? Not so-together Gloria. Lana sighed – she wouldn't have to face the indignity of having the card cut up in front of her, would she?

Jenny returned, accompanied by a security man and a man in a dark suit, whom Lana took to be a manager. Jenny's kindly smile was completely replaced by a cold and frosty glare.

"Could you accompany us to the office, please?" instructed the manager.

"The office? But why?" Lana remained cool.

The security man stepped close to her. "Just move. We don't want a scene."

After being frogmarched through the store, complete with customers staring, she was escorted to an office on an upper level.

"Could we see some identification that you are Gloria Reagan, please?"

"Identification? I don't have any with me." Lana forced herself to remain cool.

The manager looked at her handbag. "What, no driving licence or photo ID?"

"No, nothing . . . What is this about? I have an appointment at three!" Lana snapped.

"Yeah – with the Guards." The manager held up the credit card. "This card has been reported stolen, and unless you can produce identification right now that you are Gloria Reagan, I'm calling the Guards."

Lana thought quickly. "Did you say Gloria Reagan?"

She gave a little laugh. "Now it all makes sense! Gloria's a good friend of mine! I saw her only at lunchtime – I must have taken her card by mistake!"

The manager looked at her sternly. The security man left the office.

"How could I have been so stupid?" Lana said. "I was in a rush and must have picked it up by mistake."

"What's your name?" asked the manager.

"My name?" Lana wanted to run away, to get away from these awful people. "Why do you need that?" She couldn't give her name. What if they recognised it?

"Don't bother talking to her any more," said the security man, returning. "The police are on their way. She can explain everything to them."

"The police!" Lana was panicked. "Please don't call the police. I really do know Gloria!"

"It doesn't matter even if you do. She reported the card stolen."

The damned efficient bitch! She hadn't even been gone an hour!

"Please, this could be a very embarrassing situation for me!" Lana pleaded.

"I'll say!" said the manager.

Lana felt a headache coming on. "I'm Lana Curtis!" She sat down on the chair. "Barry Curtis's daughter . . . Gloria Reagan works for him."

The men looked at each other disbelievingly and then stared at her.

*   *   *

One hour later Barry walked into the office, accompanied by Gloria.

"Hi guys, got a bit of a misunderstanding here by the look of it," he said in his normal affable way. Gloria stood beside him, staring icily at Lana.

"I'm very sorry to disturb you, Mr Curtis," said the manager. "I take it this is your daughter."

"Hi, Lana, I guess you picked up the wrong credit card by mistake, huh?"

Lana nodded, avoiding Gloria's gaze.

"I'm Gloria Reagan," announced Gloria as she marched toward the desk and reclaimed her credit card.

"The credit card has been reported stolen and we have already informed the police that we have the culprit here," said the manager.

"Don't worry about that," said Barry. "We'll put a call through to them and explain the misunderstanding."

"It's just if you are pressing charges, Ms Reagan, there's a format we have to go through here," explained the manager.

Gloria glanced at Lana before looking at the manager. "I won't be pressing charges."

"Well, we'd better make a move. We've wasted enough of your time." Barry moved forward, put his arm around Lana and directed her towards the door. Gloria followed.

"Would you ladies just excuse me for a minute, please?" said Barry and he went back in to the men, closing the door behind him.

Lana and Gloria were left standing in a corridor together.

"Such a silly mistake, I –" Lana began but was withered by a look of disgust from Gloria.

Barry seemed to be in the office for an eternity, leaving the two women in an icy silence.

The office door opened and Barry turned back to the

men. "Thanks again, guys, for all your help."

"No problem at all, Barry, no problem at all," said the manager in a joyous mood.

Barry, Gloria and Lana walked through the store.

"They've really done this place up great, don't you think?" said Barry. He continued to make small talk as the women walked in silence.

"My car's parked in the carpark," said Lana as they walked into the Grafton Street sunshine.

"Don't worry about it," said Barry. "I'll get someone to collect it and bring it back to you. I'll give you a lift home. Gloria, are you okay for a lift?"

"Yes, I'm parked around the corner."

"That's fine then. I'll see you tomorrow."

"See you tomorrow." Gloria gave Lana one final cold stare and then walked off.

Lana just wanted to get to her own car and drive herself home, but she didn't want to create a fuss.

Barry drove them through the traffic the short journey to Lana's house, making small talk along the way.

"So it looks like I'm gaining in the polls, but it's a long haul yet," he informed her as he pulled up outside her house.

She sat there is the car for a second. "Thanks," she said as she undid her seat belt, and stepped out of the car.

"Oh, and Lana," Barry said as she turned to close the car door. "I'm going to have a word with Jeffrey – you know, our accountant, very nice guy – about your allowance being increased." He smiled at her. "It looks like you probably need it."

She nodded and closed the door.

*　　*　　*

Kathryn felt good as she walked into The Four Seasons. Simeon seemed to be emerging from his deep depression and she was so relieved. They had spent the afternoon holding each other. He still wasn't able to talk too much, but at least it was a start. She felt emotionally and physically exhausted, but the small change in him that day had given her lots of new strength. Even the prospect of eating an hour of humble pie for Cathal Fitzgerald didn't seem too stomach-churning. People glanced at her as she checked around the bars to see if she could spot him. Not only did she cut a striking figure in her black trouser suit, but people knew who she was. Satisfied he hadn't arrived yet, she positioned herself in a corner seat and ordered a gin and tonic.

She spotted Cathal coming into the bar. Somebody immediately called him. Smiling, he had a few words before moving on. As he made his way through the bar, somebody else called out to him and he went over and pulled up a chair and sat down for a minute chatting amicably. As he spoke he spotted Kathryn and waved at her.

Getting up, he hurried over to her.

"Hi, Cathal," said a man at a nearby table.

"How's it going, Tom?" Cathal shook the man's hand.

"Fine, we'll have to catch up soon," said Tom.

"Sure, give me a shout and we'll meet for a drink," agreed Cathal.

Cathal reached Kathryn's table and sat down opposite her.

"Sorry, I think I'm late," he said.

"Popular guy," she commented.

ell, you get to meet a lot of people in this

do. Drink?"

"A Carlsberg would be nice."

She called a passing waitress and gave ̣̇ her order, relieved that Cathal seemed to be in good form. M̲ ̲ she wouldn't have to spend even an hour with him ̣ ̣ there were lots of things she needed to do at the club.

"Thanks for meeting me, Cathal." She tried to look apologetic. "I've been so upset over this situation. The last thing I wanted was for us to fall out."

He sat back in his chair as the waitress delivered his drink.

"It did cause me a lot of hassle," he then said. "The other band members think my personal life spread across the papers cost us the No 1 spot for our new song."

Kathryn arched an eyebrow. "And do you think that?"

"No – I think we didn't get to No 1 because it was a shit song." Cathal suddenly smiled. "How simple was that to say? Everybody's been blaming my personal life, or the video or any other fucking excuse when in fact we released a terrible song. I wish I had just come out and said that at MPI when they forced us to put it on the album."

Kathryn was intrigued. She was expecting a sulk and begrudging forgiveness, and in fact she was getting an interesting conversation. "So why didn't you say it at the time?"

"Because everyone else thought it was great, I suppose." He didn't want to say any more to someone whom he only really knew on a social level but suddenly his pent-up anger with the situation was flowing out. "I reckoned they knew more than I did."

"You don't strike me as being shy, Cathal, or unable to get your own way."

"Yeah, with most things, but well, you know, the other guys are great musicians, so musically I would tend to

169

...ow them and what MPI dictates."

"You don't think you're a great singer or musician?"

"No, I'm not. I'm very much a support in the band."

"Don't you feel a little guilty about that?"

"I've just been very lucky in life. My cousin who's a great musician gave me a break in his band. Do I feel guilty? No way. I work like a dog every day making sure Affidavit is a success. It's my life and I'm totally dedicated to it. You can have all the talent in the world but if you don't work at it like a dog and not weaken you won't get anywhere."

She was becoming angry with him now but was determined not to show it. His honesty was refreshing, but that didn't stop her thinking about Simeon and a true talent that had never got the opportunity to be recognised. She felt he was insulting Simeon implying that his lack of work ethic had stopped him from getting the credit he deserved. But she didn't want to fall out with Cathal a second time. "Well, let's hope your next song will do better."

"We need to make a few changes, but I've already instigated them."

"Well, I hope we can put the photograph business all behind us and be friends again. If you could apologise to Joanne for me as well –"

"You might have to do that yourself. We're finished."

"So soon? But the papers had this down as the big romance of your life!"

"So did Joanne!"

Kathryn smiled and couldn't help giggling.

"What went wrong?"

"I wasn't at all serious about her, simple as that."

She was curious. "And when was the last time you

were 'serious' about someone?"

"I think we're getting a bit deep here, don't you?" Cathal emptied his drink. "I'd better go. I just wanted really to meet you, Kathryn, to say sorry to you."

Kathryn was confused. "Sorry to me?"

"Yeah. I overreacted a little that day when we rowed. I know it wasn't your fault that the photographer took our photo."

Kathryn was surprised. "What happens in my club is my responsibility, Cathal."

"Yeah. But accidents do happen – and, as you said, we really should have got a room. Sorry for being so mean. Now that wasn't too bad, was it?"

"What wasn't?"

"Having to have a drink with me."

"What do you mean?"

"Let's be honest with each other, Kathryn. You only rang me up to apologise because you were frightened our falling out might affect trade at Exclusive."

"That's not true . . ." she trailed off as he smiled knowingly at her.

"Let's cut through the bullshit. I know the score. And now we've met we can continue to pretend to be pals, me and my crew will keep going to Exclusive and everyone's happy."

Kathryn felt herself go red. Cathal's blatant honesty was unusual and unnerving in the fake business they lived in. She leaned back in her seat and crossed her legs. "That's very hard."

"Hard but true. If I wasn't in Affidavit and I spoke to you the way I did, you would have fucked me out of it. I know your reputation." He spoke freely and matter-of-factly. He finished his drink in a gulp and stood up.

"Anyway I'll see you around."

"In Exclusive?"

"Only if you can guarantee me my favourite table," he smirked.

"You can have any table you want at any time," she said smiling.

He winked and walked away. As somebody else called him and he went over to have a few words with them, Kathryn found herself wishing he could have stayed a little longer.

*   *   *

A stunning girl with long sleek black hair and a haughty look about her was seated waiting to meet Ralph. Tony recognised her immediately from her photo in *Hi Life*; she was Ruth Davitt, the magazine's Social Diarist. He remembered that she was a former model.

"Ruth, this is Tony, our new –" Vivienne paused for a second, "staff writer"

Who never writes, Tony could almost hear Vivienne think.

Ruth put out a perfectly manicured hand "How are you finding him?"

"Ralph? He's really good. I'm enjoying it."

Ruth nodded and smirked over to Vivienne.

The door opened down the corridor and Diana Parker came into reception looking flushed.

"He says for you to go in, Ruth," she said.

"How is he today?"

"Doesn't seem to be too bad. But you can never tell, you know yourself. I've just spent the last hour devising a new diet for him."

CHAPTER 14

The day after Lana had been caught for credit-card fraud, she still felt terrible. When Barry had left her off she had come into the house and drunk half a bottle of whiskey straightaway to settle her nerves. Then she had crawled into bed. She thought she might feel better the next day but actually felt worse. She had never felt such embarrassment and shame. She had been treated like a common criminal. What must her father think of her? She knew he would deal with the situation the way he always did. Cool and calm. And his way of dealing with his situation was to give her an increase in her allowance. She never felt so low and bad about herself.

Patricia was away on business so she wouldn't even have her to talk to during the day. Not that she could tell her what had happened anyway. Patricia would have been shocked. Not at what she had done, but that she had been stupid enough to get caught and, even worse, not to then have been able to wriggle out of it without calling her father.

She would have to go out that night and paint the town red to try and get over the whole incident.

*　　*　　*

"So, we'll book that interview on Tuesday morning for you then?" Gloria wrote the appointment in a diary. She and Barry were in his office at Kildara.

"Yes, you'll have to brief me about EU taxation law beforehand," said Barry.

"That's no problem. I'm having that info compiled for you at the moment." Gloria closed the diary. "Barry . . . could I talk to you about something of a delicate nature?"

"Of course, fire ahead!"

"It's just about the incident that occurred yesterday . . . at the store."

Barry nodded.

"I'm just concerned about Lana."

"Concerned?" he said, looking unconcerned.

"Yes . . . can I speak frankly, Barry?"

"Of course."

"Lana is a lovely girl, and I have nothing but respect for her . . . but she obviously has a problem."

"A problem?"

"Yes. Credit-card fraud is a very serious issue."

Barry looked slightly uncomfortable.

"And we just managed to avert a major scandal yesterday. If she had used somebody else's card who decided to press charges –"

"Somebody else's?"

"Yes, Barry, my knowledge of this kind of thing is it isn't a one-off situation. I hate to cast aspersions but from a behavioural point of view, it is extremely likely Lana has done this kind of thing before and, unless she gets help, will probably do it again."

Barry nodded and looked down at his desk pensively.

"This kind of crime is closely linked to shop-lifting," Gloria continued. "I suspect Lana may have shop-lifted in the past, or if she hasn't it will only be a matter of time before she does." She paused. "If Lana was caught either trying to credit-card fraud or shop-lift, the effect on the election campaign would be devastating. You're a multi-millionaire and the main weapon the opposition has against you is the notion that you are not in touch with the ordinary people and ordinary life. If your daughter, the daughter of one of the country's richest men and who wants for nothing, is caught shop-lifting – it will destroy the campaign. Your enemies' slurs that you represent corrupt big business with no regard for morals or respect will be confirmed. You would have to withdraw from the campaign."

Barry placed his hands together in temple form and nodded. "I understand the seriousness of the problem . . . and what would you say we should do about it, Gloria?"

"I strongly recommend that Lana receives therapy about this issue. It's the only way she can overcome it, and that we can be assured the situation is being tackled. I've taken the liberty of investigating some good therapists and have the name of one who has been strongly recommended. If you agree, I can make a booking for Lana immediately."

* * *

Lana cursed Patricia for being away. She really was in the mood to party that night and nobody could party like Patricia. She received a text from a friend called Johnny, who she had a fling with a couple of months ago. He was about twenty years older than her and had wanted to put their fling on a more permanent basis, but she had declined. If nothing else she suspected Johnny, a successful businessman in his own right, was in awe of the Curtis name. She ignored the text. Her mobile rang and she paused for a second, not recognising the number. She shrugged and answered it.

"Hello?" she said.

"Lana, hi. Cathal Fitzgerald here."

"Cathal," she repeated his name in confusion.

"Now, don't do this 'who are you?' shit with me again." He kept his voice light.

"No – no. I remember you – of course." She had flashbacks to the park in London and shuddered. She had gone way over the top that night.

"How are you keeping?" he asked.

Shit, she thought. "Fine."

There was a very awkward silence.

"Well, I was just ringing really to arrange to meet up as we planned."

"Hmmm . . ." She felt awkward. She didn't want to meet him. She had sailed way too close to the wind in London and didn't want any reminders of it. "Look, Cathal, you are very sweet . . ." Sweet! he thought. That's a new one.

". . . but I've had a lot of hassle recently, and I really wouldn't be good company."

"Try me! I'm great at coaxing people into being good company. Come over to mine and I'll cook you dinner. As you said yourself, if you're bored you can leave any time."

*   *   *

176

"I thought Exclusive was off the agenda," objected James as he, Seán, Rob and Cathal made their way up the steps to the entrance.

"I met up with Kathryn yesterday and we made up," said Cathal.

"Not that I would have stopped going just because Cathal said so anyway," Seán said into James' ear.

"Follow me up," said Kathryn, beaming when she saw them. "I have your usual table reserved."

"Busy night?" asked Cathal.

"You know what Exclusive is like on a Friday night," said Kathryn, then she leaned forward and whispered to Cathal, "Just to warn you – Joanne Bailey is here tonight."

Cathal rolled his eyes and muttered, "Just what I need!" as he followed her up the stairs and through the club into the members' lounge.

Seán spotted Joanne seated at the bar giving Cathal a killer look. "There's your girlfriend," he said. "Aren't you going to invite her over?"

"We broke up," said Cathal.

"Did you?" said James, surprised. "Donna was just going to invite the two of you over for dinner next week."

"Well, it will be an invitation for one now," said Cathal.

"She doesn't look too pleased with you," Rob observed.

"You don't want to join us ?" Seán asked Joanne as he went up to her at the bar.

"I'd rather not!" She almost spat the words. "Cathal's an asshole, do you know that?"

"You don't like him?"

"You can say that again!"

"Then we've got something in common. Can I buy you a drink?"

"He's just such a bastard!"

"I know, I know," Seán commiserated.

"I mean I have sacrificed so much to be with Cathal . . . here I am, a serious music journalist and suddenly I find myself in a compromising position on the front of a newspaper . . . can you imagine how that made me feel?"

"It's a terrible invasion of your privacy."

"Suddenly people stopped taking me seriously and all everyone was asking me was about my relationship with Cathal. It was so awful for me, being the very private person that I am."

"I totally understand," Seán nodded.

"And then he finishes our relationship without even an explanation!"

"That's Cathal for you. No regard for other people's feelings, only cares about himself."

"I thought you were friends?" she said.

"We used to be. But Cathal pushes everyone away in the end."

"Selfish to the end! I can't stand him!"

"Do you know what would really piss him off?" said Seán.

"What?"

"If you came out to dinner with me."

*   *   *

Stephen Rourke lay on his bed in his cell looking at the photo of Cathal and Joanne in the newspaper. It wouldn't be long until he was released and he couldn't wait to escape this hell-hole. But he was also gripped with fear. What would he do outside? Who would want anything to do with him after being on the inside. He looked at the photo again.

*   *   *

Tony watched as the senior staff assembled in the reception area of *Hi Life* for the weekly Friday meeting. He sat at his desk, as usual trying to look busy at his computer. All he had done in the two weeks at the magazine was run errands for Ralph who was often rude to him. He was feeling low and was almost missing his last job – at least he was always busy there. *Hi Life* was proving to be a big disappointment.

He looked at the assembled staff, waiting nervously for the phone call to send them into Ralph's office. There was Gavin, the head of advertising, nervously looking through his advertising figures for the week. He was a man in his late thirties. There was Susan, also in her thirties, head of design, looking through the design sheets. Then there was Clive, who was the chief photographer and seemed to be more confident than the others. Diana and Ruth were present also. Vivienne, who like him was never invited to the meetings, was typing away furiously.

"Is Maggie coming in today?" Diana asked Vivienne, under her breath.

"Yeah, she's supposed to be in later."

"All tanned from her holiday, no doubt," said Gavin.

Vivienne's phone buzzed and she answered. "You can all go in," she said.

And they all nervously filed down the corridor. Vivienne gave Tony a sympathetic look, because of his not being included again. Tony had found Vivienne to be polite and very helpful but she kept her distance. All the staff had so far kept their distance from him as if they were very suspicious of him. But he had observed there was a bond between all the staff which seemed to be based on a mutual dislike of Ralph.

Vivienne's phone rang again. "Yes," she answered. "Sure, no problem." She put down the phone and turned to Tony. "He wants you to go into the meeting."

"What?" Tony was completely taken by surprise. He nervously got up and grabbed a notebook and pen.

Tony bounded down the corridor, knocked on the boardroom door and entered. He glanced around the room and saw all the staff were seated around the board table. Ralph sat at the head.

"T-t-take a seat," Ralph ordered.

By this time Tony had noticed that Ralph often stuttered when under pressure.

Diana indicated for him to sit down beside her.

"Right, where are we?" said Ralph. "Gavin, these advertising sales are down this week!"

"Yes, I was two staff down this week, so it affected my overall figures," explained Gavin.

"W-w-why were you down two staff?" asked Ralph.

"Maureen had flu and Tommy is having some personal problems."

"Are you sure she had flu or was she making it up?" demanded Ralph.

"Oh no, I spoke to her on the phone regularly. She sounded terrible – and as for Tommy, he's –"

"I'm not interested in his personal problems," Ralph said loudly. "Tell him to leave his problems at home and get his ass into work."

"I've told him that," Gavin said, nodding. "I phoned him at home and told him if his problems continue to affect his job, he won't have a job."

"Good, good, and I want to have these figures up twenty per cent by next Friday, okay?"

"I'll hopefully have full staff on Monday so we can get there next week." Gavin nodded nervously.

"Susan!" snapped Ralph.

"Yes, Ralph?"

"Have all the articles come through from London for the next edition?"

"They have and I'm just setting them out now into our edition."

"Good, send a copy of them up to me so I can read through them."

"I've already organised that."

"What is the Beckham interview like?"

"Very good, actually. All the stuff the readers love."

"Ruth, what have you got for me this week?"

"Quite a bit actually," said Ruth, looking through her notes and pushing back her sleek black hair. "Had a première of the new Tom Cruise film on Tuesday, U2 concert on Wednesday, and special fundraising party on Thursday at Exclusive. Lots of names at all events –"

"And photos?" Ralph looked at Clive.

"And photos," assured Clive, who looked exhausted.

"And my little pièce-de-résistance this week is that Cathal Fitzgerald has broken up with Joanne Bailey." Ruth smiled happily.

"W-w-what?" shouted Ralph, causing everyone in the room to jump.

"I heard through one of my sources that their relationship is over," explained Ruth meekly.

Ralph slammed his hand on the desk. "When are you people going to understand that we don't do that kind of story!" he shouted, causing everyone to jump again. "You are not a gossip columnist; you're a social diarist! We don't report idle chit-chat – leave that to the *News of The World*. The stars t-t-t-t-trust us and we will never do anything to break that t-t-t-trust. In this day and age where stars are hunted down wherever they go, who can they rely on? Only us at *Hi Life* magazine. They are my friends and I won't let them down, do you u-u-understand?"

Ruth nodded meekly.

Tony noticed that Ralph's stutter got worse the more people there were around.

"Diana, your column, what's going on in 'Eaten Bread Is Soon Forgotten'?" asked Ralph.

"A new diet actually. A reader discovered a regime based on coconuts while travelling through the Caribbean and sent it on to me. I've done some research and it seems to work a treat!"

"Good. Send me up a copy of that to take a look through as well. Okay, I've got an itinerary of items coming up from the Hartons in London and it's pretty exciting stuff. Let's discuss what we've got coming up ourselves." Ralph looked through his notes. "We have the feature on Affidavit as they begin to record their new album. This will be one of our biggest stories this year and will not only be syndicated to the UK edition but also to the other European editions. According to Sylvia Henderson they are going in a new direction and will be talking very honestly to us about their careers, lives and –" he shot Ruth a filthy look, "loves."

"I should be able to get massive advertising for that edition," Gavin assured him.

"Then we have the Joanne Bailey and Cathal Fitzgerald interview," Ralph gave Ruth another dirty look, "which maybe is in jeopardy according to our source. I have a meeting with her on Monday morning. And have we completed our *Hi Life* Personality of the Year Award shortlist? Everyone take a look through the shortlist and give your opinions." He handed copies to Gavin who passed them around.

Tony took his copy and tried to study it. He had sat looking on in amazement at the way Ralph had run the meeting. He had conducted it at a very fast speed, only halted by his stutters which seemed to hold everyone's attention as much as when he spoke normally.

As Tony glanced through the column of names, he saw it was filled with the usual suspects of socialites, politicians and ladies who lunched. Everyone voiced their approval of the list.

"Right, everyone back to work," snapped Ralph. "Tony, come up here. I need you to do something for me."

When Tony approached, full of expectation, he was dashed to discover Ralph simply wanted him to go to the shop to get him a paper. But as he made his way there he still felt elated at having been included in the meeting.

Arriving back with the paper, Tony knocked on Ralph's door and opened it. To his surprise he saw a dark-haired woman seated opposite Ralph at the desk.

"Tony, this is my wife, Margaux," said Ralph, stroking his chin.

The woman stood up and turned around. He was mesmerised by her beauty. She was average height, in her mid-forties, with exquisite features and dark hair to her shoulders. She was dressed immaculately and smiled warmly at him.

Tony smiled back at her and put his hand out. "Really, very nice to meet you," he said, putting as much charm as he possibly could into the greeting.

"Welcome to *Hi Life*," she said. "I hope you are settling in all right." She exuded charm, confidence and warmth.

Tony was also struck by her accent which sounded very upper-class. "Yeah, just about," he said.

"That's good," smiled Margaux.

"Well – I'll head back to my work," said Tony smiling still. Work, that was a joke.

Back at reception, he sat down at his desk. "I met Margaux," he said to Vivienne. "She's lovely, isn't she?"

"Maggie?" said Vivienne with a smirk. "Yeah, she's fine."

CHAPTER 15

Kathryn stepped out of the shower and began to dry her hair. It was two o'clock on Saturday afternoon and she was getting ready to go over to the barbeque at Kelly's. She hadn't mentioned it to Simeon as she knew he wouldn't want to go.

The front door slammed. "Hello!" Simeon called.

Kathryn went out to the main room.

"Hi there, gorgeous!" he said, grabbing her and planting a big kiss on her lips.

"Where were you?" she asked smiling.

"Out for a jog. Beautiful day!"

Kathryn felt uneasy. Though she was delighted he had come out of his deep depression, he had still been quiet and sullen yesterday. It usually took him a couple of weeks to gradually emerge. This sudden turnaround usually indicated something was amiss.

"Do you know what? I'd love to do something today. A drive in the country or something – are you on?" He took off his T-shirt and headed for the shower.

Kathryn thought quickly. She would love to spend the day alone with him more than anything else, but she really couldn't let Kelly down.

"I'm sorry, love, I promised Kelly I'd go to a barbeque at their place. If I had known –"

"A barbeque?" asked Simeon, sticking his head around the corner of the bathroom. "And I wasn't invited?"

"Well, of course you were invited, but I didn't think you would want to go."

"Not want to go? But I'd love to go! What time are they expecting us?"

*   *   *

Lana dropped a painkiller into her glass of water. Was she having a terrible time recently or what? The horrible incident at the store. And the incident in the park in London. God, nothing like that had happened to her before. The convulsions had really scared her. She shuddered to think what would have happened if the ambulance had been called. Imagine her father arriving into hospital to see her, no doubt accompanied by Gloria. She'd had a lucky escape. As for this guy Cathal, she didn't know what to make of him. He wasn't part of their set, but judging from his house in London, he wasn't short of money. And he also had a place in Dublin which she was due to visit that evening. She wished Patricia was back so she could get the lowdown on him. Now he wanted to go on a date with her. A date ! She didn't go on dates. She just ended up with guys at parties and stuff. She wondered if he knew who she was and was a golddigger.

Her doorbell rang and she went up the stairs from the basement kitchen to answer it.

When she opened her door she was surprised to see her father standing there, his driver parked in the small gravel driveway. He never visited her house.

"Dad!"

"Are you alone? Is it okay if I come in?"

"Of course!"

He walked in, kissing her on the cheek. "I just came by for a chat really." He walked into the living room and sat down.

She sat facing him. You never come by for just a chat, so what do you want, she wanted to ask. "Really? That's nice," she said pleasantly.

"It's about that unfortunate incident in the store."

Lana felt herself go bright red. "The store?"

"You see, we're in a little bit of a predicament really. We owe Gloria quite a lot for not pressing charges."

"It was just a simple mistake!"

"I know that. Of course I know that."

"So what's the problem then?"

"Well, it's just Gloria is insisting on you receiving therapy." He smiled at her.

"I see," Lana said, wanting the earth to open up and swallow her. Or better still to open up and swallow Gloria Reagan.

"I don't know much about these things. But she says it will be good for you . . . and, well, we don't have a choice really, do we? Considering the position we are in."

Lana wanted to scream and shout and swear and call Gloria every name under the sun. Instead she sat there calmly. "There's no way out of it then?"

"Not really. When you think you could have ended up in court over it. We have to do what Gloria says, don't we?" He smiled kindly at her again.

"I don't think I need a therapist," she said smoothly.

"I know. Of course you don't." He frowned. "But if we

could pacify Gloria?" He stood up to leave. "She's organised everything already. You'll be getting a call from the therapist to organise an appointment."

Lana stood up and walked her father to the door.

"Call up to Kildara during the week and we'll have lunch," said Barry as he kissed her goodbye on the cheek.

Lana smiled and nodded and closed the door after him.

She paced up and down furiously. Therapy ! How could he agree to it? She didn't need therapy! She wasn't mad. The only therapy she needed was retail therapy ! That super-confident, self-assured over-achieving bitch Gloria and her meddling ways! All she was doing was having a bit of fun, for God's sake! Where was the harm in that?

* * *

As Simeon drove out to Castleknock, Kathryn felt extremely nervous sitting beside him. He seemed in great form and was laughing and joking, but she couldn't remember the last time her family and Simeon had mixed together.

In a funny kind of way her life was much compartmentalised. She had her family, her work which included all the social events she was invited to, and then she had Simeon. She rarely mixed them and that suited her fine. She didn't know how the situation had developed but she supposed it had happened due to Simeon's mood changes and also the unsociable hours of her work.

As Simeon pulled into the driveway of Kelly's lovely house, she wished the afternoon would pass quickly.

"Have I told you recently how lucky I am to have you?" smiled Simeon as he reached over and kissed her.

"Not for a while," she said truthfully, her heart leaping to hear him say the words. She went to get out of the car.

"Don't move another muscle!" commanded Simeon as he jumped out of the car and ran over to her side. "Madam!" he said, opening her door.

In spite of herself, she giggled and hugged him when she got out.

He got the wine from the boot and they walked up the steps of the house.

"I see the carpet trade is showing no sign of a slow-down," commented Simeon as he looked through the glass panels at the side of the door at the expensive furniture. Kathryn felt nervous again. She knew Kelly's husband Jim and Simeon had absolutely nothing in common and the guests at the barbeque would probably only be talking business, a subject Simeon had no interest in. She also didn't want Simeon to be intimidated by Jim's success.

"Hi there," said Kelly and seeing Simeon looked delightedly shocked. "And Simeon! There's a surprise! Kathryn, you never said Simeon was coming!"

"Last-minute decision," said Simeon, smiling from ear to ear.

Kelly linked arms with both of them and led them through the house to the back garden. She opened up the patio doors and said, "Look who's here, everyone!"

Kathryn looked around at the dozen people seated and standing around the extensive garden. They all seemed exactly like her sister and brother-in-law. The men looked well off and big-headed and the women bored and bejewelled.

Sara came running over to Kathryn and gave her a big hug.

"I'll slap on some extra burgers then, with your

appetite, Kathryn," joked Kelly's husband Jim, who was dressed in an apron, and was cooking away at the barbeque.

"Less of your cheek!" said Kathryn and she laughed.

Kathryn went over to her parents, Maeve and Arthur, who were seated at a garden table, and gave them both a kiss.

"Simeon, we weren't expecting you," smiled Maeve who reached up to give Simeon a kiss on the cheek.

"No, I can see that from everyone's shocked expressions," said Simeon, who now looked uncomfortable.

"Simeon." Arthur nodded over, rather coldly.

Kathryn went over and put her arm around her father. "You're looking well, Dad."

"I wish I could say the same for you!" said Arthur.

"Thanks a lot!" said Kathryn, bemused.

"Arthur!" admonished Maeve.

"Well, it's true. You look as beautiful as ever, of course, but you look bloody tired! And why wouldn't you be looking exhausted – all those bloody late nights, not getting in till all hours. That was okay when you were younger, but you're getting on now."

"Thanks again!" said Kathryn, looking less bemused.

"Well, it just annoys me that you have to go out to work." He shot Simeon an irritated look.

"I don't have to go out, Dad. I choose to," Kathryn said firmly, before leaning close to her father's ear. "Dad, please, just drop it, and I mean it, okay?"

He looked at his daughter and smiled and nodded. "Okay."

"Well, I'm starving. I'm going to go and try out Jim's supposedly excellent cooking," she said, linking her arm through Simeon's and leading him to the barbeque.

"What are you stirring it for?" Kelly snapped at her father once her sister was out of earshot.

"Well, it's true. I never heard the likes of it. Her out working till five in the morning while he does nothing all day but pisses around messing with his music!"

"This isn't the time or the place," said Maeve, "so shut up! For Kathryn's sake."

Kathryn delicately balanced a hamburger in her hands and tried to eat it without letting any of the contents drip onto her suit. "So how's business going?" she asked Jim as he busily flipped burgers.

"Can't complain. Well, if I did, who'd listen to me, anyway?"

"True for you," said Kathryn.

"Just opened a shop down in Athlone. First shop outside Dublin."

"Fair play." Kathryn smiled. "You're going nationwide now?"

"That's the plan. Another burger, Simeon?" asked Jim.

"Yeah, why not?"

A woman tapped Kathryn on the shoulder. "Can I just say I love what you're wearing?"

"Oh, thank you," smiled Kathryn.

"I always love what you wear when I see your picture in the magazines."

"That's very kind of you."

"I was telling Kelly the other day I hope you win *Hi Life's* Social Personality of the Year."

"Thanks, but I haven't even been nominated yet!"

"Oh you will be. You always are. And is this your husband?" The woman smiled at a sulky Simeon.

"This is Simeon, my partner."

"You're a very lucky man to have such an elegant woman. What do you do yourself?"

"Simeon is in the music industry," answered Kathryn.

"I can speak for myself!" snapped Simeon.

"Sorry," said Kathryn quickly, feeling embarrassed.

"Oh, really? What exactly do you do?" asked the woman.

"I have an unusual name – don't you recognise it?" he asked, wiping sweat from his brow.

The woman looked confused "Er . . . no . . ."

"You might remember some of the songs I had . . . 'Drifting Over To You'?"

The woman looked even more confused. "No."

"'A Pocketful of You'?" pressed Simeon.

The woman shook her head. "No"

"'After The Clouds Came Love'?" Simeon spoke with urgency.

"Can't say I've heard of any of them."

"Well, you obviously don't know the music scene at all then!" Simeon snapped harshly and suddenly he was squeezing his hamburger too tight and the burger and sauce fell down his shirt. "For fuck's sake!" he shouted. "My fucking shirt is ruined!"

Kathryn grabbed some tissues and started to clean the sauce off.

"Will you leave me the fuck alone?" Simeon shouted at her.

Everyone went silent as they stared over.

"Sorry!" said Kathryn meekly.

Arthur went to stand up but Maeve grabbed his arm, pushing him down and giving him a warning look.

Kelly walked over quickly. "It happens to me all the time," she laughed. "I've told you before, Jim, you put too much barbeque sauce in those damned burgers. But it's okay, it'll wash out fine. Jim, pop upstairs with Simeon and lend him one of your shirts, will you?"

Jim stopped staring and smiled. "Sure thing – just follow me up and I'll get you sorted out, Simeon."

"Probably give me some damned designer shirt!" snapped Simeon, following Jim inside.

"Are you okay?" Kelly asked to Kathryn, full of concern.

"I'm perfectly fine," insisted Kathryn.

Two hours later and Kathryn was sitting at a table looking on while Simeon was holding court with five other guests around him.

Arthur and Maeve had left. Maeve, seeing Arthur's fury, had insisted on it.

"Yeah, well, I had Van Morrison on to me three days ago asking me to take a look at some of the new material he was writing," Simeon was saying. "It's excellent stuff. Then I had Sylvia Henderson on, plaguing me to produce Affidavit's new album. I told her straight. I said, Sylvia, I admire them and everything but I wouldn't touch anything coming out of MPI with a bargepole. They are just so commercial . . ."

Kelly walked up to Kathryn. "Can I join you?"

"It's your house."

Kelly sat in silence for a minute listening to Simeon.

"How much longer are you going to let this go on?" she asked.

"What?"

"You know what I'm talking about – you and Simeon."

"There's nothing wrong with me and Simeon."

"Oh, for God's sake, face up to reality. He showed you up today. When he wasn't being completely rude to you, he was ignoring you and living in fantasyland about some sort of fame he thinks he has."

"He was well known on the music circuit –"

"A long time ago, and nothing came out of it. He needs to move on and get over it. And he needs to let you move on too."

"The talent is still there. It just needs to resurface."

"You're as deluded as he is! Do you know what everyone here today was asking me? They were asking how a woman as bright, intelligent and successful as you could waste your time with such a loser."

"Oh, yes, much better for me to be a housewife with a husband who sells carpets, or furniture or whatever all these people do for a living. They wouldn't recognise talent if it hit them in the face!" Kathryn was angry.

"At least they're living in the real world instead of stuck in a rut like you, paying all the bills and listening to his delusions!"

"It's all about money with you lot, isn't it? Don't try to sit here in your perfect garden, with your perfect house, your perfect marriage and condescend to me!"

"Kathryn, I'm not being condescending. There's certainly nothing perfect about my life. I'm married to a workaholic who's obsessed with his fucking carpet shops, leaving me home alone most of time with only these –" she jangled her jewellery, "for company – but at least I'm someway happy. You're totally unhappy."

Kathryn massaged her temples and then looked up at Kelly. "It's not as simple as you all seem to think it is. I'm not some woman who refuses to leave a bad relationship. Simeon's not well, Kelly. He hasn't been for a long time."

"What do you mean?"

"He suffers from manic depression."

"Oh!" Kelly was visibly shocked.

"When he first started getting depressed, I managed to get him to go to some doctors and they diagnosed him. It's just a series of very high highs and very low lows with him. I don't know if losing his musical ability triggered it, or the disorder made him lose his musical ability."

Kelly stared at her sister. "But what kind of life does that leave you?"

"If something happened to Jim tomorrow, would you walk out on him? You wouldn't and you couldn't – you'd just get on with it. It's nearly eight. We'd better be going." She got up and walked over to Simeon.

"I know it sounds hard," Simeon was saying to his group of assembled listeners,"but I can't do Kathryn any favours when it comes to getting people into her club. She's always asking me to get my friends to go into Exclusive because it would be good for her profile and the club's profile. But I say to her, sorry, babe, no can do. I can't use my contacts just to give her career a lift."

* * *

"Wasn't so bad after all, was it?" said Simeon as he got into the car.

"Yeah, it was fun," said Kathryn opening her door. It was only later when she got into the club and went to her office, locking the door behind her, that she collapsed in tears.

* * *

Cathal stood at the stove in his kitchen adding sauces to the steak he was frying in the pan, simultaneously having a conversation with Sylvia on the phone.

"The beauty of doing the feature with *Hi Life* is that they syndicate it to their UK edition and rest of Europe as well," explained Sylvia.

"Yeah, of course it's brilliant PR. It's just they follow you around for quite a bit, don't they, and take photos of us at home and that kind of shit?"

"Yeah, but we have total say of what gets published. And let's face it, *Hi Life* magazine only wants to portray any of their stars in the best possible light." Then she asked irritably, "What is all that sizzling and crackling sound in the background?"

"I'm cooking dinner. I've got someone coming over."

"Joanne?"

"No, we're finished."

"There's a surprise. Anyway I'll talk to you later." Sylvia hung up.

Cathal concentrated on his cooking. He looked at the time. It was quarter to eight. He had told Lana to drop by at eight. That was, if she turned up at all. He shook his head. He hadn't a clue what he was doing. He was inviting this crazy girl, who seemed bent on self-destruction, over to his house for dinner. After the episode in the park, he should run a mile. He was in the public eye; he couldn't afford to be associated with undesirable people. He knew if Sylvia or MPI knew he was meeting her they would put him under house arrest. But he didn't care. Lana seemed different to anyone he had met before. It had been a long time since he had met someone who hadn't been fake with him, or tried to impress him. Lana obviously didn't care who he was.

* * *

196

Lana irritably walked down the quays to Cathal's apartment block. She felt incredibly low. All the week's events had been compounded by her now having to see a therapist. It was the worst thing she could imagine having to do. And her father should realise that. That night all she wanted to do was go out with her usual crew and get mindlessly drunk. Instead she had to go around to this guy's apartment for dinner. She wouldn't have bothered going but for the fact she had made the mistake of giving him her number. And she was sure he would phone her relentlessly if she didn't show up. So, she would go to his apartment, suffer his cooking, and get mindlessly drunk there instead, before heading out to Exclusive later. Preferably without him.

She rang the buzzer of his apartment.

"Hello," said Cathal's cheery voice.

"It's me," Lana answered in a bored tone.

"Come on up." He buzzed her in.

When she got to the top floor she was surprised he had left his front door ajar, instead of being there to greet her. She pushed the door open gently. "Hello," she said, and was immediately greeted with a wonderful aroma from the kitchen.

"Hiya!" Cathal shouted from the kitchen area. "Come in, and make yourself at home."

Walking in, she could see him busy at work over several frying pans. She was immediately curious as to what he was cooking. She loved food and she hadn't eaten all day. She took off her coat and threw it on a chair. Glancing around, she admired the apartment. And the views across the city were great. She figured he must work in IT. Lots of people were making huge money in that sector.

She sauntered into the kitchen and stood beside him, studying the culinary delights being cooked in four different pots and pans on the stove. There was one pan of sizzling beef in a rich sauce. Another pan had strips of chicken mixed with vegetables.

"You look busy," she said, her mouth watering at the food.

"Cooking is a hobby of mine," he said.

"Really? That's a coincidence. Eating is one of mine." She had to admit, the food looked fantastic and she couldn't wait to try it. "Where's the drink?"

"Over there in the cupboard by the sink."

"Sorry for not bringing a bottle, but I was in a bit of a rush," she said, opening the cupboard door.

He waited for her reaction as she looked through the bottles.

"But these are all empty!"

He smiled to himself. He had emptied out all the alcohol before she arrived. "Are they? I must have run out."

"Where's the nearest shop?" she asked, alarmed.

"Just around the corner. But it closes at eight. And it's quite a walk to the next one."

She slammed the cupboard door closed. "Wonderful !" She walked to the breakfast bar and sat down. Reaching into her purse, she pulled out a joint.

"I'd rather you didn't," he said.

"You'd rather I didn't what?" she asked, placing the joint between her lips.

"I rather you didn't smoke that."

"What the hell is this place ? Oh, I get it!" she nodded and smiled. "You emptied out all the booze before I came, didn't you? I've got a bloody puritan on my hands."

"I'm as bad as anybody. But I've met you twice and each time you've been out of it. I thought it would be nice to actually talk to the real you for a change."

"Nice try. Now, goodbye." She got up to leave.

"Okay. But I'm just about to serve the starters." He pointed to the sizzling pan.

Lana looked at the food, and as she sat down again cursed herself for having an addictive personality.

They ate the chicken starter without another word, Lana enjoying every morsel. Then Cathal served the main course, which didn't disappoint either.

Lana stole a look at him as he happily ate away. She could kill for a drink.

"Exclusive is a great place, isn't it?" she said eventually. She supposed that was the kind of thing said in these circumstances.

"Yeah. Kathryn's great."

"The girl at the door? I've never spoken to her much. So . . . Cathal . . . what do you do for a living?"

He looked at her suspiciously, trying to decipher whether she was trying to be clever or deceitful. But no, he knew she was, as ever, being totally honest. He liked the position they were in and he was so tempted to let her continue not knowing who he was. But lying was not his style. He put down his fork and looked at her directly.

"I'm in a group."

"A group?" She looked confused.

"Yeah, you might have heard of us. Affidavit?"

She looked at him and it all made sense. That was why he looked familiar. "Oh, yes," she answered nonchalantly. "Now I know where I knew your face from. I don't really follow the pop scene that much."

"We're a rock band," he corrected.

"Whatever."

He stared at her, not sure whether to be angry or delighted by her lack of excitement about his information. "What about you? What do you do?" he pressed.

She was enjoying the meal so much she didn't want to ruin it with too much information. She studied him carefully. Did he really not know who she was? Well, at least if she told him it would either frighten him off or reveal him as a gold-digger and she wouldn't have to be bothered with him any more.

"I'm a professional daughter," she said.

"Huh?" He was totally confused.

"I don't really work at anything. I just enjoy my life. All funded by my father."

"Your father?" asked Cathal.

"Yes. You might have heard of him. Barry Curtis."

Cathal put down his fork and stared at her. "*The* Barry Curtis?" he asked, surprised.

"Yes," she answered.

They looked at each other intently for a minute and then both burst out laughing.

*   *   *

"But you must get exhausted. All the coming and going and giving interviews and touring and everything," said Lana. They were sitting in the lounge drinking coffee.

"Of course. Sometimes you just want to run away from it all and hide. But the pros far outweigh the cons. I have a brilliant life. I have everything I could ever want. So I have to put up with hard work and some press intrusion? I can live with that."

"Press intrusion?" Lana suddenly looked alarmed. "It

won't be in the paper or anything that I'm here having dinner with you, will it?"

"Would that be so bad?"

"I don't know! Would it?"

He loved her attitude. "Don't worry. They don't even know where I live. Don't you get any press attention, you being who you are?"

"No, no one's interested in little old me. My father is the star in our family."

"Don't you get bored doing nothing all day?"

"I don't get bored. I'm very busy with my friends and my social life. And I'm involved in charities . . ." Liar, she thought to herself. The only charities you're involved in are attending Charity Balls and getting pissed at them.

She glanced at her watch. She couldn't believe it was nearly twelve. "I have to go!" she said, standing up.

"Go where?" he said.

"To Exclusive. I'm meeting a group of friends there."

"Oh!" He looked disappointed.

"Well, you can come too," she said.

"No, thanks."

"Why? I thought you loved Exclusive."

"I do. I take it you'll be drinking there?"

"Of course."

"I just don't want to see you out of it again."

She looked at him, surprised.

"It was hard enough seeing you like that before. Tell me – why does such an intelligent person do such stupid things?"

She looked at him and didn't know what to say. She took her coat, wrapped it around her and walked to the door.

"Why do you look sad?" she asked as he opened the

door for her.

"Because I'm picturing what you'll be like in three or four hours' time."

She looked at him intently and then reached forward and kissed him on the cheek.

"Thanks for the dinner." She turned and walked down the corridor to the elevator.

Then she looked back and said, "Give me a call."

CHAPTER 16

Joanne Bailey swept into the reception at *Hi Life* dressed in a long black leather coat, tied firmly at the waist, high-heeled black leather boots and oversized sunglasses that hid half her face. Her usual flowing dark locks were tied back severely into a bun.

"I'm here to see Ralph and Margaux," Joanne informed Vivienne, who was taken aback by Joanne's change of image.

"Take a seat and they'll be with you shortly."

Joanne sat down, pulled out a packet of cigarettes and started to smoke.

Vivienne contemplated telling her about the no-smoking policy, but decided to let it drop. No doubt Joanne would only go moaning to Ralph and it would be she who would be dragged over the coals.

She picked up the phone. "Ralph, Joanne Bailey here to see you . . . sure," She hung up. "Joanne, you can go in . . . and Tony, you're to go in as well."

"He probably wants me to run out and get her some cigarettes," Tony whispered to Vivienne as he followed Joanne down the corridor.

Joanne pushed open Ralph's door. Ralph and Margaux were seated on one of the couches and smiling invitingly as Joanne walked in.

"Joanne!" exclaimed Margaux as she leapt to her feet and gave her a kiss on the cheek. This was followed by a kiss and a hug from Ralph.

"Close the door!" Ralph said to Tony, who immediately did what he was told.

"Joanne, this is Tony, our new staff writer. He'll be helping us cover the feature," said Ralph.

Joanne turned around and briefly shook Tony's hand.

At last, thought Tony, recognition!

"That is if there is going to be a feature," said Joanne.

"Is everything all right?" Margaux asked, full of concern.

"Not really." Joanne shot a cautious look at Tony through her sunglasses.

"Don't mind Tony. He's just like part of the furniture around here," said Margaux.

The description wasn't exactly flattering, Tony thought.

Joanne sat down on the second couch. "It's just that me and Cathal have broken up," she said in a distressed voice.

"No! You poor thing!" said Margaux, who immediately got up and sat beside her, putting her arm around her.

"Get some water for Joanne," Ralph barked at Tony who jumped up, ran over to a decanter and filled a glass.

"What happened?" asked Ralph, full of concern.

"I don't know," said Joanne, taking the glass of water from Tony and wiping away a tear that had fallen from beneath her sunglasses. "Work commitments, I suppose . . . they're starting work on their new album."

"I really thought it would last the distance," said Margaux, her exquisite features showing distress.

"I'm just worried now about the feature in *Hi Life*," said Joanne.

"Don't worry about that. That's not important – you just think about getting over this break-up," said Ralph soothingly.

"But I *am* worried. How does this affect the feature?" asked Joanne.

"Well, there can't be a feature, can there?" asked Margaux, "We can't have an 'At Home with Cathal and Joanne' when there isn't a Cathal and Joanne any more, can we?"

"Damn!" Joanne threw her cigarette into her glass of water, extinguishing it. "The stupid bastard! If we had even just kept going another couple of weeks, we could have at least got the feature done."

"It's hard for you." Margaux rubbed Joanne's back.

"Unless we just concentrate on Joanne," Ralph said excitedly.

"What do you mean?" asked Joanne.

Ralph stood up and started pacing up and down. "An interview with Joanne about life after the break-up."

"A kiss and tell?" asked Joanne.

"No!" both Ralph and Margaux exclaimed in unison.

"God forbid!" said Ralph. "W-w-we would never do anything like that. Just a straightforward interview with you about what it was like living under the media pressure of being Cathal's girlfriend. How work commitments broke you up, how you are still the best of friends and about your career hopes for the future,"

"That would be excellent!" exclaimed Joanne. "And would I still get the front cover?"

"You'd get the cover of the Irish edition – but it was really the Affidavit connection that was getting you the cover in the UK," Margaux smiled sympathetically.

"But it will be featured in the UK.? I'm really trying to raise my profile there."

"I understand," said Margaux. "The feature will probably be slimmed down but I'm sure it will appear."

"I'll put a call in to the Hartons today and see what they say," promised Ralph,

"But stop thinking about business at this time and think about yourself," urged Margaux.

"You're right." Joanne wiped away a fake tear.

"Why don't we go back to your place?" said Margaux. "And pack a bag and you come and stay with us for a couple of nights?"

"It would be too much of an intrusion," said Joanne.

"Nonsense. You're like family to us – if we can't be here for you during this difficult, time, who can be?" said Ralph.

"Well, if you're sure," said Joanne.

"Positive," confirmed Margaux.

*   *   *

"I'm heading home," said Tony to Vivienne.

"If you're passing a postbox, would you drop these in for me." She handed him twelve envelopes. "They are the letters to our nominees informing them they have been shortlisted for our Personality of the Year Award. How lucky are they?" Vivienne's voice dripped sarcasm.

"Have Margaux and Joanne left?"

"Yeah, they headed off together."

"They seem very close,"

Vivienne stifled a laugh. "They only met for the first and only time a couple of weeks ago to discuss this feature."

"You're joking!" Tony's mouth dropped. "I thought they were best friends for years."

Vivienne jerked her head to Ralph's office. "That's what he and Maggie are like with everyone – everyone who's rich or famous, that is."

*　　*　　*

Nicole took out the file of her next client. The case had been referred to her by a colleague who was too busy to take her on herself, a friend of the woman who made the appointment, Gloria Reagan. She quickly read through the short notes inside. Lana Curtis, daughter of Barry. Caught doing credit-card fraud. An interesting one, thought Nicole. She wondered what Barry Curtis's daughter would be like and what could have possibly driven a woman from such an affluent family to try and steal. Having said that, nothing surprised Nicole any more. She had dealt with everything in her work.

She had received an excited call from Tony. He had been at a meeting with the Conways and Joanne Bailey. She had prayed so much that the job would work out for him and now it was beginning to come together. She laughed to herself. When things were going right for Tony he was like an overgrown child. If only everyone could be as uncomplicated as him.

There was a knock on the door.

"Come in, please," she said.

The door opened and Lana walked in.

"Hello, I'm so pleased to meet you." Nicole smiled warmly at her and put out her hand. Lana shook it idly.

"Please, take a seat," urged Nicole.

Lana looked around the office and sat down.

"And how are you today?" smiled Nicole.

"I think I should point out immediately that I have absolutely no interest in being here whatsoever. I'm being forced to be here because I was subtly informed I would otherwise have charges pressed against me for the alleged credit-card fraud . . . which you, no doubt, have been told all about."

Oh dear, thought Nicole, as she forced the smile to stay on her face. "I certainly do not want to be part of anything done against your will, Lana. Because then we would be wasting both your time and mine."

"What do you care? You'd still get paid," said Lana.

"I would like to think that money isn't my main motivation for coming to work each day."

"God help me! Another worthwhile person. Easy known you're a friend of Gloria Reagan."

Nicole placed her hands together. "Just for the record. I'm not a friend of Gloria Reagan. I've never met her, or even heard of her before this. She is an acquaintance of the colleague who referred you to me."

They sat in silence for a while.

"Why aren't you saying anything?" Lana asked eventually.

"I'm waiting for you to make the decision to either stay or go."

"I've told you I have to stay. Otherwise I end up in jail or something."

"Why did you try to charge things on Gloria's card?"

"I've told everyone it was a mistake. A simple, straightforward silly mistake –"

"According to Gloria you went into her office, into a drawer, into her wallet and found the credit card before taking it."

Lana laughed. "She really hasn't held back, has she?"

They sat in silence again.

"I would like to assure you that anything that is said in here never goes out. If you are frightened that anything you might say will go back to your father or –"

Lana stood up abruptly and looked at her watch "Look – I've come along and signed the register, so to speak. So why don't we just say I stayed the full hour, and you'll get paid accordingly and I can go and do some shopping, okay?" She turned and walked to the door before turning around. "See you next week." Then she was walking down the corridor and feeling free.

But as she reached the top of the stairs, she stopped. She was remembering the park in London, the convulsions and the fear that had gripped her. It wasn't even the fear of the fit she'd had that frightened her, but the fear of what her life was about. What was it about ? She remembered Cathal calming her down. And she remembered how sad he had looked when she had left his apartment to go to Exclusive. And what got her was that it was her life that had caused the sadness in his face. You can't go on like this, she told herself.

She turned slowly and walked back down the corridor.

Nicole was surprised to see the door open and Lana come back in and sit down.

"I took Gloria's credit card because she pisses me off," said Lana, looking down at the floor.

"Pisses you off? Why?"

"Everything about her pisses me off. Her hair, her make-up, her clothes, her voice, her body movement. It's all such a statement of 'I'm so in control and so perfect'."

"And why should that upset you?" probed Nicole.

"Because I'm not!"

Lana looked down at the ground in desperation. Nicole didn't say anything for a while, and then gently moved the conversation on.

"How many times did you do it altogether – the fraud?" asked Nicole.

"I can't remember . . . a lot. That was the first time I did it on my own. Usually my friend was with me. It was her friends and acquaintances we mostly did it on."

"You took Gloria's card because she 'pisses you off'. In these other cases, was it just about getting something for free?" asked Nicole.

"It was the buzz of it. The fear almost . . . knowing that you were doing something wrong and dangerous and knowing you could get caught any minute . . . it was an amazing feeling."

"And was the reality as good as what you imagined?"

"What do you mean?"

"When you were finally caught? Did that excite you?"

"No, I was appalled. Especially when Dad and Gloria came into the store to rescue me. I felt so small."

"Your disdain for Gloria. Do you want to talk about that?"

"She just walks around Kildara, my home – my father's home – as if she owns it. She's only a bloody employee. I know my father runs his businesses from Kildara, so it has a feeling of business about it, but it's still my family home and should be respected as such. And not have her running around and setting up an office there."

"And how does your mother feel about your family home being treated as a business centre?"

Lana looked at her watch. "The hour's up. I'd better go. I don't want you charging overtime."

* * *

Lana felt dazed as she walked down the street. She couldn't believe she had spoken like she had to the therapist. And in a strange kind of way she had got relief from it. It was like there was so much stuff pent up inside her, it was great to just be able to talk about how she felt. Not just to talk about parties or shopping or holidays or gossip, but how she actually felt.

Her phone rang and she answered it.

"Hi there!"

She recognised Cathal's voice. "Oh hi," she said in what she hoped was a friendly manner.

"What you up to?"

"Just been shopping, you know."

There was an uncomfortable silence. She could hear music in the background. "Where are you?"

"In the studio. We've started to record our new album today. Long rocky road ahead. Just wondered what you were up to tonight? I was thinking you could come over and I could cook us something."

"Oh." she was taken aback. Why did he want to see her again? "Well, actually, Patricia is back this evening, and we were supposed to be going to a party later."

"Okay." He sounded disappointed.

She thought for a moment. "But I suppose I could catch up with her tomorrow."

* * *

Cathal opened his door smiling. The smile dropped when he saw Lana was holding a bottle of wine in one hand and a bottle of vodka in the other.

"I thought I wouldn't leave anything to chance this time," she said, walking in past him. He was going to say something about the alcohol, but decided against it. She walked into the kitchen and looked at the food cooking on the stove.

"You really are a good cook," she complimented. "I can't boil an egg."

"Well, who cooks for you at home?" he asked, sprinkling some seasoning on the food.

She opened drawers until she found a corkscrew. "I have a housekeeper who doubles as a cook. I endure her cooking as opposed to enjoying it." She uncorked the bottle and reached for two glasses.

"Not for me, thanks," he said.

"You don't drink?"

"Funnily enough, I can drink like a fish normally. But, don't you think it nice to have intelligent conversation without being drunk?"

She poured the red wine into her glass. "No."

He served the food onto plates and brought them over to the breakfast bar. As he placed the plate in front of Lana, he leaned over and kissed her lips.

She looked at him, a little startled.

"I just thought I'd kiss you now before you downed all that and then you wouldn't remember tomorrow if we kissed or not."

"It was a little presumptuous of you," she said, picking up her fork. "I haven't decided yet whether I fancy you or not." She ate a few mouthfuls of food in thought. "So what was it like recording your album today?"

"A fucking nightmare. We're trying to decide which material to put on. MPI – that's our record label – has all this stuff they want us to put on it. Meanwhile James and Rob, two of my band-mates, have written all this new stuff they want to use. So they're all screaming at each other. And I'm trying to act as peacemaker in the middle of it all." He felt strange having to explain who James and Rob were.

"And which of those was the charmer I overheard that morning after Patricia's party?"

"That was James. He's also my cousin."

"Keep it in the family, hey?" Lana asked.

"Something like that."

Lana suddenly put down her fork abruptly "What is going on here?"

He looked at her, concerned. "What do you mean?"

"Why have you been pursuing me?"

"Well, I fancy you, for a start." He smiled at her. "I did from the first moment I saw you."

"So you just want a shag?"

"I'd like to get to know you. I can't remember the last time somebody treated me as normal. Everyone is always running after me and wants a part of me, and you don't give a shit."

"I'm not really in a good place at the moment to have a relationship, if that's what you're looking for."

"Look, when I hear the word relationship I usually run ten miles. So don't think I'm going to be put you under any pressure like that or anything."

She studied him intently "I'd say we have absolutely nothing in common," she warned.

"I'd say you're right," said Cathal. "At least on the surface. But I recognise something in you. Something like I was years ago. I probably understand you better than you'd think."

Lana reached over for the vodka, unscrewed the cap and filled herself a glass mixed with orange juice. "Well, it's a free country. If you want to hang around me for a while, I can't stop you."

Three hours later, Cathal was looking down on Lana passed out on the sofa, the empty bottles of vodka and wine on the floor beside her. Sighing, he went and got a blanket and put it over her.

CHAPTER 17

Kathryn tried dialling Simeon's number for the hundredth time that day. As always it just went through to his voice mail. She flung her mobile onto the sofa out of frustration. Simeon had gone off to meet some old friend from the music business on Saturday night, after they had returned from Kelly's barbeque. When she had got in from work in the early hours of Sunday morning, he wasn't back. That was three days ago and she hadn't heard a thing from him since. Her mobile rang and she grabbed it in the hope it was Simeon. But she saw it was Ralph Conway's number. "Hi, Ralph, how are you?"

"I'm great, Kathryn. How are you keeping?" asked Ralph's cheerful voice.

"I can't complain."

"I'm just checking if you got your letter from us?"

"I did, thank you very much." She riffled through the letters on the coffee table and picked up the letter telling her she was nominated for Ireland's Personality of The Year. "I was going to ring you later to thank you."

"Not at all, no list like that would be complete without you."

"You're very kind," she said. And full of bullshit, she thought.

"We are announcing the nominations in the next edition and some photos of the nominees in stylish outfits. I just need to take some photos of you for the feature."

"Yeah, that would be fine."

"And we know you well enough to be able to put a small biography together about you. Style icon, manager of Dublin's top night spot, friend of the stars, that kind of thing – will that be okay to print?"

"Very flattering of you, Ralph."

"I'll get my secretary to call you to organise the photos."

"Sure. Thanks, Ralph. Give Margaux my love."

She hung up the phone and started pacing again.

*   *   *

Sylvia studied the young woman seated opposite her in her office, her long brown hair lank and styleless, her clothes hippy, her face miserable. Tina Cawley had been signed with MPI for four years and her first two angst-filled albums, *This Is Me, So What?* and *I Enjoy The Rain* had sold phenomenally well.

"If I can remind you, you are contracted to do two further albums with MPI," said Sylvia.

"I'm not a conveyer belt for music," Tina scowled. "I'm not one of your crappy manufactured acts."

"I wasn't suggesting for a moment that you were." Sylvia kept her patience. "I'm just concerned you're going to miss all your deadlines."

Tina folded her arms and scowled even more. "There you go again trying to dictate to me, to confine me, to limit me."

"Well, if you could just get back to us asap about what you have written so far I'd appreciate it. I'm sure there's plenty of anger left in you to give us some great songs."

216

"Screw you!" Tina whispered under her breath.

"Now, a couple of offers have come in for you." Sylvia spoke in a positively and upbeat fashion. "*Hi Life* are interested in doing an interview with you."

Tina threw her eyes to heaven. "Are you kidding me? Nothing on this earth would force me to have anything to do with that rag. All those people in their false lives!"

Sylvia sighed. "Okay . . . and you've been invited to the party at Exclusive for a première next Tuesday."

Tina laughed loudly before becoming serious and leaning forward. "If the world was covered in piss and the only chance of survival was climbing those stairs up to that hole, I'd stay swimming!"

*   *   *

Thinking of Tina, Sylvia shook her head as she headed towards the recording studio. She bumped into Cathal on his way in.

"Hiya!" He smiled brightly.

"You seem in good form."

"I am,"

"New woman on the scene?" she asked knowingly.

"Maybe. You don't look too happy."

"Would you if you had spent an hour listening to Tina Cawley's anguished view of the world?"

Cathal pulled a face. "No."

"And now I have to face what's coming next," said Sylvia as she pulled the door open and walked into the studio. "Hi, everyone!"

Everyone greeted her. She sat down amongst the guys from the band.

"Now, I want everyone to keep calm about what I'm

going to say next."

"What's wrong?" asked Rob as he folded his arms.

"Jack Better doesn't like the last two songs recorded."

"What?" they all shouted in unison.

"He says they're not right for Affidavit . . . they aren't what the fans will expect or buy."

"But me and James wrote those two songs," objected Rob. "We're really proud of them!"

"I know, I know and I'm sorry. I know how you feel. But there's nothing we can do. They've got some new music specially commissioned and they want those songs on the album instead."

"Oh man!" shouted Rob. He got up and stormed from the studio.

"I'll give Jack a call myself," said Cathal. "See what I can do."

"You're wasting your time," said Sylvia. "He isn't going to change."

"He's such a bastard. This is our band with our music and we decide what goes on it!" said James.

"He says it won't sell records," said Sylvia.

"Fuck him! I'm going to find Rob." James walked out.

"They won't accept it," said Cathal. "This new music means too much to them."

"They'll have to accept it," said Sylvia. She looked at Seán who was tossing a pen around and looked like he was daydreaming. "What do you think, Seán?"

"Huh?" said Seán, woken up out of his thoughts. "Oh, whatever!" he shrugged.

*   *   *

The Conway house was a beautiful Victorian townhouse overlooking the sea at Monkstown. They had bought it ten years previously when they had taken over *Hi Life*. It was falling into dilapidation and and they had lovingly restored it. It was now a fitting abode for a couple who saw themselves as the confidants and friends of Ireland's elite.

"You look fantastic!" said Margaux as Joanne came down the staircase into the open-plan Spanish-style downstairs.

"Thanks, you've been so good to me," said Joanne as she admired herself in the huge mirror over the fireplace.

"What time is Seán collecting you?" asked Ralph, pouring himself a drink at the bar.

"Any minute now,"

"Time for a drink?" he asked.

"No, thanks. Listen, I just wanted to say I'll be leaving tomorrow."

"But you are more than welcome to stay for however long you want," said Margaux.

"I know, and thanks. You've been more than good to me already. But it's time I went back to my little apartment." She frowned as she went and sat beside Margaux. "And while on the subject of my apartment . . . when I was with Cathal, we were going to use his penthouse for the feature, but now I'm worried that my little place might not be impressive enough for the photo shoot."

"Don't worry about a thing," said Ralph. "I'll have a word with a property developer I know who'll lend us his show house for the day – we'll just say it's your home."

Joanne's eyes widened. "Can we do that?"

"Of course – who'll know the difference?"

Everyone who knows me, thought Joanne, but then, did she care? "You've just been so good to me." She went and kissed the two of them.

There was a beep from a car outside.

"That'll be Seán," said Joanne.

"Won't he come in for a drink?" asked Margaux.

"No, I think he's a bit shy – and don't worry, I'll make sure nobody sees us. Like I said, we're only going around to his house. We don't want to jeopardise my 'Life After Cathal' feature by my being seen out with his band-mate, do we?"

*   *   *

Lana sat in her car looking at the building Nicole's practice was in. She glanced at her watch and it was a couple of minutes to three. She anxiously tapped her fingernails on the dashboard, trying to decide whether to go in or not. Her phone rang and she saw Cathal's number come up. Now she didn't know whether to answer that or not. Why was her life full of indecision?

She flicked the phone open and said, "Hi!"

"How's it going ?" he asked cheerfully.

"I'm fine. What are you up to ?"

"Just recording the new album at the moment, or trying to. Lots of shit going on."

"Really ?"

"Yeah, tempers are flying. What are you doing ?"

She glanced over at her therapist's building. "Just doing a bit of shopping."

"Just wondered if you wanted to come by this evening?"

"To eat more of your cuisine? I'll be fat as a fool!" she laughed.

"So what?"

"So none of my clothes will fit me and I'll have to buy a new wardrobe!"

"You'd enjoy doing that."

"True."

There was silence for a while.

"Well?" he asked.

"I don't know." She ran her fingers through her hair and didn't speak for a while, then said, "Okay, I'll be over around eight." She closed over her phone.

She stared at Nicole's building. It was now nearly five past three. She started the car and began to drive down the road.

*   *   *

"I nearly didn't come here today," Lana told Nicole.

"Really?"

"I was driving away and turned back."

"Why didn't you want to come?"

"Because this is a nightmare for me – having to come in here and talk about me. I hate it . . . for me, to be in therapy is the worst possible thing."

"Why is talking with someone about yourself for an hour so bad?"

"It just is. I just want to get on with my life, and enjoy myself and have fun. I don't want to stop and have to think or talk about me."

"So why did you come back today then?"

"Because, deep down, there's some little part of me telling me I need to."

They sat in silence for a while before Nicole asked "What do you want in life, Lana?"

"I don't know . . . to have a purpose, I suppose."

"I'm sure you have lots of – purposes. What do you enjoy doing?"

"I enjoy going out, getting off my face."

Nicole nodded. "Anything else?"

"I enjoy shopping. I love clothes, I suppose."

"Did you ever think of getting more involved in that?"

"In shopping ? I don't think I could spend any more

221

than I do."

"I don't mean that. I mean you could somehow get involved in fashion or retail?"

Lana sighed "I think it's took late for me to do something like that."

* * *

Nicole thought about Lana as she walked home. This was going to be a difficult case. The girl had everything but nothing. She felt deeply sorry for her. Lana had been extremely cautious in talking about herself. A lot of her clients had so much stuff built up that by the time they came to her, they couldn't get the information out quick enough. And from there it was a case of going through all the details and trying to come up with conclusions. But Lana was reluctant to divulge any information.

She put the key in the door and banished all thought of work from her mind as she looked forward to a night in with Tony beside the fire.

Tony got up from lighting the fire and enveloped her in a hug. "How was your day?"

"It was all right. What about yours?"

He rolled his eyes. "So so. Sit down and I'll bring out the pizza – it's only just been delivered."

Nicole took off her coat, kicked off her shoes and collapsed onto the couch.

"I had to collect Margaux's dry cleaning today," said Tony, coming back with the pizza.

"Oh, Tony!"

"I'm still the staff writer who has never written. Anyway, we're doing the interview with Joanne Bailey tomorrow, so we'll see if I'm invited along to that." He shrugged as he bit into his pizza.

CHAPTER 18

"We're making a bit of a habit of this," said Lana as she refilled her glass in Cathal's lounge. She held the wine bottle over his glass. "You want some?"

"No, I'm fine, thanks."

"So, you were telling me things aren't so good at work," she said, nestling back into the large armchair.

"You can say that again. MPI refuses to let us use some of James and Rob's songs on our album and so Rob is refusing to go back into the studio."

"He's on strike?"

"Kind of, yeah."

"And what part do you play in all this?"

"Peacemaker as usual. Trying to come up with a solution and get everyone happy . . . that's my role in the band."

"It must be strange," mused Lana." Having your life full of so many appointments. Having to be everywhere all the time, with such a hectic schedule." She felt envious.

"Well, I'm never bored, that's for sure."

"And everyone knowing who you are. Being instantly recognisable."

"Except by some," he reminded her with a smile.

"Never mind me." She smiled back. "But so many people knowing who you are, like you could never be lonely – you only have to walk down the street and everybody knows you." The thought was appealing to her. In a way it was like her father and the recognition he enjoyed. He was never alone.

"I suppose . . . but they say you can be at your loneliest in a crowded room, don't they?"

She nodded and sighed.

He felt anxious. He had never met anyone like Lana before. Everyone he had gone out with before was declaring undying love by now. So he hadn't a clue how to act with her.

"Do you want to sit over here beside me?" he asked.

She downed her drink. "I don't know if I do."

"I see."

"You seem very nice, and you seem to want some kind of a relationship with me . . . which I'm surprised about and, if I thought about it, I suppose I'm flattered. But I don't do relationships."

"Neither do I," he said quickly.

"We're from two different planets."

He looked at her as he refilled her glass. "We've more in common than you think. I think I understand you."

"How so?"

"You're lost."

"And now I'm found?" Her eyes suddenly blazed. "Now everything is clear to me! I've been sitting around all my life waiting for Cathal Fitzgerald to come and rescue me!"

"I wasn't saying that!"

"I have to go and meet some friends." She jumped up

224

angrily. "You know, if you want to feel better about yourself, why don't you go and find a stray dog?"

He stood up. "I'm fine with my life. And for the record, I wasn't feeling sorry for you."

"Feeling sorry for me?" Her voice rose. "I'm Barry Curtis's daughter! I have had a privileged life. Feeling sorry for me doesn't even come into the equation when I'm dealing with low-class types like you who just got lucky in life!"

His face clouded over. "All right, fuck off then. I only spent time with you because I actually liked you. You can't deal with that, so fuck off back to your ivory tower! You won't be hearing from me in the future."

"Good!" She grabbed her bag but picked it up the wrong way round and all the contents spilled over the carpet, including make-up, money, a joint and cocaine.

"Says it all really, doesn't it?" said Cathal looking down at the contents. "Pick up your things and clear off."

She stood staring at the spilled contents.

He was unnerved by her look of distress. "Are you okay?"

"I walk the streets," she said quietly.

"What?"

"At night, I roam around for hours through the streets."

"Why?" He looked shocked.

"I don't know. I just walk and walk for ages. Main streets, back streets, everywhere, just walking for what seems an eternity."

"But – that's so dangerous."

She still stared at the contents of the bag. "I don't care."

He looked at her for a long while and then slowly approached her, expecting her to pull back any second. But she stayed still, allowing him to put his arms around her and envelop her into a hug. As he held her tightly, he felt her body relax as if all the pressure and tension had disappeared.

* * *

Tony and Vivienne sat listening to Ralph roar at the top of his voice in his office. They grimaced at each other as the ranting and swearing continued.

Then the office door opened and was closed gently and the young guy from the advertising department walked through reception, looking red-faced and very upset.

"He's just been fired," Vivienne informed.

"Really, why?" asked Tony.

"Didn't meet his target." Seeing Tony was frowning, she said, "You get used to it. There's a very high turnover of staff here. Anyone who displeases the royal couple is quickly shown the door."

"It'll probably be me next."

"You?" said Vivienne, trying to sound surprised, but failing. The thought had crossed her mind too.

"Well, let's face it. I don't seem to be doing anything. I'm obviously not impressing Ralph enough to give me anything to do but run errands."

Vivienne nodded. "It must be frustrating for you. Well, if it makes you feel better, when I came for my interview here I was promised I'd be out on photo shoots all the time. Instead I'm chained to this desk, banging away at this –" she pointed to her computer, "and answering that –" She pointed to the phone.

"Really? Actually, that doesn't make me feel better at all."

They heard Ralph's door open and they both started tapping away at their computers.

"I'll be gone for the rest of the d-d-d-day," he informed Vivienne. "Only contact me if it is urgent."

"Fine," she smiled brightly.

"Tony, come with me," he ordered.

"Oh! Sure." Tony stood up, startled.

"Bring a notebook and pen with you!" snapped Ralph.

"Okay, of course." Tony looked around for a notebook. Vivienne handed him one from her drawer. He mouthed "Thanks!" to her and hurried off after Ralph.

*   *   *

Cathal sat in the studio, deep in thought, as the others experimented. Rob still refused to come back to the studio and so they were unable to continue to record the album.

Cathal was allowing his thoughts to drift back to a couple of nights ago, when Lana was saying how she wandered aimlessly for hours at night, and how he had held her in his arms for ages. Finally they had somehow lain on the sofa and, as tiredness had crept over them, had fallen asleep in each other's arms. The next morning they had woken up like that and they both had seemed somehow embarrassed by it. Because Lana hadn't had much chance to get off her face the night before, she hadn't been hung-over and they had chatted for a while about nothing in particular. She seemed shy without the armour of drink in the mornings. And then she had left. He hadn't really been able to stop thinking about her since. He couldn't understand what was happening to him, but he wanted to spend time with her. He had nervously rung her that morning to ask how she was and they had spoken for a while about the album and its problems. And then he had finished the call by jokingly saying he gave her permission to ring him as well, but only if she wanted to. She had laughed and promised she would.

"What the fuck is going on here?" screamed Sylvia as she marched into the studio, face like thunder, jolting Cathal back to reality.

"Nothing," answered James hesitantly.

"Exactly! Why are we paying for studio time for an album to be recorded when it isn't being recorded? Where the fuck is Rob?" She turned to Cathal, as if he was the culprit.

"No one knows. He won't answer his phone. Me and James drove out to his house last night, but he wasn't there. Even Heidi won't answer her phone."

"He's holding up the whole recording!" snapped Sylvia.

"He's really angry about those songs not being on the album. I've never seen him so pissed off."

"Tough. He needs to get over it, and himself. Jack Better is hitting the roof over this. Well, you can all go home. I'm not paying for studio time for nothing."

"Really?" asked Seán.

"I shit thee not. I suggest we all work on trying to get Rob's ass back in here asap before Jack Better gets really pissed off."

* * *

Tony sat nervously beside Ralph as he drove out to an exclusive new housing development on the west side of Dublin.

"Are you a fan of classical music?" asked Ralph as he

turned a bend.

"Er . . . I listen to it a bit, but I'm not a major fan," answered Tony.

"Margaux and I were at a recital last night."

"Really?"

"We were invited by the German Ambassador. We're very good friends of his, you know."

"That's . . . nice."

"He's always inviting us around to the embassy for dinner."

Tony nodded.

Ralph pulled his car into the show house of the new estate. Tony stared at the beautiful five-bedroomed detached as he got out of the car. He followed Ralph into the house

Inside, Tony was gobsmacked by the luxury of the open-plan interior.

Joanne Bailey was lying on a couch, looking resplendent, while her make-up was being touched up by the stylists. Clive was setting up his cameras and looked hassled. Margaux sat on another sofa, speaking in turns to Joanne and an over-excited young female estate agent, who couldn't believe her luck in getting *Hi Life* to feature her development.

"I think you should put a little more bronze on her cheeks," advised Margaux.

Irritated, the stylist did what she was told.

"How's everything going?" asked Ralph, smiling broadly.

"Everything is under control," Margaux assured him. "Hello, Tony." She smiled encouragingly at him. "This is Sally, who represents the selling agent."

"Mr Conway." Sally was up and shaking Ralph's hand

over-zealously."Thank you so much for choosing Cedar Falls for this photo shoot."

"That's all right. You're welcome," Ralph smiled.

"As long as it never gets out that I don't live here," Joanne sounded a warning note, while trying not to move too much facially, in case her thick make-up cracked.

A worried and honest look appeared on Sally's face. "I can assure you, Ms Bailey, under no circumstance will that fact ever escape from our source."

"Good," said Joanne.

Tony wasn't sure what he was supposed to be doing. He picked up one of the brochures carefully arranged on the coffee table and looked at the dreamy cover that announced: *"Fall into heaven - Fall into Cedar Falls!"* He glanced through it and hoped that one day he and Nicole would end up living in a place like this.

"Tony!" Ralph called over. "Help Clive set up his equipment."

"Sure." Tony walked over to Clive, who seemed to be struggling with his lens. "What do you want me to do?"

"Here, hold that, mate," said Clive and handed him a big silver board."Just hold it up to the window to block out the light." He looked through his camera and started adjusting the lens. "Hold it a bit higher, mate. That's it."

"You look under pressure," Tony said softly – the others were busy talking.

"I am under fucking pressure. Maggie's been issuing orders for the past two hours, all in the sweetest possible way of course. Then there's Judy fucking Garland spread out like the Queen of Sheba," he nodded over to Joanne, "and now Ralph is going to be issuing orders how he wants the shots done for the rest of the afternoon. I've just about had enough of this lot. They won't even pay for me to have an assistant. I want to go back and work for the tabloids."

"Clive, are we ready?" Margaux asked sweetly.

"Just coming," he said gruffly back. "Right, let's start."

*   *   *

Donna beeped the horn of her car as she saw James and Cathal come out of the MPI. building.

"Hi, doll!" said James, getting into the car and kissing her.

"Do you want a lift home, Cathal ?" asked Donna.

"Sure," he said and got into the back of the car.

"Still no word from Rob?" she asked as she took off.

"No. Sylvia is really pissed off and cancelled the studio until he's back," said James.

"That's reflecting really badly on you all," said Donna, worried. She always believed in smiling and pandering to corporate bosses. It was a strategy that had served her modelling career well.

"Well, Rob's so passionate about his music," said Cathal.

"And so am I!" James reminded him.

"Yes, my love," said Donna, smiling, "but if you tried to go on strike over a principle, you know I'd kick you up the ass and send you in."

He leaned over and kissed her cheek. "I can always rely on your support. Anyway, we've got a couple of unexpected days off. Any plans, Cathal?"

"Not really," mused Cathal, looking out the window.

They drove in silence for a minute.

"Any word from Joanne Bailey?" Donna enquired.

"Oh, no. That's firmly in the past," said Cathal.

"Anyone else on the scene?"

He was about to say no, when he stopped himself. "Actually, there is."

"Is there?" James sounded surprised. "Who ?"

"I've been seeing a bit of Lana Curtis recently."

"Lana Curtis!" Donna asked incredulously. "When did this all happen?"

"We kept bumping into each other, like over at that bash in London."

"And you're seeing each other?" James was shocked.

"Well, yeah. In a casual way."

"How casual?" demanded Donna.

"She's been over to mine a couple of times for dinner –"

"You cooked her dinner?" James' voice was rising all the time.

"Sure, why not?"

"You kept that very quiet," said James.

"And have you managed to understand her slurred speech?" Donna asked and James giggled.

"We've actually had very intelligent conversations. She's a very bright person."

"You are joking me." Donna's voice was giddy but harsh. "Any grey matter she had was killed off years ago in a swimming-pool of vodka. I bet she was passed out on the floor by the time she'd finished eating!"

"You've got her all wrong." Cathal felt himself become tense and angry.

"Oh no, I haven't." Donna shook her head, falsely smiling. "I've warned you about her before, Cathal. You're making a big mistake getting involved with her. She doesn't know her arse from her elbow. She's all over the place and she'll drag you down."

"Save your breath," advised James. "Cathal never

could resist the allure of danger. I thought he had learned from his mistakes by now but –"

Cathal saw red and said loudly, "You can –" he was stopped by his mobile ringing. He grabbed it angrily from his pocket and snapped, "Yes?"

"Oh, have I caught you at a bad moment?" said Lana, surprised by his tone.

He was taken aback that she had phoned him, but delighted. And her timing couldn't have been better. "No, not at all. How are you, Lana?" he said brightly, noticing the two front occupants of the car were shaking their heads in disbelief.

"I'm fine. I hope you don't mind me phoning. I only did because you said to –"

"Of course I don't – I'm glad you did. What have you been up to?"

"Oh, the usual, you know . . . How's your album coming along?"

"It's not. We're not going back into the studio for a couple of days until the problems are all sorted out."

"That's a bummer."

"Sure is. So I've some time to kill on my hands . . . Do you want to hang out with me?"

"Hang out? What exactly would that entail?"

"Anything you wanted. Eat, drink and be merry!"

Lana thought for a while. She didn't have anything else on and maybe she would enjoy herself. "Sure. Why not?"

"Cool. I'm heading home now, so make your way over to my place." He looked up at James' horrified face and Donna's eyes looking at him through the mirror. "What?" he asked innocently, enjoying every moment.

* * *

Joanne came into the bathroom wearing nothing but a skimpy bikini. Clive and Tony stared as she tested the water, which was piled high with suds.

"This fucking water is freezing cold!" she screeched.

"I'm so sorry." Sally stepped forward. "This house hasn't been hooked up for hot water yet." Her face looked very apologetic.

"How the hell am I supposed to look sexy and sensual in a bath full of fucking cold water?" Joanne shouted.

"There's nothing I can do." Sally looked on the verge of tears.

"Just let the professional in you take over, Joanne," urged Margaux sympathetically.

"For fuck's sake!" Joanne shouted, stepping into the bath. She slowly slid into the water, screaming and cursing all the way.

Then the stylists rushed in to fix up her hair and make-up.

"Hurry up, before I get hypothermia," she snarled.

The stylists rushed out.

Clive checked the view through his camera as Tony held the board to block out too much sunshine.

"Fame had better be worth all this!" Joanne screamed and then smiled brightly and seductively as Clive began to click the camera.

CHAPTER 19

"It was fantastic," Patricia trilled down the phone. "Two weeks in the Caribbean. Amazing!"

"I thought it was supposed to be only a few days?"

"It was but there were lots of technical hiccups, so the shoot just went on and on. Anyway, what's been happening in my absence?"

"Well, I've been seeing a bit of that guy from that band, Cathal."

"Cathal Fitzgerald?"

"Yeah."

"When did this all happen?" Patricia sounded shocked.

"I don't know. Went over to his house a couple of times and things started to happen."

"I'm really surprised," said Patricia. "Well, he's not exactly one of our scene, is he?"

"He's not a surgeon in the Blackrock Clinic like Henry, if that's what you mean."

"And do you want to get caught up in that media thing when people discover you're seeing each other?"

"We're not seeing each other . . . even if we were, the press might be interested in him, but I doubt anyone would bother with me."

Not because of you, darling, but who your father is, thought Patricia.

"Do you know anything about him?" asked Lana.

"Well, to be honest, from what I hear, I don't think he's a very nice person. He went out with a model I know and he dumped her after two months. He has a reputation for fucking people out of it when he doesn't get his own way."

"Well, I haven't seen that side of him. And there's nothing wrong with not suffering fools gladly."

"Well, no doubt he's just a passing fancy for you – this time next week, you'll have moved on," Patricia giggled. "You know what you're like!"

"Maybe."

"Anyway, are you around tomorrow, to do some shopping?" She giggled again. "The lovely Imelda has just signed up for MasterCard!"

Lana felt herself tense. "Actually, I told Cathal I'd spend the day with him."

"What ? How very strange," said Patricia.

*   *   *

Kathryn finished going through the accounts at her weekly meeting with Barry Curtis.

Although Exclusive was only a small part of his empire, he still made sure to meet Kathryn without fail for their regular meetings. He always impressed her with how agile his mind was, how quickly he could read figures and absorb them. And she knew he dealt with all of his businesses the same way. He had such a work ethic, it was hard to believe that Lana was his daughter.

"Everything seems to be in order there." He closed

over the accounts. "What else is happening?"

"We're booked for the after party of the première of the new Colin Farrell film. And I have a few after-show parties booked in for concerts."

"Excellent. Should be good PR for the club." He looked at her. "I heard you got nominated for Social Personality of the Year."

"Oh yeah," she said, wondering how he found out.

"That's something we don't see often – you blushing. Anyway, should be great PR for the club."

Barry, thought Kathryn, was the ultimate professional and he trusted her to run the club without any problems and also to provide a glamorous image.

"Any luck in getting yourself an assistant manager?" he asked.

She shook her head. "I've given a couple of interviews, but I haven't met anybody I feel I could trust."

"Well, keep trying – you haven't had a holiday for at least a year."

She smiled. "You don't hear me complain, do you?"

"No, but you hear me complain. I don't want you working six nights a week and no time off. So get yourself an assistant. Okay?" He smiled at her in a fatherly fashion.

She smiled back. "Yes , I'll make it a priority."

Gloria Reagan came into the room. "Sorry for interrupting, but I need to go through a few things with you, Barry."

Kathryn thought Gloria didn't look one bit sorry for interrupting. Kathryn didn't like this new addition around Kildara. But by the look of Gloria, she was here to stay.

"Ah, I think we've more or less finished, haven't we, Kathryn?"

"Yes." Kathryn closed over her folder. "I'll see you next

week, Barry." Getting up, she nodded to Gloria and left the office.

Gloria sat down in the vacated seat opposite Barry and waited till she heard the door close before she spoke. "I'm getting good results back from the polls. But I think we could do better. I think we need to do some big publicity event." She clicked her fingers.

"You think so? And what kind of ideas did you have in mind?"

"Well, I understand it's your birthday soon. Fifty-five, I believe? I think we should throw you a birthday party. A glamorous affair, with stars present. Something that will get you plenty of press. Raise your profile. You see, in this country everyone knows your name but not everyone knows your face yet."

Barry thought for a minute. "We could hold it in Exclusive – get Kathryn Foy to organise it."

"That sounds an excellent idea. And instead of having an array of press there, why don't we invite just one magazine to do an exclusive. With just a few choice photos passed on to the newspapers. Then we can control the press that goes out?"

"Uh huh . . . I know Ralph Conway at *Hi Life* well . . . what about them? They have the highest circulation in the country."

"Excellent."

He picked up his phone. "Cáit, get Ralph Conway at *Hi Life* on the phone for me."

Gloria sat back a little and examined Barry as he chatted away on the phone to Ralph. She found his mind very exciting. She had never met anybody who could be so bright and so charming. His very presence excited her. She found their meetings to be sexually charged. For the thousandth time, she wondered what the story was with his wife. Where the hell was she? Barry was no fool and, as many times as she had tried to draw him out about her, he had expertly avoided the subject. She wished she knew what the story was, so she could understand what kind of a chance she had.

Barry hung up the phone and said, "All arranged. Ralph thought it a great idea."

"Good. We'll get to work arranging it straight away. Barry, people will be expecting to see Barry Curtis the family man there. If you could make sure Mrs Curtis is available?"

He hesitated. "Of course . . . although the dates Ralph mentioned there . . . I think she's away then. I'll check it out. Anyway, we can have Lana there." He smiled reassuringly.

What an asset! thought Gloria wryly. I must remember to leave my handbag at home.

*   *   *

"I have to leave early today. I'm meeting a friend," Lana said to Nicole.

"I see. Well, thank you for coming in anyway."

"The only reason I did was because I'm sure Gloria Reagan is checking up on me."

Nicole decided to push the conversation in a positive direction. "Where are you going with this friend?"

"Nothing planned. Whatever takes our fancy."

Bit of credit-card fraud? Nicole wondered. "That's nice."

"Is it? I don't know what it is . . . I sometimes feel so lonely."

"You seem to have a lot of close friends and a loving family."

"I do, to a degree. But ultimately I feel I'm alone. And I feel I'll always be like that. I wonder what it feels like to have somebody who you can trust with anything."

Nicole thought of Tony and realised that was how she felt about him, and he about her. She felt so lucky. "Why do you think it will never happen to you?" she probed.

"Well, it hasn't happened yet, has it?"

"That's not a reason. What kind of relationships have you had in the past?"

"Numerous casual flings."

"And none of them have wanted any more?"

"I'm genetically programmed to pick men completely unsuitable who I know I won't see again."

"Why?"

"You tell me. You're the shrink."

"I'm not here to give you the answers, Lana. I'm here to help you figure the answers out yourself."

"Sounds a lazy way out for you."

"Well, when you employ a personal fitness instructor, they don't lose the weight for you; they just show you how. I do the same thing for the mind."

They were silent for a while, then Lana said, "I've never really wanted a relationship, I suppose. So I can't really blame anyone but myself for feeling lonely, can I?"

"Have you spoken to your friends about how you feel, or your family?"

"No! God forbid. I'd hate them to think this is how I feel."

"Then you're not being yourself with them. Is it a male friend you're meeting later?"

"Yes. And to be honest, I don't know what I'm doing. I

met him at a party, and I've done absolutely everything to push him away. But he seems to keep coming back"

"Is that such a bad thing?"

"I enjoy his company, I suppose, in spite of myself. And I guess I do find him attractive . . . even though he's from a very different background from me . . . that sounds horrible, doesn't it?"

"It sounds narrow-minded."

"What I'm trying to say is, he's completely different from the people I usually know."

"Well, the people you know don't seem to be providing you with much happiness, so why don't you look beyond that small pool and see what else is out there?"

*   *   *

Nicole thought about Lana later as she lay wrapped up on the couch with Tony, listening to his day's tales. She just felt so grateful for everything in her life as she thought about Lana's emptiness. She was even breaking her own rule of not thinking about clients after work time. She knew how risky it could be if you didn't switch off. A colleague of hers had allowed the guard to come down with a client, and it had a very bad effect on him.

"Are you listening to me?" Tony said, seeing the faraway expression in her eyes.

"I'm sorry, I drifted off. What were you saying?" She hugged him tighter.

"This house where the photo-shoot was, you never saw anything like it."

"Gorgeous?"

"Cedar Falls. Amazing. I was just thinking of our cramped little rented house here and thinking one day we'll live in a place like that."

She smiled. "I love our little cottage!"

"Yeah, but let's face it. We need to move on soon. And we shouldn't be setting our standards low."

"You're right, I guess."

"I was looking at an old edition of *Hi Life*, and the Conways had welcomed the magazine into their own home to do a photo shoot there. It was amazing."

"That's a curious way of describing it – welcomed?"

"You know what I mean. Anyway, their house is this big old pile. Fantastic. And they just looked so classy. Like something from a different world."

Nicole looked up at him. "You sound like you admire them."

"Well, in a way you have to, don't you? Living their life the way they do."

"It depends on what you want in life. Money isn't everything."

"We've been without it long enough. I think it's about time we tried to follow through on our aspirations, don't you?"

CHAPTER 20

Ralph dumped ten filled copy books and four cassette tapes on Tony's desk.

Tony looked up at him curiously.

"There you go. You can start straightaway," said Ralph.

"Er . . . what's all this stuff?" Tony questioned politely.

"That's all the interview stuff from Joanne Bailey. The notebooks c-c-c-ontain notes we took from talking to her, and the tapes just have her in conversations."

Tony looked at the mass of material "And you want me to –?"

Ralph looked angry. "Just w-w-w-write the feature. You've got till Friday." He turned and walked into his office.

Tony took up the notebooks and glanced through them at the almost illegible scrawl.

He looked over at Vivienne. "Three days to do all this?"

Vivienne sighed. "That's them for you, Tony. That's how they work. No organisation and then expect miracles. And they use aggression to get what they want."

"They?"

"Maggie's as bad as him under her sweet smile."

"But I don't know what the format should be, how long he wants it . . . or even what order these copy books and tapes are in." He stood up. "I'm going in to have a word with him."

He walked down the corridor and knocked on the door.

"Come in."

"Can I have a quick word?" Tony asked good-naturedly.

"What?" Ralph looked uninterested.

Tony came up to his desk and sat down opposite him. "It's just all the notes and the tapes you gave me, I'm not sure what order they're in. What's the beginning and what's the end?"

"It's your job to go through it all and see how you want to run it. There is no beginning or end as it stands."

"It's just that there isn't much time to sort through it all."

Ralph shrugged.

"And I don't know what format you want the feature in. What angles do you want me to take –"

"You either can do the job or you can't!" snapped Ralph. "If you can't, let me know and I'll get someone else to do it."

Tony was taken aback by his attitude.

"Let's put it this way," Ralph said coolly. "By Friday I'll know whether you can do the job or not."

Back at his desk, Tony started trying to read through the notebooks. "I can't believe this. I'm working in the dark here."

"Tony, if this job means anything to you, then try your damned hardest to get that feature done by Friday," Vivienne advised.

* * *

Kathryn felt weak and exhausted as she opened the apartment door. Simeon had been gone for five nights, the longest he had ever disappeared for.

It was seven in the evening. She had spent every night after the club had closed alone, pouring out her pain and her worry into her singing.

As she turned on the lights she saw Simeon sitting on the sofa staring into space.

"Simeon!" She ran over to him and sat beside him. "Where the hell were you ?"

He ignored her.

"Simeon! Are you all right?" she pleaded.

He nodded and stared down at the floor.

"Oh Simeon!" Tears started to pour down her face. "I was so worried! What's wrong? You were in such great form last Saturday at the barbeque!"

He ignored her.

"Simeon, don't freeze me out like this. I want to help you, but I need you talk to me."

"I'm going to bed." He got up and walked into the bedroom.

* * *

After Cathal had collected Lana after her therapy session, they had driven out to Howth and gone for a walk on the cliff. Then that night they found a quiet restaurant.

The waitress, on recognising Cathal, gave Lana a double look.

"She's assuming there's something going on between

us," said Lana.

"Would that bother you?"

"No, apart from the fact there isn't anything going on between us."

He glanced over at her, looking half-amused and half-irritated. "You know, you don't have to keep saying that – as if I'm going to push you into something. If you knew me at all you'd know how much I'm not like that."

"I'm sorry, I guess . . . I just wonder why we're here . . . you've been very nice to me . . . Are you always nice?" She looked at him sceptically.

"What have you heard?" He looked irritated.

"What do you think I've heard?"

"Probably that I can be a bit of a bastard and, yeah, I can be. I don't take shit from anyone, and I let them know that fairly quickly. If that's a crime so be it."

* * *

"For God's sake, Tony, you haven't been to bed at all," said Nicole as she came down the stairs and found Tony scribbling notes as he listened to Joanne's interviews on a Walkman.

He pulled the Walkman off. "I have. I grabbed a couple of hours' sleep on the couch."

"This is too much pressure on you. The job's not worth it. Nothing's worth this. The job has been a disaster since you started."

"I can manage it." He started filing his notes.

"Look, just leave the job. You'll find something else."

"No!" he snapped. "I'm not giving up on this, Nicole. It means too much to me and it's the last chance I might get."

* * *

"You look desperate!" commented Vivienne as she arrived into work and found Tony slaving away at his computer.

"Been up all night doing this fucking feature."

"How's it going?"

"Shit so far."

A door opened and closed down the corridor.

"He's in early," she whispered.

"He's been in there with Diana," Tony whispered back.

Diana came into reception, dressed in a designer track suit and looking radiantly healthy.

"Hi, all," she said, smiling. "I was just in with himself devising his new diet for him"

Tony had a bag of doughnuts on his desk, and was munching through one while he typed furiously.

Diana looked in horror at him. "Tony!" she squealed.

"What?" he asked, surprised.

"You won't find happiness in the middle of a doughnut, you know." She looked over his slightly tubby frame. "It's no wonder you're putting on weight, having those for breakfast. I'll tell you what I'll do: I'll sit you down when I have a spare moment and devise a diet regime for you. How about that?" She smiled encouragingly.

"I didn't think I was that overweight." He looked horrified.

"You need to nip it in the bud, straightaway. You probably eat pizzas and takeaways all the time, do you?"

His face reddened guiltily.

"A minute on the lips and a lifetime on the hips! Don't

worry. We'll sort that out for you!" She leaned forward and put a hand on his shoulder. "If you're around long enough, that is."

*   *   *

Cathal and Lana spent the next day walking around town, shopping, going for lunch. In the afternoon they went to the cinema. Lana found herself to be completely relaxed and enjoying Cathal's company. She also was intrigued as he told stories about Affidavit. It wasn't so much the stories about after they became famous, but what happened to them before that fascinated her. She was impressed by how Cathal had risen from an average background to where he was today.

"You mentioned your family were there for you when things were bad. What did you mean?" she asked.

"Ah, nothing, you know, normal teenage stuff," He looked defensive.

She reached over, took his hand and gave it a squeeze. "I'm in no position to judge anybody with my track record."

He thought for a long time. "I just fell in with the wrong crowd – it happens."

"And how did it happen with you?" she gently pushed.

He didn't want to talk about it. But sitting there in the restaurant on a sunny afternoon, holding hands, it seemed normal to talk. She seemed interested in him as a person.

"When I was seventeen I just fell in with an older crowd. They seemed really cool to me. And I just wanted to fit in with them. I guess I lost my sense of what was right and wrong . . ."

248

"Go on." She squeezed his hand tightly. "Please go on. I won't think anything different of you."

"We broke into a couple of shops and stuff, stealing cigarettes and some money. Stole a car once and . . ." He stopped talking as he registered the look of surprise on her face.

"I shouldn't have said anything. I never talk about this shit. It was so long ago –"

She squeezed his hand. "Please, go on."

"We drank a lot and experimented with drugs a little . . . you know. One night we were stopped by the guards and found to have dope on us. I was expelled from school, never sat the Leaving Cert. I knew taking dope was wrong, but I just went along with the gang."

"And your parents?"

"They went mad constantly at me."

"So what happened then?"

"I worked in a carpark as a kiosk attendant for a long while. James and everyone else were heading off to college and I was left behind. I realised I'd fucked up my life. And I felt terribly guilty for the damage I'd done and the trouble I'd caused. I got a job in a nightclub for a couple of years. Then James started the band and invited me to join . . . I owe him a lot."

"You don't have to carry that guilt around with you any more."

"I don't carry it," he said defensively.

"I think you do."

They spent the next day in the same easy-going manner. They went for a drive down the country in the afternoon and in the evening stopped off at a pub. There was live music and they had something to eat.

"Right, everybody!" one of the guys on stage shouted

into his microphone. "Welcome to Hennessy's! I hope you all know who we are: I'm Jim, that's Keith and Jake and that gorgeous lady beside me is Vera!"

A huge applause erupted from the crowd. Cathal looked at the girl and did a double-take. She was so similar to . . .

The band started to play, their booming music enveloping the whole bar. Lana was carried away with the music and the crowd who were dancing and clapping.

"It's great, isn't it?" said Lana, turning to Cathal. She was surprised to find him sitting back, with a strange look on his face, staring at the band.

"Are you all right?" she asked and he nodded.

For the next song, Vera took the microphone and sang, coming down off the stage and mingling with the crowd. As they watched her, a drunken man hit off a table beside Cathal and Lana, knocking over two women's drinks.

"Sorry . . .sorry," said the man, stumbling away.

The two women looked at Lana and pulled a face as they started mopping up the spilled drinks.

Lana smiled back at them, and watched as they cleaned up the mess.

"There's no need to feel sorry for them," said Cathal, leaning forward.

"What?"

"Those two girls beside us, you don't have to feel sorry for them."

"No, I wasn't," objected Lana.

"Yes, you were. You were sitting there and staring at them and thinking 'Poor them in their little lives in their little town. Not particularly good-looking and out socialising in a shithole like this'."

"What are you now, a mind-reader or something?"

"And do you know why you shouldn't feel sorry for

250

them? Because they will probably end up far happier than you or me. Because they don't have the same expectations, they won't always be searching for something to satisfy them. They probably have very good pensioned jobs, nice homes, and when they meet a guy they won't be looking at him and thinking 'No, he's not good enough for me – I'll see what else comes along'. They'll give it a chance, end up very happily married with kids and have perfect lives."

"You really think you know everything, don't you?"

"It's her you should feel sorry for," He nodded at the singer, busy belting out a Shirley Bassey song.

"Why her?"

"Because she was the type who had massive expectations for herself. Who thought she was too good for this place and everyone in it, because she was going to go far. But you know what happens to her? Time goes by. Time passes her by. And nothing happens for her and she's pushing a pram around on her own during the day and still singing in joints like this at night. That's who you should feel sorry for. These people beside us will know when to grab happiness when they have the opportunity. She up there never will."

"You don't know anything about that girl up there," Lana objected.

"I know exactly what she's like – every town has a girl like her. I used to go out with a girl who looked just like her and she used to sing in pubs as well . . ." He got up. "I've had enough of this place. Let's go."

Lana grabbed her coat and followed him out.

They started walking through the street back to the Jeep.

"Who was she?" asked Lana following him.

"I don't want to talk about it."

"Oh, so Cathal Fitzgerald doesn't want to talk about it – so that's that then!"

"Well, yeah, actually."

She grabbed him by the arm and turned him around. "Why won't you talk about it?"

"It's in the past."

"Well, I don't want to be around somebody who doesn't open up. I mean it's all very well you talking about your latest album and the problems you are having in the studio, but that's not what interests me."

"Tough."

"So I get it. You can see me at my absolute most vulnerable. You can see me lying on the ground in a park nearly choking to death –" She put a hand quickly to her face to stop herself from being emotional. "Forget it!" She turned and started to walk away.

He watched her walking down the street. "Okay," he called after her. "Let's talk."

*   *   *

They were back in Cathal's apartment. Cathal got himself a beer and opened it before sitting down across from Lana.

"Well?" she asked.

*   *   *

"What are you going to do?" demanded his parents, after he had been expelled from school.

"I'll get a job," said Cathal optimistically.

"As what? You have no experience and no qualifications. You won't get anything," said his father.

Cathal didn't know what he wanted to do, but he was so relieved to be finally finished with school. Over the past year he had wised up a lot. He knew the group he hung around with were bad news as they steadily did worse things. He had distanced himself from them a huge amount. The trouble was that none of the other kids wanted much to do with him because of past events.

He went off one Saturday and headed to the shopping centre and asked around the shops if they were taking anyone on. Nobody was, but somebody suggested he try the general manager's office. Nervously he knocked on the door and met the manager, who was a kindly middle-aged man.

"What kind of job are you looking for?" he asked.

"Anything you have. I'll try anything."

"You ever handled money before?"

"Not really."

"I do have a job, and I'll give you a try, but if you mess it up you're finished on the spot, okay?"

The job involved sitting in the kiosk of the shopping centre carpark, taking in the money and giving out parking tickets in exchange. He was delighted. His parents were horrified.

"Your cousin James is up studying engineering at university in Dublin and you're in a dead-end job!" his father had shouted when he announced his good news.

In fact, his father had a point. It was the most boring thing he could have imagined, sitting there in the kiosk, day after day, taking in the money and handing out the ticket and saying "Thanks". Every night his arm ached from the repetitive action and his mind was numb from the boredom. He went out at the weekends when his friends were back from college, but as time went by he found he had less and less in common with them. He felt everyone was moving on and he was being left far behind. If he ever managed to get his life back on track, he swore he would never fuck up again.

As he sat in the kiosk a sports car pulled up and the window came down. A hand came out and handed him fifty pence. Cathal gave the man his ticket.

"Thanks," said Cathal putting the coin into the till. He looked down at the man in his car and recognised him as Stephen Rourke. Rouke ran the Tuxedo nightclub in the town. Aged in his mid-twenties, he was very flash and considered to be something of a hero among the town's young. He often came into the carpark and was always very polite to Cathal.

"You look bored," Stephen said.

Cathal was surprised he was chatting to him. "Oh no, I'm fine." He smiled.

Stephen handed him his card. "If you're looking for a career change, give me a call some time."

Cathal stared down at the card. "A job at Tuxedo?"

"No, the United Nations!" Stephen laughed lightly and drove off.

All that night at home Cathal had stared at the card, barely letting it out of his hands. He wondered if Stephen had been serious. Well, there was only one way to find out.

Next day, he phoned the number on the card.

"Hi, is that Stephen?"

"Sure is."

"This is Cathal Fitzgerald. You gave me your card yesterday and said to ring you about a job."

"Cathal . . .Cathal . . .?" Stephen mused.

"I work in the kiosk at the carpark." Cathal reminded him.

"Oh sure! Why don't you drop by the club some time and we'll have a chat."

"When would suit?"

"Drop by after you finish work this evening. I'll be here."

* * *

Nervously, he pushed open the door of Tuxedo and walked in past the cloakroom and through to the huge nightclub. He had been there a couple of times and it so looked different empty.

"Hello!" Cathal called.

"Be with you in a moment," came Stephen's voice.

Cathal looked up to see him on top of a ladder fixing a sound system. Stephen came down the ladder, went up to the DJ box and started flicking switches on the equipment. Suddenly music was booming out from the speakers.

"That's better!" he shouted and turned off the music. He then went behind one of the bars, grabbed two Cokes and handed one to Cathal. "Come over here and we'll have a chat."

He sat down in a booth. Cathal joined him. Cathal remembered seeing Stephen at the door the couple of times he had been to Tuxedo and remembered him looking very cool and commanding respect.

"So how long have you been at the kiosk?"

"About eight months."

"You like it?"

"It's a living."

"What did you do before that?"

"I finished school."

"You seem a bright kid – you didn't decide to head off

to college then?"

"I can't stand all that studying."

Stephen laughed out loud. "I was the exact same myself. Working in a nightclub might sound fun, and it is great crack, but there's an awful lot of hard work and you're working nights so it'll disrupt your social life."

"That's no problem."

"Okay, you can start whenever you want. You can start on the ticket desk, same really as what you're doing at the kiosk. The punters hand you in the money and you give them back a ticket, only you're dealing with larger amounts of money. We'll try that for a while and then we'll train you up on other things, cloakroom, behind the bar, some promotional work. How does that sound?"

"Sounds great," Cathal smiled.

*　　*　　*

"A nightclub?" shouted his father.

"Yeah, it's giving me a chance of a real career," defended Cathal.

"For fuck's sake, you nearly ended up in prison when you were in the safety of school! Where the hell are you going to end up working in a club?"

"Thanks for the vote of confidence."

"I'm serious, Cathal. You're too easily led, you always have been. You don't have a strong enough personality to know when to bail out when things are dangerous."

"I'm nearly nineteen and you can't stop me. You know I'm happy about this opportunity – why can't you just be happy for me as well?"

*   *   *

Cathal pushed the door of Tuxedo open and walked in. Walking through to the main club area, he found it a hive of activity. People were walking around setting up the club for the night, cleaning, putting out ashtrays, changing kegs behind the bars. Stephen was in the middle of it all.

"Jason, check if the Heineken keg needs changing, will you? Tim, this ashtray is chipped over here. Do me a favour and get a new one. Frank, there's some paint spilled on the floor. Try and get it off, will you? Ahh, Cathal, come over here!"

Cathal walked to the middle of the dance floor where Stephen was.

"This is Cathal, everybody. He's starting work here tonight," announced Stephen.

Everyone shouted hello cheerily.

"Right, follow me," Stephen said, leading Cathal out to the ticket desk. He ran through the procedures with him. "If you've any problems, just call me." He handed him a walkie-talkie. "I'll be at the end of this. When the punters stop coming in, go to the cloakroom and start helping out in there, okay?"

"Stephen, I'm heading out now!" said a female voice as a girl came through from the club.

"Cool – where you are heading tonight?"

"The usual suspects – all the normal bars and there's a new one opened over on Pearse Street so I'll try that one as well."

"This is Cathal. He's starting here tonight. Cathal, this is Michelle."

Cathal realised he was staring at her and quickly

looked away. He thought she was incredibly beautiful with her long black sleek hair. He guessed she was around twenty-one. She oozed confidence.

"Hiya," she said and walked out the door.

"See you later back at the ranch," said Stephen. "That's Michelle. She's our promotions girl. You know – goes around handing out flyers to all the pubs and putting up posters and placing adverts in the papers – that kind of thing."

"She's gorgeous, isn't she?" said Cathal.

"Well, she thinks she is!" laughed Stephen. "She sings in a band as well – she's only working here till she gets the big break. They play here occasionally."

Cathal was run off his feet all night. He had to work very fast at the ticket desk as people were swarming in. After the last customers arrived, he helped out in the cloakroom and then Stephen started calling him on the walkie-talkie asking him to do lots of jobs from emptying ashtrays to helping out behind the bar.

By 2.30, when the club was at last empty, Cathal was exhausted.

"How did you find it?" asked Stephen.

"Great," Cathal said truthfully. "Anyway, I'll see you tomorrow night."

"Why? Where are you going?" asked Stephen.

"Home, I guess."

"No way. All the punters have had their fun: now it's time when we have ours. Come and join the party."

Confused, Cathal followed Stephen through to the main club, where all the staff were sitting around the bar drinking and soft jazz music was playing.

"Every night after we close, we let our hair down," said Stephen.

* * *

The weeks flew into months and Cathal was having the time of his life. For the first time in his life he felt totally at ease with a place. He loved working at Tuxedo and became great friends with everyone working there. He would go in every night and work like crazy and then party till dawn and arrive home at seven or eight in the morning. Stephen seemed to be very fond of him and trained him up on everything from the bar to cashing up at night. Cathal found himself doing a little bit of everything. And he hero-worshipped Stephen whose life was so together. He seemed to have a variety of different glamorous girlfriends and he lived in a swish new apartment block.

Cathal could barely speak when Michelle was around as he found himself falling in love with her. The first time he saw her perform with her band on stage at Tuxedo he had been completely gobsmacked. If she knew of Cathal's feelings for her she certainly didn't show it.

One night, the staff were all partying and the music was blaring as people were dancing.

Stephen came and sat beside Cathal. "Look, why don't you just ask her out?" he said.

Cathal realised he had been staring over at Michelle. "What do you mean?"

"Oh come on. You're fooling nobody. You're obviously interested in Michelle."

"Is it that obvious?"

"Yeah. Go over and ask her out."

"No way. She wouldn't be interested in me."

"You'll never know if you never try."

Cathal shook his head.

"Well, if you won't, I will," Stephen said, getting up and walking across the dance floor.

"No, wait!" Cathal called.

He cringed as he saw Stephen pull up a chair beside Michelle and start talking closely to her. Michelle seemed to be listening, nodded a few times and then glanced over at Cathal. She nodded again, got up and walked across to him.

Cathal didn't know what to say or do as she stood in front of him.

"Do you mind if I join you?" she asked.

"Er, no. Be my guest."

He was mesmerised by her as they spoke. Although it was mainly her talking about her career as a singer and what she wanted to do.

Finally she turned around and said, "Do you want to come back to my place?"

"Yeah, but only if you want me to. I don't want to put you out or anything."

She looked at him and raised an eyebrow sceptically.

* * *

She lived in a two-storey cottage down a back street.

"Do you live here alone?" he asked.

"Of course," she answered, pouring herself a whiskey.

She sat beside him and resumed talking about her singing career. "Music is such a tough business. We've sent away so many demo tapes to record companies. But I know I have the talent and it'll only be a matter of time before we're signed up."

"Of course," he nodded. "You're too talented not to make it."

"You're nice," she said and leaned forward and kissed him.

Cathal had had a few flings but they were nothing to the intensity he felt for Michelle. He started staying at her place a lot. And he felt really happy. He loved work, he loved the social side to it and now he had Michelle. All the trouble he had seemed a distant memory. The only thing stopping his complete happiness was his parents' constant disapproval and Michelle's insistence that their relationship wasn't going anywhere.

"I am fond of you, Cathal," she would say as they lay in bed at night. "I really am. But one day I'll be gone and that'll be the end of that. One day, when I get that recording contract, my life will change so much."

"I know it will."

"So you know the score."

"Yeah, I do."

He did everything she asked. Everything from giving out flyers for her band, to cooking her dinner every evening before they went in to work.

"What's wrong?" asked Stephen one night as they stood at the door, the music thumping out from inside. He allowed Cathal to do the door now. "Is it the job?"

"No, I love it here," Cathal insisted.

"It's Michelle then," Stephen said.

"Yeah," Cathal nodded and looked at the floor.

"You know I'm always here to talk to."

"I know, you've been a great friend to me."

"You love her, don't you?" said Stephen. "Go on. Just admit it to me. You're in love with her."

"Yeah, I am. I have been since I first met her."

"I know you have. So what's the problem then? You're going out together and everything's fine. No?"

"No. Love seems to be a dirty word as far as Michelle is concerned. She just sees this as filler in until she moves on to bigger and better things."

"Oh, I see, when she becomes famous," Stephen said cynically.

"Yeah."

"Does she know how you feel?"

"No. How could she? She made the rules clear from the beginning and as far as she's concerned I'm happy with that."

"Well, maybe you should tell her how you really feel."

That next night Cathal and Michelle were together in her house.

"Cathal, I'm so miserable," she said, putting her head on his shoulder. "Another rejection from another fucking record company. When am I going to get the break, Cathal?"

"It'll happen for you. Just be patient."

"I just want it so bad."

"Maybe if you didn't spend so much time chasing it, it might come to you quicker. Maybe if you concentrated on other things in your life?"

"Like what?"

"Like me . . . Michelle, I love you. I really do, and I want you to know that I love you."

She didn't say anything but continued to rest her head on his shoulder.

"Did you hear me? I love you."

She closed her eyes quickly and pretended to go to sleep.

*   *   *

Stephen had put him on the door for the night with instructions not to leave his post for any reason, as he had heard it through the grapevine that some known troublemakers intended to turn up that night. So when a girl cut herself severely on broken glass, Cathal didn't leave the door to deal with it – instead he tried to contact Stephen on the walkie-talkie. There was no reply. He tried again and again. He urgently needed the first-aid kit which was in Stephen's office but he also felt Stephen should come and deal with the matter personally. After all, the girl might decide to sue – someone should drive her to the hospital or at least offer to do so – or offer her free admittance to the club for a year – but would that be admitting culpability? Cathal didn't know how to deal with the situation. Where the hell was Stephen? Without his walkie-talkie? The other staff said he was not in the club. He *must* be in his office.

Cathal raced out the back to Stephen's office, barging through the door without knocking first. There was no-one there. Cathal grabbed the first-aid kit and left.

It was then he heard the sounds from the nearby storeroom. He opened the door.

Michelle and Stephen were lying on some stacked boxes, semi-clothed, his head nuzzling her breasts. She screamed when she saw Cathal, causing Stephen to jump up.

Cathal stared at them as Michelle grabbed her top and pulled it on, before he turned and ran out of the club, shoving the first-aid kit into the hands of one of the other staff as he passed.

He walked through the town's streets home, a pain that felt worse than physical pain tearing through his chest. Almost as if his heart was breaking. What hurt most of all was the fact they hadn't even bothered to lock the door of the storeroom – he mattered so little to either of them they just didn't care about the risk.

He sat up all night feeling totally lost, finally falling asleep the next morning out of exhaustion.

The next evening he didn't go in to work. He lay out on the couch and decided what to do. He and Michelle were finished as he realised she cared absolutely nothing about him. As for love, the joke had been on him to think that it could actually exist and that he could have it. That was it, he told himself, and he would never allow himself to feel that way about somebody again. He'd never let himself get close to anybody.

He could live without love. As for Stephen's betrayal, part of him never wanted to even hear his name again. But he couldn't just walk away from the club; it was too important a part of his life. And besides this, Stephen had been such a good friend to him in the past. He had rescued him and given him a purpose.

The next night he went in to Tuxedo and started getting ready for work as usual. His workmates looked at him curiously.

Stephen was seated in a booth going through paperwork. "Cathal!"

Cathal went over to him. "Hi."

"You okay?"

Cathal nodded.

"Er . . . me and Michelle . . ." Stephen began.

"It's okay," Cathal said, staring down at the floor.

"I know how it looks . . . I mean it was her. She has a terrible reputation around town. I should have known better, I suppose. But I'm glad you found out about her now rather than later . . ." He trailed off. He put out his hand. "No hard feelings?"

Cathal took his hand, shook it and looked him in the eye. "No, none at all."

Later that night Cathal was doing security, walking through the crowds, when Michelle arrived in. She immediately saw him and came over to him.

"Cathal, I –" she began.

But he looked right through her and walked past her. From then on, they avoided each other and never spoke again.

* * * *

"I guess Michelle never got the recording contract?" Lana asked.

"No. She just continued playing gigs around town. I heard she got pregnant a couple of years back and the guy ran out on her. I believe her mother minds the kid while she goes out singing at night."

Lana got up and went to sit beside him. She started to kiss him.

* * *

Cathal groped for his ringing phone.

"Yeah?"

"Where the fuck are you?" Sylvia demanded.

"In bed."

"Well, get your sorry ass back into the studio asap. Rob has decided to show up and we're recording today."

"I'll come in right away." Cathal turned off his phone, leaned over and put his arm around Lana in the bed.

"What's up?" Lana asked wearily beside him.

"I have to head back into the studio."

"Pity . . . what will I do without my playmate now?"

*   *   *

Tony stood over Ralph's desk, feeling tired and exhausted. "There it is, the finished feature." He put the papers down in front of Ralph.

"Okay, I'll look at it later," said Ralph, who then yawned and stretched and picked up his phone to make a call.

Tony stood there, unable to believe it. After all his hard work, he wasn't even getting a response.

"You can go," Ralph said.

Turning, seething, Tony walked out.

*   *   *

"Not even a fucking 'well done'," Tony muttered down the phone to Nicole.

"It's not fair, after all your hard work!"

"And now I'm worried he'll pick fault with it and say it's a load of shit."

"He won't say that."

"How do I know? I was practically asleep when I was writing last night."

"It'll be fine. Just relax."

*   *   *

"I'm just making myself clear," said Rob as they sat around the studio. "I'm extremely pissed off with the way MPI have treated us, dropping my songs like that and I'm still reviewing the situation."

"Okay, review away as much as you like, but please

266

let's start making some music!" Sylvia pleaded.

*   *   *

Clive from *Hi Life* focused his camera. Kathryn was sitting at the bar in Exclusive, dressed in an elegant black dress, smiling.

Clive snapped. "Okay, that wraps it up then."

"You look fantastic!" Margaux enthused. "I'd say you'll get lots of votes."

"Well, it's a bit of fun, isn't it?" said Kathryn, getting down off the high stool.

"This could be your year," said Ralph, smiling happily.

"Fingers crossed," said Kathryn, who enjoyed being nominated and knew the publicity would be good for the club, but wasn't too concerned about winning.

"So maybe we'll just go through the proceedings for the big night," suggested Ralph. "Doors open at eight. Strictly invitation for the night. Champagne Reception on arrival. Clive will be circulating taking photos of guests –"

"I'm sorry – what are you talking about?" quizzed Kathryn.

"The big party. Barry Curtis's birthday party here at Exclusive."

"A birthday party?" Kathryn looked confused.

"Didn't Barry tell you?" Margaux was surprised.

Kathryn didn't show her anger. "Ah, yes, the party. But I'm sorry, I have an appointment. Could we go through this another time?"

"Of course, I'll give you a call," said Ralph.

Kathryn walked quickly to her office, seething. She slammed her door, sat down at her desk and dialled Barry's direct line.

"Barry, what is this about a birthday party being held at Exclusive?"

"I was going to give you a call about that today."

"Don't you think you should have discussed it with me before arranging it all with the Conways? I'm kinda pissed off about this, Barry."

There was silence on the other side of the phone. Then, "I take your point, Kathryn. It just happened very fast. Gloria suggested it and it was all very spur of the moment."

I might have thought she was involved somehow, thought Kathryn.

"Why don't you come over to Kildara tomorrow and we'll discuss it properly?"

*   *   *

Simeon was seated on the couch in a bathrobe, looking at the television with the volume turned down.

"Hi, love!" she greeted him.

"You're looking smart," he said quietly.

"Yes, *Hi Life* were in taking my photo for the next edition," she said, hurrying into the bedroom to change her clothes. "You know how I've been nominated for that Personality Award."

"Oh yeah."

"Did you get down to the doctor today?" she called from the bedroom.

"He gave me these new sleeping pills."

"Did he offer any reason why you can't get to sleep?"

"No."

"Hopefully these new pills will work," she said, hurrying to the kitchen, now dressed in a black trouser suit. It was nearly seven and she was expecting a delivery in to the club at eight. "It's just spaghetti bolognese, as I'm in a hurry tonight!" she called.

Suddenly she heard a crash from the sitting room. In panic she ran in to find Simeon looking distraught and a glass vase on the ground.

"What happened?" she asked.

"Why are you even bothering to cook anything? Just go in and forget about me."

"Simeon –"

"Here I am, not able to sleep for five nights and you don't give a shit! All you care about is having your fucking photo in that magazine and mixing with the stars in Exclusive!"

"Oh, Simeon!" She rushed to him and held him in her arms. "I'm so sorry. I'll stay with you tonight and call in sick. You're my priority. You always have been and you always will be."

CHAPTER 21

Nicole looked through the papers on her desk, making notes, on the Monday morning. She was dying to find out about the response to Tony's feature. That bastard Conway had swanned out of the office to a photo shoot on the Friday afternoon without even wishing Tony a good weekend after he had put in so much work to reach the deadline. Their weekend hadn't been very good. Tony had been exhausted from the lack of sleep and so had been cranky and tired most of the time. She was tempted to give him a quick call before her next client, Lana Curtis, arrived in. But decided against it.

The door opened and Lana walked in.

"You look very refreshed," Nicole commented as Lana sat down.

"I feel refreshed."

"What have you been up to?"

"I've just spent the last couple of days with Cathal. You know, the guy I was telling you about. I didn't even drink that much."

"Have you established a relationship?"

"Well, insofar as two emotional cripples can establish

anything, I suppose we have. I really admire him."

"In what way?"

"Before, I just thought of him as a guy who got lucky. But now, having found out about him, knowing where he's come from, it's amazing how far he's come. It kind of made me ashamed."

"In what way."

"Because of all the golden opportunities I have in my life. My background, my contacts – but what have I done with it?"

"It sounds like you're ready to start looking at different options for your life."

"I'd like to, but what can I do at this stage?"

Her esteem is very low, thought Nicole.

*   *   *

Tony looked at his feature on the desk in front of Ralph. His heart sank as he saws the number of red marks Ralph had scribbled through the pages.

"It's very good," said Ralph, looking up and giving a brief smile.

"Really?" Tony beamed.

"It needs tidying up and editing obviously, which I'm doing. But other that that, it's very good. I want you to start writing the profiles for those nominated for Personality of the Year." He passed him a bunch of papers.

"Sure, I'll start straight away."

*   *   *

"He loved it," Tony said down the phone to Nicole as he walked down the street.

"That's fantastic!" said Nicole.

"He gave me the next thing to work on already."

"Tony, I'm so happy for you!"

"For us, darling, and this is only the beginning."

*   *   *

Nicole lay on the couch looking at Tony stretched out on the floor in front of the fire, busily writing and talking at the same time.

"Of course, Kathryn Foy had to be nominated. Remember, the bitch who threw me out of Exclusive?"

"Yeah."

"Listen to this crap: *Kathryn Foy has long reigned as the social doyenne of Dublin's social scene. Kathryn is friend and confidante of the stars. She manages Exclusive, Dublin's No 1 nightspot and so named because it's full of stars. No social event in the capital would be complete without Kathryn. Immaculately turned out on every occasion —*"

"Stop already!" Nicole shrieked as she buried her head in a cushion. "I can't bear to listen to any more!"

"I know, I know," laughed Tony. "It's cringe, isn't it?"

"I'm not mocking your style of writing – you have it perfect for *Hi Life*. But how can people bear to read it?"

"You know, they don't just read it, they live their lives by it. They totally admire the people who appear in *Hi Life* and want to live their lives the same way."

"Who else is on the list?"

"The usual suspects: a couple of models, the President and a couple of politicians, an actress, a TV presenter and a host of society wives."

"Who do you think will win?" asked Nicole.

"I haven't a clue, and couldn't care less. Whoever is of

most use to the Conways, I suspect. Who knows, in another couple of years it might be us being nominated for this kind of award."

"Are you for real?"

"I can see it now. Award-winning journalist and his beautiful wife, therapist to the stars," Tony said and looked dreamily into the fire.

Nicole looked for some sign of irony in Tony's expression, and was scared when she couldn't find any.

* * *

Diana sat down at Tony's desk with a notebook and pen. "And then last night what did you have?" she asked.

"We had lasagne for dinner."

"No garlic bread?"

He looked embarrassed and nodded. "With garlic bread."

"And to follow?"

"There was a box of chocolates there, so we kind of munched our way through them for a while watching TV."

Diana shook her head. "I'm just looking back on what you've eaten over the past week, and it makes for sad reading," she said in a melancholy fashion. She took her pen and started drawing quick sharp lines through her notes. "All this should be off your agenda from now on. Out with chocolates, sweets, doughnuts, pizzas and fizzy drinks. In with salads, fruit and lots of water."

Tony nodded.

"What about your girlfriend, does she put on weight too?"

"No. She can eat anything and not put on any weight."

"People like that are a curse to have around when

you're on a diet. Right, what I'm going to devise is a special diet for you and I want you to adhere strictly to it. Okay?"

"All right. Thanks."

"I also want you to keep a notebook with you at all times and jot down everything you eat, so you can keep a record of what's going into your mouth because," she smiled sadly, "eaten bread is soon forgotten."

"Write down everything?" He pulled a face. "That sounds like hard work."

"Being fit is hard work," snapped Diana.

A door down the corridor opened and she jumped up, realising Ralph was coming out.

"So, I'll leave you my column for next week and you might just check it for me," she said loudly and winked at Tony.

*   *   *

"Hiya," said Nicole struggling through the door with her briefcase in one hand and a giant pizza box in the other.

"What's that?" Tony said, staring at the pizza.

"I thought I'd pick it up on the way home instead of cooking us something tonight."

Tony shook his head. "I've already eaten. I had a chicken salad."

She looked at him, confused. "You eating a salad?"

"Yeah. I was talking to Diana today and decided to go on a diet."

"Oh well, more for me," she said as she put the pizza down on the table. "What's brought this on?"

"Well, I think I've needed to go on a diet for a while." He sighed.

"I don't think so."

"Come on, Nic. If I don't take action now, my weight will spiral out of control."

"Does it really matter if you're a few pounds overweight?"

"Well, yes. Especially now I'm working at *Hi Life*."

"Why? Is everyone stunningly beautiful with perfect bodies at *Hi Life?*" she giggled.

"Of course not. But they try to be fit because they're out meeting celebrities all the time and stuff."

"Sounds like you're going on a diet for other people rather than for yourself."

"You know that therapist in you can be really annoying sometimes."

"I'm sorry," she said, sitting down beside him with a plate of pizza. "You're right. We should try and eat more healthily. I think I'll start next week sometime." She bit into the pizza and smiled at him.

"I've got something to show you," he said mysteriously and produced a copy of *Hi Life* from the coffee table. "An early copy of *Hi Life*, on sale tomorrow morning."

"Oh, show it to me!" she said excitedly. "I can't wait to see your name in print."

He opened up the magazine and under credits pointed to *Editorial Staff* and to his name.

"Fantastic!" she said, hugging him and grabbing the magazine. She went to the main article about Joanne Bailey and then paused, confused. The feature was credited to Ralph and Margaux Conway without any mention of Tony.

"Tony, they haven't given you credit for the feature you wrote," she said, full of concern.

"They have, at the beginning under editorial – I just showed you."

"I know that, but after the feature it says it was written by Ralph and Margaux."

"So?"

"So, you went without sleep to try and get that feature ready on time and you're not getting any credit." She felt herself becoming angry.

"Well, let's be honest. It was Ralph and Margaux that provided all the information. I just edited it."

"What is this? Why are you defending them, Tony? They've taking credit for your work. It's plagiarism, almost."

"Well, I don't see a problem with it, and I don't know why you're getting upset. Look, they've mentioned me in the front so I'm happy."

"They also mention everybody in the front except the window cleaner. Why aren't you fuming? Before you started working at that damned magazine you would be going berserk over something like this. Now, you seem to be content to let these horrible people walk all over you."

"I'm not letting anybody walk over me, Nic." Now he was becoming angry. "I'm just really happy to be working as a journalist, and I'm really upset you can't be happy for me as well. I've been published in *Hi Life*, and you should be happy for me."

"You're settling for less –"

"I'm not settling for less!" he snapped and looked at her with the most determined expression she had ever seen on him before. "Far from it. I want more than I've ever wanted. But if I start rocking the boat, I'll be out on my ear. So I'll keep smiling, because that's how I'll get there. Why should I be asked to leave tables at Exclusive, or not be invited to premières? Why can't I live in a house like the Conways? I've as good a chance to get these things as everybody else, and this job is my passport there."

Nicole shrugged "I didn't realise how committed you had become to all this." She lifted the magazine into the air.

"I want it, Nic. I want it for us."

* * *

Cathal walked down the street to the shop, smiling to himself. He had been giving Lana cookery lessons because she had never cooked a thing in her life before. He had left her in his kitchen in charge of some scrambled eggs while he went to get the morning papers. It was 8.30 and he was due in the studio for ten so he had lots of time yet. He thought about Lana. Here at last was somebody who was with him because she wanted to be. Somebody he enjoyed being with. Somebody he felt needed him. She reminded him so much of himself years ago. He saw so much potential in her but she had been on a self-destructive course for so long. He loved spending time with her. He found the way she viewed the world hilarious, if a little strange and unsettling at times.

"Hi, Hakaam," he called, entering the shop.

"Morning, Cathal."

Cathal grabbed some milk and the papers.

"How's your new album coming along?"

"So so." Cathal grimaced.

"My daughter can't wait to hear it."

"Really? I'll give you a signed copy for her when it's finished."

"Thank you! Did you want to get a copy of *Hi Life*? It's just in this morning." Hakaam looked uncomfortable. He nodded over to the shelves that carried the magazines.

Cathal looked over and saw blazing from the front cover of *Hi Life* a photo of Joanne with the heading *My Life After Cathal*.

* * *

"I can't believe what she did!" Cathal shouted, coming into the apartment.

Lana got a shock. "Who?"

"Joanne Bailey!" He threw the magazine on the coffee table. "She's gone and done this big feature about the two of us!"

Lana picked up the magazine and looked at the front cover.

"It's full of her saying shit like we were in love but our work commitments kept us apart, and how I told her she would always have a special place in my heart and how we'll always have this bond nobody can take away!" He was practically yelling.

Lana went to the feature, spread over several pages, full of glossy photos of Joanne interspersed with the odd photo of Cathal.

"I'm going to ring her." He grabbed his phone, went into the kitchen and dialled Joanne's number.

She answered immediately.

"What the hell do you think you're playing at?" he shouted down the phone.

"Ah, Cathal, you've seen the feature I take it. I'm very pleased with it," she cooed.

"Who gave you permission to talk about the two of us and to build it up into something it never was?"

"Well, I did, actually."

"You had no right! You're trying to get publicity on the back of my success."

"I would have thought you'd be delighted to be

associated in the press with a beautiful girl like me." She kept her voice smooth as velvet throughout.

"You're a conniving, manipulating bitch!" he shouted.

"Yep! All that and a great ass too! I even got a nice spread in the UK edition as well, although not the main billing, unfortunately. Still the phone has been hopping from London already with offers."

"You've used me!"

"Oh, get over yourself, Cathal. I know I have." She hung up.

He came storming into the sitting-room.

"Cathal, calm down, I've never seen you like this before," Lana pleaded.

"I can't. I'm too pissed off."

She went over to him and held his head firmly. "I said calm down!"

He said nothing and then removed her hands. "I'd better go to the studio. I'll see you later." He turned and walked out.

Still taken aback she went, sat down and took up the magazine. She was struck with how much interest there was in Cathal and Affidavit. She scrutinised the photos of Joanne and thought she looked beautiful. She felt intimidated by the knowledge that Cathal had gone out with Joanne and wondered what he was doing now with her. She flicked through the magazine and saw all the beauties posing at different events. She stopped when she saw a photo of Kathryn Foy, and saw she had been nominated as Social Personality of the Year. Because Lana had been born into the family she had, she had never craved this kind of attention. But as she sat back and studied the magazine she became intrigued.

CHAPTER 22

"The question is, are you tough enough to do the job?" Ralph asked, as he swung slightly in his chair.

"Of course I am!" Tony answered enthusiastically.

"Are you capable and tough enough?"

"You can trust me," Tony assured him.

"Myself and Margaux have to go to New York for a couple of weeks. We're guests of Calvin Klein, you know. But we have to get this article about Affidavit under way. So you'll have to be with them, putting together the material, while we're away."

"No problem at all," said Tony, feeling empowered.

"Okay – you can go – oh, and take this." Ralph threw a card at him.

Tony picked it up and looked at it. It was a member's card for Exclusive with his name on it.

"They give them out to all the staff here at the magazine," said Ralph.

"Thanks, Ralph." Tony was delighted.

* * *

"This is madness," Nicole said as she and Tony approached the steps of Exclusive. "It's a Wednesday night, we both have early starts in the morning and we're going clubbing!"

"We're not just going clubbing, Nic. We're entering Exclusive as members!"

So fucking what, she wanted to roar. But she didn't want to upset him. He had come home so excited about covering the Affidavit story and being given membership of Exclusive. He had quickly talked her into going to try out their membership. But as she walked along in high-heeled shoes, all she could think of was her warm bed at home, and the long day of clients ahead of her tomorrow.

"There she is!" Tony whispered to Nicole as they climbed the steps and saw Kathryn on the door.

*   *   *

Kathryn had a photographic memory for faces. You had to in her job. She instantly remembered Tony and the argument they'd had.

"Sorry, folks. Members only," she said.

"I am a member," said Tony, reaching into his wallet and showing her his card.

She glanced at the card which seemed legitimate. She made a mental note of his name so she could check the membership was valid with the members' secretary the next day.

"That's fine. Go on through," she said, waving them in.

*   *   *

"Did you see her face?" said Tony excitedly as they put

in their coats.

"I saw a woman who was too much of a professional to let us see a flicker of emotion when you produced your card."

"I think she looked really pissed off," said Tony happily.

Two hours later and Nicole was feeling really tired. They sat in the members' lounge drinking champagne while Tony pointed out the celebrities.

"Tony, we're really going to have to go. I have to get up in the morning."

"Ah, come on! This is fantastic. We've arrived!"

"If feeling tired and exhausted in an overcrowded place while music booms into my ears – if this is being arrived – I wish I'd never set off!"

"Ah, come on, Nic. This is our dream!"

"No, Tony, it's your dream!" she snapped. She saw the hurt on his face and she reached over and took his hand. "I'm tired and irritated. Sorry."

"Okay, let's head home." He nodded and squeezed her hand.

* * *

Barry had come in to *Hi Life* to discuss ideas for his birthday party at Exclusive. Kathryn was there too and was none too pleased to see Gloria Reagan in attendance.

"Thank you so much for taking some time out of your busy schedule to visit us, Barry." said Margaux, sounding like they were all just having afternoon tea together.

"It's good to see you both again," said Barry. "And this is my campaign advisor, Gloria Reagan."

There were much smiling and charm going both ways.

Even for the Conways, they were being particularly fawning, thought Kathryn.

"We've been following your election with the greatest of interest," enthused Margaux.

"I'm so glad. And I can't tell you what having a publication with *Hi Life's* reputation covering this launch party means to me."

Gloria was getting bored with the chit-chat and mutual admiration society and decided to hurry things up a little. "I'm sure Barry may have briefed you about the nature of our visit. We are planning on having an exclusive party at Exclusive . It's basically his birthday party, but unofficially we are using it as a vehicle to gain publicity for his election campaign. It will be the party of the year. If your magazine does an extended feature on the night, then your readers will not only get exclusive shots of where Barry Curtis lives, but a guest list which will include the following." She handed Ralph a page with printed names on it. Ralph quickly read through the list and felt himself salivate.

"You can guarantee these people will attend?" he asked.

Gloria looked at him condescendingly. "Of course".

"I didn't mean to insinuate anything – it's just that these people would have heavy schedules –"

"They are also close friends of Barry's and will, of course, make the effort to be there for him."

Kathryn looked at Gloria in fury. It looked like she would now take over the whole show.

"We would of course be delighted to cover the event," smiled Margaux, not particularly warming to Gloria herself.

"Of course, that's only a few of my own personal contacts. I would like for you to add maybe some more showbiz stars," explained Barry.

"Of course," Ralph said. "I can get bands like Affidavit to attend."

Big deal, thought Kathryn. They practically lived in Exclusive anyway.

"We want to give the public something special to look at," explained Gloria. "We want to give them glamour and excitement – to show them that Barry Curtis entering politics means Irish politics entering a new era."

"Indeed!" Margaux clapped her hands together in excitement.

*   *   *

Margaux came quickly up the stairs to reception at *Hi Life*.

"Hi, everybody," she said as she hurried down the corridor to Ralph's office.

"Er, Margaux, Ralph's with somebody." Vivienne called after her.

"Who's he with?" Margaux asked, irritated, returning to reception.

Tony looked up at Margaux from his computer and got a shock. Her normally smooth and youthful features seemed suddenly much older and more lined.

"I thought he was supposed to be free this afternoon," Margaux's normally sugar-sweet voice was almost venom.

"Sylvia slipped a meeting in. I'm sure they wouldn't mind you joining them."

"I'm sure they wouldn't either!" Margaux snapped, causing Vivienne to blush.

Tony tried not to stare, but it seemed to him that the locks of her thick hair were carefully arranged to fall over her forehead and cover part of her face.

"I'll leave it for now," said Margaux. "Get Ralph to give me a call." She raced down the stairs.

"Is it me, or does she look much older than usual?" he asked.

Vivienne was about to respond when the phone rang on her desk.

"Yeah? Sure." She hung up and turned to Tony. "He wants you in there."

Tony got up and walked down the corridor, feeling nervous at the prospect of meeting the legendary Sylvia Henderson. Pull yourself together, he told himself. You have to get used to meeting celebrities. He knocked on the door and entered.

Sylvia was sitting opposite Ralph talking rapidly. "So I said to Cathal, get over the whole Joanne Bailey thing and concentrate on the feature you're doing on Affidavit."

"Is he very upset?" Ralph was concerned.

"Not with you, Ralph. He knows it wasn't a kiss and tell. He's just pissed off that she's getting publicity for her career on his back." She turned to Tony and put out her hand. "Hello."

Tony shook her hand. "Hi."

"Sylvia, this is Tony O'Brien. He's going to be spending some time with Affidavit over the next few days while Margaux and I are in New York. I'm so sorry we can't be there ourselves. It's just the Irish Ambassador is having a fund-raising party at Fitzpatrick's in New York and insisted we go – he's a very good friend of ours, you know."

"Margaux will be fitting in a bit of shopping as well, no doubt," said Sylvia. "Okay, you can just work away behind the scenes, Tony. I want the feature to heavily publicise the new album we've started working on. Now, Ralph, have you guaranteed it will make the front cover of *Hi Life* in the UK and Europe?"

"Definitely – I was only speaking to Victoria Harton today and she's very excited about it all," said Ralph

"Good. It should be excellent PR all around." She handed over her card to Tony. "Give me a shout if you've any problems."

Ralph opened his drawer and gave a handful of envelopes to Sylvia.

"What are these?" she asked, glancing through them and seeing them addressed to some of her most prominent acts.

"Invitations to the party of the year being held in Exclusive for Barry Curtis's birthday."

"I see." She opened the envelope addressed to herself and looked at the invite.

"If you could put a word in to make sure they all attend, I'd be grateful," pushed Ralph.

"I'll do my best. I won't be going myself though. I don't want to get associated with any political candidates."

Ralph looked at her curiously. She never went to any social do's and kept her life very much private. "This isn't just any political candidate, Sylvia; this is Barry Curtis."

"Just because he's loaded doesn't mean he's any better than the rest of them – probably worse in fact."

"Oh, Sylvia, you're so cynical!" Ralph shook his head and smiled.

"Too right . . . Ha!" She had just spotted an invitation addressed to Tina Cawley. "You can forget about her as well. I'm afraid she's far too busy getting in touch with her inner anger to go to something as superficial as this."

"Can't you force her?"

"No, Tina has her own mind," she sighed before adding, "unfortunately."

*   *   *

Nicole really felt the need to gently push Lana to open up about her family, especially her mother. But any time she attempted to do so, she was met with a brick wall. Unlike this new guy she was seeing, who she seemed very willing to talk about.

"Can I be honest with you?" Lana asked, looking concerned.

"I was hoping that was why you were seeing me."

"The guy I'm seeing isn't just Joe Bloggs. He's well known."

"In what way?"

"He's a member of Affidavit – Cathal Fitzgerald."

"I see." Nicole sat back surprised.

"You've heard of them?"

"Of course."

"You know, I hadn't. I mean, of course I'd heard of Affidavit, but I wouldn't have been able to give you the names of the band members or say what they looked like."

Lost in a privileged world of her own, our Lana, thought Nicole.

"Funnily enough, since we've started going out, I've gone out and bought their CDs and looked them up on the internet and everything."

"Understandable. And sometimes it can take a little while to get to know somebody we start a relationship with." Except for Tony, thought Nicole, who was such an open book she knew him inside out almost immediately. It was only recently that she felt he was becoming more complex.

"You know, I think he's the first person who hasn't just accepted and tolerated my behaviour because I'm Lana Curtis, who was born into such wealth that she can do anything she pleases without consequence. But he hasn't just dismissed me either for being selfish and spoilt, but has tried to get to know the real me and tried to get me to understand myself and see the potential that exists inside me."

Now we're getting places, thought Nicole.

*   *   *

After her therapy session Lana sat into her car and checked the messages on her phone. There were two from her father asking her to call him. She wondered what he wanted. Ever since the unfortunate incident with Gloria's credit card, she had steadfastly avoided visiting Kildara. The shame was too much for her to face. This in turn annoyed her, as she was literally handing free rein of Kildara over to Gloria.

She dialled her father's number.

"You were looking for me?"

"Yeah, I want to invite you to a party."

"Party?" She was perplexed.

"My birthday party. It's in Exclusive, your favourite. Will you come?"

"I'm not sure . . . I might be in London or –"

"It would mean a lot to me," Barry pushed.

She sighed. It was obviously important for her to be there as some strategy, no doubt devised by Gloria, especially since her mother wouldn't be there. But, how could she refuse? Her father never asked her for anything.

CHAPTER 23

"Right, I'd better go if we're to catch this plane," said Ralph. "Have you double-checked you haven't missed anyone on the invitation list I drew up for the Curtis party?"

"No, everyone has been included," Vivienne confirmed, trying to keep the irritation out of her voice. He had asked her the same question fifty times that day alone.

"Tony, when you finish doing that, you're going straight over to the MPI studio," said Ralph. "You're to give me a call if there are any problems at all."

"Of course," Tony agreed.

"Right, I'll see you in a few days."

"Have a nice time," said Vivienne.

They waited until he was safely down the corridor.

"Good riddance!" Vivienne whispered.

"You really can't stand him, can you?"

"Can you blame me? They are the most self-centred, snobby, egotistical people you could meet!"

"I suppose they are very connected and know lots of influential people."

"And don't they like the world to know!"

* * *

Nicole ate a chicken sandwich at her desk as she went through her notes. She was pleased with her work. She found her clients extremely challenging but she was progressing with them. Especially Lana. Her outlook on life had improved so much. And now she wanted her to feel comfortable with that outlook and herself before starting to delve further into her life.

She picked up the phone and called Tony to wish him luck starting work with Affidavit that day. She was consumed with guilt over not being happier for him in Exclusive the other night. This was his dream come true and she should be more supportive. But she also was alarmed to see the change in him and she resolved to do everything to make things like they were before between them.

"Hi, where are you now?" she asked when he answered his mobile.

"Outside MPI's studio, just about to go in, and feeling nervous."

"Why?"

"Well, before, Ralph was always there or Margaux, but I'm on my own now."

"You'll be fine. You know how talented a writer you are."

"Yeah, but it's meeting all these people is intimidating me a little. Ralph and Margaux are so at ease with celebrities. I'm not."

"It's just practice, that's all."

"Thanks, Nic. Anyway I've walked into reception so I'll phone you later. Love ya." He hung up.

*   *   *

Cathal turned off his mobile and shook his head, smiling.

"Who were you talking to?" asked James, coming down the corridor.

"Just Lana."

"I thought you'd have given her her marching orders by now."

"No way. We're enjoying ourselves too much."

"Aren't you frightened the press will get wind of it? Like what happened with Joanne?"

"No – Lana's more paranoid about being spotted together than I am."

James handed Cathal an envelope. "Speaking of which, Sylvia asked me to give you this. It's an invitation to Lana's father's birthday party. It's going to be the party of the year seemingly – aren't they all?"

"Are you going?" Cathal asked, opening the envelope and looking at the invite.

"I'll have to check with Donna."

"Excuse me," said a voice behind them. "I'm Tony O'Brien from *Hi Life*."

"Oh yeah, Sylvia said you were going to spend a bit of time with us doing the feature. I'm Cathal and this is James."

"Eh, hi," Tony said awkwardly.

"I hope you're not going to do some nasty exposé on us," James said and winked.

"Hardly, with the sugary features we do," laughed Tony.

"Come on into the studio. I hope you like Affidavit,

because otherwise you'll be bored listening to us over the next couple of days' recording."

*   *   *

Tony looked at his watch. It was nearly ten o'clock. He hadn't left the studio all day. He had sat on the sidelines, fascinated, as he watched Affidavit record. They worked so hard, and when they got it right the music was excellent, but when the numerous mistakes or difficulties emerged tempers would fly.

"Oh, for fuck's sake!" roared Rob, interrupting the rhythm of music as he threw his drumsticks on the floor.

"What's wrong now?" asked James, turning around exasperated to him.

"Is it only me or does nobody else think that we were off-key with that last piece?" Rob was angry.

"Do you know what I think?" asked Cathal, looking equally irritated. "I think you hate this song, because it's not your song, and nothing is going to make you like this song and so you're just looking for excuses to disrupt us from recording the fucking thing and finishing the fucking day's recording!"

"Are you accusing me of sabotaging?"

"That's exactly what I'm accusing you of."

"You'd want to watch what you're saying, Cathal," Rob snapped.

"Gentlemen, please!" Sylvia marched into the studio. "In case you had forgotten, you have a member of the press in your presence."

They all looked over at Tony.

"He's reporting for *Hi Life*," said Seán. "He's hardly going to report we all hate each other."

294

Cathal was surprised by Seán's comment. Did they?

"It's late. Why don't you all go home and start again tomorrow?" advised Sylvia.

"I'm going home to my wife and child. At least I'll get some peace with them," said Rob, marching off.

The others started tidying away their stuff.

"That was a bit strong – saying we hate each other," Cathal said to Seán.

"We're hardly the best of mates any more, are we?"

"Aren't we?"

"Wake up and smell the coffee, Cathal. You and James may still be close, being family and all, but the magic is gone from the rest of this band. Rob hates the music we are recording and as for you and me . . . well."

"Let's go for a drink and try and get to the bottom of what's wrong," suggested Cathal.

"Forget it. I've more important things to do with my time."

Cathal felt as if he had been slapped across the face.

*   *   *

Tony tried unsuccessfully to flag down a taxi as he came out of the studio. Then he phoned home.

"Tony, where have you been ? I've been worried sick about you!"

"I'm so sorry. I was in the studio with Affidavit all day. Can you believe that? I had to keep my phone off."

"You could have popped out and phoned me. I cooked us a beef meal and yours is all ruined now."

"Oh sorry, love. But I wouldn't have eaten it anyway with this diet I'm on. You know, I think I've lost a couple of pounds. And Diana is getting me sorted to join a gym next week."

"You! In a gym !"

"No pain, no gain!"

*   *   *

"You know, I think I nearly hate him at this stage," said Seán. He was in his townhouse having dinner with Joanne.

"Because of the way he treated me?" Joanne asked, casting her eyes down in a shy manner.

"Yeah, but not just that. The way Cathal treats everybody. He railroads over everybody to get his own way, but pretends to be everyone's friend at the same time. He's done it with us for years. He slowly took over the management of the band and started making the decisions, and we were so busy making good music that we allowed him that role and that power."

"It's Diana Ross and the Supremes all over again!" said Joanne, shaking her head sadly.

"He doesn't care that Rob and James are not happy with the music MPI are forcing us to make for this album. All he's concerned with is getting the album out and keeping the whole show rolling so he can continue basking in the limelight."

"Well, you just remember you owe him nothing. The only one you owe loyalty to is yourself – and me, of course."

"I can't wait to see his face when he realises we're seeing each other. Why don't we tell eveybody about us now?"

She reached out across the glass dining-table "Soon, my darling, but not just yet. The timing has to be right."

"When were you thinking?"

Joanne picked up the invitation for the Curtis party

which Seán had shown her earlier

"Maybe we should arrive together for this party? That would give the press something to photograph, wouldn't it?"

* * *

"I've had such a lovely night," said Lana as she and Cathal curled up in bed.

"I'm glad you did." He hugged her tightly.

"Are you all right, Cathal – you seem kind of distant tonight."

"Just this album, it's causing so many problems. I kind of had an argument with Seán tonight. Anyway, I don't want to think about that. Let's change the subject. Do you think your father will get elected?"

"I don't know," she shrugged.

"You don't sound very excited. My God, if my father was running for public office I'd be excited!"

"That's because it would be so out of the ordinary for your father to do that. Ever since I can remember, my father has been doing amazing things. I just accept it and expect it now."

"I got an invitation to his birthday party today," Cathal informed her.

"You did?" She sat up quickly and rested on her elbow. "How did that happen?"

He chuckled. "I'm a member of Affidavit – I get an invitation to the opening of a bin in this town."

"I see." She lay on her back and looked at the ceiling.

He looked over at her. "You never mentioned the party. Are you going?"

"Ah . . . I'm not sure . . . I suppose so . . ." Her voice was cool.

He tried to fathom her. "Would you like me to go?"

"Why would you want to?"

"I'm not saying I do."

"It's just that this is nice, isn't it, the way we are – with nobody knowing about us. Why would we want to ruin that?" Lana seemed uncomfortable.

"Wouldn't you ever like me to meet your mum and dad?"

"You know my family are very busy and – well, why bother?"

Cathal looked at her and half-smiled. "I hope you're not saying I'm not good enough to meet them?" He put out an arm to embrace her.

"Why are we having this ridiculous conversation?" Lana pulled away from him. "Of course, I'm not saying that. But what's the point?"

"My God, I was only joking but I think I hit a grain of truth there. *Do* you think I'm not good enough to meet them." He looked angry.

"You're being ridiculous!"

He jumped out of bed and pulled on his jeans. "I get it. Obviously because I don't come from the same background as you, I'm not good enough!"

"Of course not!"

"No way will I get to meet your mum and dad – that's the story, isn't it? They'll look down their noses at me. I might have money and some degree of fame, but I'm still not good enough!"

"Will you calm down and –"

"No, I fucking won't! Answer me truthfully, Lana: have you never had those thoughts about me?"

"All right, all right – maybe when I met you first, I did. But now I've got to know you, I admire you so much more than somebody who was born into it like me. You've done it yourself and –"

Cathal became very angry. "That's why you kept running away from me when we first met?"

"I ran away from everybody then!"

"I refuse to allow you to look down on me! I refuse to allow you –" he tried to control his anger, "to look at me as in any way inferior."

"I don't –"

"Who the fuck are you to try and be superior to anybody? Look at yourself! You're a fucked-up junkie!" He turned and stormed off into the lounge.

Lana sat on the bed, a tear rolling down her face, totally wounded by his words. Just go, she told herself. Walk out and leave him. How dare he? But she didn't want to leave him. And that felt very strange to her. Not wanting to run away as soon as the going got tough. Not wanting to grab the nearest bottle of vodka or line of coke to help ease the pain.

She tried to understand how he had reacted like that. Then she remembered about Michelle back in Castletown and how inferior she had made him feel and how people had looked down on him back then. She got up, put on a dressing-gown and walked into the lounge. She saw Cathal sitting on the couch, staring down at the ground. She went over and sat on the coffee table in front of him and took his hands.

"I have problems with my family," she said. "I've had them for years. I'm not close to them . . . I wish I was. I'd love to be as close to them as you are to yours, but I'm not. So no, I wouldn't feel comfortable introducing you to them right now. And that's nothing to do with you or who you are. I just don't feel I can let them into this part of my life.

I'm sorry if you got the impression I didn't think you were good enough. That's not true." She squeezed his hand tightly.

He stared at her for a while and then squeezed her hand back.

CHAPTER 24

Over the next couple of days, Tony spent as much time with Affidavit as possible. He tried to grab conversations with them when he could during breaks in recording.

Having coffee with Rob in the canteen, he asked: "How are you finding combining fatherhood with making the new album?"

"To be honest, the baby screaming all night and changing nappies at three in the morning is child's play compared to making this album."

Tony stopped scribbling down notes and looked up at Rob. "I'll just say you're finding the two roles challenging, but you're enjoying the new experience of fatherhood more, will I?"

"If that's what your readers want to hear, fire ahead." Rob sat back in his chair and folded his arms.

"Your management has said this new album is going to take Affidavit into a new direction. Are you excited about that and can you tell us a little about that new direction?"

"Oh, man! The management speaks shit! The management are ramming crap songs onto our album to sell records."

"I see." Again Tony stopped writing and twiddled his pen. "Will I rephrase that to something like . . . MPI have been playing a very hands-on role on the new album and you've selected some excellent songs together?"

"Whatever!" Rob yawned.

*   *   *

Tony found James talking on his mobile in the corridor.

"Okay, Donna, I'll see you later." James turned off his mobile.

"Er, James, I wonder could I have a few words with you? I just haven't managed to speak to you alone at all yet."

"Sure." James opened the door beside him and, seeing the room was empty, they went inside and closed the door.

"If it's okay I'll put the dictaphone on while we speak – I can do notes from it later."

James nodded.

"James, you're the person who first thought of the idea of Affidavit and put the band together all those years ago. It must give you a particular sense of satisfaction to see how far you've come."

"You know it does. We've come a long way."

"But you never lose sight of where you come from?"

"Not at all. I could never be away from Ireland for long and it gives me great pleasure to get home."

"You're now seeing the model Donna McCarthy. There has been talk of a wedding next year – anything confirmed yet ?"

"Well, yeah, here's an exclusive for you – we're hoping to get married next June. She's out shopping for wedding dresses as we speak."

Tony's face lit up. "Thanks for that, James – that's a brilliant exclusive."

"My pleasure."

"So what kind of wedding do you want?"

"I would like to say we just want a small family wedding, but both of us have so many friends in show business it wouldn't be right not inviting them."

"And I suppose there will be another tour once the album has finished?"

"I guess so. MPI will insist on it. Though I'll want to spend more time with Donna. And also I've started writing more music with Rob, so who knows where the future will take us."

* * *

"So is this going to be done like just a normal friendly chat, but you'll be recording it and taking parts for the feature later?" checked Seán.

"Yeah, if that's okay?" Tony turned on the tape. "Seán, when it comes to publicity, you tend to keep your private life private. We all know about Rob and Heidi, and James and Donna, and Cathal's love-life has been well documented, but you prefer to keep out of the headlines. Anyone special at the moment?"

"There is actually."

"What's her name ?"

"I'm not going to disclose that at the moment. We're trying to keep it private for now."

"Your fans would love to know."

"They'll have to stay in the dark for another while. But I will say that I've never felt so strongly about anybody in the past."

"So you're ready for settling down?"

"Maybe, if she accepts me."

"How will that affect your commitments to Affidavit and the heavy touring schedules?"

"Well, I think there comes a time in everyone's life where they have to make decisions about where they want their lives to go. We've all worked like dogs over the years but I guess every dog has its day. You have to remind yourself what is right for you now."

"And what's right for you now?"

"For me to put me first. To put my personal life first."

"And your career to come second?"

"If it has to, yes."

*   *   *

Tony put on the dictaphone. "Cathal, you're the one in the group who's always seemed to get the most media attention – would that be fair to say?"

"I guess so. I never seek it; it just kind of happens."

"Does it annoy you?"

"Sometimes, like when I'm out in a nightclub or something and next thing a photo appears the next day – that can really piss me off."

"What about the new album? Are you pleased with it so far?"

"I'm delighted with it. It's the best we've done so far."

"And are you ready to tour next year again?"

"Of course. We're all really looking forward to touring again."

"It's great you're still so enthusiastic about the band after all this time."

"It's my life. I love it and so do we all. The four of us

are one hundred per cent committed to the band and committed to putting the band first before everything else. Because that's what's got us to the top and what will keep us at the top."

*   *   *

Tony pushed the door of the *Hi Life* building open and ran up the stairs, carrying loads of paperwork under his arm. He stopped suddenly when he reached reception at the sight that greeted him.

Vivienne was sitting back on her chair, her legs up on her desk, a bottle of gin on her desk and a glass in her hand.

"Oh, hi !" she said, raising her glass. "Are you finished over at the studio for the day?"

"Er, yeah." He walked slowly over to his desk.

"Good ! Then you can join me in a drink." She held up the bottle of gin.

"I don't think I will." He sat down at his desk, feeling disturbed. He had only ever seen Vivienne composed before.

"Oh, don't be stupid! Ralph and Maggie are in New York – they aren't going to catch us. They work us fucking hard enough usually, don't they ? Let's relax while we can."

"I might as well have one." Tony took the glass from his desk and held it out to her and she poured in some gin, then topped it up with tonic, before putting her feet back up on her desk.

She raised her glass. "Let's drink to Maggie's facelift!"

"Facelift?" Tony was confused.

"That's what they've gone over for, you know. All this ambassador's guest story, my arse! They've gone over for herself to have a facelift."

"I don't believe it!"

"It's true." She crossed her heart. "She goes over every few months for this special treatment they do on her face. It's excellent – it should be – it costs a fortune. It only has one problem – every few months it gives out and she ages ten years overnight. You must have seen her the day she came in before they headed off."

Tony nodded enthusiastically. "I saw she looked much older."

"That's why. But she'll look all young again in time for the Curtis party and they can be the centre of attention and mix with all their rich and famous friends. And I use that word 'friends' in the loosest possible terms."

"Why do you call her Maggie behind her back?"

"Because that's who she is or at least who she was. Maggie Doyle from some foul slum somewhere."

Tony's mouth dropped open.

"I know, hard to believe, isn't it? With the way she looks and dresses and that posh accent, you would swear she was royalty. And he's no better. They started at the bottom and crawled their way up. He started working for some magazine. They saved every penny they could – you know how tight they are, and finally went out on their own."

"I'm gobsmacked!"

"I know, so was I. And you know, I would really admire them apart from the fact they became really horrible and reinvented themselves and became these horrible snobs."

"It's amazing they managed to come so far and that they had the same target in life."

"Oh, they had the same target all right, to be at the top

and look down on everyone else. Of course they nearly went off target a few times."

"How so?"

Vivienne knocked back her gin. "A little case of Ralph's affairs along the way."

"Affairs?"

"Sure, remember Gina who worked here before you? You met her when you came in for the interview? They were having it off for years. Maggie came in like the north wind one day and fired her and kicked her out. Still it's an ill north wind that doesn't blow somebody some good – you got her job!"

*   *   *

"Tony?" called Nicole as she came down the stairs. It was three in the morning and she had awoken to find Tony not in bed.

The lights in the sitting-room were on and Tony was sitting at the table, concentrating on his laptop screen.

"Tony what are you doing?"

"I'm just looking up property on the internet," he said, not taking his eyes from the screen.

"Property? What are you talking about?"

"Property. A house for us to buy, or an apartment. We've been renting long enough. I think we should seriously start looking for something to buy, don't you ?"

"Yes, but why are you looking for something at three in the morning?"

"The way they describe houses is hilarious. Listen to this – they say this house has great personality. Isn't that a weird way to describe a house? It makes it sound like an ad in a personal column or something. They'll be

307

describing houses as having a great sense of humour next."

"Tony, don't you think you're putting the cart before the horse? We have no mortgage approval whatsoever, and we haven't even been saving for a deposit or anything."

"Do you know something, Vivienne was telling me today that the Conways are from real working-class backgrounds and worked their way up to where they are now. I was shocked. I mean they act as if they were born to it. And if you see where *they've* got to in life, imagine where *we* could get to!"

CHAPTER 25

Tina Cawley sat in Sylvia's office, arms crossed, legs crossed and chewing gum.

"So I've decided to go to India for a while."

"India?" Sylvia was incredulous. "I'm waiting for you to start writing music for an album and you're going to India?"

"That's what I said, didn't I?"

"Why are you going to India?"

"I feel a calling."

"And you're answering, I suppose?"

"Smart bitch," Tina muttered under her breath.

"Sorry?"

"An itch," said Tina. "Me going to India is like an itch that needs to be scratched."

"Well, could you scratch it another time and start concentrating on music, please? All that anger and anguish in you must surely need to be directed into your art."

"I'm sorry. I've made up my mind. I feel by going on a spiritual tour of India I will be able to discover my inner light – in turn, that will bring my music to a higher plane."

"So you'll be writing music while you're out there?"

"Only if the calling happens – but if that makes you feel better, think of me out there creating beautiful music."

"Tina, I don't know what to say to you. Do you know how many people would love to be in your position now, signed up to a major label?"

"Well, go sign them and then everyone will be happy. I can't live my life on other people's terms – I have to be true to myself."

"All right – all right – I'm going to give you six weeks to go to India and discover your inner light, but that's it, Tina. You have to realise this is a business and you have to play by the rules. I want a follow-up to *I Enjoy The Rain*."

Tina yawned. "So gracious of you." She picked up an envelope on the table and opened it. "What's this?"

"An invitation to Barry Curtis's birthday party at Exclusive. I told them you wouldn't be going."

"Maybe I might want to go."

"Hardly your scene, I would have thought."

"There are many facets to me."

"Ain't that a fact!"

*   *   *

Cathal came into the canteen at MPI. as the canteen woman was busy cleaning the shelves before she headed off for the evening.

Grabbing a coffee from the machine, he looked around and saw Tony over at a corner table, scribbling away.

"Do you mind if I join you?" Cathal asked.

"Er, no." Tony was surprised and started clearing away his notes. "I'm just trying to get some stuff together for the feature."

310

Cathal sat down opposite him. "How's it going anyway?"

"Really good, so far. You've all been great – thanks for all the help."

"I guess some people you interview are fairly egotistical," said Cathal, thinking about Seán.

"Yeah, you know yourself." Tony put down his pen. "Actually, I've only started this job a while back, and you're really only the second feature I've worked on."

"Really? Fair play to you – you're very on the ball with everything."

"Do you think so?" Tony was delighted.

"Yeah, totally. You observe and take everything in, but aren't being pushy or too obvious. I sometimes think it's journalists who think they are the real stars."

"There you are! I was looking for you everywhere!" James had come into the canteen. "Come on, Donna's already at the restaurant and the table is booked for 8.30."

"Okay." Cathal stood up and started to follow James, before turning back to Tony. "We're going out for something to eat, maybe catch a club later. Do you want to join us?"

"Er . . . I had planned to go home." Tony thought for a second. "Sure, why not?"

* * *

The taxi pulled up outside Shannahans On The Green. They walked into the restaurant and saw Donna with a friend sitting beside her.

"How's everyone?" James said, kissing Donna.

"Fine," said Donna. "This is Jayne who's working with me on a shoot at the moment." The smiling girl beside her was obviously a model. "Hi, all," she said.

Cathal nodded and sat down, aware that his cousin and Donna were obviously trying to set him up with Jayne. "This is Tony," he said.

Donna looked up at Tony. "Oh, hello, sorry, I didn't realise you were joining us. I thought you were waiting for an autograph or something."

"I just have to make a quick phone call," said Tony, irritated by her comment. Then seeing the waiter hovering, he said: "Order something for me, Cathal, will you?" Reaching for his mobile he headed out of the dining room.

"Why did you ask him along?" asked James.

"Why not? He's a nice guy and we're working with him."

Tony didn't feel like staying. He felt excluded from this circle and awkward. You have to stay, he told himself, and this is what your life is going to be about in future. He dialled his home number.

"Hi, Nic, it's me."

"Where are you? I was expecting you back ages ago."

"Yeah, look, I'm sorry, I had to go out for dinner with the guys from Affidavit."

"Oh . . . I see."

"It's part of the job, love. I have to make them comfortable enough to open up to me and so they have to get to know me and trust me."

"I understand . . . What time will you be home?"

"I'll come home straight after dinner."

"Okay, I can't wait to see you."

"Yeah, me too," said Tony. He headed back to the table.

"I just loved your last song!" gushed Jayne.

"You're about the only one who did!" said Cathal.

312

"Oh, you're so funny!" Jayne started to laugh loudly.

"Tony is writing the feature about us for *Hi Life* magazine," said Cathal to the table at large.

"Oh really?" Donna put down her menu and flashed a megawatt smile at him. "You must be new there, are you?"

"Yeah."

"How are Ralph and Margaux?"

"They're in New York at the moment."

"They're brilliant, aren't they? They've been so good to me along the way, you can't imagine." Donna adopted a grateful expression.

"I can imagine, yes."

"I love *Hi Life*," said Jayne, smiling over at Tony. "There's nothing I like more than curling up in front of the fire with a bar of chocolate and a copy of it."

Tony looked at the woman who looked as if she had never eaten chocolate in her life.

"I'm starving!" said Cathal as their starters arrived. "I ordered a warm chicken salad for you, Tony, okay?"

"Great."

"Jayne's just after landing a big contract with L'Oreal, Cathal," said Donna.

"Well done!" said Cathal.

"I'd love to take a look around the studios where you're recording," said Jayne. "Maybe you could invite me in?"

"I don't believe it!" said Donna looking over at the entrance.

Lana and Patricia were entering the restaurant.

"Who's that?" asked Jayne.

"The blonde one is Patricia, a friend of mine. The other one is Lana Curtis," Donna looked at Cathal, "a floating gin palace"

"She likes her drink?" asked Jayne.

"Let's just put it this way – if they cremated her it would take three days to put out the fire."

*   *   *

"I haven't eaten here for ages," said Lana, handing her coat over to a waiter at the door.

"Really? I had lunch here the other day." Just then Patricia spotted Donna and waved to her. "How are you?" She went over to Donna, who stood up and they kissed each other on both cheeks.

Lana froze as she saw Cathal.

"You're back from your shoot in South Africa?" asked Patricia. "How was it ?"

"Very tiring," said Donna."The director was a bastard who forced us to get up at five each morning to catch the sunrise on film." She tossed back her mane of honey-blonde hair. "This is Jayne, Patricia, who was working on the shoot with me."

Deciding Patricia was an advertising executive who could put work her way, Jayne smiled broadly at her and shook her hand.

Lana and Cathal looked at each other and smiled.

"You know my friend Lana?" said Patricia.

Donna sat down and nodded. "We've met."

Lana, remembering the comments she had overheard the morning she stayed at Donna's house, stared icily at her.

Patricia glanced around the table. "And James and Cathal! The gang's all here! Why don't we get them to join the tables and we can all have dinner together?"

"Good idea," said Donna.

314

Patricia went off to find a waiter.

Donna looked at Lana. "I suppose we'd better order more wine in that case."

Patricia arrived back with two waiters and they set about putting the tables together. Tony was glad of the distraction. He felt even more uncomfortable since the overbearing Patricia and Lana Curtis joined them. He was in way over his head with these people.

Still, he had to try. When they were all seated again, he turned to Lana. "Are you all set for your father's big party next week?"

"Should be a bit of fun," Lana answered, watching how Jayne was intent on trying to isolate Cathal in a private conversation. She felt the whole situation was odd. Patricia, James and Donna were the only people in the world aware that she and Cathal were seeing each other. Tony and Jayne hadn't a clue. So they had to pretend nothing was going on.

"There's a surprise!" Donna smiled. "You out for a bit of fun!"

If you think I'm going to let you sit here and be a bitch to me, you've got another think coming, thought Lana. She looked at Donna with an amused smile. "Oh, sorry, I forgot you're a model. I suppose your days are filled with serious issues like breaking nails and false tan streaking."

Patricia, sensing trouble, jumped in. "Has anyone seen the new play in the Gaiety? Amazing!"

"You know, I used to kiss you every night before I went to sleep," Jayne said, looking seductively at Cathal. "I used to have a poster of you on my bedroom wall."

"Really?"

She reached forward and stroked his hand. "I always dreamed of meeting you."

315

Cathal pulled his hand away and sat back in his chair.

Jayne's mobile rang and she answered it.

Lana, seizing the moment, leant back in her chair and said to Cathal behind James' back, "Who's your friend?"

"She isn't a friend," Cathal whispered back.

Lana threw her napkin on the table and walked off to the toilets.

Cathal waited a moment before going out after her. He paced up and down the corridor, waiting for her to come out.

"Oh, hi," said Lana as she emerged. "I'm so sorry to have interrupted your cosy little dinner date."

"How could it be a dinner date with three other people there?"

"Well, I think somebody should tell Jayne that."

"Oh Lana!" He went to hold her.

"Fuck off!" she snapped.

He saw an exit door out the back. "Come on out here and we'll talk."

*   *   *

Nicole sat at home looking at the clock and feeling increasingly worried.

What was happening to Tony, to her relationship, her life? She had to be honest with herself and realise he was changing so much. The man who loved nothing more that curling up with her and a pizza was now happier having dinner out with Affidavit. She needed to talk to him. She picked up her mobile.

* * *

"Now what's wrong?" asked Cathal as they stood out in the back alleyway.

"That silly bitch is touching your hand constantly and flirting with you."

"I get a lot of that being who I am."

"I just feel we're in some kind of strange half-relationship. I mean, understand where I'm coming from. Sitting at the same table with you and that going on."

"I do understand. Okay, I honestly didn't know she would be there. Donna obviously brought her along to try and set us up."

"But does Donna not realise we're seeing each other?"

"Of course she does."

"Then she's being an absolute bitch!"

"They're just concerned that we're not suited to each other."

"Tell them to get over it – haven't they got their own wedding to organise or something? Jayne seems like the type you've always gone out with before."

Cathal sighed. "She probably is the type I went out with."

"So why don't you just go off with her now and we can all just get on with our own lives?"

"Do you know how boring she is compared to you? She's just another model on the make. I've never met anybody like you before."

"I'm sorry for being emotional. But I've never let myself get this close to somebody before."

"I know." He reached out and hugged her.

*   *   *

Tony's phone rang and he saw it was his home number. "Excuse me for a second, please." He got up and headed out of the dining-room. "Hello?"

"Hi, Tony, it's me."

The reception was poor and her voice sounded muffled.

"What's up, Nic?"

"Just wondered when you'd be home?"

"We're still on the main course. There are some real good contacts here."

"I know, and I'm glad for you, but I just got to wondering when was the last time we actually went out for dinner, other than to your parents' on a Sunday afternoon?"

He could barely hear what she was saying. "Hold on. It's a bad signal in here." He opened the back exit door and stepped into the alley, only to be confronted with the sight of Cathal and Lana kissing passionately.

They both turned their heads and stared at him, shocked.

"Oh, I'm s-s-s-sorry," stuttered Tony, retreating quickly back into the building. "Shit, Nicole, I just walked into something I shouldn't have." He was flustered. "I'd better go. I'll talk to you later." He turned off his phone and quickly made his way back to the table.

*   *   *

Tony let himself into their house. The rest of the evening had passed in a strange discomfort. Cathal and

Lana had been cautious with him. Donna and James had been openly hostile to Lana who was well able to defend herself. Jayne had been embarrassingly flirtatious with Cathal and Patricia had been oblivious to everything.

As he came in, he threw his keys down on the sideboard.

"You're back very late," commented Nicole. "But what happened earlier when you hung up on me?"

"Ah, for fuck's sake, I'm after making a major boo-boo."

"How?"

"When you rang me I went out the back of the restaurant to get a better signal and caught Barry Curtis's daughter Lana and Cathal Fitzgerald snogging the faces off each other."

"Oh!" Nicole relaxed. "Is that all?"

"What do you mean – is that all? I walked into something that I wasn't meant to see."

"So what?"

"You obviously can't see the repercussions of all this. If it got out to the press they were seeing each other it would be a major story – daughter of one of Ireland's richest men and the member of one of our most successful bands."

"But it's not going to get out." Nicole felt strange that she had personally known the secret for ages.

"I'm a member of the press and both of them are going to be hostile to me in case I tell their secret."

"But you aren't, are you?"

"Of course not. But they aren't going to believe that. Fuck's sake! They're powerful people – they might organise to have me fired or something."

"You are being utterly paranoid and ridiculous. Just take Cathal Fitzgerald aside tomorrow and tell him you won't tell anybody."

"And he's going to believe that, from a member of the press?"

"Look, I wanted to talk to you about a few things tonight, but I'm too tired by this stage and you obviously are a little more concerned about Cathal Fitzgerald and Lana Curtis to concentrate on anything I have to say." She walked to the staircase. "Are you coming up?"

He was pouring himself a drink. "I'll be up in a short while. I need to think about all this and chill out with a drink."

*   *   *

"Will he say anything?" asked Lana as she drove them back to her house.

"I'll have a word with him tomorrow. Tony seems a decent enough kind of fella."

"This is all very weird for me. I'm used to doing whatever I want whenever I want without giving a thought about anything. Suddenly I'm dating somebody famous and we have to hide all the time in case people find out."

"Welcome to being a public figure." He reached over and rubbed her leg.

"But it feels so strange. I feel I have to watch what I do and say for the first time in my life. How do you cope with the attention all the time?"

"People leave you alone most of the time. You kind of have private time and public time and learn to separate them. We are private time."

CHAPTER 26

"Do you mind if I have a word?" asked Cathal as he found Tony writing in the studio's canteen.

Tony looked up, embarrassed. "Sure."

"Did you enjoy last night?"

"Yeah, thanks for inviting me."

"No probs. Listen, I wanted to have a quick word with you about what you saw in the alley."

"That's none of my business, Cathal. I won't say a word to anyone."

"I would appreciate that. It's just it's early days and we don't want too much attention, to give us some breathing space."

"I totally understand. I'm not a member of the gutter press. I'm a feature writer."

"Thanks, Tony," Cathal stood up. "We're all going to Exclusive tomorrow night – why don't you come along?"

*   *   *

"His cousin James and this bitch of a girlfriend called Donna obviously can't stand me," Lana confided to Nicole.

"What makes you say that?"

"Well, first of all, in the early days before anything happened between me and Cathal, I stayed over at their house and overheard them talking about me. It left me in no doubt of their opinion of me. And last night at dinner she was really hostile to me and he was barely civil."

"How does that make you feel?"

"I couldn't give a fuck. I'm going out with Cathal not them. But they obviously care a great deal about Cathal and think I'm bad for him."

Nicole toyed with her pen. "And who else was out to dinner last night?"

"This model who flirted outrageously with Cathal all night."

"What was she like?"

"She was like Arizona – you wouldn't want to go there. But it didn't stop her demanding Cathal's attention. Myself and Cathal ended up arguing out the back of the restaurant and then we made up – and then this guy from *Hi Life* who was also having dinner with us came out the back for some reason and caught us kissing, stupid idiot!"

Nicole coughed slightly in surprise. "And then what happened?"

"He apologised and went back in. We were obviously concerned he might talk about us. Cathal said he'd have a word with him today – the last thing we want is for our relationship to be in the papers . . . or so we said."

"What do you mean?"

"Well, when I saw that silly bitch flirt with Cathal, I wanted to shout over: 'Hands off. He's mine!'"

"Do you think the guy from the magazine will say anything? Is he the kind of guy who would say it?"

"I haven't a clue. He was just insipid, in the

background."

"I see." Nicole blinked a couple of times. "Did you drink much last night?"

"Only a glass of wine."

"You weren't tempted to get hammered?"

"No, I was too busy making sure that Cathal stayed away from Jayne."

That's good, thought Nicole; she cares about more things now then just being pissed.

*   *   *

Tony helped bring Clive's equipment down the corridor to the studio.

"Thank God, Ralph and Maggie aren't here anyway. I can take the photographs without those two getting in my way." He swung through the doors. "Hello, everybody!"

"Hi, Clive!" said Cathal. "How are you keeping?"

"Struggling." He put down his equipment.

Tony quickly guessed from the friendly banter that they had all met Clive numerous times before.

"Right, lads, you know the kind of thing I want," said Clive. "At the beginning I'm just going to take your photos as you're recording, so I want to make them look as authentic as possible. And later I'll take some of you relaxing around the studios, okay?"

*   *   *

Kathryn stood at the door of Exclusive, talking to Simeon on her mobile.

"Did you take the sleeping pill I left out for you?"

"Yeah, I took it an hour ago, but it's had no effect on

me." Simeon's voice was low and depressed.

"Where are you now?"

"Just lying in bed in the darkness."

Kathryn felt a knot in her stomach from anxiety. He was really in a bad way this time. She couldn't remember him being this low for so long. Every time she came home she expected him to have bounced into hyperactivity or off on his adventures for a few days. But this time he was in such a dark pit of despair.

She saw two cars pulling up at the footpath and recognised some of the guys from Affidavit as they stepped out. "Listen, I'm going to have to go now, but I won't delay tonight after work. I'll be back as soon as possible."

"Okay." He hung up the phone.

"Busy tonight, Kathryn?" asked Cathal as he came up the steps.

"Yeah, a nice crowd. Hi, James, hi, Seán. Clive, we haven't seen you for a while."

"Too busy working or being broke."

"Aren't we all!" said Kathryn, smiling.

The fifth guy was Tony O'Brien. They gave each other a cool nod.

She thought it was strange how the man she had turfed out previously, so she could give his table to Affidavit, was now sharing their table. He obviously held a grudge. If he wanted to be cool with her, she could be twice as cool back.

"Follow me up to the members' lounge," she said, leading them inside. Upstairs she beckoned a hostess over. "The first bottle of champagne is on the house," she said.

"Thanks, Kathryn," said Cathal, sitting down.

"If I sit down I won't be thrown out halfway through the evening?" Tony whispered sarcastically to her.

"Not if you observe house rules and do what the management ask," she said back coolly, "and that goes for whatever company you're in, or whoever you work for."

*   *   *

All the guys had been ordering bottles of champagne all night. Tony remembered reading recently about a French champagne house who objected to all the American rap stars quaffing their precious product, feeling they were giving a down-market image to their brand. As Tony looked at all the empty bottles of champagne around the members' lounge, he thought the product had descended from a drink for the refined to a drink that merely reflected bling culture. Especially since Affidavit were half-filling their glasses with champagne and then topping them up with Red Bull. Glancing at the price list, he nearly passed out when he saw the cheapest one available. But it was his turn and so he reached for his credit card and beckoned over the hostess.

Cathal leaned over to Tony and whispered, "Look, nobody expects you to buy a round here. You're here as Affidavit's guest."

"No, fair's fair. It's my round."

"Put your card away. Just make sure we all look good in print, okay? And thanks again for not saying anything about me and Lana. I told her today and she was pretty relieved."

"Of course I won't tell anyone. It must be hard having a relationship under those circumstances."

"It's harder having one under the glare of publicity."

"I guess."

Tony spotted Kathryn gliding through the members'

bar. "I don't like Kathryn Foy much," he suddenly felt the
need to say.

"Kathryn's all right. She's just come up the hard way in
a man's world and making sure she stays at the top and if
that means treading on toes, she doesn't care."

"She trod on my toes once. She fucked me out of here."

"Did she?" Cathal laughed lightly. "Yeah I had a run in
myself once and she's made of stern stuff all right. We
made up though. One of the advantages of being in the
position I'm in – people want to stay friendly with you."

"Do you think people just like you because of who you
are?"

"It just comes as part of the territory." Cathal took the
fresh bottle of champagne from the hostess, telling her to
put it on his bill. He then started filling everyone's glass.
"There, that might put a smile on your face," he said to
Seán who was next to him, as he filled his glass.

"Are you trying to be clever?" snapped Seán.

"No, it's just you look pissed off," said Cathal quietly.
"Do you want to tell me what's up?"

"You, that's what's up," sneered Seán. "You're so up
your own arse, I can't stand being around you any more."

Cathal was shocked. "How has it come to this? We
used to really get on."

"People get on with you, Cathal, when they do what
you want. After that you're not interested."

"All right, Seán." Cathal sat back in his chair. "I've
really tried hard with you for months now and I'm not
going to bother any more. You have some problem with
me, but it's your problem, and we're stuck in this band
together so you'll just have to get on with it. But I'm not
taking any more of your rudeness or your crap."

"Well, don't then," Seán jumped up and walked off.

*   *   *

It was nearly three in the morning when Nicole heard Tony's key in the lock. She put aside the notes she was working on as he came in.

"Hey love!" he said as he walked over to her and kissed her. She realised he'd had a few drinks. "You had work to do?"

"Not really, but I thought I'd better get through some paperwork while I waited for you."

"You shouldn't have bothered waiting up for me."

"I waited up for you, Tony, because I feel we need to talk."

"What about?"

"About us and what's been happening to us since you started working at that damned magazine."

"What are you talking about?"

"Slowly but surely you're changing into somebody else."

"Somebody else? Do you mean somebody who is actually happy with what they do for a living?"

She rubbed her temples. "Look, I know how much this job means to you and how long you've needed the break but it's like it's taking over your life."

"I am dedicated to a job I enjoy. What is your problem with that?"

"The man I used to relax with, eating pizzas and watching videos, laughing about everything, is suddenly on an obsessive diet, never laughs, talks about fame and money all the time and is out partying with rock bands every night. Can't you see how I'm a little concerned?"

"You could have come to Exclusive tonight as well,"

Tony lied.

"The last place in the world I would want to be is in Exclusive with a bunch of egotistical stars. And as for these Ralph and Margaux characters, instead of hating everything they stand for you want to become just like them!"

"That's not true!"

"It is! You're suddenly dreaming of becoming rich all the time."

"And so what if that is true?"

"Look, I don't want to take your dreams away from you, but you've become so driven and it's affecting our relationship. We're losing sight of each other, and I love you too much to let what we have go. I just want us to be like we used to be."

"You know what? I think my mother was right."

"What has your mother got to do with this?"

"She mentioned that you seemed happier when I was miserable in my job, because then you were the superior one in our relationship. Instead of trying to analyse everybody else's feelings and thoughts and lives, why don't you take a good look at yourself and analyse your reaction to my success?" He strode out and up the stairs.

CHAPTER 27

"How is everyone?" Ralph came swaggering into the Reception.

"Everything's been fine," Vivienne reassured him, beaming a false smile.

"No problems at all," said Tony. "How was New York?"

"Amazing. We met so many great people including Bill and Hillary Clinton – we invited them to stay with us next time they are in Ireland."

"Isn't that great!" Vivienne blinked and smiled.

"They got on very well with Margaux – they adored her."

Vivienne shot Tony a very quick amused look.

"Anyway. Tell Gavin I want to see the advertising figures for the past week immediately. Bring into my office the RSVPs for tomorrow's Curtis party. Also Victoria Harton is flying in especially tomorrow for the party – have a car arranged to collect her at three and bring her straight to my house." He marched off down the corridor.

"Yes, sir!" Vivienne said as she heard his office door slam.

"Victoria Harton is attending?" said Tony. "I didn't know that."

"Oh, she likes to make at least one visit a year to the far-flung corners of their publishing empire. This is just her annual Irish visit. It gives Ralph and Maggie the excuse to fawn over her for the night and show her how popular they are."

*   *   *

Cathal tasted the food that Lana was cooking.

"Well?" she enquired.

"Not bad at all. You're a natural."

"Only under your supervision." She turned around and faced him. "Cathal, I want you to come to Dad's birthday party tomorrow."

"I thought you didn't want me to meet him."

"I'd like you to be there. I mean, it's not like anybody will know we're seeing each other anyway – so it won't be anything heavy or anything."

"A relief to both of us then." He bent forward and kissed her. "I'll go."

*   *   *

Stephen Rourke walked down the road from the prison, squinting in the sunshine. He didn't know where to go or what to do. He took out a piece of paper and looked at a couple of names and numbers on it: people who helped ex-prisoners try to get their lives back on track. He reached the end of the road and stopped, looking left and right, trying to decide which way to go.

*   *   *

Kathryn dropped into the chemist's to get some pills for Simeon, went back to the apartment where she gave him his medication, then tucked him up in bed before racing into Exclusive. By seven in the evening she was double-checking to ensure the Curtis party that night was a success – everything from making sure the bar was fully stocked, to having a special stage area inserted that afternoon and checking the sound system was working perfectly.

"I don't care what excuses you come up with – we ordered those flowers a week ago and I want them at Exclusive within an hour!" Kathryn blazed down the phone before hanging up, confident the flowers would be delivered in the time frame. Barry had been very specific about how he wanted the club decorated.

She looked around the club which was a hive of activity. Cleaners were making sure everything was spick and span. Barmen were busy making preparations. Technicians were testing equipment and carpenters building a temporary stage.

Ralph arrived with Tony in attendance. As *Hi Life* had an exclusive for the night they had been very involved in the organisation as well. The invitations had gone out with the *Hi Life* logo on them and *Hi Life* would be in charge of the door that night. This was fine by Kathryn, as it was their problem if they let in any other press by mistake.

"Are we all set for tonight, Kathryn?" asked Ralph.

"I think we are."

"This is Tony –"

"We've met," Kathryn said quickly.

Ralph looked confused for a second before looking around and exclaiming, "The place is looking amazing! How is security?"

"I have my best men on the job."

"There are going to be a lot of celebrities here tonight and I don't want any other press taking photos. It's an event exclusive to *Hi Life*. Vivienne from my office will be at the door checking the invitations. She knows exactly who's been invited so there will be no fuck-ups. And since myself and Margaux will be up at the top mingling, can you arrange for Tony to have a walkie-talkie as he will be keeping an eye on proceedings?"

Kathryn looked at Tony coolly. "Consider it done."

*   *   *

Lana had changed outfits ten times that afternoon. Finally she decided on a classic beige dress. She was dreading the night. She usually stayed out of her father's affairs and she liked it that way. As she looked at herself in her full-length mirrors in her dressing-room, she reached over for a decanter filled with whiskey and poured herself a shot.

*   *   *

Tony fixed his tie and glanced at his watch. It was 5.30. "Fuck, I'm running late! You might give a call to that taxi firm and ask them what's holding up that cab, will you? I have to be over at the Conways in thirty minutes."

"So let me get this straight." Nicole sat on the bed looking at him. "You're going all the way out to Monkstown to drive Ralph, Margaux and this Victoria

Harton back into town to Exclusive?"

"Yeah."

"So you're now their chauffeur on top of everything else?"

"Well, they can hardly be expected to drive themselves in when Victoria Harton is with them."

"Why not?"

Tony turned around and looked at Nicole in a slightly exasperated manner. "Victoria Harton owns the whole *Hi Life* empire – it's all about impressing her. And I feel pretty happy that Ralph thinks I'm cool enough to go out to their house and be introduced to her."

Nicole didn't know whether to laugh or cry. "After all those Nobel Peace Prizes Victoria won, I know it's such a privilege for you to pander to her every need."

A car beeped outside.

Tony looked at Nicole, visibly annoyed. "That's my cab. It will be a late night so don't bother waiting up for me."

* * *

Joanne Bailey took a look at herself in the mirror. She was wearing a ruby-red dress that was cut down to her waist, and split up to her thighs. If that didn't make her the centre of attention for the night then nothing would. And when she arrived on the arm of Seán and announced they were an item, there would be shockwaves throughout Dublin. Move over James and Donna, a new celebrity couple is about to be launched! And fuck you, Cathal Fitzgerald, as well!

Her mobile rang and she recognised the number as Seán's.

"Hi, babe, where are you?" she asked.

"Should be with you shortly and we'll head straight over to Exclusive. We can grab a cab together and go Dutch on the fare." He smiled to himself, testing her reaction, as he knew Joanne believed the man should pay for everything.

"Dutch?" she cooed. "Baby, this chick doesn't wear clogs!"

*   *   *

"When the guests come in, make sure they are immediately served with champagne." Kathryn instructed two hostesses. She quickly glanced at her watch and realised she'd better get moving and change outfits or else the guests would arrive and see her in jeans and a black T-shirt.

She closed the door of her office behind her, stripped off her clothes and put on the gown that was hanging on the back of the door.

*   *   *

Tony vaguely wondered why the Conways never had children. Too busy chasing celebrities, he mused. His eyes widened as the cab turned through the huge gates of their house.

"Some gaff," remarked the taxi-driver as he pulled up outside the front doors.

"Sure is," said Tony.

He stepped out, staring at the house, then climbed the steps and nervously rang the echoing doorbell.

After about a minute the double oak doors unlatched

and there stood Margaux, smiling, a vision in sequins, looking remarkably refreshed and about ten years younger since her trip to New York.

"Tony! Step in!"

He smiled awkwardly and walked in.

"Come and join us for a drink!"

He followed her down the steps into a huge lounge room with massive arches which looked out onto a balcony. Ralph was standing beside a blazing fire and a woman was sitting in an armchair in a regal fashion.

"Victoria, this is Tony O'Brien," Margaux smiled. "Our latest acquisition at Irish *Hi Life*, and somebody who is turning out to be a little treasure."

Victoria didn't move but held out her hand almost as if for him to kiss it. He edged forward and shook it lightly.

"How are you finding working for *Hi Life*?" she asked.

"Oh, I'm really enjoying it, you know."

"I'm so glad."

"Tony, get the decanter and refill our glasses," ordered Ralph. "Fix yourself a soft drink since you're driving."

Tony did as he was bid and then sat down with his orange juice.

"I've instructed my design department to leave a page aside in our next issue to cover tonight's events," informed Victoria.

"In British *Hi Life*?" Ralph was hugely excited.

"Yes, well, Barry Curtis has done a lot for charity in the UK, so this night should be of interest to our readers as well."

"Oh, thank you, Victoria!" Margaux reached forward from her seat and kissed Victoria on both cheeks.

Tony sat transfixed by Victoria. What amazed him most were the similarities between her and Margaux, despite her being ten years Margaux's senior. The way they looked, their upper-class accents, their dress styles, their expressions and gestures were identical. She's been your role model, hasn't she, Maggie? he thought. You reinvented yourself and became a Victoria Harton clone.

* * *

Ralph, Margaux and Victoria climbed the steps where Kathryn stood waiting to greet them, a security guard on either side of her. Vivienne was in position behind a table where the open guest book rested.

"I think we're fashionably late, Kathryn," declared Margaux. "Have you met Victoria Harton?"

"No, it's a privilege to meet you. I've heard a lot about you." Kathryn shook her hand.

"How is it looking upstairs?" asked Ralph.

"Pretty packed. I think most of the guests have arrived."

"No matter what happens, don't leave this table tonight," Ralph said to Vivienne. "I don't want anyone in here tonight who shouldn't be."

After he was safely out of earshot, Vivienne muttered sarcastically "Make sure you have a drink after all your hard work, Vivienne!"

Tony, who had gone to park the car, came hurrying up the steps at this point.

"Right, here's your walkie-talkie," Kathryn said, handing it to him. "Any trouble at all, give me a shout immediately."

* * *

Lana pushed the main door of Exclusive open and

336

surveyed the club packed with designer-dressed people being served champagne while music played overhead.

She looked through the crowd for Cathal, but couldn't see him.

*　　*　　*

"Well, look over there! I don't believe it!" said Donna. All the others at the table followed Donna's gaze across to the club's entrance.

There, posing for a photo for Clive, were Joanne and Seán. Kissing.

"Did you know they were seeing each other?" James asked Cathal, mouth open.

"Of course not," said Cathal, feeling very uncomfortable with the situation and suddenly realising a lot of things were suddenly making sense.

Joanne and Seán walked arm in arm over to their table.

"Hi, everybody!" Joanne smiled broadly.

"We didn't realise you two were an item," said Donna.

"Well, you know me." Joanne looked at Cathal pointedly. "I like to keep my private life private . . . and it's so hard to keep anything secret in this town. Even since arriving here this evening with Seán, my mobile has been ringing non-stop with the press wanting to do interviews."

"Well, we must all meet up for dinner soon," suggested Donna.

"That would be nice. Anyway, we have to go. Clive wants to take lots more photos of us. I feel really bad because I think we're going to get more publicity than Barry Curtis tonight!" She began to lead Seán away.

Cathal got up and followed them. "Hey!" Joanne and Seán swung around. "It all makes sense now. The hostility coming from you, Seán, has been stirred up by *her*."

"*She* has a name," said Joanne. "A soon-to-be-very-famous name, may I add."

"You're a fool, Seán. She's using you for her own ends."

"And you are so bitter and cynical, Cathal," said Joanne. "You just can't stand to see two people in a happy and fulfilling relationship, because you're so weary of life."

"And just because she dumped you for me, Cathal, no hard feelings, huh?" said Seán.

"She dumped me? Is that what she said?" Cathal was incredulous.

"We don't have time to stand here and talk to you. Run back to the safety of your little gang, Cathal!" With that parting shot, Joanne turned and led Seán away.

*   *   *

"A whiskey, please," Cathal said to the barman.

"Make that two," said Lana, coming to stand beside him. "You look stressed."

"It's just that some things are suddenly beginning to make sense." He looked at her nervous face. "I'll tell you later. How are you?"

"I want to run a million miles from here."

Looking at her, he wondered what the situation was with her parents to make her so uneasy. He discreetly reached forward and squeezed her hand. "I'm here for you, okay?"

The music stopped and the DJ began to speak. "Ladies and gentlemen, we're all here for a special reason tonight and that reason is here now: Barry Curtis!"

Music started blaring and the crowd applauded as the double doors into the club opened and Barry stepped through with Gloria. The two of them stood there smiling and waving to the crowd.

"What the fuck is she doing standing beside him like his running mate?" spat Lana. "Or even worse – his wife!" She turned around and snapped at the barman. "A double vodka and no ice!"

*   *   *

"Kathryn, could I have you for a few photos, please," Clive asked as she whizzed past.

"Sorry, Clive, I'm up to my eyes. Can it wait a little? Jill, there's a bottle broken over in the far corner – will you clean it up at once, please?" she ordered a passing waitress.

*   *   *

Barry and Gloria were mingling through the crowd, shaking hands with everybody and chatting. Clive followed them everywhere, taking photos as they posed with the different guests.

"Okay, everybody, and a big smile!" he urged as they posed with Ralph, Margaux and Victoria. "You can guarantee that photo will have pride of place in the spread," he then whispered to Tony.

"Hopefully the next party we have will be a celebration party when Barry wins the election!" Gloria said loudly.

At this moment, she spotted Lana at the bar. Unfortunately, it was necessary to take the girl's photo and include her in an interview to give Barry that lacking family-man image. Seeing Barry was distracted with some guests, Gloria turned to the Conways. "Barry's daughter is over there by the bar. Can we organise a photo of her and a quick interview?" she urged.

"Of course," said Ralph. "Tony, Clive, follow us!"

*　　*　　*

"He's riding her!" Joanne stated, looking at Lana.

"What?" asked Seán.

"Cathal is sleeping with that girl over there, Lana Curtis."

"No, he's not," scoffed Seán.

"Oh yes, he is. I can spot these things a mile off – call it woman's intuition. I spotted it immediately. The little looks they've been giving each other, the way he talked to her at the bar. He even squeezed her hand when he thought nobody was looking. Yep – he's riding her."

*　　*　　*

"Lana!" Gloria put a hand on Lana's shoulder.

Lana turned and came face to face with Gloria's uncompromising expression.

"This is Ralph and Margaux Conway from *Hi Life* and they want to have a few words with you about your father's birthday and his forthcoming election."

Margaux stepped forward and kissed Lana on both cheeks. "Absolutely delighted to meet you. Let's take the photo first before we have our little chat."

Clive lifted his camera.

"Wait!" said Gloria. "I don't think the background of the bar, though telling, is very appropriate."

"True," said Margaux. "Let's go over to that booth in

the corner."

Margaux and Ralph each took one of Lana's arms and led her over.

"We're great friends of your father's," said Ralph. "Once Clive has taken his photos we'll ask you some questions – Tony here will take notes."

I feel like a secretary, thought Tony, following them with his notebook.

"I'm not sure about this. I don't really want my photo taken or to give an interview," objected Lana.

"Nonsense. Our readers would love to meet Barry's daughter."

"Well, I don't particularly want to meet them." She shook off their hands as she reached the booth.

They looked at her in surprise.

Gloria stepped forward. "Lana, your father wants this. Can't you do this small thing for him?"

Lana felt complete loathing for Gloria as she stared at her. She threw her hands in the air. "Oh, whatever you want!"

"Thank you," Gloria said before heading off back to Barry.

"Okay, give me a big smile!" said Clive, aiming his camera at her.

Clive left after finishing his work, while the others settled into the booth.

Tony poised pen over notebook.

"So tell us a little about yourself, Lana," said Margaux.

"What kind of things do you want to know?"

"Well, what do you do for a living?"

"I . . . I . . . eh . . . I'm involved in the Charity circuit." Attending Charity Balls and getting pissed, she thought. "And I, eh . . ."

"You're not working in a full-time job at the moment?" asked Ralph.

"Well, I'm very busy canvassing for my father's election at the moment." Oh yeah!, she thought to herself.

Sensing Lana's discomfort, Margaux said, "Yes, I think we should concentrate on Lana's thoughts on her father's election. Your mother must be very excited about it?"

Lana started feeling very stressed. "Of course."

"What's your mother's name again?" asked Ralph.

"Eh, is that important?" She saw their surprised expressions and quickly added, "Ann."

"Do you inherit your sense of style and elegance from her?" asked Margaux.

"I guess so," said Lana, feeling the whole situation was entering into the bizarre.

"You're going to have to give us a little more to go on here," said Margaux.

"Relationships!" said Ralph. "Who are you seeing at the moment?"

This is hell, thought Lana, wishing she had stood up to Gloria. She couldn't mention Cathal.

"I'm not seeing anybody at the moment." Okay, so you haven't a job, or a relationship, and won't talk about your family. They'll think you're a freak.

Margaux tried to search for something to talk about. "You have a lovely complexion. What's your secret?"

"A bottle of vodka a day seems to do the trick," Lana said.

Margaux and Ralph looked at her as if she were mad.

"It's been such a pleasure meeting you," said Margaux quickly.

"And do call in to *Hi Life* any time for a chat," added Ralph. "Okay?"

Lana nodded.

"We're your friends and we're here for you if you need anything," said Margaux.

"Thanks," said Lana, feeling uncomfortable.

"Well, we'd better mingle. More people to interview!" Margaux said and they moved off.

Lana raced for the bar.

"She seems lost," said Ralph.

"Doesn't she? She needs a role in life. And we might be just the people to give her one." said Margaux smiling.

*   *   *

Barry was on the stage giving a speech while Gloria stood beside him.

Cathal looked on intrigued. Since going out with Lana, he had followed Barry's political campaign with extra interest. Barry was a traditionalist from what Cathal's could see. He believed in people doing a hard day's work and getting a decent wage for it. He believed in a society that rewarded talent and hard work. And to encourage such a society he was proposing large tax cuts, particularly for business enterprise. He believed in a meritocracy, which was hardly surprising since Barry himself was a spectacular example of a self-made man. He was proposing to be tough on spongers and criminals and illegal immigrants. In many ways, Cathal could see Barry as an elected representative would benefit people like him. However tax cuts were all very well, but Barry wasn't proposing any extra revenue for hospitals or education or any social services, or even infrastructure. In fact, he was proposing to start a massive privatisation programme of such services that people assumed were the responsibility of the state. Barry Curtis maintained such an act would make these services much more cost-effective and efficient and therefore automatically release extra revenue that could be reinvested in them. There was a huge fear with Barry's opponents that such a move would lead to the deterioration of these services. A meritocracy was all well and good, but it might not cater for the people who were caught in between, wanting to work but not being able to find work, or for people who wouldn't have the resources to look after themselves if they got sick or found themselves in other difficult positions. Cathal suspected that Barry's policies might make society more hard-edged and greedy and weaken the safety-net that Cathal believed every society should provide.

"I knew it!" said James to Cathal as Barry continued to speak. "I knew Curtis would use this party as an excuse to talk about his manifesto."

"It's his party, as the song goes," said Cathal.

"The man just makes me want to puke! All his policies will do is make him and his mates richer . . . I mean how much money do they fucking need?"

"He's just trying to encourage business," Cathal felt the need to point out.

"At the expense of the poor and the old and the sick!" said James.

Cathal knew that James was much more political than he himself was and, to be fair to him, James campaigned hard for his charities, but his holier-than-thou attitude could be irritating sometimes.

"Look, maybe you should vote for him – he will protect your assets," Cathal smirked.

"I don't want to protect my assets if it means other people suffer," said James.

344

"Think about that when you buy your next matching His and Hers Mercedes. You know something? *You* are a real champagne socialist!" Cathal chinked his glass against James'.

"I never said money was wrong, only the misuse of money." James was annoyed.

"If you felt so strongly, why did you bother coming tonight?"

"Donna insisted, saying everybody who was anybody would be here. But there's no way I am posing for any photos to endorse that man's campaign."

*   *   *

Lana looked on, still standing at the bar.

"I wouldn't have thought you were his type," said a voice beside her. She turned to see the speaker was Joanne Bailey.

"I'm sorry?" Lana said.

"I didn't think you were Cathal's type. You are together, I take it?"

Lana looked at her. "I suppose they told you." She nodded over to James and Donna's table.

"No, I didn't need to be told. I just knew. I mean, don't get me wrong, you're lovely-looking and everything, but Cathal usually goes for the more glamorous types – you know, models."

"And television presenters?" Lana viewed her coolly.

"He usually goes for the same type as himself – people who rely on a bit of ambition, looks and luck to make it. Not somebody who never had to fight for anything. But I wish you the best of luck with him. You'll need it. Because I think he's a bit fucked up to be honest. I mean – why else would he let someone like me go?" She smiled and walked away into the crowd.

* * *

Gloria looked at her watch and saw it was getting late. "Barry, I wonder should we go? I need to go through tomorrow's schedule with you."

"Yes, we've stayed longer than I expected. I just want to find Lana – I haven't spoken to her all night."

"Barry," Gloria voice was stern, "I had a long conversation with her earlier. She was in great form, posed for photos, gave an interview and everything. I really need to verse you that interview tomorrow with RTÉ."

The tears stung Lana's eyes as she saw Barry leave the club with Gloria. She looked over at Cathal who had a couple of model creatures all over him. He smiled sympathetically at her. She turned around to the barman. "A double whiskey," she ordered.

Joanne was standing next to Seán, posing for yet another photo for Clive.

"Well, I don't know how you have the cheek to stand there as if you're something," said Lana loudly.

Joanne turned around. "Lana?"

"Look at yourself, with your cheap ruby-red dress and your trashy hair colour!"

Joanne realised Lana had had a few drinks but people were beginning to stare.

"Lana, why don't you get reception to order you a taxi and go home?"

"Don't you dare try to be condescending to me! I'll go home when I'm good and ready!"

"I'm disappointed in you, Lana. I didn't realise you'd

be so threatened by Cathal's ex. Jealous of me!"

"Me, jealous of you? I'm the daughter of a multi-millionaire – why should I be jealous of you?"

"Jealous because I'm somebody who's achieved what I have achieved off my own bat!"

"On your own back, you mean! Yeah, by the look of you the only thing you've ever achieved was on your back!"

"I work extremely hard all the time. Why don't you try to sometime?"

"All you've done is make a name for yourself by dating Cathal."

Across the room, Donna tapped Cathal on the shoulder. "Well, it looks like your friend is up to her old tricks!"

Cathal looked around and saw what was happening.

"Well, as they say, you can't change a leopard's spots or make a silken purse out of a pig's arse," concluded Donna.

Cathal began to move towards Lana.

"Where are you going?" demanded James.

"I'm going over to stop her."

"Don't be stupid, Cathal. Don't get involved!" James pleaded.

"I can't just leave her!"

"Why? Why can't you? You know you've always been your worst enemy. For once in your life recognise trouble and stay away from it!" snapped James.

Cathal looked at James with a mixture of anger and hurt and continued over to Lana.

*   *   *

Vivienne stood behind the reception table smoking a cigarette. She looked at the time – it was after eleven. Nobody was going to arrive at this stage and yet Ralph insisted she stay in reception all night. She was desperate to go upstairs and take a look at all the celebrities and have a drink. But no, she had to stay put. She really had to think about getting a new job.

Just then, to her surprise, she saw Tina Cawley and a group of five others come up the steps.

"Hi, guys, sorry we're late," said Tina to the two security guards as she walked past them.

The security guards, realising who she was, said nothing but gave Vivienne a concerned look.

"Hey!" said Tina to Vivienne and threw her invitation on the table. "Where do I sign in?"

"Er, Tina, we weren't expecting you . . . you didn't RSVP."

Tina sat up on the table casually. "Oh, I'm sorry. I thought I was only to let you know if I wasn't coming."

Vivienne looked Tina up and down. She was as ever very dressed down in a black hippie-style outfit, as were her friends. "You've missed most of the evening," she said.

"Well, we'd better hurry up so we don't miss any more then, huh?" Tina grinned.

Vivienne looked at the five others "The invitation said Tina Cawley and guest. All invitations were only for two people."

"Really?" Tina yawned and picked up the invitation. "Well, honey, my invitation reads 'guests', and so I'm not telling my friends they can't come in, okay?"

Vivienne looked at it and realised somebody had written an 's' in pen after the word 'guest'. She thought quickly. They really did look unruly, but Tina Cawley was a big star and she could imagine what Ralph would say to her if she upset her.

"Okay, if you could just all sign the guest book, please," she said.

"There's a good girl," said Tina and yawned again.

*   *   *

Cathal put his hands on Lana's shoulders. "Come on, Lana, calm down," he said.

"No, I won't! This bitch came up to me at the bar and started stirring it!" She turned and hugged Cathal. "She started to bitch about you. I'm not taking it from her. You deserve more. You're much too nice –"

"Nice! Ha!" scoffed Joanne loudly.

Cathal gave Joanne a warning look.

"You know, you two really suit each other," said Joanne. "Shit finds its own level."

"Why don't you shut up!" Lana snapped at her.

There was a flurry of excitement around as people realised Cathal and Lana were an item.

Kathryn, noticing the disturbance, quickly made her way over. She saw how upset and agitated Lana looked. She quickly figured out the scenario.

"Take her home, Cathal," advised Kathryn. "Now!"

At that moment, the double doors of Exclusive burst open as Tina Cawley and her entourage burst in, waving banners.

"*Down with capitalism!*" screamed Tina. "*Fuck the elite!*"

People started pulling back and screaming as the six ran through the crowd, shouting anti-capitalist slogans. One of the gang took out a copy of *Hi Life* magazine and set fire to it. Commotion erupted as people tried to get away in fear.

Kathryn pulled out her walkie-talkie. "*All security to the main club area immediately!*"

"Come on. Let's get out of here!" Cathal grabbed Lana

and they headed to the door.

Tina got up on the stage and grabbed the microphone. "This is a protest against capitalism! Against you! You congregate in this temple of bad taste, spend millions on shite dresses and then give yourselves awards for vulgarity. Instead of realising there are people who need help, not only in our own country but throughout the world. And if you could all stop being so fucking vainglorious –" she took up a copy of *Hi Life* and waved it in the air, "if you could stop caring what brand of coffee useless vacuous so-called stars drink and started thinking about the real issues in the world, the world might become a better place!"

Havoc reigned throughout the Club. A demonstrator lunged at Margaux and Victoria, but Tony jumped in the way and pushed him to the ground.

Kathryn quickly went through the club with her security. "How the hell did they get in here?" she shouted, dialling the police on her mobile as the crowd scrambled to leave.

As Cathal and Lana headed down the steps to the front door, he phoned Matt. "Where are you?" he asked.

"Just around the corner from Exclusive," Matt informed him.

"Come around to the front door immediately. All hell is breaking loose in here!"

Cathal and Lana reached the front door, and seeing Matt pull up in the car, they began to descend the steps quickly.

"Cathal, this way!" called a man's voice.

Cathal turned to look and a camera flashed in his face.

The press photographers that had gathered outside to get photos of the VIPs leaving the party, had been tipped off and they all descended on Cathal and Lana, snapping as they made their way to the car.

*   *   *

Back at her apartment, Lana rested her head against Cathal's chest, crying softly. "I made a complete fool of myself! I just couldn't help myself."

"After that riot people will have forgotten about your little scene pretty quickly," said Cathal.

"She came over and provoked me at the bar earlier, and then later after I'd had a few drinks I lost my cool."

"Joanne's good at provoking."

"That's not the point!" She pulled back and looked at Cathal. "I should have stopped myself from doing it."

She walked over to his cabinet, took out a bottle of vodka and poured herself a large drink. Then she took a joint out of her handbag and lit up.

"It didn't take you long to slip back into your old ways," he said sullenly.

She fell back on a sofa. "Wanna drink?" she asked, holding out the bottle.

"No, thanks. You're a good advertisement not to drink."

"Only from where you're standing. From where I am, I think I'm a great advertisement to drink as much as I possibly can."

"I thought you were cutting down on all that. You've been doing really great."

"That was then and this is now," she said in a sing-song fashion.

"I think I'll go for a walk."

"No, don't go!"

"What's my other option? Sit and watch you get

drunker and drunker and baby-sit you for the night? I thought I was dealing with an adult. I was mistaken." He turned to go.

"Wait, Cathal! I had such a shit day!"

He stopped. "Because of Joanne? I know she's a bitch but –"

"Not just her." She took a long drag from her joint and then stubbed it out. "Everything. The Conways from *Hi Life* insisted on interviewing me. They just seemed so superior and I could tell they thought I was a loser."

"Why do you think that?"

"What do you do for a living? Pass. What are your interests? Pass. What about your personal life? Fucking pass ! You know, I really didn't need those people coming in and holding a big magnifying glass up to my life to show everyone that there's nothing in my life of any significance. And, you know, my father didn't even come over to speak to me all night. Didn't even come to see how I was. I only went to support him. There he was swanning around with Gloria."

"Who's Gloria?"

"His Campaign Director – or some such nonsense. She's really going to laugh when she reads what *Hi Life* write about me."

"*Hi Life* doesn't write anything bad about anybody. And what do you care what she thinks of you anyway?"

"Same way you care what people down in Castletown think of you, when you've obviously left them far behind a long time ago."

He went red. "I don't care what they think."

"You care! You shouldn't, but you do!"

He sat down on the couch opposite her. "Stop it right there, Lana."

"I'm not criticising you. I think you're fantastic, what

you've achieved, I really do. And I really found you inspirational. And I want to do something with my life when I see what you've done with yours. And my therapist said I should try it —" She went red and looked up at him.

"Therapist?"

"There, it's out!" she said, sitting back in the couch.

"How long have you been in therapy?"

"Not long. I didn't want to go, and still don't want to go."

"Why are you there then?"

"Because I did a couple of stupid things and I was made to go. The kind of stupid things you did years ago but had the excuse of youth behind you. I have no excuse."

He went and sat beside her and put his arm around her. "I know all about making mistakes. But I also know about getting another chance."

"I can totally understand if you don't want to see me again."

"Why? Because you're seeing somebody who's helping you work out a few issues? I respect you for that."

"Really?"

"Yeah. And you know it took me so long trying to get you to meet me, I'm not going to walk out now, am I? Well, everybody knows we're going out together after tonight."

"I'm sorry, Cathal. I know how much your privacy means to you."

"I think it's about time we let people know anyway."

"Really?"

"Yeah, we can't hide away forever. Besides, everybody will be talking about that riot that Tina Cawley was causing. What kind of nut is she? Your father won't be too pleased with that. Where was he during that anyway?"

"Oh, himself and Gloria had left before that started. Of course, they would have. You could dip those two in a pit of shit and they'd come up smelling of roses."

*   *   *

"You stupid fucking bitch!" Ralph shouted at Vivienne in Reception.

Tony came into reception after putting Victoria Harton safely into a taxi.

"I'm sorry, Ralph. I'm sorry," said Vivienne who was crying.

"How could you be so fucking stupid as to let that crowd of knackers in?" shouted Margaux, who seemed to have lost her grand accent and returned to her working-class roots in her anger.

"Tina Cawley had an invitation."

"An invitation for two, not six, you eejit!" shouted Margaux. "You have single-handedly ruined a magnificent night. It will be in all the fucking papers tomorrow. And all in front of Victoria Harton as well!"

*   *   *

Joanne sat on the stage, her lips set in an angry line, looking around the club, now empty apart from staff cleaning up.

"There will be a taxi to collect us in about five minutes," said Seán, coming back from the bar.

"Can you believe that?" she said, full of anger.

"What?"

"Here I am, dressed in a knockout dress and looking gorgeous and announcing our relationship to the world. My big moment ! And what happens ? First of all Cathal and that lunatic Lana are exposed as seeing each other. And then, as if all that wasn't bad enough, there's a full-scale riot! I won't even get a look-in in the papers tomorrow!"

CHAPTER 28

Tony sat at his desk listening to the roars coming from Ralph's office. Vivienne had been in there for half an hour and Ralph hadn't stopped shouting once. As he heard Ralph's door open and close, Tony turned to his computer and pretended to be typing.

Vivienne came into the office area, her eyes red.

"Are you okay?" he asked as he watched her start clearing out her drawers.

"He's such a bastard!" she said, fighting back the tears.

"Did he . . . fire you?" Tony found it hard to ask.

"No, it would have been easier if he had. I'm demoted, for want of a better word. In future I will be strictly manning the phones down at the switchboard in the advertising department. He doesn't want me even up here. I'd leave if I didn't have a mortgage to pay."

"I'm really sorry," said Tony. And he meant it. Vivienne had been very nice to him since he had started. The phone rang on his desk, causing him to jump. He picked up. "Yeah?"

"Come in here," ordered Ralph.

Tony hurried down the corridor, knocked and entered.

"Sit down," Ralph ordered.

Tony did as he was bid, feeling nervous that he was about to suffer a similar fate to Vivienne's.

"I have never worked with such an i-i-incompetent idiot in my life. I don't want her in my sight any more. I've sent her downstairs. She isn't up to the job."

"We all make mistakes," Tony said.

"I don't!" Ralph slammed his table with his hand. "And I won't allow for mistakes in other people. I will not accept mistakes from anyone!"

Tony nodded.

Ralph didn't say anything for a while. "You impressed me greatly last night," he said at last.

Tony looked up.

"You impressed both me and Margaux. You kept a cool head throughout and were on the ball at all times."

Tony managed to smile.

"Since you started, you've been doing a great job. It's people like you that I need around me, not people like Vivienne. I'm giving you a pay rise."

"Thanks, Ralph!"

"I'm going to be relying on you more now that Vivienne is gone. You could go places. If you watch and learn and do what I say, you will become somebody. Do you want that?"

"Yes!" Tony said enthusiastically.

*　　　*　　　*

Sylvia picked up the phone and dialled Tina Cawley's mobile.

"Well, you have surpassed yourself," she said once Tina answered, "and that takes some surpassing."

"I regret nothing," Tina responded. "Somebody needed to point out their vacuous existence to those assholes."

"And you're just the girl to do it."

"I sure am."

"It's in all the papers today. *Tina Cawley Stages Demonstration at Curtis Party*. Luckily there were no photos as only *Hi Life's* photographer was present. "

"At least I can sleep well at night, knowing I'm being true to myself."

"Where are you now?"

"At the airport, en route to India as I told you I would be."

"So you caused havoc, and are now just calmly heading off into the sunset?"

"Yes, on my voyage of self-discovery. See you in a few weeks." Tina hung up.

*   *   *

Cathal braced himself as he went into the shop.

"Hi, Hakaam," he said. "Anything in the papers of interest?"

"You could say that," said Hakaam.

Cathal looked down at all the newspapers and saw photos of him and Lana leaving Exclusive on the front cover of all the tabloids.

"Cathal and the Heiress!" screamed the headline in *The Mirror*.

*   *   *

Lana opened her eyes and looked around Cathal's bedroom.

"Cathal!" she called, before remembering he had said

he'd be heading off to the studio early. She ran her fingers through her hair and wished she'd had a blackout the previous night so she wouldn't have to remember how she had made such a fool of herself. What was she thinking of, attacking Joanne Bailey like that?

She got out of bed and pulled Cathal's dressing-gown around her, feeling utterly miserable. Barry's ignoring her had really got to her. Gloria's presence had really got to her. And then looking at Joanne Bailey's beauty and confidence – well, how long till Cathal would get bored of her because she did nothing, had nothing to talk about, nothing to offer?

She saw a handwritten note from Cathal on the coffee table and picked it up.

It read: *"I'm sorry about this – talk to you later – Cathal."*

She was puzzled, not realising what he was talking about and then she saw three newspapers on the table. She picked them up and was greeted by the photos of herself and Cathal on the front pages. She felt confused, and then terrified.

* * *

Gloria Reagan paced up and down the top of the lecture hall, looking out at the several hundred faces hanging on her every word, whose average age was twenty.

"Today's world has become so much smaller. The improvements in transport mean we can be in Australia in a day, or pick up the phone and have live contact with somebody on the other side of the world in an instant. Our economy has become global, our telecommunications industry has become global, our politics are global. So it follows that our gossip has become global as well."

There was a wave of laughter through the lecture hall.

"When we lived more local lives, before the improvements of telecommunications and media, everybody in a small village or town would know each other. And people talked about Mary down the road, and Tom in the next street. But at the same time that there has been a breakdown of local community, there has been a pulling together of the global community. So even though many of us do not even know what our next-door neighbour looks like, we all know intimate secrets of people like David Beckham, Madonna – any celebrity you want to name, we know about them. And this is what has ushered in this age of celebrity. It's what brings us together; it's what people immediately have in common. They can talk about celebrities, or gossip about them. When people meet they no longer talk about Mary down the road, they talk about Kylie Minogue. A breakdown of local community and a strengthening of the global." She stood behind her desk and picked up some magazines. "And these are the reporters of our new celebrity gossip. The highly glossy *Hello*, *OK* and *Hi Life* magazines and the tabloid press. It is these publications that allow us to be, in our own minds, close to these people. To see them inside their homes, feel what it's really like to be them." She dropped the other two magazines and held up *Hi Life* with Joanne Bailey smiling dreamily from the front cover. "And so here we see a minor TV star telling us about her break-up with a singer. And also in today's celebrity culture, we are led to believe that anybody can become that celebrity. Let's take a quick glance through this morning's tabloids. Look at this, a weather girl who's has become a household name . . . " Gloria paused as she looked at the front of the next paper and saw the photo of Cathal and Lana leaving Exclusive. She did a double-take and saw her name printed. She started reading the article.

The students started murmuring.

"Miss Reagan, are you okay?" asked a student in the front row.

Gloria looked up sharply. "Excuse me . . . and also an industrialist's daughter."

*   *   *

Gloria sat at her desk in her office in UCD and closed over the essay she had corrected. The writer of the essay, a student aged twenty, sat the other side of the desk, biting her lower lip, nervously awaiting the verdict.

"This is shit," Gloria announced, handing the girl her essay back.

The girl went bright red.

"I suggest you tear it up and start from scratch."

The girl nodded, took the essay and exited quickly.

Gloria sat back in her chair and began to contemplate.

Gloria Reagan had never failed at anything in her life. However, after studying the latest polls on the Barry Curtis election campaign, she knew she could be facing failure. Barry was lagging behind in the polls. He was not trusted by the general public because of his tycoon status. He was admired, respected, liked, adored even . . . but not trusted. Whatever the implications of Barry failing to get elected were for him, Gloria now considered what the implications would be for her. She would become the laughing stock of the academic world. All her colleagues, anxious for her to trip up over the years, would delight in her embarrassment. But it didn't stop there. Gloria had always been an overachiever and she had seen this step as Barry Curtis's political advisor and strategist as the beginning of a successful and powerful life in this field. Barry's failure would also bring a quick and sudden end to any such ambitions.

She was an expert in behaviourism. There was no point in pretending Barry didn't have the money he had and so she had decided the best approach should be to try and project him as having a glamorous lifestyle and to show him as being a friend of stars. These connections bought votes. She opened her drawer and took out the day's papers and again looked at the photos of Lana with the guy from Affidavit hurrying from a nightclub. This new development was very interesting and perhaps, handled the right way, hugely beneficial.

*   *   *

"That Tina Cawley sure is one fruitcake," said James, as they broke from recording.

"Yeah, I was talking to Sylvia this morning and she's hopping mad over it," said Cathal.

"Did she do it as a publicity stunt?"

"No – anyone else, maybe, but not Tina. You know how self-righteous she is – she believed in what she was doing."

"Are you coming to the canteen for a coffee?" James asked Seán as he walked past.

Seán stopped for a second, gave Cathal a withering look and walked off. They hadn't said a word all morning and you could cut the atmosphere with a knife.

"You're going to have to come to some truce," James advised Cathal as they walked down the corridor.

"Whatever chance there was before, it's finished now that he's seeing Joanne. She's so manipulative and such a user. He can't see she's using him for her own ends – as she used me,"

"I saw the papers today," said James cautiously.

"I know, fucking bastards. After we were so careful to hide our relationship as well."

"Well, I suppose that's the end of that then."

"What do you mean?"

"Well, I know how you hate the press hanging around you and now they know about Lana they'll be after you like a pack of hounds if you stay with her."

"No, nothing changes at all." Cathal walked into the canteen, leaving James staring after him.

* * *

"She's nothing but a bitch!" Ralph said down the phone.

Sylvia sat in her office listening to Ralph Conway's rant down the phone about Tina Cawley. She had been fielding calls from the press all day, looking to get in contact with Tina who was now flying away from the furore and leaving her to deal with the mess as usual. Now she had to pacify Ralph Conway. Experience had told Sylvia that Ralph was very nice when things were going well, but it was a different story when he was unhappy.

"You should have seen it!" continued Ralph. "That bitch Cawley and this trashy mob with her running around Exclusive like a bunch of wild animals."

"I can imagine. But luckily there were no photographers present – except your own."

"Screaming, shouting, setting fire to editions of *Hi Life*.

One of them nearly hit Victoria Harton!"

"It's unforgivable."

"The biggest event of *Hi Life*'s calendar destroyed."

"There's no excuse. MPI are prepared to make a donation to your favourite charity in an attempt to make amends." Sylvia had heard rumours that a lot of money from the Conways' charity affairs ended up in their own coffers.

"It still doesn't help the situation I am in," Ralph's voice had softened somewhat on hearing this news.

Sylvia tried to think hard. She was so busy trying to do damage limitation on Tina Cawley that she hadn't had time to digest the information that had been exposed – that Seán was seeing Joanne Bailey and that Cathal was seeing Lana Curtis. "I suppose you saw the papers today," she said, picking up the *The Star* and looking at a photo of Cathal and Joanne.

"How could I miss them?"

"To be honest, the fact that Cathal is seeing Barry Curtis's daughter overshadowed Tina's antics."

"What's your point?"

"I'm just pointing out the level of interest there is in Affidavit and their lives. What we could do is expand the feature being done at the moment to an at-home with the guys and their partners. There's always massive interest in James and Donna and now Seán's dating Joanne, I think we're offering you quite an exclusive."

"Yes, yes," Ralph was becoming excited, "and I know Joanne well – she'd love it. And if we could get Cathal and Lana Curtis it would be the coup of the year."

Sylvia became weary. "We'll see how it goes. I have to run to a meeting. Talk to you later." She hung up the phone on a delighted Ralph.

*   *   *

Tony and Diana were jogging after work. Tony couldn't remember the last time he had taken exercise and was exhausted.

"I'm too old to be doing this," he gasped.

"And you're too young to be that fat. Keep moving!"

"I can't!" Tony stopped and bent over to catch his breath.

"But you have to! Look, if you're Ralph and Margaux's new blue-eyed boy, then you better look the part as well. They aren't high on bad aesthetics."

"I'm not their blue-eyed boy," he objected.

"That's not what I've heard. I hear they have big things planned for you."

"I'm exhausted!"

"You could always try the Atkins diet. This guy I train went on Atkins and he managed to lose three stone . . . and then he looked so well he went on and lost a further eleven stone . . . his wife!"

Tony pulled himself up. "Okay, let's give it another ten minutes."

They jogged off. They passed a woman who stared at them as they ran by.

"Come on and join us!" Diana called out to her.

*   *   *

Nicole turned off the television. It was nearly seven and no call from Tony all day. He had told her over breakfast about some stupid scenario concerning Tina Cawley staging a demonstration at Exclusive and then he'd headed off to work. The man who used to ring her constantly when they weren't together hadn't bothered to tell her he would be late home tonight. Since her outburst when she'd attempted to get him to realise what was happening to their relationship, he had acted normally enough, obviously choosing to ignore it.

She had gone to lunch that day with a couple of friends and she hadn't been able to concentrate on the conversation. They were close friends, but Nicole felt she couldn't open up about what was happening between herself and Tony. Oddly, for the profession she was in which entailed people telling everything about themselves, she wasn't comfortable talking about herself in that way. Except with Tony who she had always told everything to.

"I'm fucking shattered!" Tony declared, coming into the house.

"Where were you?" she asked.

"Out running with Diana. She's one hard taskmaster." He headed into the kitchen and got some milk from the fridge.

She had to admit, since he went on his health kick, he looked really well.

"I'm going upstairs for a shower and then I'm going to spend some time editing the Affidavit feature." He ran upstairs.

She thought about how Tony used to tell her everything. He used to spend hours telling her every detail of his day. Now he just went up for a shower.

I'm losing you, she thought. I'm losing you to a magazine.

* * *

365

Cathal put a forkful of food into his mouth. He and Lana were eating in his kitchen.

"I just kept my mobile off all day, haven't even bothered to listen to any messages," he said. "I know that it will be just messages from journalists asking about the two of us and are we seeing each other."

"What are you going to say to them?"

"Nothing. It's none of their business."

"This whole thing is very scary for me, Cathal. I've never had this kind of attention before. I didn't even leave the apartment all day in case someone recognised me. I'm just worried that, now everyone knows, we'll change. That you'll change towards me."

He leaned over and hugged her. "That's not going to happen." He kissed her and went back to his eating.

*   *   *

Lana and Patricia mingled through the crowd at the private party of a première being held in The Westbury Hotel. Lana had her hair piled high on her head and she was wearing a long flowing white gown. She was consumed with nerves, aware that people were giving her second looks, recognising her from her photo in the papers.

"I have an overwhelming desire to knock back fifty of these," Lana said to Patricia as she tapped her cocktail glass.

"Don't you dare! That's my boss over there and these tickets were very hard to organise. I don't want you showing me up!"

"Oh, so I can misbehave fully usually, on your encouragement I might add, but because this is a work-do I have to behave?" Lana raised a quizzical eyebrow.

"Something like that. Welcome to the real world, darling."

"Can I take your photo?" asked a passing photographer.

"Sure. What's the publication?" asked Patricia as she put her arm around Lana and they both posed.

"*Social and Personal*," said the photographer, who took the photo and moved on.

"You can kiss goodbye to your anonymity now, darling," said Patricia.

"I just don't understand why anyone would be bothered being interested. Okay, I know Cathal is a well-known singer, but why would anyone be interested in me?"

Not you, darling, thought Patricia. It's who your father is that interests them. "We live in fickle times," she sighed as she gave a passing actress the once-over. "Anyway, I'm sure Cathal will be a tower of strength – he's used to all that, isn't he?"

"Well, he hates it when the press get involved in his personal life. And I have to respect that. And to be honest, that really frightens me, having the press write about us and photograph us."

"Well, you seem to be taking to your fifteen minutes of fame with amazing ease."

"Sorry, Miss Curtis, can I take your photo?" asked another photographer.

"What publication are you with?" Patricia enquired.

"*The Herald*"

"That's fine." Patricia put her arm around Lana and smiled.

"Sorry, Miss. I just wanted a photo of Lana," explained the photographer.

"Oh!" Patricia's face dropped and she pulled away.

"I'd hate to get in the way!"

Lane finished posing and her mobile rang. Looking down, she saw her father's number.

With all the stress of being on the front pages, she had forgotten about what he might think of the whole situation.

"Hello?"

"Hi there. Just ringing to apologise really for missing you the other night at the party."

"Oh, that's fine . . . you were busy and . . . um . . ."

"Anyway, I appreciated you being there, meant a lot to me. And from what I see you've got yourself a boyfriend."

She cringed and felt herself go bright red. "Well, I – ah –"

"He looks nice. Anyway, I'll call over for a chat with you soon."

"Okay –" The phone went dead. She put her mobile away.

"Excuse me, would you mind posing for a photo?" asked a photographer.

CHAPTER 29

Lana sat in Nicole's office, her legs crossed and arms folded casually.

"What made you attack Joanne Bailey like that?" Nicole asked.

"She had came over and provoked me earlier and I was in no mood to be provoked."

"Earlier? Then why didn't you attack her at that time?"

"Um . . . I guess I hadn't been drinking too much at that point."

"Have you thought of apologising to her?"

Lana looked confused. The thought had never crossed her mind. "No, why should I? I don't regret it. I just regret doing it in public. She's not a nice person."

You've never had to ask, apologise, or explain yourself ever in your life, have you? thought Nicole. However, she was intrigued; she was finding out more about the launch party from Lana than she did from Tony. "So what happened then?"

"Well, to my surprise and great delight, Cathal came over to me and tried to calm me down. I couldn't believe he did it, because he hates his private life exposed. But he

369

cared more about me that he did about his privacy. Then there was this big commotion and we left and as I told you photographers took our photo and we were all over the papers."

"What did you think when you saw those photos?"

"I thought I'd hate it. But all my life I've been in the shadow and suddenly there I was on the front pages, not in my father's shadow. "

"And how did Cathal feel about it?"

"Angry, furious, apologising to me constantly that I was in the papers because of him."

*   *   *

Margaux, Ralph and Tony sat around the board table counting the nominations that had come in by post for Social Personality of the Year.

"It's very close," declared Margaux as she looked at the final figures. Kathryn Foy has done really well, but it's Edel Gordon who wins out."

"For fuck's sake!" shouted Ralph.

"Now, Ralph," Margaux looked displeased. "You know how I hate to hear bad language."

Tony knew Edel Gordon was a lady who lunched, who did considerable charity work and was aged around sixty.

"We can't put her on the front cover of *Hi Life*!" said Ralph. "Not with a face like hers – we'll sell no copies!"

"I take your point." Margaux nodded.

He reached over and took a group of Edel's votes and put them on Kathryn's instead. "As you can see Kathryn Foy is our clear winner. She would look great on our front cover."

Tony looked on silently as Ralph picked up the phone

and dialled Kathryn.

"Kathryn! I've wonderful news for you."

"I need it, Ralph, after the terrible lapse of security at the launch party. I gave you complete control of the door and I don't know how those people were allowed in. It's been very bad for the club's image."

Ralph shifted uncomfortably. "Yes, that stupid secretary of mine let them in. Anyway, it's in the past now. And there was no press present except our photographer and *we* sure as hell aren't going to publish any of the r-r-r-riot photographs."

"Still, it's taught me a lesson, I'll never allow someone else's staff in charge of the door at Exclusive again."

Ralph looked at Margaux and raised his eyes to heaven. "Yes, yes. Anyway the reason I phoned you was because you won the Social Personality of the Year Award!"

"Oh – right!" Kathryn was genuinely shocked.

"A wonderful privilege to be bestowed on you by the people of Ireland – don't you agree?"

"Yes – I'm flattered."

"Now, what I want to do is organise an interview and photos of you at your home."

"At my home?"

"Yes, that is what we do every year for the winner. We put you on the front cover and have a full-length feature on you inside. Maybe we can organise a time now?"

"You know, I'd really have to check my diary on that one. Can I call you back?"

* * *

Kathryn closed over her phone and sat down at the bar and looked around Exclusive. She was alone there in the afternoon. Photos at home? How could she allow that to happen with Simeon the way he was? She hadn't expected or wanted to win the damned award. What would Simeon say? She knew what kind of crap they wanted. Her, curled up lovey-dovey with her partner. Which could be not further from the truth.

* * *

"How much further to the hotel?" Barry Curtis leaned forward from the back seat of his car and asked his driver.

"Should be about another ten minutes, Barry."

As the car made its way through the lush Meath countryside to The Marriott, en route to a meeting with an environmentalist group, Barry sat back into his seat and looked at his daughter smiling from a photo in *The Herald*, and under it the caption: *"Lana Curtis, daughter of Barry, shows us some style at the première last night."*

Gloria, sitting beside him, scanned through some paperwork. "We're still lagging in the polls," she sighed.

"What do you think the problem is?" Barry was concerned.

"I maintain that Joe public is still nervous about electing a man of your wealth. They believe that a vote for you is a vote for big business and tax breaks for big business."

"How can they be so naïve? Why can't they see that my policies will make the economy continue to boom. And if the economy is happy, then everybody is happy."

"I think we need to work on you as a person. Not just Barry Curtis, the tycoon, but Barry Curtis the man. Despite the huge pressure from the press, we still see no personal life from Barry Curtis. Your candidates are being promoted as family men and women devoted to their families. We just are not getting that from you, and I don't know how much further I can hold the press off without you being seen with your wife."

"And what do you think would be a way around that, Gloria?"

Gloria reached forward, took the paper from Barry and studied the photo of Lana.

* * *

Lana looked down at her ringing mobile as she made her way home. Two calls from Barry within a couple of days – she was honoured. She answered and they did their usual chit-chat routine, before Barry asked, "How's Cathal?"

"Cathal – eh, he's fine, thank you."

"I was just wondering if the two of you would like to come over to Kildara for dinner soon?"

"Dinner? Kildara?" Lana was filled with a mixture of terror and confusion.

"Sure. I'd like to meet Cathal." He gave a laugh. "Check out if he's good enough for my girl."

You never bothered checking out the dozens who came before him, Lana thought.

"Well, when were you thinking?"

"How about tomorrow night?"

"I'm not sure. I'll have to check it with him."

"Around eight would be just fine."

* * *

Cathal stood in front of the mirror in his bedroom trying to knot his tie. He was all sixes and sevens and couldn't manage to do it. He felt very stressed at the thought of meeting Lana's family. He wished he hadn't agreed to it. He looked at Lana applying her lipstick in another mirror. He realised their relationship had developed very quickly and he was the kind of person who liked to step back and have a firm grasp on what he was doing in life. But all he knew was that he really enjoyed being in Lana's company. She excited him, intrigued him and often confused him, and it had taken him so long to get her to give him a chance that he didn't want to risk it by saying he didn't want to meet her family. Besides, he knew how easily hurt she was and didn't want to upset her.

"This fucking thing!" he shouted, giving up on tying the knot.

"Here, let me try," she said, coming over and doing the job for him.

"Will I call your father Mr Curtis or Barry or what?"

"Everyone calls him Barry."

"And what about your mother?"

She began to blush. "It's just going to be my dad there tonight."

"Oh, why?"

"Mum's been on a shopping trip to London, and her flight was delayed, so she's decided to stay on another day."

"I don't know why your father wants to meet me," Cathal fretted.

"Well, that's what people do, isn't it? Meet each other's family when they're seeing each other."

Cathal's face creased with worry. He never really thought about Lana's family. He knew they weren't close and she never bothered speaking about them much. He never even thought about her as the daughter of the legendary Barry Curtis.

"You know . . . I think I'd rather not."

"But why not?"

"Look we're doing fine, aren't we? Just the two of us. Or we were before the press found out about us . . . and now meeting your father and all that . . . I'm just not at ease with it."

"You once got very upset when you thought I didn't think you were good enough to meet my father, remember?"

He nodded.

"And now I want you to meet him. Don't worry. You'll love him," she sighed. "Everyone does."

* * *

Cathal drove out from the underground carpark of his apartment and paused, checking to see if the coast was clear of traffic before swinging out onto the street.

Suddenly there was a loud banging on his window and man's voice shouted "Cathal!"

Both Cathal and Lana looked startled as a photographer took their photo.

"Fuck off!" Cathal shouted before tearing off in the Range Rover down the street.

"What were they waiting there for?" Lana asked, her voice high with upset.

Cathal's mobile rang. "Yeah?" he snapped.

"Cathal, it's Tony here at *Hi Life*. I just have the feature ready now and I wanted –"

"I can't talk now," Cathal snapped rudely down the phone and hung up.

*   *   *

Tony hung up the phone on his desk, feeling dejected. He was amazed to hear Cathal talk so ignorantly. He was just like all the rest of them. He looked out his window. It was nearly eight and he was working late, trying to get through things. Since Viviene's demotion he seemed to be working non-stop. He had been trying unsuccessfully to get through to Kathryn Foy to organise her photo shoot. He thought he'd try again and dialled her number.

"Hi, Kathryn?"

"Yeah?"

"It's Tony O'Brien here from *Hi Life* magazine."

Kathryn tensed. "Yeah?"

"I'm just phoning on behalf of Ralph, just wondering when you could come into the office to have a chat about the feature we're going to do on you."

"I'll have to phone you back about that – I'm tied up all this week."

Tony heard the phone go dead on the other end.

Replacing the receiver, he felt himself become annoyed. That Kathryn Foy really thought she was someone, the way she spoke to people. He had a head role in *Hi Life* magazine; she should at least try to be pleasant to him. He deserved some respect.

*   *   *

"Who was that?" asked Simeon as he walked into the kitchen.

"That? Oh, just a guy from *Hi Life* magazine. I won that stupid little award from *Hi Life*. I forgot to tell you." She felt tense.

He shrugged and headed back out to the lounge.

And they want to do an eight-page At Home with us incidentally, she thought, as she counted out Simeon's pills to take to him.

* * *

Donna lay out on the couch, her hair tied up loosely, as she flicked through *Hi Life* magazine. James sat at the bottom of the couch, rubbing her feet, slightly distracted.

"I can't understand Cathal," mused Donna. "I'd have thought he would have dumped her straightaway."

"As I've always said, he always has to be different and is always attracted to danger. He's going over to her parents tonight for dinner."

"What?" Donna cast *Hi Life* aside to give this piece of information her full attention. "He's going over to have dinner with Barry Curtis?"

"Yeah."

She was impressed. "I can't understand how somebody as dynamic and successful and brilliant as Curtis could have ended up with such a disaster for a daughter."

"He probably spoiled her rotten!" grinned James.

"I'm not being funny. And you know I love Cathal and everything. But what is a man like Barry Curtis going to have in common with our Cathal? He will probably just dismiss him as one of his idiotic daughter's latest fads."

"I suppose." James continued to rub her feet.

* * *

As Cathal pulled up outside the Curtis house, he couldn't but show how impressed he was by the residence.

"What's wrong?" she asked.

"Well, when it's just you and me alone in my apartment, I forget that you come from all this." He noticed she looked nervous and reached over, took her hand and squeezed it.

"It'll be fine. Don't worry," he said.

The front door of the house was, as ever, unlocked.

"Hello!" Lana called.

"Hi there!" said Barry's strong voice.

Cathal looked up and saw Barry come down the circular staircase. He was hit immediately by the man's presence and realised everything people said about Barry Curtis was true.

"Thought you might be a bit late with the traffic and everything," Barry said. "Hiya, darling." He enveloped his daughter in an embrace. "And Cathal!" He took Cathal's hand and shook it warmly.

"Nice to meet you, er, Barry."

"You know, I heard a couple of your songs on the radio today and I think I'm just going to sign myself up to your fan club," said Barry in his easy-going manner and backed it up with a genuine smile.

"Cool. You can get free text alerts now telling you when our next concerts are on!" Cathal joked.

"Great. I can be ahead of the pack and get good seats," Barry laughed and stepped between them, putting an arm around each of them and leading them towards the drawing room.

Lana felt the tenseness in her fade as she noticed both men seemed to be relaxed in each other's company. But as they entered the drawing room, Lana felt herself go cold.

Gloria was seated on a couch, dressed in a shimmering evening gown, coiffured to perfection.

"Hi, everyone," said Gloria brightly, standing up.

"Gloria, this is Cathal Fitzgerald," said Barry. "Cathal – Gloria Reagan."

Gloria walked across the room and shook Cathal's hand, before approaching Lana and kissing her on the cheek. Lana froze.

"Right," said Gloria, taking charge as ever. "What's everyone drinking? Cathal? Lana?"

*   *   *

The dining table could seat fourteen, and so with just the four of them at it, they were spaced out considerably. Which was just as well, thought Lana, considering how angry she was. This was supposed to be a private family moment. An opportunity for her father to meet the only man she had ever felt anything for. How and why Gloria was not only present but also seemed to have taken on the mantle of hostess for the night was beyond her.

"How did you ever end up being in a rock band?" Gloria asked with amused interest.

"I kind of fell into it really," he said, "but I don't know any other life now."

"And what were you studying before you formed the band?" pushed Gloria.

Cathal shifted uncomfortably and really wished he hadn't come. These people were way out of his sphere. "I didn't go to college," he answered.

"I love it!" said Gloria, smiling broadly. "I love the way the whole celebrity culture enables people to rise so quickly from nowhere to fame and fortune." She cut into her beef.

Lana sat toying with her food, trying to contain her growing anger. So her father thought so little of her he had included his political advisor in such an intimate family event!

Gloria looked over at Barry and nodded at him carefully, indicating that he should push the agenda she had suggested. He shook his head, meaning it was too early for that.

"You certainly have been getting a lot of press attention since your relationship with Lana was revealed," remarked Gloria, deciding the time was right to push her agenda, with or without Barry's approval.

"Unfortunately," said Cathal.

Ignoring Barry's warning looks, Gloria continued. "Barry is having a fund-raiser at the Radisson Hotel on Thurday evening for his campaign. Why don't both of you come along?"

"Thursday evening? I'm not sure what I have on," said Cathal.

"I'm sure you could find some room in your diary," Gloria pushed.

"What kind of sport are you into, Cathal?" Barry asked abruptly, seeing Cathal was uncomfortable.

"Er, soccer, golf –"

"Golf, my favourite pastime. I'd love to have a game with you. When are you free?"

"I'm not sure –"

"Could you be around for a couple of rounds tomorrow afternoon?"

Cathal was surprised. He had expected Barry to tolerate him for Lana's sake, be coldly polite and then try to get rid of him. But he had been nothing but nice to him and also he had this strange way of making you want to please him. "I suppose I could get out of the studio for a couple of hours," he said, feeling honoured that a man of Barry's status would want to spend any time with him.

Lana's agitation increased as Gloria's presence continued to infuriate her. She sat at the table almost as if she was Barry's partner. Maybe that was Gloria's plan, it dawned on Lana. And as she watched Barry work his magic on Cathal, a burning anger developed inside her. Yes, he was being charming to Cathal. But that was his problem: he was charming to everybody. She wanted her father for herself, not to be shared by everybody. And she realised once he was elected and became a political figure, he would become even more public property, whose time would be carefully controlled by Gloria. Lana was a runner. Whenever she didn't like a situation, her overriding emotion was to run. And as all these thoughts crowded her head, she felt suddenly clausrophobic and needed to get out of there.

Lana put down her fork and gave a quick look at everybody, before reaching down for her handbag and standing up. "I'm sorry – I forgot to do something back at the house."

She quickly walked out of the room.

"Lana?" Cathal said, startled.

He felt a hand on his arm as Barry said, "It's okay. I'll go after her."

The tears streamed down Lana's face as she walked out the front door. She just wanted to get into the car and drive home, but she realised she couldn't leave Cathal there.

"Lana, wait up!" came Barry's voice behind her.

She quickly tried to wipe away her tears as she turned to look at him.

"What's wrong, honey?" he asked.

"Nothing."

"Come on. Tell me. Was I rude to Cathal or something?"

"Oh, course not. You're never rude to anybody." The tears started to roll again.

"Then what's the problem?"

"Why is *she* here?"

"Gloria? I thought it would be nice for her to come along."

"This was a private family affair, Daddy. God knows, it's taken me long enough to find anybody I can relate to and, now that I have, I wanted *you* to meet him not bloody Gloria as well!"

Barry was shocked. "I'm sorry. I didn't think."

"No, you didn't. Cathal's somebody very important to me and you're treating him, and me, like one of your employees!"

"I've always treated you as special."

"You treat everyone as special!" she shouted. "You're Barry Curtis. Everyone who meets you loves you because you treat them as special. And you can't distinguish me from everybody else!"

"I'm sorry. I never meant for you to feel like that. I just wanted you to be happy, that's all. I just wanted for you and your mum to have everything and never need for anything."

"Don't even go there !" She shot him a warning look. "You gave us everything but you!"

He sat down on the steps in front of the house. "I just wanted you to be happy, that's all," he repeated.

"Well, I'm not – I'm *not*. I have no purpose in life. Except for Cathal."

"What do you want from me?" He looked up at her.

"I don't know . . ." She looked up and saw Cathal come quietly out of the house and stand looking at them.

"I want you to need me," she said.

She turned and started to walk back to the Range Rover. Cathal ran down the steps and came alongside her, putting his arm around her.

"Eh, thanks, I'll see you again," said Cathal to Barry as they got into the Range Rover.

Barry nodded and gave a small wave.

They drove away, leaving him sitting on the steps.

*   *   *

Lana dried her eyes after sobbing for an hour in Cathal's arms in his apartment.

"I'm sorry I had to leave like that," she said.

"It's fine." He rubbed her arm.

"You probably wonder what kind of a freak you're involved with here. But Gloria! How dare he bring her along to something as important as tonight! And there she was, looking at you like some amusing sociological project!"

He had to admit Gloria had seemed to view him in a condescending fashion. He wanted to probe further and ask Lana about her mother. But he didn't want to push her any further that evening.

"I'll tell you this –" She mopped her eyes with a handkerchief. "I bet you're glad you come from such a normal background after seeing that tonight. You don't know how lucky you are."

*   *   *

Stephen Rourke looked around the miserable flat in the north city centre of Dublin. His euphoria about being released from prison after so many years had quickly turned to anger as he realised how hard life was on the outside. He looked at himself in the cracked mirror in the tiny bathroom and decided that despite his time on the inside he still looked good. But his life was as cracked as the mirror. He strolled out of the bathroom and looked at the unkempt bed squeezed into the corner of the room. He had had everything going for him when he was young. Everything. He was a big man around Castletown; everyone looked up to him. He had money, talent, connections. And it had all been cruelly swiped from him. He looked down at the newspapers spread out over the coffee table, all with photos of Cathal and Lana on the front. All his time in prison he had watched Cathal Fitzgerald's rise, feeling increasingly angry. It was Cathal's fault that he had ended up there. And now he had hooked up with an heiress. Cathal Fitzgerald's life was sweet, and he owed it all to Stephen. Now it was payback time.

CHAPTER 30

Ralph slammed his fist on his desk, making Tony jump. "What do you mean she said call her back next week?" he demanded.

"She said she was too busy to talk and she'd talk later," explained Tony.

"I can't wait around for people to fit me into their schedule. You should have forced Kathryn Foy to make an appointment there and then!"

Easier said than done when she hung up on me, thought Tony.

"I need to schedule her feature as soon as possible. Get her on the phone again and force her to come in. You have to be more forceful."

Tony nodded and got up and left the room. He felt totally stressed. He had gone from hardly doing anything to doing everything. He sat down at the phone at his desk and contemplated phoning Kathryn. He didn't fancy getting through to her ice-queen manner again. He picked up the phone and dialled but it rang through to her voicemail.

*   *   *

Kathryn ignored *Hi Life's* phone number coming up. But she knew Ralph Conway and knew there was no point in trying to avoid him. The more she did it, the more he would plague her.

Simeon had made great headway over the past couple of weeks and he was better than he had been for a long time. She was so very nervous the feature would in some way unbalance him.

She went into the lounge and sat in an armchair opposite him. "That was *Hi Life* magazine on the phone."

He put the paper down. "Yeah ?"

"Just congratulating me on the win for that award."

"That was nice."

He stared at her and she felt herself staring back at him intently. He got up and moved slowly to her, then bent down to her. Expectantly she raised her face to him. They gazed at each other at close range for a long moment. He bent and kissed her lips. She put her arm around him and kissed him back. He pulled away from her and stared down at her again. He went back to the couch and started reading the paper, leaving Kathryn still staring at him.

*   *   *

Cathal's phone rang while he was driving through town. "Yeah?"

"Cathal, how are you ? It's Barry Curtis here. Can you talk?"

Cathal swerved the car slightly, he was so surprised to hear from Barry. He wondered how he got his mobile number. "Yeah, Barry, er, thanks for dinner."

"It was really nice to meet you. I've eh –" he gave a little laugh, "even gone out and bought one of your CDs! Cathal, just wanted to know what time you want to meet up for that round of golf today?"

I thought you were only being polite, Cathal thought. "Er, any time that suits you."

"Drive out to Kildara around lunchtime"

*   *   *

Cathal parked his car in the carpark of MPI and made his way to Sylvia's office. Checking his messages on his mobile, he realised all of them were from journalists wanting interviews about himself and Lana. Sighing, he turned off the phone and knocked on Sylvia's door.

"Come in," she called. Entering, he found her swivelling on her chair behind her desk and talking on the phone.

"I'll pass the message on but I doubt he'll agree." She hung up the phone and looked up as Cathal sat opposite her. "That was a journalist wanting to do an interview with you about Lana."

"Yeah. I've had a lot of enquiries too."

"Have you considered any of them? Or have you already finished with Lana?"

"No, I haven't finished with her," he snapped, looking angry. "I wish everyone would stop saying that. It's pissing me off."

She held her hands up in mock surrender.

"I don't want to give any interviews, and neither does she. It's nobody's business but ours."

Sylvia sat back in her chair and joined her hands. "Cathal, you're very in the public eye and now you've met somebody who because of her family is very high profile. The press won't let up."

"I know," he sighed and leant back in his chair. He knew Sylvia well enough to know that she probably already had a plan in place. "Go on, Sylvia. What do you suggest ?"

She leant forward. "An exclusive with *Hi Life*. I was talking to Ralph Conway and he's willing to extend the feature with Affidavit to include photos at home and personal interviews. We're talking about it dominating a whole issue, and it will go out across Europe to all *Hi Life* franchises."

"You know I hate that kind of thing," he grimaced.

"You have to give them something, Cathal. That's the price for the money, and the recognition and the lifestyle you have. This way you have control over what is said and done."

"You know, even if I was in favour of it, Lana's very different from everyone I've ever met. She's very private and . . . fragile. She'd hate that kind of intrusion into her life."

"Well, either that or every time you leave the house together you'll have a photographer snapping a camera in your faces looking for an exclusive."

"I suppose." he sighed again.

"I mean, all the other guys in Affidavit are more than willing to include their partners in the feature."

"Of course they are. Donna already lives her life as if there's a permanent photographer from *Hi Life* in her house. And now that Joanne Bailey is on the scene – well, she'd jump up and down naked for a photo if she thought it would get her press attention."

*   *   *

"I just couldn't help myself," said Lana, bending forward and putting her face in her hands. "I just felt so angry and disappointed."

Nicole looked at her, thinking she was on the verge of a major breakthrough. She knew there were issues in Lana's family which were fundamental to her unhappiness but, no matter how hard she had tried in the past, she had just come up against a brick wall. But now things seemed to have come to a head.

"It was like years of anger and frustration suddenly came spilling out to my dad."

"But that's a good thing. For the first time you communicated with him."

"No, I didn't. I came across like a spoilt child angry at not being the centre of attention."

"Do you not think you deserve to be the centre of your father's attention?"

"Yes . . . but he's so busy and, well, you know who he is." She ran her fingers through her hair. "He told me all he has ever done is try to give me everything."

"In a material sense, yes. But you were just letting him know you want more. And what's wrong with that?"

"Nothing, I guess."

"What's wrong with him seeing the real you? The real you with needs and wants and insecurities?" She couldn't help from giving a small sigh."Just like everyone else."

"I just don't know where we are going to go from here. Do we just pretend nothing happened? Do we sit down and talk everything through?"

"Maybe you should just go with the flow."

"As for Cathal, I don't know what he thinks of the whole situation. Him from his nice safe cosy background."

Nicole twirled her pen in her hand, studying Lana. "You seem to be getting on very well."

"I don't know what I'd do without him."

Nicole put down the pen. She knew Lana had an addictive personality. I hope you're not swapping one addiction for another, she thought.

* * *

"Good shot!" praised Barry, watching the golf ball Cathal hit fly over the green.

"I haven't been playing that long really," admitted Cathal as they walked over the grass. He had driven out to Barry's house at lunchtime and left his car there. Then they had been taken over to the golf club by Barry's driver.

"Did you tell Lana you were meeting me today?" Barry asked.

"Er . . . no. I didn't know whether to or not. So I decided against it."

"How has she been?"

"Okay, I guess."

"I'm sorry you had to witness that."

That was pretty mild compared to a lot of the things I've witnessed with Lana, Cathal thought.

Barry positioned himself at a tee, judging the ball for a while. "I was thinking. You're the first official boyfriend Lana has ever introduced to me."

"Really?"

"Well, I've met loads of her friends over the years and I could never keep up with her to know what the story was between all the people she hung out with."

Did you ever think of asking, Cathal thought.

"You're not really what I expected Lana to go out with."

Here we go, Cathal thought. "No?"

"No. I thought she would end up with one of those guys from Patricia's gang. You know Patricia?"

"Yeah." Cathal didn't try to keep the hostility out of his voice. "I know Patricia and her gang. Spoilt rich kids who had everything handed to them on a plate. And they end up totally vacuous or fucked up in the head. But they come from the right families and have the right position in life. So I'm sorry I must be such a disappointment for you . . . Mr Curtis."

"Whoa !" Barry called with a smile. "You're a touchy fella. Do you usually fly off like that?"

Cathal looked down at the ground.

"I take it you do," Barry said. He put a hand on Cathal's shoulder. "What I was going to say was that I'm very glad Lana didn't end up with somebody like that."

Cathal felt uncomfortable. He was ready for a fight but this man had totally disarmed him. He nodded and they walked off across the green.

"I wasn't born into all this, you know," said Barry. "I did it all myself. Built it up from very little. And you came from nowhere and did the same."

"You used your mind to get to where you are – I just got lucky," said Cathal.

Barry looked at Cathal, perplexed. "I'd like the opportunity to get to know you better, Cathal." He sighed. "And I would like the chance to get to know my daughter as well. Will you help me get to know her, Cathal? Could you put in a good word for me?"

*   *   *

The doorbell rang. Lana switched off the television and went to answer it. When she opened the door she was surprised to find Margaux and Ralph there.

"Lana!" Margaux approached her with her hands stretched into the air.

Lana felt herself enveloped in a huge hug and being kissed on both cheeks. This was followed by Ralph doing the same thing.

"This is a surprise," said Lana, wondering what on earth they were doing there and how the hell did they get her address.

"We thought we'd personally bring you over a copy of the issue. It hits the stands tomorrow," said Ralph, holding up a copy of *Hi Life*.

There on the front cover was a photo of Barry waving at his birthday party.

"Won't you, er, come in?"

They followed her into the lounge. Lana went to sit down and to her surprise Margaux sat on one side of her, and Ralph on the other. Lana felt slightly claustrophobic.

'Now – look at this!" Margaux quickly opened to the feature on the launch and Lana was greeted with a full-page colour photo of herself taken on the night by Clive, under the heading *'Barry's Stunning Daughter – Lana'*.

Lana took the magazine and looked at it in shock. "I thought you were just going to include a small photo of me!"

"You must be quite used to all the attention now since your relationship with Cathal Fitzgerald was exposed – you're quite the dark horse!" said Margaux, taking Lana's hand and holding it.

"You know, we've been thinking about you a lot since we met you – we felt we had a great rapport." Ralph patted her knee. "We were wondering if you had given any thought to your future."

"My future?" asked Lana, confused.

"Well, you know we think you've a big future ahead of you – with the right guidance." said Margaux.

Ralph took Lana's other hand and held it tightly, and now she sat between them, both her hands being held on either side.

"We would like you to come and work for us at *Hi Life*," said Ralph.

"You're offering me a job? As what?" Lana's head was spinning with confusion.

"We were considering you might join us in our Marketing Department."

"Marketing?" Lana was stunned. "Well, yes, but I've very little experience in the publishing business." Or anything else for that matter, she added silently to herself.

"A girl with your brains, charm and connections will quickly learn the ropes and become a shining light in the magazine industry." Ralph nodded reassuringly.

"But what would I be doing?"

"You'd be promoting the image of *Hi Life*," explained Ralph, "and that means everything from designing sales slogans to shop posters. You would be responsible for tying in brands to our image and coming up with advertising directions. And you'd also have a say in editorial – you know, coming up with ideas for features that you think would suit our market and advertisers."

"A truly exciting and diversified role!" exclaimed Margaux.

"I really don't know . . . I'd have to give it some real

thought." Lana's face was filled with concern and worry.

"You take all the time you need." Margaux smiled and squeezed her hand.

* * *

Joanne Bailey lay stretched out on Seán's couch, on the phone to Jason, her new agent in London.

"This At Home feature with Affidavit is going to be huge, Jason. There will be lots of photos with me and Seán and not only in the Irish and UK edition of *Hi Life* but across Europe as well."

"A real PR coup," acknowledged Jason.

"We have to strike while the iron is hot, Jason. If I don't get some high-profile TV-presenter role after this, then I never will."

"I'll start making my calls immediately."

"I was also thinking of raising my profile in the UK by doing some photo calls for free for charity. What do you think?"

"Good idea."

"You know the kind of thing, some children's charity. Me, surrounded by some kids, looking gorgeous for the cameras with low cleavage – the press would love it."

"You're all heart!" scoffed Jason.

"Listen, mate, Snow White doesn't live in my gaff!"

Joanne clicked off her phone and looked around Seán's spacious sitting room. She liked Seán's house, but she much preferred Cathal's apartment. She would have to get Seán to do the place up before *Hi Life* took their photos. Not that they would be competing against Cathal, because there was no way he would pose for any photos. As for Rob and Heidi, there was no glamour stakes there any more since they had their sprog. Having said that, she didn't want to be outdone by James and Donna. She stretched her arms in the air. She couldn't believe her luck.

She heard the front door slam. "Seán?" she called.

A hassled-looking Seán came in and bent over to kiss her before sitting down.

"How was the studio?" she asked.

"We only did a couple of hours this morning and then we all needed a break. The atmosphere isn't getting any better. Me and Cathal are barely civil to each other."

"Don't let him push you around, the bastard. Show him you're the boss." She threw some magazines in his lap.

"What are these ?"

"Interior designer books. I've marked the pages I like. We need to get working on this place quickly for the photo shoot."

*   *   *

After their round of golf, Barry had insisted that Cathal come back to the house for something to eat. Cathal surprised himself by going along and enjoying a sumptuous salad spread. He found Barry fascinating and good company and one of the nicest people he'd ever met. Eventually, looking at his watch, he realised it was getting on and so he said his thank-you's and left.

As he made his way to his car he came face to face with Kathryn Foy. She was dressed in a business suit and carrying a folder under her arm.

"What are you doing here?" he asked, surprised.

"Here to go through the books for Exclusive with Barry."

"Of course," he said, remembering that Barry was a major shareholder of Exclusive.

"It's kinda funny seeing you in daylight," he said and laughed.

"You too." She smiled back.

He realised he hadn't seen Kathryn smile much. She always seemed so serious and businesslike at Exclusive. He wondered how to broach the subject of Lana's outburst. He hadn't been looking forward to seeing Kathryn since as he knew he couldn't just ignore the situation. This was an ideal opportunity to try and paper over it as they were out of the usual environment.

"Listen, just about the *Hi Life* party. I'm sorry Lana made a bit of a scene with Joanne Bailey."

She was taken aback. The last thing she'd expected was an apology from Cathal. "You have an amazing knack of surprising me," she said.

"Huh?"

"Remember the time we had our big bust-up, and we met up to have a truce – I didn't expect you to apologise then either. It's not your role to apologise for her, Cathal. In fact, if anything, I should be thanking you, for coming over and taking her away."

"I don't think she'll be apologising to you in person." He pulled a face.

"I'd be very surprised if she did. Anyway, I'd better go in. I don't want to keep Barry waiting."

"See you tonight."

"Fine."

Cathal watched her go. He had arranged to go in to Exclusive that night and had persuaded Lana to go as well. Better for her than sitting home moping, he had said. He had rung Tony from *Hi Life* and apologised for cutting him short the night before. Tony had been cool at the beginning of the conversation, obviously hurt, so Cathal had suggested he come into Exclusive that night and he could look through the feature there. Tony had seemed genuinely delighted by this suggestion and readily agreed.

*   *   *

Lana had breezed in past Kathryn Foy at the Exclusive front door that night, barely nodding to her, and gone straight to the members' lounge. Luckily, James was the only one from the group out that night – the rest of the gang were with the crowd working on the album. She wasn't in the mood for Donna. And as for Seán and Rob, there seemed to be a definite split in the group and they didn't socialise together with Cathal any more.

Her head had been full of the job offer at *Hi Life* all day. She didn't know what to make of it and was at the same time excited and terrified. She hadn't had a chance to talk to Cathal about it yet. Cathal had invited the guy Tony from the magazine along with them that night. She studied him intently as he talked to Cathal while Cathal read through the stuff he had done so far. Tony was really excited by his work and this made her wonder even more what it would be like working at *Hi Life*.

"What do you think?" asked Tony as Cathal finished reading the feature.

"Really good. I think it's brilliant."

"Really?" Tony was delighted with the praise.

"Couldn't be better," nodded Cathal.

"Good. That's that finished then." Tony glanced over at Lana who at that moment was busy talking to a friend who had been drinking at the next table. "Have you given any more thought to including Lana in the photos for this feature?"

Cathal frowned. "From your expression, it's all been arranged already behind my back. Did I ever have a say?"

"Don't say I said anything!" Tony looked alarmed.

"No – I won't. I don't know – Lana doesn't like that kinda thing."

"It's gonna look weird if everyone else has his partner in the photos and you don't. It will make the press hound you even more."

"I know. I thought about all that. I'll have a word with Lana and see what she thinks."

* * *

"I've something to tell you," Cathal said to Lana.

"What?" she asked, her mind still on the *Hi Life* offer.

"I played that round of golf with your father today."

"Did you?" She looked at him. "You never said."

"I didn't know whether to go or not, or whether to tell you or not. Are you angry?"

She thought for a moment and sighed. "No. I know what Barry's like. No one can resist him."

"I didn't go because I wanted to meet the great Barry Curtis. I went because I wanted to see if I could help after the falling-out the other night."

"What did he have to say for himself?"

"I think he's surprised and shocked after what you said. He had no idea how you felt."

"Well, he should have thought about me more then." The anger came through in her voice.

Cathal took her hand. "He really wants to make a go of it with you. A fresh start."

She reached forward, grabbed her whiskey and knocked it back in one go.

Kathryn, walking around the members' lounge, spotted Cathal and Lana. She was surprised to learn they were an item. Lana wasn't his normal type. She'd had quite a heated discussion with Barry at their meeting that day as she expressed how she felt the Tina-Cawley-led riot had affected the club's image. She had explained that, between the Conways, Gloria Reagan and herself, there had been too many chiefs and not enough Indians on the night which had caused an insecure door policy allowing what had happened to happen.

Kathryn spotted a hostess heading over to Cathal's table with a tray of drinks and she intercepted her. "I'll take them for you," she said, taking the tray. She moved over to the table. "Hi, everyone." She smiled and started putting the drinks down on the table.

"Thanks, Kathryn," said Cathal with a smile, then turned and continued his conversation with Tony.

Kathryn looked at Lana, who was viewing her coolly. "Your whiskey?"

Lana nodded. Kathryn put the drink in front of her.

"I just want to say one thing to you," Kathryn said, just loud enough so only Lana could hear. "You ever try causing a scene like you did the other night with Joanne Bailey in Exclusive again and I'll have your ass thrown out of here so quick you won't know what's hit you."

"I beg your pardon?" Lana was incredulous.

"And I don't give a shit who your father is or who your friends are – you won't be getting back in here again, you understand me? I run a tight ship here and I will not tolerate troublemakers in Exclusive." Kathryn turned and walked away.

*   *   *

Nicole lay out on her bed in darkness, her mobile against her ear, listening to the message Tony had left earlier.

"Hi, Nic, it's me. Listen, just letting you know I'm going out for the night with Cathal and the guys to Exclusive. It'll probably be a late night, so don't bother waiting up."

She had been replaying the message over and over again to herself as the tears fell down her face.

*   *   *

Tony went over to have lunch with his parents on Sunday by himself. It felt so weird because Nicole always came too. He thought about the problems they were having. He loved her, but she seemed to want to undermine him as he tried to forge a new career for himself. She seemed to resent that he wanted a bit of a social life with the people he dealt with like Affidavit. And when they tried to discuss things they just got nowhere.

*   *   *

Nicole had gone over to her parents for Sunday lunch and the whole family – her two sisters and two brothers – were there.

Nicole had had such a happy upbringing. There had never been any arguments or stress in the house. And all her siblings got on most of the time. She couldn't explain it but she still had always felt slightly alone in spite of all this. She had been very popular growing up and had loads of friends. But she had this feeling that there was somebody out there waiting for her that would make her feel complete. When she met Tony, he made her feel like that immediately.

And they did everything together from day one. She hadn't felt alone since she had been with him. But suddenly that feeling was creeping back to her.

*   *   *

Cathal and Lana were curled up on the sofa at his apartment.

"Did you give any thought about what I said the other night about your father?" he said.

"Of course I have. I'm going to have to see him again soon, no matter what. After my outburst, I don't want to have any awkwardness though."

"C'mon! He's your dad – just pick up the phone and call him!" Cathal reached for the mobile and forced it into Lana's hand.

She reluctantly took it and stalled for a while before dialling his number.

'Hi, Dad – it's me," she said quietly.

"Lana!" He sounded delighted. "How are you?"

"Okay, I guess."

"Good. Listen, I want to see you real soon. I miss you. What are you doing Thursday?"

"Eh, nothing, I guess."

"Well, you are now. You're coming to my rally at the Four Seasons. Not only do I want you there, I *need* you there."

Lana felt her heart jump. "Okay, Dad, I'll see you

401

there." She closed over the phone.

"Wasn't so bad, was it?"

She hugged him tightly. "Thank you!" She looked at him. "He wants me to come to his rally on Thursday. Would you come with me?"

"Ah no, I don't think so. That wouldn't be my scene at all."

"But I need you there. Oh, please, Cathal, come with me!"

"You want me there that much?"

She nodded.

"Okay then. I'll go."

She gazed at him seriously. "Cathal, what would you think about me working?"

"Working?" He laughed lightly. "As what?"

"Ralph Conway has offered me a marketing job at *Hi Life*."

He was surprised. "Really?"

"What do you think?"

"I think it would be very good for you to work. But are you sure you'd want to work at a place like *Hi Life*? There would be so much bullshit there."

"I don't know. I'll have to think about it."

*   *   *

Nicole rubbed her temples as she tried to concentrate on Lana Curtis talking about her relationship with her father. She had hardly seen Tony at all over the weekend. He was either at his parents or partying with his new friends. When he was at home, he was writing his articles. She had hardly slept and was feeling exhausted and emotional.

"So we're going to my father's political rally this week. Cathal's agreed to go as well."

"And how do you feel about that?"

"Well, it will break the ice between us and we might even be able to talk a little, which I think is important. Nicole . . . I have a decision to make."

"What about?"

"I've been offered a job."

"Where?" Nicole tried to look interested.

"At *Hi Life* magazine."

Nicole perked up and sat up straight.

"As a marketing executive. I would be involved in everything from editorial to advertising to promotional stuff. I don't know what to do."

"Where would you be working from?"

"Their office here in Dublin. But I've hardly any experience – in fact I've none."

"I see." Nicole steadied herself. "And what do you think you'll do?"

"I'm not sure . . . What do you think?"

Nicole sat back in her chair. "I can't give you any direct opinion, Lana."

Lana nodded, her mind a million minds away. So was Nicole's.

*   *   *

"You okay?" Cathal asked, squeezing Lana's hand as they walked into the reception of The Four Seasons Hotel.

"I think so," she said, feeling nervous.

As they walked into the function room, they saw it was already filled with party supporters, press and celebrities.

"I didn't realise there would be so much press here,"

said Cathal, concerned, as he recognised faces from the media.

"Ah, there you are!" said a familiar voice and they turned to see Gloria Reagan in evening dress. "Lana, your dad's dying to see you." She took Lana's arm and drew her through the crowded room, Cathal in tow, until they came face to face with Barry.

"Lana!" Barry said, his face filled with joy on seeing his daughter. He enveloped her in a huge hug and whispered in her ear "Thanks for coming. You don't know how important it is for me to have you here tonight . . . we'll talk later, all right?"

She blinked back tears and nodded.

"And, Cathal, thanks for getting her to come."

Gloria looked on with delight. Who would have thought that Lana Curtis could be the key to winning this election? Since she had got herself a rock-star boyfriend, there seemed to be a huge amount of interest in her. Gloria was an expert in behaviourism. She knew what people wanted. She could use Lana and Cathal's relationship to its best advantage during the campaign. So many people supported that group he was in – it was a sure vote winner. She had discussed it with Barry and he seemed enthusiastic. She turned to round up journalists to interview the Golden Couple.

*   *   *

"So you are completely in agreement with all your father's policies?" asked a journalist.

"Eh – yes, of course." said Lana, unsure. "I think he will make a wonderful representative for his constituency and for this country."

"What about you, Cathal? Bit of a change of direction for you from music to politics."

Cathal nodded and smiled, careful not to say anything.

A microphone squealing cut through the noise and everyone looked up at the platform as Gloria tried to amend the sound.

"Ladies and gentlemen," she said, "you are all welcome here tonight – and now without further delay, I introduce to you our soon-to-be-elected representative, Barry Curtis!"

Cathal manoeuvred himself and Lana to the sidelines at the front, regretting coming. It would be in all the papers tomorrow that he was here. What had he been thinking of? He didn't want to be associated with Barry's policies. But Lana had seemed delighted with the attention her father had lavished on her all evening.

Barry finished off his speech. Gloria immediately came on stage with three press photographers.

"Barry, if you could just stand over here," said one of the photographers, positioning Barry in front of the backdrop bearing his campaign slogan: *"Together We Can Achieve It."*

"Wait!" said Gloria, fully aware the photographers would take just one or two photos and then rush off to their next job. She wanted the photos they took to be right. She scanned the crowd until she saw Lana positioned over at the bar. "Can you wait for just one second, guys?" she pleaded as she hurried down the steps from the platform.

"Lana, quick, your father wants you for a photo," she said authoritively.

"A photo?"Lana asked.

"Come on. We don't have time. The photographers will be off in a minute."

Lana downed her drink and set off to the platform.

"Come on. You too, Cathal," ordered Gloria.

"No, I don't think so," Cathal said, smiling and shaking his head.

"You have to!" Gloria grabbed his arm and started pushing him towards the stage.

"Will you let go of me?" Cathal demanded, shaking her loose.

"Cathal, I thought you cared about Lana,"

"I do. But I'm not posing for some photo."

"If you do, you'll get some brownie points with Barry," Gloria whispered insistently. "You should get your ass up on that stage right now!"

"I don't want to get brownie points with anyone here," Cathal said, half-smiling and half-concerned.

"What's keeping you two?" Lana had come back, wondering at the delay but unaware of the struggle that had taken place between them.

"Your father was thinking it would be nice to include Cathal in a photo," said Gloria. "What do you think? You, with the two men in your life?"

Lana smiled at the thought. "Yeah, I'd like that. Come on, Cathal. I want you to be a part of this as well." She held out her hand to him.

"Go on, Cathal," Gloria insisted, smiling, but her eyes were hard.

"I don't . . . er . . ."

But Lana had grabbed his hand and pulled him after her.

Gloria looked on triumphantly as the photographers posed Lana between Cathal and Barry. She was oblivious to Cathal's obvious discomfort as she anticipated getting some front pages with the shots tomorrow.

*   *   *

The crowd had mostly filtered away and Cathal was putting on his coat in the function room, waiting for Lana who was hugging her father.

"Thanks, baby," Barry said. He remembered Gloria's words. "Eh, Lana. The other night you said I don't need anything from you. Well, I actually do. I need you to be with me and part of this campaign – do you think you could do that for me?"

"I'd love that." She hugged him tightly.

"Your car's waiting out the front," a porter informed Lana.

Lana gave Barry a kiss and they walked out to reception.

Cathal waited for Lana out by the lobby, feeling angry. He hadn't wanted to be in any photos and he had been bullied into it.

"I really enjoyed every minute of the night," smiled Lana as she joined him. "Thanks for coming and everything."

He was happy she was happy. "It was no problem."

Word had got out that Cathal was at the hotel and four or five fans had gathered outside, wanting him to sign autographs. As Lana made her way into the car, Cathal stopped, took a pen and started signing for them.

"Thanks," said a male voice, as he wrote his signature on a piece of paper that had been handed to him. "I'm a big fan of yours. I've been following your career with interest over the years."

Cathal looked up smiling, to thank the fan. He froze. He felt himself go cold and the background noise went silent as he looked into the face of Stephen Rourke.

"Your car's waiting, Mr Fitzgerald." The porter placed a hand on Cathal's arm and started directing him to the car.

Cathal turned and walked to the car like a robot. As he sat in, he looked over to the fans, but Stephen Rourke had gone.

CHAPTER 31

Lana sat in the Unicorn restaurant with Patricia, having lunch, as they both looked at the photo of herself, Barry and Cathal from the previous night on the front page of *The Independent*.

"So you enjoyed the night?" asked Patricia.

"It was brilliant. I think myself and Dad are at the beginning of a new phase of our relationship. I'm meeting him later for dinner."

"And Cathal gets on with him?"

"They've already had a game of golf. You know Dad, everyone loves him."

"Any decisions on the job offer at *Hi Life*?"

"No. I think I'll give it another couple of days to decide."

Patricia took up the paper and examined the photo closely. "Well, you two are certainly the new Golden Couple."

"Are we?" Lana laughed lightly.

"Yes. I've heard lots of people talking about you."

Lana took the paper from her friend and peered closely at the photo. "I wonder, if Cathal and me had children, what would they look like?"

"Have you got to that stage?" Patricia's mouth opened.

"No!" she laughed. "But do you think we would have the right genetic mix?"

"Darling, he wears Armani and you wear Gucci – that's the only genetic mix you need to worry about!"

*   *   *

Cathal had had a very bad night's sleep. He'd tossed and turned all night. He'd got a terrible shock seeing Stephen Rourke like that. He was the last person in the world that he'd expected to see. When Affidavit first become famous, he had been worried sick that Stephen would track him down. In fact when Affidavit were offered their first record deal, Cathal had given considerable thought to pulling out, he had been so worried that the attention he would receive would bring Rourke back from his past. In the first couple of years of fame, as Affidavit become more and more well known, he'd lived on his nerves over the situation. But as time passed, he'd become more occupied with the present than the past. And he had become confident that if Roukre hadn't come forward by then, he never would. From time to time he did wonder what had become of him, but he just assumed it hadn't been particularly nice. And then suddenly, there he was, standing there waiting for him outside the hotel last night. What did he want? What would he do? When would he make contact next? So many questions had been whirling around in his mind that even when he had finally fallen asleep he'd woken in a cold sweat, shouting, giving Lana a shock.

The next day he parked his Range Rover in the carpark

of the recording studio and made his way in.

"Well, here he is!" said Seán, smiling smugly.

Cathal glanced at James and Rob, who looked unhappy. Sylvia was there as well, looking concerned.

"Take a look at that," said Seán, tossing a copy of *The Independent* at Cathal.

Cathal took the paper and saw the front page. "I didn't plan this," he said, looking at the photo of himself with Lana and Barry.

"Do you know how bad this looks – associating yourself with a politician like Barry Curtis?" demanded Seán.

"I couldn't help it. I attended as a guest and they took the photo."

"Without you knowing?" Sylvia raised an eyebrow. "Come on, Cathal. That's a posed photo."

"Whatever about you being photographed with Lana, her father's different," said James. "He's running for office, and I don't know if you've studied his manifesto in detail, but a lot of it is about protecting big business. Not the kind of thing our fans want us to be associated with. I'm really pissed off about this, Cathal – a lot of that guy's policies are directly opposed to the charities I work with. You just never think before you do things!"

"You know how we feel about this music MPI are forcing us to put on this album," said Rob. "Your love life has stopped us from being taking seriously in the past and now you've become political arm-candy. It's going to go from bad to worse!"

Cathal felt exhausted from lack of sleep and worry about Stephen Rourke and the last thing he wanted was listening to this lot giving out hell to him for the day. "Look, I can get photographed with whoever the fuck I want to!" he said angrily..

With that, he turned and stormed out.

*   *   *

Lana took out the copy of *Hi Life* the Conways had dropped over and started to leaf through it at home. She studied the features entitled *'At Home with Lord and Lady Hatcombe'* – *'Fresh from His Hollywood Success, Jack Donavan Tells Us His Plans for the Coming Years'* – *'Having Shed Three Stone, the Beautiful Model Francesca Lawlor Tells Us the Secrets of Her Success'*. The magazine was a brilliant blend of international and Irish stories, Lana thought. She marvelled at how she and her life had changed for the better, what with Cathal and now her new understanding with her father. He wanted her to campaign with him – she felt honoured. She would take the job at *Hi Life*. She wanted to continue improving her life, and this was an opportunity too good to miss.

*   *   *

Cathal went to the quiet pub around the corner from the recording studio, ordered a pint of Guinness and sat in a corner out of the way. He wished he hadn't attended the bloody function. And then that bitch Gloria Reagan forcing him into a situation to have the photo taken! He understood the other guys' fury. He wasn't happy about it himself.

It crossed his mind that the whole thing might have been planned. Maybe he was a pawn in Barry's political game. The thought alarmed him greatly. He couldn't suggest this to Lana, as she was in such hero-worship mode regarding her father. As he thought about it more deeply he reckoned and hoped that Barry wasn't such a using bastard. Whatever about Gloria Reagan.

But a bit of support from Sylvia and the guys wouldn't have gone amiss. He knew when he got involved with Lana that she wasn't going to be plain sailing. But he had thought that would be more to do with her and her problems than her father. The truth was that he hadn't allowed himself to get close to anyone for years, but he had with her. He had had a lot of relationships but he always knew they wouldn't go anywhere long-term. He had felt that way since Michelle.

And now Stephen Rourke was back. He couldn't get his face out of his mind and he let his memory drift back . . .

* * *

After Cathal had caught Michelle and Stephen together something changed in him. He couldn't believe what a fool he had been, running around after her. After what happened, she stayed clear of him. She soon left Tuxedo nightclub and did promotions for another club, still playing music wherever she could in her spare time. They passed in the street and never even acknowledged each other. Cathal was wary of Stephen for a long while but Stephen behaved normally to him and even started giving him more and more responsibility. Cathal kept wondering over and over again, in bewilderment, how somebody as sound as Stephen could have done something like that to him. How could somebody so supportive and encouraging have betrayed him? In the end he looked for excuses, and it was easy just to blame Michelle for the whole thing.

Cathal had learned a lot of lessons through Michelle. He wasn't going to allow himself to get bogged down in anything that wasn't real again.

Life was good. He worked hard and partied continuously. And Stephen was so good to him that in the end he had to put aside what had happened with Michelle. The fact was Stephen still totally impressed Cathal. He admired everything he did, the way he dealt with people and how he carried himself, and he wanted to be like him.

One day, Cathal was called into Stephen's office.

"How would you feel about becoming assistant manager here?" Stephen asked.

"Are you serious?" Cathal's eyes opened.

"Sure am. Pay increase. You get to wear a nice suit and have some more responsibility. What do you say?"

Cathal couldn't believe it. Everyone told him he wouldn't amount to much and now here he was being offered a managerial position. "I'd love it."

"Well, welcome to the management team." Stephen beamed and shook his hand.

"You've been really good to me, Stephen," Cathal was actually telling the truth. "I don't know where I'd be if it wasn't for you. Still taking in change at the carpark or something."

"Well, Cathal, you're loyal. I know I can trust you, and that's everything in this game."

*   *   *

Cathal stopped himself from thinking any more of the past, before his mind started to wander to more unpleasant memories. He got up quickly and left the pub.

*   *   *

Tony knocked on Ralph's door and entered his office. Seeing Ralph was on the phone, he hovered for a while.

"That's fine! Looking forward to working with you. Bye, darling!" Ralph hung up the phone. He was smiling from ear to ear. He slapped his hands together and rubbed them gleefully. "Do you know who that was?"

"No."

"Lana Curtis – she's coming to work here."

Tony's face was filled with confusion. "As what?"

"As a marketing executive."

"Oh!" Tony didn't know how to take the news.

"You know who her father is. It's going to be such an asset for us! His companies are worth millions. The amount of business she can direct our way is unbelievable. And she is so connected. She'll be working with you. I want you to look after her, okay? Go very easy on her. Be very nice to her and let her find her own pace. I want her to be completely happy with us."

*   *   *

Tony came in the door and threw his briefcase on the coffee table

"How's everything?" Nicole asked, realising her voice sounded as if she was addressing a stranger on a bus.

"Fine. You know Barry Curtis, who we did the feature on? Ralph has only gone and offered his daughter Lana a job. She's going to be working with me."

Nicole cleared her throat. "As a writer? Will she be a threat?"

415

"Only to the English language. No, not as a writer, although I read her job spec and she will have a say in the feature articles."

It felt strange that she knew this information already, but Nicole felt he was beginning to talk to her and felt excited.

"I'd better go upstairs to the computer. I have to finish an article by the morning."

*   *   *

Lana surveyed herself in the mirrors in her dressing-room. She had chosen a black suit for her first day of work at *Hi Life*. Her first day of work ever, she reminded herself. She had butterflies in her stomach. She hadn't a clue what she was letting herself in for. But she remembered what Cathal had said to her. If she didn't like it, then she didn't have to go back. As she heard Cathal beep outside, she quickly left her house.

"All set?" he asked as he drove out of the driveway.

"I'm absolutely terrified."

"There's no need to be. You'll be great. And Tony works in there, you know, the guy I'm friendly with – he'll look after you."

"Yeah. I know. You know, if somebody had told me a few months ago I'd be going to work at a magazine, I wouldn't have believed them." She reached over and put her hand on his. "And it's all because of you. You've given me such confidence in myself. You're everything I ever wanted, even before I even knew what I wanted. If someone told me I'd have found somebody like you and be in a stable and happy relationship, I'd have laughed in their face."

* * *

As Cathal drove towards the studio, after dropping Lana off, he tried not to think about Stephen Rourke. He couldn't allow himself to dwell on him. It was a one-off encounter, he decided. Stephen had never been the kind of guy who played games – he just came out and said whatever he wanted. And if he wanted anything from Cathal he would have made it known by now.

He mustn't allow himself to think of Stephen Rourke or the past again.

* * *

"Lana, Lana, Lana!" said Ralph entering reception with Tony and holding his arms out to her.

She stood up, and uncomfortably allowed herself to be embraced by the man.

"You're so welcome to *Hi Life*. It's like a member of the family coming to work for us!" He smiled broadly.

"Thanks, Ralph,"

"You remember Tony?"

"Yes, how are you again?" she smiled.

"You're going to be working here with Tony. He's here for you at all times. Anything you want or need, just ask Tony. He'll explain everything to you – he'll be at your beck and call."

Tony felt himself becoming angry. He didn't want to be at this rich bitch's beck and call. It was bad enough being at Ralph's. He also marvelled at the difference between her reception and his when he started working there. He had been left on his own and made to feel very unwelcome.

But then again, she was Barry Curtis's daughter, he reminded himself. Big difference.

"This is your desk here," Ralph said, pointing to Vivienne's old spot.

She moved forward and sat down, feeling comfortable.

"Is it okay?" Ralph asked.

"Yes. It's fine, thank you." She looked up at him and smiled awkwardly. "What exactly do you want me to do today?"

"Er, whatever you feel like. Take a look through those past issues and get a feel for the magazine." He smiled warmly and headed back to his office. "Tony, bring me a coffee. And ask Lana if she wants one as well."

*   *   *

"You turn it on here," Tony said, switching on Lana's computer.

"What do you do then? It's been years since I used a computer."

"Well, it depends what you want to do. Which file you want to access or create."

She returned to flicking through an edition of *Hi Life*. "Who writes all these articles?"

"A lot of them come from head office in London. We do the Irish features."

She nodded and took up another edition to read it.

*   *   *

"I'm heading out," said Ralph, coming through the office. "Myself and Margaux have been invited to Gay Byrne's for dinner. We're going to do a feature on him soon."

"That's great," Tony smiled.

"Speaking of features, when are we doing your photo shoot?" Ralph asked Lana.

"My photo shoot?" Lana was curious.

"Yes, the Affidavit photo shoot. All the band members with their partners at home."

Lana went red. "I don't know . . . I'll have to ask Cathal about it."

*   *   *

Tony switched off the light as he and Lana walked down the stairs that evening.

"I have an appointment in the morning with the dentist, so you might let Ralph know I'll be late," Lana informed him.

Tony couldn't believe her attitude. "Er, okay."

He closed the front door behind him and locked it, then turned to see Cathal waiting there in his Jeep.

"How did it go?" Cathal asked as Lana got in.

"It was fine," she shrugged. "Not too difficult."

I'll say. All you did was drink coffee and read past issues all day, thought Tony.

"Tony, how are you?" Cathal asked in a loud and friendly manner.

"Good." Tony smiled back.

"Keeping an eye on this one for me?"

"Something like that."

"We'll have to meet up for some drinks soon. Give me a call." Cathal started the Jeep and drove off.

As Tony watched the Jeep drive away, he was filled with a resentment. A resentment towards Lana Curtis. He had worked so hard since coming to *Hi Life* to gain respect and be trustworthy. He had networked and charmed as much as he could. And then she had just arrived and everyone was fawning over her just because of who she was. He knew Ralph wouldn't give a damn that she'd be late in the morning. And he had built up friendships with a lot of the people like the guys in Affidavit. But she would now become the contact with them and others just because of who she was.

* * *

"Cathal, what's this all about a photo shoot for us?" Lana asked as Cathal drove out to Malahide.

Cathal cursed to himself. "I meant to say it to you, but didn't want to bother you about it. Sylvia was talking about *Hi Life* doing a photo shoot with us all in our homes. But I hate that kind of thing, and I knew you wouldn't like it."

Lana digested the information. "But it would be good publicity for Affidavit?"

"According to Sylvia, yeah."

"Well, from what you were saying, Cathal, you need all the help you can get. Your last single failed miserably, and it just sounds like a nightmare in the recording studio. I mean, if this went out across Europe, millions of people will be reading it, which could only be good for the group, no?"

"I guess. But I hate that kind of shit."

"Cathal, sometimes we have to do things we don't want to. I certainly have no problem participating in it." She nestled back in her seat. In fact, she thought, she would love to do it.

*   *   *

Cathal, Lana and Barry sat close together at the top end of the dining table.

"So, you enjoyed your first day at work then?" quizzed Barry as he sipped his wine.

"I guess so." Lana pulled a face. "I hadn't a clue what I was supposed to be doing."

"You'll be fine there. You're my daughter, aren't you? You were born with a business brain."

Lana blushed as she took up her glass and sipped from it. She reached over and grasped Cathal's hand. "And *Hi Life* are doing an exclusive on Cathal's group and going to take photos of the two of us."

Barry sighed in fake melancholy. "I never expected to have a celebrity for a daughter."

"No, I'm not!" She laughed out loud.

"Cathal, when are you going to give me an opportunity to beat you at golf after the last time when you thrashed me."

In fact it was the other way round, thought Cathal. "Any time you want, Barry."

*   *   *

"Did you enjoy tonight?" Lana asked as she stepped out of her dress.

"Yeah. I really like your father," said Cathal who was lying in bed looking through a magazine.

"He's a great guy, isn't he?" smiled Lana, taking out her earrings. "I just can't believe how well we're getting on after all these years."

Cathal was burning with curiosity and had been for

some time. He decided now was the right time to ask. "Lana . . . are your parents separated?"

Lana went bright red, and threw her earrings onto her dressing-table, not looking at him.

"Lana?" he pushed gently.

"No, they're not," she snapped, beginning to brush her hair vigorously.

"Well, where was she tonight then? Where is she all the time?"

"Where do you think we should take the photos for *Hi Life*? At your place or mine? Or both?"

"Lana, I asked you a question."

She continued to brush her hair.

"Lana. I thought we'd reached a level here between ourselves. One that neither of us had reached with anybody before. And that means trust and opening up about everything."

Lana slammed the brush down on the dressing-table and swung around. "Since you are obviously not in a sleepy mood, and I will not be getting any sleep here tonight, I might as well get my new marketing books out and go learn something." She turned and walked quickly out of the room.

* * *

Lana sat at her desk at work and scrutinised the photo of her father on the front cover of *Hi Life*. All the photos were glamorous and in neither them nor the feature was there any hint that the event had descended into a full-scale riot. That's what magazines like *Hi Life* did, Lana thought: hide the truth of life under an illusion of beauty. She studied the photo of Joanne Bailey taken with Seán at the birthday party. She saw at the bottom of the feature that it had been written by Tony. She started flicking through the article, trying to blot out Tony's constant phoning and typing that was distracting her. She skimmed through the headings and photos. *'Beautiful Model Katie Mondeo invites Hi Life to her Fairytale Wedding – Exclusive'.* *'Stunning Television Personality Sandra Fallon Invites Us to Take an Intimate Look at her Fabulous New Home'.* It went on and on. In spite of herself, she was unable to put the magazine down. She didn't particularly like it and certainly didn't respect it, but it was intriguing to see these people at an intimate level. She looked at her watch. It was 5.30. Time to go home.

Diana came bounding into the office in her track suit, and was surprised to see Lana sitting there. "Oh hello!" she said.

"Diana, this is Lana Curtis, our new marketing executive," said Tony.

Lana stood up and shook her hand. She remembered Diana's diet and health columns in *Hi Life*, all advocating a regime of nuts and grains and other starvation food policies. Certainly none that would appeal to Lana. She felt Diana's eyes sweep over her, checking her out and judging her figure and appearance.

"Welcome to the team!" Diana smiled before turning to Tony. "Are you ready for our jog?"

"Just give me a minute to finish this off," he said, typing furiously.

"You're going running?" Lana looked perplexed.

"You wouldn't believe how unhealthy Tony was when he first came to work here. But he's made such progress!"

Lana felt Diana's curious and slightly disapproving eyes sweep over her again. "Good luck to you. It's a gin and tonic and a cigarette for me, I think," said Lana, grabbing her handbag. "I'll see you tomorrow." She walked down the stairs.

"Hmmm, not in bad shape, I suppose," Diana mused. "Although I'd say that owes more to good genetics than any attempt on her part at a healthy lifestyle. What's she like?"

"Stand-offish, if you ask me. And not interested in anything. Ralph and Maggie are all over her, of course."

*   *   *

Kathryn drove herself to Exclusive for work that night. That guy, Tony, from the magazine had been leaving constant messages on her phone asking her to come in to talk about the feature. She dreaded the invasion into her life – into their life. She would have to broach the topic with Simeon soon.

CHAPTER 32

Lana sat at the board table looking at the staff of *Hi Life* gathered around for their meeting. Ralph was at the top of the table, looking angry and giving out about the advertising sales figures to Gavin who looked terrified. Diana started speaking and saying that she was exploring a new diet based on carbohydrates, a kind of anti-Atkins diet. Her words seemed to have suitably impressed Ralph who smiled with interest. Then it was Ruth, the social diarist's turn as she started listing out the list of premières and openings she had been to. As far as Lana could observe, the only person who didn't jump when Ralph spoke was Clive the photographer, who managed to look suitably bored.

"Any luck with Kathryn Foy, Tony?" Ralph demanded.

"She hasn't returned any of my calls."

"For fuck's sake!" Ralph slammed the table, causing everyone except Lana and Clive to jump. "Where the fuck is she? She can't keep avoiding us. She's going on the front cover of the magazine and we have a time schedule to follow. Get in contact with her soon and no excuses."

Tony nodded.

"Speaking of schedules. Where are we at with the Affidavit schedule?"

"Everything was finished until we expanded it for the home photos as well," explained Tony.

"We need to get our asses in gear on this immediately. The Hartons are waiting for this in London. It's going to be our biggest feature this year."

"I'm ready to rock n' roll with taking the shots whenever I get the go-ahead," said Clive.

Ralph picked up his mobile and dialled Sylvia's number. "Sylvia, Ralph here. Just trying t-t-t-to tie up the Affidavit feature. We're running out of time."

Sylvia's voice sounded carefully controlled. "Well, I can let them off from the studio whenever you're ready. James and Donna are ready to go, as are Seán and Joanne. We've got a problem with Rob and Heidi, however."

"What problem?"

"Between ourselves, Rob has a lot of problems with the new album and he refuses to do any commercial publicity at the moment. He says it'll affect his artistic standing."

"Oh, for fuck's sake! Who gives a fuck about them anyway? Rob was always the most uninteresting of the group, and who wants to see a photo of his housewife and their sprog? And Cathal?"

"There's another problem there. You know how Cathal hates that kind of PR. I've pushed it with him, but he's not committing."

"What?" Ralph looked agitated. "Hold on, I've got Lana here. Lana, are you not doing the photo shoot for us?" His voice was filled with concern.

"Er, yes. I spoke to Cathal about it and we're perfectly fine. Whenever you're ready, we are."

"Did you hear that, Sylvia? Lana's our new marketing

executive."

"Oh, I see." Sylvia was genuinely surprised. "In that case, give me an hour and I'll check everyone's schedules and call back to fix dates."

Ralph hung up the phone. "That's the way to do business. N-n-n-no messing. Moving on. Our new slogan. Has anyone come up with any new ideas since those shit ones you gave last week?"

There was an uncomfortable silence.

"I was thinking something like '*Hi Life* – The Way Forward'," suggested Diana.

"We're not a political party! I'm going to give you all one more week, and I want some good suggestions by then. We need a new marketing slogan and we need it quick. Okay, have we managed to get in contact with David Shorely?"

David Shorely was an Irish playwright who had written a film script that was now tipped for Oscar glory.

"I left loads of messages with his agent, but no response," said Tony.

Ralph started humming a song and kept it up for ten seconds. "Ask me why I'm humming," he demanded.

"Why are you humming?" Tony asked awkwardly.

Ralph slammed the table. "I'm humming along because I've heard this tune before! With all your supposed brains and contacts, you haven't managed to get in contact with this guy!"

Lana remembered meeting David Shorely at a party a few months previously. He had known Barry for ages, and had followed her around all night asking her for a date, and insisting she take his number. She took out her mobile and looked through the numbers. Sure enough it was still there.

"Let me just try this," she said, dialling the number. "Hi, David? It's Lana Curtis here, remember me? How are you keeping? Listen, David, I'm working at *Hi Life* here, and we want to do an interview with you – how about it?" She sighed. "Okay – but only if you agree to the interview . . . all right then, it's a deal . . . I'll see you there tomorrow at one, and don't be late!" She hung up the phone and smiled. "Yep, he says he'll do it, no problem. If I go to lunch with him." She looked around the table.

Everyone looked shocked except for Ralph who looked excitedly happy and Tony who looked annoyed.

"I'll probably have to spend the afternoon charming him, so I'll doubt I'll be back after lunch," said Lana.

*   *   *

Nicole had been faced with a huge dilemma since finding out that Lana had accepted the job at *Hi Life*. This was all too close for comfort. She didn't know what to do. She felt very uncomfortable that her partner, albeit an estranged one, would be working with one of her clients. She considered having Lana move to a colleague. But this would be a disaster. The main point was that Lana hadn't come looking for help, she had been forced to. Most people who came to therapy wanted to get better. Lana hadn't. With Lana it had been a slow uphill battle to get her to open up and trust and now eventually she was getting somewhere with her and there had been a great improvement in her wellbeing. She knew if Lana was transferred, it would be a massive step back that would affect her development. In fact, Nicole knew in her heart that Lana would just stop coming to therapy and, since the real issue of Lana's troubles hadn't been addressed, it would only be a matter of time before she slipped back to where she was before. As is the practice in Nicole's business, she met with a colleague every week to discuss different clients and get a second opinion on any problems or issues she had. Last time she had discussed Lana getting a job with Tony with her colleague. The colleague had advised her to continue seeing Lana, but to proceed with caution. Nicole couldn't bring herself to explain that her relationship was also in serious trouble.

Nicole maintained her usual professional air at her therapy session with Lana.

"So you're enjoying *Hi Life* so far?" she probed.

"Yeah. I guess. I mean, I haven't really done anything – just been left to my own devices."

Same way Tony was at the beginning, thought Nicole.

"I've just been reading past issues and getting acquainted with the whole set-up. But I secured an interview with David Shorely and everyone seemed delighted."

Nicole wondered if that was the reason Tony had been in such a bad mood the previous night. She knew he'd been trying to set up an interview with Shorely for ages. Curiosity got the better of her. "So where are you exactly in the building?"Careful, she told herself, this line of questioning really has nothing to do with Lana's therapy.

"I'm in this kind of open-plan area where everyone comes in and out. I share it with this guy called Tony."

Nicole cleared her throat. This was making her feel extremely uncomfortable and yet her curiosity overcame that. "And what's he been like?"

Lana shrugged. "He's seems really busy all the time."

"Has he been helpful to you?"

"Yes, but he hasn't gone way out of his way or anything."

That's because he sees you as a threat, thought Nicole.

"And – eh – what are the politics like in there? Does he get on with the boss?"

"Tony? Seems to be totally up Conway's arse, as far as I can see. Running around trying to please him all the time. I can't understand how anyone could allow themselves to be a lapdog like that."

Nicole had feared that. "Does he seem – happy there?"

"Yeah, he seems to love it."

Nicole felt the answer was like a slap. She wanted to hear he was miserable at this stage and wanted to leave. She quickly cleared her head and got the session back on track. "So how's your relationship with Cathal progressing?"

"Great – good, I suppose. He's spent loads of time with my father and they get on great . . . but this has led him to be curious about my mother."

Nicole felt excited as she felt she was reaching that elusive breakthrough but wouldn't allow her manner to show this.

"He wanted to know where she was," continued Lana.

"And what did you say?"

"I told him it was none of his business and stormed out."

"Don't you think he was entitled to ask?" Nicole questioned.

"I guess. We barely spoke the next morning and haven't been in contact with each other since."

"Why won't you discuss your mother?" Nicole probed Lana's face for details.

Lana tried to speak but stopped herself. She tried again, but the words didn't come out.

"I'm sorry." She stood up and headed to the door. "I'm

going to have to go."

"Lana," Nicole called, stopping her for a second. "You can't run from this for ever."

Lana nodded and left.

*   *   *

Lana walked to her car deep in thought. She opened the door and sat in. Slowly she reached over and took her mobile from her handbag. She looked at the mobile for a long time before dialling the number.

"Hi, Eileen . . . it's Lana here . . . I was just thinking of dropping down for a visit."

*   *   *

Lana's car sped down the dual carriageway, the countryside whizzing by her. She slowed down slightly. Glancing at her watch, as she took a turn off the main road onto a country one, she realised it was nearly two hours since she left the capital. It was a beautiful day, and the overhung branches from the trees shaded parts of the road from the sun as she manoeuvred the twists and turns. She drove on for another ten minutes before she pulled into a large gateway, the iron gates firmly closed. She got out of the car, steadied herself, and then went over to the intercom and pressed the button.

"Yes?" asked the woman's voice on the other end.

"Eileen, it's Lana."

The intercom clicked off and after a few seconds, the gates opened electronically.

Lana drove up the tree-lined driveway. As she turned a corner, the house came into view. It was a beautiful old period manor house. It was large, without being too big or stately. She halted the car outside the house, looking up at its ivy-clad walls.

Her heels crunched on the gravel drive as she made her way to the front door. She rang the doorbell and waited. Through the glass panel of the door, she saw Eileen approach.

"Hello, dear," said Eileen, opening the door and giving Lana a kiss on the cheek. She was a middle-aged woman, homely and kind-looking.

"Hi, Eileen." Lana smiled down at her. "It's a beautiful day, isn't it?" She walked into the grand hallway, which was all marble and furnished in antiques.

"Isn't it?"

"Where is she?" Lana asked, her smile not as pronounced.

"She's out by the river. There's tea and sandwiches out there as well for you."

"You shouldn't have bothered!"

"No bother. Come on and follow me through. She can't wait to see you."

Lana walked with her through to the drawing room that had patio doors open onto the lawn, then stopped and put a hand on Eileen's arm.

"Eileen . . . how is she?"

Eileen smiled kindly and patted Lana's hand. "She's fine, just fine."

The lawn big and long with a river running at the bottom of it. As she followed Eileen across the grass, Lana could see the lone figure seated beside a table, gazing at the swaying water.

"Look who is here, Ann!"

Lana braced herself as her mother turned slowly

432

around. Lana was immediately struck, as ever, by her fragile beauty. Her unlined but pale face was totally free of make-up. Her soft, thick fair hair was pulled back with just a slide. She wore a simple beige summer dress over her slim frame, a simple beige cardigan resting on her shoulders. For a woman who never dressed in anything but simple clothes, whose beauty routine consisted only of soap and water and combing her hair, Ann's beauty was tantalising, but almost breakable.

A smile broke out on Ann's face. "You never said you were coming," she said, her voice soft.

"I thought I'd surprise you." Lana leaned down and kissed her mother's cheek while placing a hand on her shoulder. Ann placed a hand on Lana's, and squeezed it gently.

Eileen poured tea while Lana sat down on the free chair across the small garden table.

"I'll leave you two alone – let me know if you want anything." Smiling broadly Eileen left them alone.

"She's so amazing. I don't know what I'd do without her," said Ann. She gazed at her daughter. "It's been so long since you visited me."

"I know . . . I'm sorry . . ."

"Oh, I'm not giving out to you. I know how busy you are with your friends and your life and everything."

Lana nodded and smiled. "You look lovely."

"Do I?" She laughed lightly. "Have you seen your father recently?"

"Yes, we had dinner a little while ago. You?"

"He was down with me at the weekend. He's so busy now though with the election . . . I really wish he wasn't bothering with it. I've asked him over and over again to pull out. He's drawing too much attention to himself with it."

"He always had a lot of attention anyway."

"I know, but this is different. People feel differently about politicians. They inspire more passion, both good and bad."

Lana bit her lower lip and prepared herself as she saw Ann's face become a cloud of worry.

"I worry so much about him. I've read some of the speeches he makes. He's going to anger some people and you never know what they might do."

"I have a new job." Lana cut in quickly to stop Ann's flow of talk.

"Where?" Ann's face brightened with the news.

"I've become a marketing executive with *Hi Life* – you know, the magazine?"

"But that's wonderful! When did you start?"

"Just this week."

"Oh, I am glad. Do you have to go out to meetings and interviews?"

"Well, I haven't yet, but maybe."

"You wouldn't be meeting strangers on your own?" Ann's face was filled with alarm.

"No," Lana said quickly, cutting in, "There will always be other people from the office with me."

Ann's face looked relieved. "Promise me you'll be careful? Don't work late in the office on your own or anything, will you?"

"Of course not."

"You never know who might be waiting outside, knowing you're in there."

Lana blinked. "I'm so lazy, there's not a chance I'll be working late."

"Good." Ann looked relieved. "It only takes one person, you know, to ruin your life. One mad person to do something and it's over like that!" She clicked her fingers together.

There was a quiet bang in the far distance.

"What was that?" Ann was overcome with fright.

"It was just somebody banging a car door, a long way off," Lana assured her.

Ann stood up. "Eileen!" she called loudly.

Eileen immediately came out and hurried down the lawn. "What's wrong, Ann?"

"I heard something. It was something banging."

"It was nothing –" Lana started.

"No, it was definitely something. What was it, Eileen?"

"It might have been Tesco's leaving the groceries down at the gate as usual."

"No, it wasn't. They came this morning. I know because I saw you put the shopping away."

Eileen nodded. "I'll tell you what I'll do. I'll walk down to the gates and see if I can see anything and I'll make sure the alarm is activated at the gates – is that okay?"

"Would you, Eileen?" Ann still looked concerned but relieved and sat down as Eileen hurried off.

"Mum, that sound was miles away." Lana wrung her hands together.

"There are so many bad and strange people out there – you have to be so careful. The whole world is moving at such a fast pace. Here we are spinning around in the middle of space and nobody knows where we're going to . . . none of us know . . . if people stopped and realised that, we'd all stop what we're doing and hold on to each other for safety."

*   *   *

Lana drove her car through the main gates and drove

quickly through the empty country roads. It was only after she had been driving for five minutes that she pulled into a gateway on the side of the road and allowed the tears she had been holding back to flow. Then she was crying loudly.

*　　*　　*

Cathal opened his front door, his face set in a cold expression, ready for a confrontation with Lana over her lack of trust. On seeing she had been crying, his expression immediately turned to concern.

"What's wrong?" he asked, putting his arm around her and bringing her inside.

"I'm sorry about the other night, Cathal," said Lana.

"Is that what you're upset about?"

"Yes, no . . . I went to see my mother today."

They sat down on Cathal's couch, as Lana described her visit to her mother.

"But I don't understand. Your parents aren't divorced or separated then?"

"No." she shook her head. "They don't see each other as much as they should, but they are still together."

"So what are you saying? I still don't understand . . . she never comes up to Kildara? She never comes to Dublin even?"

"Cathal, she never leaves the grounds of the house she lives in. I don't know when it happened or how it happened. It wasn't sudden. It was over a long period of time. Mum and Dad met when they were young. Dad wasn't rich or anything in those days, but both of them were very much in love and very ambitious to get ahead in the world. Even when I was very young, Dad had achieved a lot of commercial success, but he wasn't at all as rich as he became later. I remember my childhood being so happy, and safe. We lived in a lovely house by the sea in Malahide. Dad worked very hard, but Mum and Dad had lots of friends – there were always parties and people coming and going. Mum was so beautiful, and full of life, although always sensitive. Then Dad started becoming very well known as his companies sky-rocketed. Mum wasn't prepared for the attention that came their way. She was just from a nice middle-class background and was expecting to have a similar life with Dad. She started becoming anxious as our surname became known not just here, but in the UK too. It began small, with her suddenly wanting a better security alarm. Then she wanted a couple of guard dogs. It was the time of the kidnappings here in Ireland and so I suppose that added to her fears. But slowly she became paranoid. She suddenly wouldn't go out shopping on her own. She was always being invited out to society events, and she used to enjoy them, but she stopped going to them as well. She didn't like meeting new people, and would only meet very old and trusted friends. This was all the way through my teenage years. By the time I was going to college, she wasn't able to function any more with people. Dad tried to bring therapists to her and stuff, and she did meet them for a long while, but it came to no good. She just didn't want to have anything to do with the world – she was completely terrified of it."

Cathal rubbed Lana's back as he listened.

"Eventually she couldn't cope with Kildara, as there were too many people coming and going with Dad's business, and so she wanted to go and live in the country. Dad bought her an old period house and installed the best security around it and she went down to stay there. We thought it would only be temporary, but we were wrong.

437

We had a housekeeper, Eileen, who'd been with us for years and she agreed to go and live there with Mum."

"And she never leaves there?"

"No. Dad goes down there regularly, and some old friends visit her as well."

"And you?" Cathal pushed.

Lana shrugged her shoulders. "Not that much any more. I get upset when I see her. The least little thing sets her off, Cathal."

"Things are beginning to make sense now." He put his arm around her. "The reason you hated being in therapy at the beginning . . . you thought you were going down the same road as her, didn't you?"

She sighed. "They say the acorn doesn't fall far from the tree."

"And all the risks you took?"

"The drugs, walking the streets alone at night? Probably all tied in somewhere. Not wanting to impose any boundaries on myself. Wanting to be fearless, but all the time I was as lost as she is."

CHAPTER 33

Tony drove out to Dalkey, to James and Donna's house. Lana was seated in the car beside him. They'd had a meeting with Ralph beforehand and he had been furious with the delay in finishing the Affidavit exclusive. Tony felt like telling the man that it was his own fault, that the feature would have been finished and put to bed by now if he hadn't decided to extend it to include the band's home life as well.

Lana opened her cigarettes and lit one. He was mildly irritated as she didn't ask if she could first. He was under huge pressure to work quickly, and now he was straddled with this lazy rich girl as well.

He tried to read directions to the house as he drove along an exclusive road.

"You take a right at the top of this road, and it's on the left," Lana informed him, remembering when she had stayed there the night she had met Cathal at Patricia's party. Little did she know then how her life would change.

Her knowledge of the house's whereabouts managed to irritate him more. Why should it, he asked himself – she's probably been there loads of times; she's one of them.

But that reasoning also irritated him.

He pulled into the driveway of the house. Clive was already there, unloading his photographic equipment.

"How are we set?" asked Tony, getting out of the car.

"All dressed up and ready to go," Clive spat the cigarette out of his mouth and carried some equipment through the open front door.

Tony and Lana followed him. They walked into the expansive lounge and saw Donna in a Gucci dress, seated on the couch, having her make-up finished off. James stood behind her speaking on the mobile, dressed in an immaculate suit. Both of them looked as if they had been groomed and pampered to perfection.

"Hi, Tony," said Donna, then her face filled with surprise on seeing Lana enter the room. "What's she doing here?"

"Lana's become part of the team at *Hi Life*, and so she'll be present during the shoot and interview."

Donna didn't try to disguise her irritation, neither did James as he turned off his phone.

"Okay, guys, time's against us. Let's get the ball rolling," ordered Clive as he fixed his camera onto the stand.

Lana sat in a corner looking on at the shoot. She watched in fascination as the two curled up together on the couch, their expressions moving from provocative to content for the cameras. She cringed with embarrassment as she realised she and Cathal would be expected to pose for similar shots. What had she got herself into? And she couldn't see Cathal doing this kind of thing with the ease that James did. There were photos of Donna, pretending to cook in the kitchen in a Versace dress. Another change of outfit, and the two were stretched luxuriantly across the king-size bed. More photos out by the pool, and then a finale with them both in their His and Hers matching Mercedes.

*   *   *

Cathal left the studio and walked down the corridor to reception. Bad enough they were behind schedule on the album, but now these photo shoots with *Hi Life* were delaying everything further.

He smiled at the receptionist, pushed open the glass doors and walked through the carpark towards his Jeep, his mind lost in thought about Lana's revelation. He pressed the zapper and his Jeep unlocked.

"Hello, Cathal," said a voice behind him.

He got a start. He recognised the voice immediately, and turned around to see Stephen Rourke standing there.

Cathal studied his face. It was still handsome, though it had changed a lot. But his eyes, the cool grey blue, were the exact same. What struck Cathal most were his clothes. He had always been used to seeing Stephen in the best expensive clothes; it was odd now seeing him looking shabby.

Despite himself, he felt anxiety. "Hello, Stephen." Cathal kept his voice even.

"Long time, no see," said Stephen, equally calm.

"You're certainly a blast from the past." Instinctively, Cathal backed away from him a step or two.

"You've probably been expecting me . . . after you saw me the other night."

I've been expecting you for years, thought Cathal. "What do you want, Stephen?" He made his voice matter--of-fact and in control.

"Just a chat."

Cathal looked down at his Gucci. "I'm really busy, I have to be —"

"You'll make time for me." Stephen walked over to the passenger door and opened it, sitting in.

"Hey!" objected Cathal.

"Get in, Cathal. We're going to my place for a talk – unless you want me to go into reception here and we can talk there?"

Cathal thought for a second, his face creased in worry. Slowly he got into the Jeep and closed his door. "Where to?" His voice was cold and tense.

They sat in silence as Cathal drove. Stephen only spoke to give directions, which Cathal followed without saying anything. What you are doing, thought Cathal. Just throw him out. He drove through a very derelict part of the city, full of run-down flats.

"Pull in here," ordered Stephen. Cathal pulled in.

"Come on up," said Stephen, as he got out of the Jeep.

Cathal stayed stationary, staring ahead at the busy street.

"I said come on!" Stephen's voice was powerful.

Slowly Cathal got out of the car. He followed Stephen into a run-down building and up a couple of flights of stairs. The building was dark inside, with bits of plaster falling off the wall. Stephen put a key in a door, opened it and stepped inside.

"Come in," he said, holding the door open.

Cathal hesitated for a while, wondering if he had any options. Then he walked though the door.

* * *

The photo shoot was finished, and Clive and Tony were packing away the camera equipment.

"Why don't you come and join us for a coffee?" Donna said to Lana, smiling, directing her into the kitchen.

442

James was there, seated at the huge island. Lana sat down across from him on a high chair, as Donna took the coffee pot and filled three mugs.

"Cathal had mentioned you were going to work at *Hi Life*, but we didn't realise you would be out on the shoots," Donna said, smiling, and handing her a mug.

Lana thought Donna was visually stunning, and full of confidence, as was James. "Well, I'm just getting to know all the different aspects of the business, so I can do my job properly."

"Marketing, isn't it?" said James, sipping his coffee.

"Yes."

"You must miss all the free time you had." Donna sat up on one of the high stools.

"I'm enjoying this," said Lana.

"You're doing some campaigning with your father, as well?" said James.

"A little bit."

"And Cathal got in on the act."

Lana nodded.

"Cathal's family to us. We love him," stated Donna.

Lana nodded. "I know that."

"Well, we're worried about him, to be honest," said James.

"In what way?"

"Because he's with you," said Donna. "You're not his type, Lana. In any way."

"And what is his type?" Lana's voice was ice.

"Well, not somebody without any direction in their life, a drug problem, and a rich daddy to clean up the mess."

Lana put down her mug in anger.

"Besides, if you knew Cathal like we know him, you'd finish with him sooner rather than later," said James.

"Go on." Lana raised an eyebrow.

"Well, do you really want to be a sympathy fuck?" Donna's face was concerned.

"I beg your pardon?" Lana was incredulous.

"He's always been attracted to dangerous and off-the-wall people," continued Donna, "and you know the reputation you have, Lana."

"I've known Cathal all my life, and you're just another dangerous situation for him," said James.

"Until it blows up in his face," Donna concluded.

Tony came in. "Okay, Clive's gone. So I'll just ask you some questions. Do you want to do it here, or in the lounge"

"The lounge, I think," said Donna, getting up, smiling.

In the lounge Tony double-checked that the miniature recorder was on.

Lana sat beside him, burning with fury, but trying not to show it.

"You've said your wedding will be next spring. Donna, any idea about dresses yet?" asked Tony.

"Actually, I have a confession, I've already got it. A little premature, I know, but a girl has to be prepared! It's in a wardrobe upstairs, under lock and key."

"And what's it like?"

"Oh, I'm a traditionalist, and I want a fairytale wedding, so it's a big meringue!" Donna giggled.

"James, Affidavit has been together a long time now – and you're all settling down?"

"Yes, we've all settled down . . . apart from Cathal, of course." James looked at Lana pointedly.

Tony felt the intense atmosphere.

* * *

444

Cathal looked around the one-room flat. It was old-fashioned with a small kitchenette and a bathroom off it. There was an unmade bed in the corner. A dirty net curtain hung over the window. Cathal felt nauseous and wanted to run away from the place.

Stephen emerged from the kitchenette with a bottle of whiskey and two glasses and filled them up. He walked over to Cathal and held out a glass to him.

"No, I don't want –"

"Take it!" demanded Stephen.

Reluctantly Cathal took the glass. He saw it was dirty, but he took a sip anyway.

"Welcome to my world!" said Stephen in a loud and happy voice as he walked around the room. "You like?"

"What do you want, Stephen?"

"I'm surprised, Cathal, you're not a little friendlier. No questions about how I've been? Where I've been? I mean, I don't have to ask you, because the whole world knows how you are. You just have to pick up a copy of a magazine to see your great life. Wealthy, famous, and now to top it all up, Barry Curtis's daughter. You've come a long way since you were pining after that hooker, Michelle."

Cathal felt himself tense up even more. "How have you been?" he sighed.

"Thank you for asking. I've been pretty bad. Miserable actually." Stephen sat down on the sofa and knocked back his drink, before filling his glass again. "When I went to prison for four years – remember, Cathal? – to prison for four years thanks to you – well, things started going wrong for me just around that time." Stephen was smiling broadly, but his eyes were full of hate. "And then when I was in prison, Cathal, I was set upon by this thug. It was pure self-defence, but the authorities didn't see it like that.

They saw it as my fault. Because he was in a much worse way by the time I finished with him."

Cathal was trying not to shiver, but it was cold in the flat, despite the heat outside.

"They gave me a further six years. For that little misdemeanour . . . and I owe it all to you, Cathal."

*　　*　　*

Cathal had been amazed to be made assistant manager at Tuxedo. He wanted to give it his best shot and show he was up for the job.

"Okay, we cash up every night and put the money into the safe," explained Stephen. "Next morning, if I'm not here, you open the safe and do a cash count before taking the money down to the bank and cashing it in."

"Okay," said Cathal as he took the piece of paper with the safe numbers on, feeling very nervous but privileged to have such responsibility.

"Are you okay with that?" Stephen noticed his concern.

"Sure."

Stephen smiled kindly. "I know your reputation a couple of years back. I know about the crowd you used to hang around. But I'm trusting you with the safe numbers. I'll also be trusting you with taking cash over to Frank Daly if he has a cashflow problem and needs a loan to tide him over – or when we need cash or change ourselves, okay?

Cathal nodded. Frank Daly ran another nightclub, Franklyn's, at the other end of town. Frank and Stephen were good friends and always helped each other out when it came to things like change or staff when the other was short. Between them, Franklyn's and Tuxedo had the nightclub business sewn up in the town.

Things went well for Cathal after that. Despite his relative youth, he was popular with the other staff and they worked hard for him. Every night after the club closed he enjoyed partying with them, as did Stephen.

He had quickly got tired of his parents' constant nagging about his lifestyle and rented out a new apartment down by the river in the town. He was earning good money, so why shouldn't he?

His cousin James was doing very well at university, getting brilliant results in his exams. He was amazed when he came home on holidays and saw the transformation in Cathal.

Cathal had gone from being somebody who was always in trouble and heading nowhere in life to looking great and having a lot of confidence.

"I've started a band up with a couple of lads at college," explained James to Cathal one night he dropped in to Tuxedo.

"Really, that's cool. Got any gigs?" Cathal knew that James had always been obsessed with music. He had gone through his teenage years forming different bands on a regular basis. He had known it was only a matter of time before James did the same thing at college.

"No, not yet."

"Why don't I see if I can get you a gig at Tuxedo?"

"That would be fantastic." James' eyes widened with amazement.

"I'll have a word with Stephen and see what we can come up with."

"Great! So what you been up to?"

"Been working every night and partying after," smirked Cathal.

"You'd want to take it easy. Your mum and dad –"

447

"Listen, I don't want to know. I'm fed up with everybody constantly going on about me. It's all right for you – your family love everything you do. Mine hate everything I do."

"That's not true."

"It is. You know, they should be proud of me. I'm twenty-one years old and look at me. I'm earning big money, got a great pad, but no – they just nag about me going to college."

"You're very young to have got the job you're in," said James, noticing the bags under Cathal's eyes.

"And I'm well able for it, okay?"

*   *   *

Cathal was walking around the nightclub. It was packed and he was looking for a security guard to put on the door, but couldn't find any. He went out the back of the club and through the fire exit to see if any of them were smoking out there.

He saw that Stephen's office door open, pushed it open and walked in.

Stephen was bent over his desk snorting cocaine.

"Fuck!" shouted Stephen, his face a mask of anger at being disturbed. "When are you going to learn to knock on a fucking door!"

"S-sorry," said Cathal, backing out of the office.

"Come in and close the door," snapped Stephen.

Cathal did as he was told. Now he'd fucked up big time. Stephen was furious with him and he would be fired on the spot.

To his surprise Stephen smiled and sat on the desk. "What's the worried look for, Cathal?"

"Nothing . . . I . . . just . . ."

Stephen laughed. "You've never seen anybody do a bit of coke before? There's nothing wrong with taking a bit of coke now and again. We work long hours; it keeps you fresh." Stephen got up, opened an envelope, sprinkled some coke onto his desk and started chopping it with his credit card. "Here, try some."

"No, I'm okay."

"What's your problem?" Stephen looked bemused. "You'd think I was offering you something bad – it's only a line of coke, Cathal."

"I'll take a raincheck." Cathal smiled and exited.

There was an immediate change in Stephen's attitude to Cathal after that. It wasn't as if he wasn't nice or anything. He just became very professional and stopped treating him like a friend. Cathal thought about the situation long and hard and realised it must have something to do with the fact that his uncle, James' father, was a guard in the town.

Cathal worked extra hard to try and regain Stephen's trust, but Stephen kept a distance between them. Cathal realised that Stephen felt exposed because of the coke. He started to worry that he would lose his job.

Cathal knocked on Stephen's office door one night. The music was booming from the dance floor.

"Yeah?" Stephen looked up from his paperwork.

"I'm feeling a bit shattered tonight. Just wondered if there was a bit of coke going spare to pick me up?"

Stephen sat back in his chair, smiled and opened the drawer in his desk.

Cathal felt disgusted with himself the next day for taking it. He felt he had sold himself to get back in Stephen's favour. He didn't enjoy it and he didn't want to use it. But Stephen was back to treating him the way he always did. It was like now Stephen felt Cathal didn't have anything over him any more. Cathal tried to avoid situations where coke was on offer. But once he had tried it, and it was known that he had used it, Stephen and his friends were very open in front of him about coke. This made him uncomfortable. He tried to avoid taking the drug whenever he could.

One summer's night, the club was very hot and so Cathal opened the back doors to let in some air. He stepped out into the alleyway to have a minute's break and was shocked to see Stephen punching a young guy who worked in the club. He stared in amazement as Stephen laid another punch into him.

Cathal stepped forward. "Stephen, what the fuck are you doing?"

"Fuck off, Cathal, and mind your own business!" shouted Stephen.

"Will you knock it off!" Cathal went to restrain Stephen.

Stephen angrily turned around and slapped Cathal's face hard.

Cathal looked at him, stunned. Stephen walked past him angrily into the club.

*　　　*　　　*

Time went on and Cathal tried to forget what he had seen and what Stephen had done to him.

Stephen acted as if the incident in the alley hadn't happened. Then one night, he called Cathal into his office and handed him the usual bag stashed with money. "Take this over to Frank and get me change, will you? I want tens, twenties and fifties."

"No problem, boss."

"Oh, and Cathal, you're off tomorrow night, aren't you?"

"Yeah."

"Could you come in and work? I need you to take some stock over to Tuxedo. You can drive my car over. Easier than making ten rounds walking, okay?"

"No problem."

Next night Cathal turned up for work early.

Stephen seemed in great form but a little on edge. "I want you to take that stock over to Frank at 11.30," he told Cathal. "And I mean on the dot, so don't go missing in action or anything, all right?"

Cathal went about his business and was at the door when a call came through the office for him at 10.30.

"Your alarm is going off and it's waking up the whole neighbourhood," Cathal's neighbour informed him. "You'd better come home and turn it off now."

"Can I pop home? My alarm is going off," said Cathal to Stephen, covering the mouthpiece of the phone.

"No way!" Stephen was angry, "Tell them to fuck off. You're delivering that stock for me in an hour."

"I'll only be half an hour," said Cathal.

"Forget it."

Cathal went back to the phone "No, sorry, I can't get off work . . . Don't be like that . . . There's no need to call the police."

Stephen stepped forward quickly. "Okay, go home and turn the fucking thing off!"

"Sorry about this," said Cathal, grabbing his jacket.

"You better be back here in time or else I'll fucking go through you," said Stephen angrily.

Cathal remembered the incident in the alley and rushed off. He raced home, got to his apartment, opened the door and quickly pressed in the code to turn off the alarm. When the wailing stopped, he turned around and saw James' father Ben and his own father standing there.

"You've been a fucking eejit for months carrying drugs over to Frank Daly for Rourke," said Ben.

"What? What are you talking about?" Cathal was in shock.

"And there's a massive assignment being shipped between Rourke and Daly tonight and you're the one supposed to be moving it. From Franklyn's it's going to be shipped around the country. There's a team from the Special Branch waiting to intercept that car when it arrives into the alleyway behind Franklyn's and if you weren't my family you'd be fucked."

Cathal turned to his father. "I didn't know . . . I swear I didn't know."

"Now, you're going to do exactly as I say," said Ben.

* * *

Stephen was red in the face with anger as he looked at his watch and there was still no sign of Cathal at eleven twenty-five. Cathal wasn't answering either his house phone or his mobile.

The phone in his office rang.

"Stephen, hi, how are you?" said Cathal.

"Where the fuck are you?" Stephen shouted.

"The alarm! I'm having terrible trouble with the alarm. Should be back there in thirty minutes. Got a fella trying to fix it now."

"Fuck your alarm! It will be too late then."

Stephen slammed down the phone. He grabbed his car keys. Frank and his contacts would be waiting in the garage of the club for the drugs in four minutes' time. And these weren't the kind of contacts you let down.

*   *   *

"You set it up just right, didn't you?" Stephen said as he downed his whiskey. "You got off scot-free. Your name was completely kept out of it and you could get on with your life as normal. When I got to Franklyn's, the guards were waiting, and me and Frank were caught redhanded. I thought I was clever but I didn't realise the stupid guy I had eating out of my hand had an uncle who set me up."

"Whatever you got, you had it coming!" snapped Cathal. "You were dealing drugs."

"So were you!" Stephen shot back.

"I was not. I thought I was carrying money for change, not drugs. You were scum, using me like that. And I admired you so much, had you up on a pedestal."

"You sold me down the river to save your own ass!"

"If I'd known what you were doing, I'd have had no part in it or you."

"Whiter-than-white Cathal! Sorry, I must be getting you mixed up with somebody else. It wasn't you who shoved coke up your nose in front of me?"

"I only did it to impress you."

"You still did it, and you ran drugs for me as well – what would your fans think about that?"

Cathal smiled. "Don't believe what you read in the magazines, Stephen, I haven't that much money. What I have is caught up in property in my apartment and a house over in London."

"Did I say anything about blackmail?"

"Well, what the fuck do you want then?" Cathal raised his voice. "Just say it so I can get back to my life. You're just a bad memory and one I don't want to remember."

"Yeah, let you get back to your life, your rich glamorous life, and leave me here in this hole! In this dump paid for by the Social and all I have to do is go over to the pub and drink with the other losers, because it's lonely down here at the bottom, Cathal. And you know what? It could so easily have been you."

"What do you want?" Cathal sighed, wishing this nightmare was over.

"I just want the exact same thing I gave to you years ago – an opportunity."

"All you gave me was an opportunity to go to prison."

"I offered you a job at my nightclub and rescued you from a supermarket carpark. I'm out of prison, with no possibility of a job or rescuing myself from this mess. I want an opportunity to make something of my life, and you owe me that opportunity. If it wasn't for you, I wouldn't have been in prison all those years."

"You dealt drugs!"

"That was going to be my final time! That night I was going to earn so much money that I wouldn't have to deal again."

"What kind of opportunity do you want from me?"

"Not from you, but from your girlfriend's father. I only know one business, the nightclub one. It's my only chance of earning a living. I want you to arrange an assistant manager's job for me at Exclusive."

"You're joking!" Cathal was incredulous.

"No, I'm not. I've had it bad enough long enough and now I want some of the sweet life." He got up from the sofa, went to Cathal and gave him a gentle slap across the face. "And you're going to get it for me. You're going to get me that job, because you owe me. Just give me this job and give me a chance to go straight, Cathal. Otherwise, I'll need money from somewhere – and I'll get it from the press, Cathal, when I tell them about how you ran drugs for me."

Cathal's face went red from a mixture of outrage and horror.

Stephen's face relaxed and he smiled. "Come on, Cathal. It's not like I'm asking for much. Just a job through a contact, and a few quid for a deposit for a car and nice pad – that's not too much for an old friend."

* * *

Cathal drove around aimlessly after leaving Stephen. Why the hell did he have to come back? After all these years of being in the public eye and going from strength to strength, always looking over his shoulder waiting for Rourke to reappear. The irony was he had at last allowed himself to think that his past would never catch up with him. And then Rourke came back. And you're still afraid of him, he told himself. God, but Rourke was good. Listening to him today, you'd almost swear he was the poor fool who was manipulated instead of the dangerous drug dealer he really was. Maybe he's gone straight, he thought. Maybe it's as he said and he just wants a chance to make something of his life after being in prison for so long? Maybe. But the bottom line was Rourke was desperate and needed a lifeline to get him out of that hole he lived in. And he would go the press route if he had to, to get money.

He imagined the headlines: *Cathal Fitzgerald Drug Runner.* His career would be over immediately. MPI would drop him without question. It wasn't just him. The other guys in the band would be severely damaged. And what about his family, who had stepped in all those years ago to rescue him? He was now a source of huge pride for them. This would destroy them. And what would it do to Lana? What would finding out he was a drug-runner do to her? And to her father's election campaign! She would lose all faith in him and herself, and go back to the way she was before.

He parked his car at the apartment and, reaching into his pocket, pulled out a load of invitations to different openings and launches that evening. He was on the guest list for most things in Dublin. He went to some and didn't bother with others, depending on how he felt. But as he considered the free bars at all the events that evening, he felt like going to them all. He wanted to numb his mind and forget everything.

* * *

That night Kathryn was surprised to see Cathal stumble up the steps of Exclusive with a bunch of people she recognised as PRs. She had seen him the worse for wear on many occasions, but never as bad as this.

"Cathal, are you all right?" she asked.

"He's fine. Just been enjoying himself all night," said a young woman with him, who Kathryn recognised as being a PR for MPI.

"Do you want me to call you a taxi and send you home, Cathal?" asked Kathryn.

"No. I want to party some more!"

* * *

Kathryn walked through the crowd in Exclusive. It was a very good night as she spotted the usual in-crowd, a couple of visiting Hollywood stars, a high-ranking politician and a highly respected British actress. She had recently employed a new DJ, a young black woman from New York with mad hair, who could really work the crowd up into a frenzy. She paused to survey the dance floor. She saw Cathal dancing with his friends and he seemed totally out of it. She shook her head and moved on.

*   *   *

The champagne kept flowing all night, but Cathal couldn't blot out the past. He kept seeing Stephen Rourke's face. And as he looked around the members' bar everyone seemed to be looking at him and laughing and shouting and then everything went blank.

*   *   *

Cathal woke up and his head thumped. He felt sick and couldn't remember what had happened. He began to piece it together. Drinking on his own in a bar until the evening. Then going to a launch party and guzzling back more alcohol. Then to a record do where he joined up with some MPI people before going on to an opening. Finally he remembered going to Exclusive and continuing to party for what seemed like forever. Then everything went blank. He tried to sit up and see where he was, but he seemed to be in semi-darkness. He pushed what seemed like a thick velvet curtain aside and looked around the main club of Exclusive. He cursed to himself when he realised he must have fallen asleep under one of the tables and the curtain was actually a tablecloth. He looked at his watch and saw it was nearly four in the morning. The place had long since closed and all he could see were half-empty drinks everywhere. How was he going to get out of the place? It would all be locked up and alarmed. He crawled out, stood up and walked across the dance floor. He could hear music somewhere in the distance and realised it was coming from the members' lounge. Thank God for that. Someone was still there.

He went behind the bar, got himself a Diet Coke and sat down to gather his thoughts. It was ridiculous getting that pissed. Why had he done it? Because of Stephen Rourke.

But how had Stephen even known he was in The Four Seasons that night?

He could hear the music and singing from the members' bar and he sat back, resting his head against the back of the seat. It was a woman's voice singing to a piano. It must be an after-hours party, he guessed. The singing was very good. He opened his eyes and concentrated, listening. It was a beautiful love song and the words, the sentiments and the timing were all perfect. It was exquisite. He got up and walked over to the members' lounge door, which was slightly ajar. He peered through.

Instead of seeing a group of people as he had expected, he saw Kathryn Foy as the only occupant. She was sitting at the grand piano, singing. He was very surprised. He didn't realise Kathryn could sing, let alone be that good.

She stopped for a few seconds, took up a pencil and wrote on the music sheets laid out in front of her. Then she tried the piece of the music again. She stopped and made another amendment, then started sifting through her papers.

*   *   *

458

Cathal glanced at his watch and realised he had been listening to Kathryn singing for nearly an hour. He had pulled up a chair and watched her from behind the door, his headache almost forgotten as he realised what a major musical talent Kathryn was. He watched as she stopped singing and looked at her watch. She then closed over the piano. She stood up and started gathering up her music sheets. Cathal didn't know what to do. He would have to make his presence known to get out of Exclusive but that would reveal he had been eavesdropping. But, more importantly, he wanted to talk to her about her singing. He stood up and knocked on the lounge door, pushing it open gently.

"Kathryn!" he called softly.

Kathryn jumped and gave a scream.

Cathal stepped in, holding up his arms. "Sorry. It's only me, Cathal Fitzgerald."

Kathryn leaned against the piano, regaining her breath. "What the fuck are you doing here?" she demanded angrily.

"I fell asleep in the main club under a table at the back."

Somebody in security tomorrow was going to get it for not doing their job properly, thought Kathryn. "I'd have thought you would have had more sense than to get into that condition!" she snapped.

"I know, I know. Been under a bit of pressure recently."

"If it was anyone else I'd be calling the guards for trespassing."

"C'mon, Kathryn, I had one too many and fell asleep. Hardly something the guards would be interested in under any circumstances."

True, she conceded.

"But never mind that," said Cathal. "I want to talk to you about your music."

"I don't know what you're talking about!"

"Kathryn, I've been outside listening to you for the past hour. Not only have you an amazing voice, but your whole understanding of music is exceptional."

Kathryn went bright red. "How dare you listen like that without telling me you were here! You had no right to!"

"Maybe I didn't. But when you hear pure talent like that it's hard to switch off."

"Cathal, you're mistaken. That was the sound system on."

"Yeah, right! You were playing and singing for over an hour."

"I was checking on the club before I locked up and just tinkered with the piano for a while, that's all."

Cathal looked down at all the pencil marks on the music sheets. "No, I don't buy it." He shook his head. "You've been doing this for ages. And you're too good to be hiding up here after hours singing the blues to yourself. Let me bring you in to meet Sylvia –"

"No!" Kathryn shouted the word, giving Cathal a shock. "Cathal, why don't you just mind your own business? You shouldn't have been here in the first place. Now just fuck off and leave me alone! And I don't want you telling anybody about this, do you hear me?"

Cathal was surprised by the anger displayed by Kathryn and he put his hands up in the air in defeat. "Okay, no problem."

Kathryn grabbed all the music sheets and stuffed them into a slim briefcase. "Now, come on. I want to lock up and get the fuck home."

CHAPTER 34

Joanne Bailey had borrowed a wardrobe of clothes from Ireland's top designers. She had brought a hairdresser friend over to Seán's house that morning who had spent two hours on her hair. Seán was fixing his tie in the mirror in his hall when he heard Joanne descend the stairs. He glanced up, and did a double-take. She was dressed in a gown that was pure gold, and very low cut. She was heavily made up, and her black hair was pumped out as far as it could be in huge curls.

"Joanne," he said staring, "you look like a – an Easter egg!"

She frowned slightly, trying not to crack her heavy make-up. "I'm not sure if that's a compliment?"

He went to her and started to put his arms around her.

"Get off!" she squealed. "I'm a precarious balancing act here! The slightest thing, and the whole thing could come crumbling down! What time are they arriving?"

"Any second now." He moved into the lounge and fixed himself a drink.

"Where were you last night, anyway?" she asked, checking herself out in the mirror.

"Just at a party?" he said, gulping back the drink.

"With who?"

"Just a couple of friends." He looked sheepish.

Smiling, she crossed over the room to him and held his chin in one hand. "This relationship means a lot to me, you know." Her expression turned cold. "So, don't fuck it up, okay?" She went back to admire herself in the mirror. "You can never have enough mirrors around when you're beautiful! Did you give any more thought to what I was saying the other night?"

"About Cathal?"

"Yes, about Cathal. I'm telling you he's taken over Affidavit – he's gently pushed you and the others out and is making all the decisions himself."

The doorbell rang, and he took the opportunity to quickly go and answer it.

"Hi!" he said smiling, on opening the door and seeing Tony and Clive. The smile faltered when he also saw Lana. James had mentioned she had come to their photo session, but he'd been hoping she wouldn't come to theirs. By the look of her, she was a stuck-up bitch. Well, with all that money, she had to be.

"Hi, again," Tony said, moving into the lounge and seeing Joanne preening in the mirror over the fireplace.

"Hi," said Joanne, still posing.

"You remember Clive from your last photo shoot with us, Joanne?" said Tony. "And this is Lana, our marketing manager."

On hearing Lana's name, Joanne swung around. "The gang's all here," she said with a sneer.

Lana watched as Seán and Joanne were put through their paces, having photos taken throughout the house, Joanne changing outfits for every photo. She had been stressed at the thought of meeting Joanne again after their confrontation, but had decided to be adult about it and face the situation. She was also very pissed off about what James and Donna had said to her. She had thought about talking to Cathal about it, but he was a little preoccupied at the moment as the band was going from bad to worse.

"Make me look beautiful!" Joanne called to Clive as she posed on Seán's bed.

"Honey, you couldn't look any other way!" replied Clive.

Tony looked on in amusement. Clive managed to always build up a great rapport with his subject – that's what made him a great photographer. But that day, Joanne and him seemed to almost have something sexual going on.

Seán felt slightly pushed aside as Joanne took over.

"You want more leg?" gasped Joanne, pushing the long slit of her dress to one side.

"Yeah, more leg!" demanded Clive, as he photographed intently.

"How much more?"

"As much as you've got, baby!"

Lana was totally intrigued by this woman. Her confidence in her own allure was breathtaking. She had star quality. She could imagine this confident young woman making a beeline for Cathal. She must have been devastated when he dumped her. But why did he dump her? She was beautiful, confident, and obviously, with self-belief like that, going to get to the top. Lana felt dowdy and uninteresting beside her.

Clive focused the camera close on Joanne's face, her mouth slightly open. "You're turning me on!" he said.

"That's what I want!" gushed Joanne.

Seán looked on with increasing anger.

Tony was relieved when Clive left as the atmosphere had turned so bad.

"I didn't realise you would be present for the interview as well," said Seán, not pleased when Lana took a seat beside Tony on the couch opposite them.

"I am part of *Hi Life*."

"And where's Cathal today?" asked Joanne, looking Lana up and down.

"At the studio, I believe."

"Really helping out there, because he's *so* talented," Seán sneered.

"Well, will we make a start?" interrupted Tony, unable to deal with any more tension.

"When will this feature be published?" asked Joanne.

"Next edition. We're really behind schedule," answered Tony.

Joanne took out her mobile. "I just want to give my agent in London a quick call." She dialled the number and waited for the response. "Hi Jason, it's Joanne here. Listen, we've just done the photo shoot for *Hi Life*, and I looked absolutely gorgeous in it! I'll be in the next edition."

Tony and Lana exchanged cynical looks.

Joanne turned off her phone.

"Now, I've already talked to Seán about the band at the studio interviews," said Tony as he turned on the tape, "so now we'll just be talking about your home life. Seán, how has life changed for you since you met Joanne?"

He put an arm around her. "Quite a bit. I've met my soul mate."

"Has it affected the way you look at your life?"

"Well, yeah – before it was all just about Affidavit. But now, Joanne's more important."

"And Joanne, how has your life changed since you met Seán?"

"It's been incredible. You know, you go through life dating these people," she looked at Lana, "thinking they might be special, and they're not. After meeting Seán everyone else paled into insignificance. You'll find that yourself someday, Lana."

"I'm sorry?"

"Well, I was just like you once, flinging from pillar to post, thinking that this might be the big one, when it wasn't."

"Joanne, I've found someone, in case you haven't realised."

Joanne threw her head back and laughed. "Cathal? As I well know, Cathal's only a starter, he could never be the main course. There's nothing to him, no substance. I should know – I looked hard enough."

"*Ahem!*" coughed Tony. "Joanne, you mentioned you had a London agent. Are you trying to get work over in the UK?"

Joanne ignored him. "I just hope you're in that relationship with your eyes wide open, love. Because you seem like a bright girl, if a little volatile judging from your performance in Exclusive that night. Somebody as shallow as Cathal isn't going to be able to offer you anything long term. I know. I found him a huge disappointment in every way. I kind of feel sorry for Cathal. Yes, I do. Because he's a shallow man with no talent and he's only where he is thanks to Seán and the others."

Lana stood up abruptly. "I think I'll wait out in the car for the remainder of this interview," she said, walking away quickly.

She slammed the door of the house behind her, lit up a

cigarette and went and sat in the car. What was it with all these people? They were all so undermining and cutting and nasty. How did Cathal put up with them? He was totally different from them. They wanted her out of their lives, that was for sure. And they felt the best way to accomplish that was to undermine her and Cathal. She thought of her mother, frightened and hiding behind her walls and gates. She thought of her father, one of life's winners and in control of everything. She was at a crossroads at her life and she could choose between two different paths. She wouldn't let these bastards put her down, or Cathal. Her mind was filled with ideas. She would fight these people on their own terms, with the only thing they understood. The photo shoot for Cathal and her was tomorrow. She picked up her mobile and dialled Eddie Haughey, her father's PR head.

* * *

Sylvia sat looking at Tina Cawley seated the other side of her desk and couldn't help from letting the shock register on her face. Tina had rung the night before to make an appointment, saying she had just got back from India. Sylvia had found this unusual, as Tina lived life by her own rules and usually never bothered with the courtesy of making appointments. She expected everyone to be available to her whenever she wanted.

Sylvia had prepared herself to go into battle with Tina over her behaviour at the *Hi Life* party, her attitude, her lack of music production. She had prepared herself for everything, but she hadn't prepared herself for this.

Tina Cawley sat opposite Sylvia with a completely new image. She had adopted the Indian look and sat there in a long flowing cotton dress, her long hair dyed black and neatly combed with a centre crease, again in a typical Indian fashion. Instead of Tina's usual outlandish make-up, she looked simple and natural. She sat poised in her chair, legs crossed, arms relaxed. However, what amazed Sylvia most was that Tina was smiling.

"So how was India?" Sylvia managed.

"It was amazing!" Tina said, her smile widening at the memory. "You know, Sylvia, it was the best thing I ever did, just experimenting with the different culture over there, really getting in tune with my spiritual self. It really was a voyage of self-discovery."

"Uh huh." Sylvia sat back in her chair. "You certainly look different – you look really well."

"Thanks, Sylvia. I feel really well. I think our outer being radiates from our inner, don't you?"

"Sure . . . you know, you upset an awful lot of people before you left."

Tina managed to look ashamed. "I know, and I've been feeling really bad about it ever since. I'm going to write to all those people individually and apologise."

Sylvia sat forward abruptly. "Okay, Tina, let's cut the crap. You've never apologised for anything in your life"

Tina looked hurt before smiling meekly. "That was the old me, this is the new. I've released all my negativity."

"And what about your new album? Have you written much in India?"

Tina nodded enthusiastically. "It's nearly finished. I can't wait for you to hear the tracks. I've kind of changed direction musically. I think you'll be pleasantly surprised."

Sylvia indicated Tina's dress. "And is this how you're going to dress from now on in public, or will you revert to your old image?"

Tina smiled brightly. "No, this is the new me, in every way."

"I just don't know if the world is ready for a Tina Cawley who isn't angry any more."

"Well, they'll have to get used to it . . . and it's Martina from now on, incidentally."

*　　*　　*

The day after Cathal's bender was a write-off. He had barely got out of bed, his head was thumping that much. But he was forced to get up early the next day as it was the day for his photo shoot with *Hi Life* and Lana. But now, as he drove to Lana's house his mind began to function again and he realised how stupid he had been allowing himself to get so intoxicated. If the press had seen him like that, they would have been delighted. It had just been the stress of meeting Rourke again and what he was asking. That mixed with the breakdown with the relationship with his band members. He thought about his encounter with Kathryn Foy. She had been really angry to see him spying on her and completely uninterested in his opinion of her singing. He would love to get her to meet Sylvia but Kathryn was so adamant, there was nothing he could do. It was too bad, because he thought she really was a great talent. It was funny, even though he had known Kathryn for years, he realised he didn't know her at all.

Lana had rung him the previous day and said to leave everything to her for the photo shoot, that they would take the photos at her house and other venues she had lined up. The way he had felt with his hangover, he was delighted for her to take over. As he drove through the streets, there were posters all over the city for the general election.

Hardly a lamppost was free from the smiling face of some politician or other. He passed a poster of Barry smiling down, the slogan promising a better future. Cathal had thought his own future was as bright as it could be until Rourke resurfaced. Rourke had given him a week to come up with the goods. Cathal was due a game of golf with Barry the next day and he was preparing himself for broaching the subject of Exclusive taking on a' new employee. He pulled into Lana's drive and saw the *Hi Life* crew were already present. Sighing, he got out of the Jeep and reached into the back for the selection of clothes that had been picked out for him for the day.

"How's it going, Cathal?" said a friendly voice behind him.

He turned around to see Tony. "Not bad, I suppose, considering I have to do this all day."

"All the price of fame," sympathised Tony.

"Listen, I hear you've been a great help to Lana. I really appreciate it."

"No bother at all. She's a great girl to work with," said Tony. When she's not yapping on the phone to her friends or skiving off early.

"So what we doing today?" asked Cathal.

"Got quite a schedule." Tony handed over a sheet of paper.

Cathal read through it out loud: *"Initial photos at Lana's house, photos at the Curtis's stud farm, a drop by at Barry Curtis's elect* – what the fuck is all this about?"

Tony shrugged his shoulders. "I don't know. Ralph gave me the itinerary this morning. He and Lana came up with it."

"Oh, for fuck's sake!" Cathal stormed up the steps of the house and in through the front door. He was amazed by the number of people in the house.

"Oh, hello, Cathal, my name is Eddie Haughey, Barry Curtis's Director of PR. We're so glad –"

Cathal walked past him and into the lounge where he found Lana perched on the couch, dressed extravagantly, and having her hair and make-up done by three people.

"Oh, hi, darling, you're late. You'd better hurry up and change – use my dressing-room upstairs."

Clive was arguing with two other photographers. "Look, I don't mind you taking photos for your records, but you can't print anything before this exclusive!" he insisted.

"It's all in hand," said one of the photographers. "We have a written agreement from Ralph Conway that in return for the use of Curtis property during the shoot, we can take photos. They won't be used until after your publication date."

Clive looked at Tony for confirmation.

"It's fine. I checked it with Ralph," confirmed Tony.

"It looks like this photo shoot is going to be more of a photo opportunity for the election," Clive grumbled under his breath.

"Lana, can I have a word with you, please?" said Cathal, looking annoyed.

"I'm just in the middle of –"

"Now!"

Lana got up nervously and followed Cathal up the stairs to her bedroom. He closed the door behind them.

"Lana, what's going on here? Who are all these people?"

"They're just employees of my dad's."

"And why are they here?"

"For the photo shoot!"

Cathal became angry. "But there's no need from them all. We just needed to take a few photos at home and leave it at that. Now we're heading off to constituency offices!"

"Oh, I'm sorry, Cathal. I didn't think!" Her eyes filled with tears.

"I don't want to be part of this circus."

Lana sat on the side of the bed. "I'm sorry. I should have realised you'd hate all this." The tears started streaming down her face.

He went and sat beside her, putting his arm around her. "C'mon, stop it. You'll ruin all that make-up."

"It's just I was at James' and Seán's photo shoots and they were all so lavish . . . and the way they look down on me, I just wanted to do something to make you proud of me."

"They don't look down on you –"

"Oh, they do, Cathal! I've been so stupid. I've just been trying to impress everyone. I thought this would impress Ralph and Margaux and all your friends. And all I've managed is to upset you."

"It's fine. Don't worry!" He hated to see her upset, so he tried to put aside his real thoughts.

"It's just, you see, I know I only got that job because of my father. I know everything's only because of my father. Except you. I know you want me for me, but I don't know why you do."

He held her face in her hands. "You've got to start believing in yourself, Lana."

*   *   *

It was an exhausting day for everyone. Cathal was used to heavy schedules, so in spite of his discomfort with

471

the situation, he swung into action. Besides, looking at Lana, he quickly realised she had bitten off more than she could chew. She wasn't a seasoned performer like Donna and Joanne, and all the posing began to quickly take its toll.

"I wish I hadn't bothered with this fucking thing!" she said through gritted teeth, as they posed beside some thoroughbreds at Barry's stud farm.

"Just smile for the camera," said Cathal.

Gloria Reagan was waiting for them at the campaign office. Cathal remembered her bullying tactics at The Four Seasons and was wary of her. But she was full of charm today.

"What about a few photos of the two of them with the election volunteers – answering phones – that kind of thing?" suggested Eddie.

"Yes, and some of Cathal on the phones, as if he's a volunteer himself!" urged Gloria.

Tony and Clive were getting annoyed. They were being shoved aside by Curtis's people.

"Don't let them take over!" Clive hissed at Tony. "You're the guy representing *Hi Life* here. It is a *Hi Life* photo shoot after all!"

"Nah, they might go back and complain to Ralph," said Tony.

"C'mon, Tony! Show some balls! Cathal and Lana look as pissed off with them as we are."

"Yeah, well, Cathal's well able to defend himself."

"There were lots of tears from Lana this morning – I overheard her and Cathal. So he's just trying not to rock the boat today."

Tony steadied himself and walked over to Eddie and Gloria. "Excuse me?"

Eddie and Gloria both looked at him as if he were unwelcome. "Yes?" snapped Gloria.

"It's just, can I remind you, that this is a *Hi Life* photo shoot? You're not calling the shots here."

The whole room was listening.

Gloria waved an itinerary in his face. "And can I remind you that there is an agreed itinerary with your boss? And the election office is part of it."

"And that's where your part ends. We're here. We'll decide what shots we're taking. Now if I could ask you to move out of the way . . ."

Gloria looked furious. "Excuse me –"

"We're behind schedule – please move now," Tony insisted.

Gloria was about to scream at him, but felt Eddie's hand on her arm.

"We'll discuss this privately," he said as he guided her away.

Tony felt a little numb after standing up to those powerful people. He turned around and saw Cathal, Lana and Clive smiling happily at him.

"Fair play to you!" said Cathal, half-laughing.

"I've never seen her look so disgruntled!" Lana was delighted and felt some relief from the stress of the day.

Tony smiled and rubbed his hands together. "Okay, we're calling the shots now. What photos would you two feel comfortable with here?"

Tony felt empowered, and he liked the feeling.

*   *   *

By the end of the exhausting day Lana had suggested that Tony and Clive come back to her house with Cathal

473

and they could order some pizza and have a few drinks. She felt it might be a good opportunity to bond with her new workmates. And Cathal seemed to be getting on really well with Tony.

Tony nearly had to pinch himself. Here he was at Lana Curtis's house with Cathal Fitzgerald eating pizza! And they liked him! He wished he could phone Nicole and tell her all about it. He wished she could be as excited about all this as he was.

They then went out to her back patio and had a couple of bottles of wine, sitting around the garden table. Before Tony knew it, the time was two in the morning. It was a Friday night, so nobody was too concerned about an early night.

"Tell me what's it like, Lana," said Clive.

"What's what like?"

"To be born into all this?"

"Same as it is to be born anywhere else, I guess."

"But you don't have to work for a living," said Tony.

"No, I don't. But I want to. I know it sounds strange but I've never felt happier than since I went to work at *Hi Life*."

"You're mad!" scoffed Clive. "How could anyone enjoy being around Ralph and Maggie?"

"Maggie?" Lana was confused.

Tony didn't know if it was the drink or the relaxed atmosphere but he was letting his guard down with Lana. "That's what everyone calls Margaux."

"Any particular reason?" asked Lana.

"Long story. Anyway, it's different for you. Because of who you are, the Conways are treating you with kid gloves."

"And how do they treat everyone else?" Cathal was intrigued.

474

"Like dirt," said Clive.

"Well, I don't want to be treated different," said Lana and she looked at Tony. "I want to be good at this job on my own merit."

Tony sat back and gave a little laugh.

"What's funny?" asked Lana.

"Nothing. It doesn't matter"

"No, go on. We're all friends here"

"Well, it's just that you've a long way to go in that case."

Lana was upset. "I thought I was doing quite well."

Tony sat forward. "What have you actually achieved as the magazine's marketing manager?"

"I got us that interview with the screenwriter."

"Okay, one thing."

"I got us all these places for shoots today!" she shot back.

"To be fair, those locations are amazing today. The UK market will love them," Clive interjected.

Tony was a little annoyed by this, but then copped on to himself. He didn't want to alienate these people. They were becoming his friends. "Yeah, I admit, you've made a good start!" he said.

* * *

Clive had gone home and Cathal had gone off to get some more drink inside the house, leaving Lana and Tony alone out on the patio.

"It seems to going well between the two of you," observed Tony.

Lana smiled broadly. "I love him to ickle bits! I've never met anyone like him. He keeps me grounded, which is important because I'm a little mad. And he seems to love me in spite of everything I am. I'm really lucky to have found someone as special as him – sorry, I'm getting soppy!"

Soon after, Lana had gone to bed, leaving Cathal and Tony drinking.

"What about you, Tony. Anyone in your life?"

"Yeah . . . no . . . I don't know."

"Sounds confusing."

Tony shook his head. "I'm just going through a rough patch with my partner at the moment."

"In what way?"

Tony started to massage his temples. Maybe he needed to talk to somebody about it. He used to discuss everything with Nicole exclusively, but he couldn't talk to her about this. "It's just we don't seem to be able to talk any more. We were so close. We never did anything without the other. Even when I was at work, I used to speak to her on the phone about fifteen times during the day."

"So what went wrong?"

"I don't know. I got the job with *Hi Life* and things changed. I had to work much longer hours and the job really needed to become a priority. Then she said I had changed, that I was hanging around with stars all the time and she stopped supporting me. And I miss that support, you know. I miss her. But there's nothing I can do."

"You're saying it's over?" asked Cathal.

"That's the last thing in the world I want. I just want us to be back the way we were."

"I'm sorry it's not working out for you," Cathal's face was full of sympathy.

"You know, you're so fucking lucky!" Tony sat back in his chair.

"Me? Why?"

"Well, look at you. You're at the top. Professionally and personally. You got it all going for you."

"Come on, Tony. The whole PR machine's job is to promote us as having it all," Cathal pulled a cynical face, "but I didn't think you were naive enough to believe your own writing!"

"PR bullshit or not, you look to be in a pretty good place from where I'm standing."

"But it's been a huge struggle getting here. Not only with my career, but with Lana as well. I spent years looking for somebody I could trust. Well, I wasn't even looking consciously. And when I did meet Lana . . . let's just say it's been a rocky road."

Cathal's mobile bleeped beside him. "It's nearly three in the morning. It's probably Lana saying to get to bed. He casually picked up the mobile and opened the text. It read *"Well?"* and it was from Stephen. Cathal began to shiver.

"You all right?" asked Tony, concerned.

Being so busy with the photo shoot had stopped Cathal from thinking about Rourke all day. But now the whole situation came flooding back, and it was made worse by all the drink he had consumed.

"Cathal?" Tony pressed.

"There's just a lot of shit going down in my life at the moment," said Cathal, turning his mobile off.

"Do you want to talk about it?"

For a moment, Cathal was tempted to let it all out. To just tell somebody all about Rourke and the situation he was in. To hear somebody's opinion. Then he shook his head. "Nah, but thanks anyway. I'd better go to bed." He got up. Looking down at Tony's worried expression, Cathal realised he had probably just shattered his image of Cathal having an ideal existence.

CHAPTER 35

Cathal and Barry were on the golf course.

"Thanks for everything yesterday, supplying all the venues for the photo shoot and all," said Cathal.

"It was nothing at all," said Barry, taking a swipe at the golf ball. "In fact, as you probably well know, you were doing me a favour."

"Yeah?"

"Well, the election is hotting up, so any publicity is good for me. Thanks for the shot at the election office. I know Gloria can be a bit heavy-handed at times, so always just say no to her if she asks you to do anything you don't want." Barry guessed Cathal knew his image was being manipulated to help him win the election.

Cathal nodded. "Barry . . ." he searched for the right words, "could I ask for a favour?" He felt himself go red.

"Sure, name it."

"It's just there's an old friend of mine from home, and he's been away for a while and now he's moved to Dublin, and he needs a job."

"Okay, what field is he in?"

"He's a nightclub manager."

"Right."

"I was just wondering if there was any position available at Exclusive for him. Maybe Kathryn could do with an assistant or something?"

Barry looked at Cathal for a few seconds before pulling out his mobile and dialling a number. "Hi, Kathryn, Barry here . . . how's things? Good. Remember you've been saying you're a little under-staffed. I think I may have something to help you solve your problems."

*   *   *

Kathryn drove her car through the north County Dublin countryside for a meeting with Barry Curtis. She felt irritated. She and Barry were due to interview this guy Cathal Fitzgerald had recommended as assistant manager at Exclusive. She didn't want an assistant. Yes, she probably needed one, but she still didn't want one.

She had spoken to her sister about it and she was delighted. "You're working six days a week sometimes," said Kelly. "You need someone there to give you a couple of nights off."

It made sense, Kathryn knew, but she was still uncomfortable with letting someone else in on her patch, even if they would be subordinate to her. And if she was going to have an assistant, she would prefer to have chosen someone herself, rather than have this guy foisted on her. But what could she say? She knew from Barry's tone that he had already made up his mind, unless the guy turned out to be clearly unsuitable. She wished Cathal Fitzgerald would stay out of her business. She felt very uncomfortable that he had heard her singing. She hoped he wouldn't mention it to anybody. She had roared at security the next day for not checking the club was empty.

"He's just a nice guy who's doing an old friend a favour by trying to get them a job," Kelly had told her.

Yeah, maybe, thought Kathryn, but why my club?

*   *   *

Even sitting beside Stephen in the Range Rover, driving him over to Kildara, made Cathal's skin crawl. If there had been any other way out of the situation, he would have taken it. He was consumed with guilt at bringing Stephen into Barry's world. It was a betrayal of Lana, and he knew it. His mind even drifted to Kathryn Foy, whom he had known for years. He was lumbering her too with Stephen. But if he didn't arrange this, then Stephen would expose him. Not only would he be destroyed, but so would Affidavit. And also Barry's campaign would be severely affected, now he and Lana were a firm fixture in the public eye. And least this way there was a chance everything might work out. Maybe Stephen had changed after years in prison and would be anxious to stay on the straight and narrow. And also Cathal knew how sharp and tough Kathryn was. If Stephen stepped out of line once, she wouldn't tolerate it. But it didn't stop Cathal from thinking he was just shifting his own dangerous mess into somebody's else's yard.

"I can't tell you how I appreciate all this," said Stephen. Cathal looked coldly ahead.

"And thanks for the suit." Stephen rubbed the material. "You have the money for the car deposit and the apartment?"

"Yes. I'll give it to you after the interview."

"We were good friends once – it's a pity we can't be again."

"We weren't good friends," snapped Cathal. "I was a stupid kid you thought nothing of. You fucked me over with the girl I loved, you threatened me, you got me to run drugs for you without my knowledge. Now, once you get this job, I never want to see you again, as we agreed, okay?"

Stephen nodded. "As agreed. You'll have to write Exclusive off as your social hot-spot in Dublin."

"It's a small price to pay. The only reason I'm doing this is because you have me over a barrel."

Stephen didn't speak for a couple of minutes. "So, tell me about Kathryn Foy. Is she the cold bitch she's made out to be?"

"She's very professional and on top of things. You put one foot wrong and she'll have you out the door."

"Do you know her well?"

"I've known her a long time, but I don't know her well." I don't think anyone knows her well, thought Cathal.

He swerved into the driveway and Stephen blew a long low whistle as they pulled up outside Kildara.

"Cathal, you've done very well for yourself, my boy!"

"Come on. Let's get this over with."

They waited in the hallway as Barry's secretary came to meet them. "He'll see you at once," she said, smiling and showing them through.

Cathal was amazed that Stephen was showing no sign of nerves.

Barry was seated behind his desk, while Kathryn sat beside him, legs crossed, pen and folder before her.

"Gentlemen, welcome!" Barry stood up and smiled warmly. He shook Cathal's hand first.

"Barry, this is Stephen Rourke."

"It's a pleasure meeting you, Mr Curtis. I've long been

an admirer of yours." Stephen shook Barry's hand earnestly.

Cathal noticed his face was pure honest and sincere. He had forgotten how good Stephen was.

"Call me Barry. I'm delighted to meet an old friend of Cathal's."

Kathryn stood up.

"Cathal, you know Kathryn, don't you?"

Cathal smiled warmly at her, but her smile back was cool. She obviously hadn't forgiven him for listening in to her singing. If he got a chance today, he'd say sorry.

"I'm Kathryn Foy, manager at Exclusive." Kathryn shook Stephen's hand. His handshake was firm but gentle, she thought.

They all sat and the others looked expectantly at Kathryn.

Kathryn realised that this guy's connection with Cathal meant he already had the job. She wouldn't even be able to check references. But she was still going to give him a normal job interview and put him through his paces. She crossed her legs and toyed with her pen.

"Stephen, Cathal gave us your background. He mentioned you have been the general manager for clubs down the country, and that you've been travelling and managing clubs abroad. I'll be honest with you. You have no experience of the Dublin nightclub scene and that is a huge minus against you."

Stephen cleared his throat. "I admit I have no experience of the Dublin scene. But I think that is an advantage. I'm a fresh face, rather than being associated with any other club in the capital. And I'm also bringing completely new fresh ideas and thoughts with me."

"As I'm sure you know, we get a lot of stars in

Exclusive. Some of them can be very demanding. So, say a Hollywood actor is in Dublin and visits Exclusive, and treats you very badly all night long, expecting you to run errands for him, being abusive. How would you react to that situation?"

"I think the best way to deal with stars is to treat them in a cool professional fashion. Just keep a little distance between yourself and them at all time. Be charming, yes, be attentive, yes, but don't be friendly. They'll respect you and the club more and be less likely to be abusive to you. And then, if they are abusive to you, you're not going to be upset, because that familiarity isn't there."

Kathryn nodded. "Okay, you're on the door all night. It's cold, you're tired, and it's three in the morning. A group of guys come up and insist on gaining entry to the club and become abusive when you don't let them in. What do you do?"

"Firstly, check that I have back-up –"

Cathal listened intently as Kathryn continued to ask Stephen a series of very tough questions. He could tell that both she and Barry were impressed. He had broken out in a cold sweat from the whole situation.

Thirty minutes later, the job had been offered to Stephen, terms discussed and agreed. Kathryn smiled to herself. Barry always made sure to be involved in the hiring of the management of any business he had. His excellent choice of management was the secret of his success. She had to admit, Stephen seemed very good and he might work out just fine, in spite of the source he came through. She glanced at Cathal. She was surprised to see he looked nervous and uncomfortable.

"If that's everything, I have to fly," she said, standing up.

"Okay, Kathryn, give me a shout during the week," said Barry.

Kathryn shook Stephen's hand. "I'll see you for your first night of work on Friday then." She ignored Cathal and walked from the room.

Cathal excused himself and hurried out after Kathryn.

"Kathryn, can I have a word?" he called, closing the office door behind him.

Kathryn turned around in the marble hall. "About what?"

"Just wanted to say thanks for giving Stephen the job."

"Did I have a choice?"

"Well, I'm sure if you put your foot down, Barry would have listened to you."

Kathryn shrugged. "I'll see you in Exclusive, Cathal." She turned to leave.

Cathal felt weird. He realised he had never got to know Kathryn on any kind of personal level. And now, since Rourke would be working in Exclusive, he wouldn't be going in any more. He felt it was the end of an era, and he wished he had spent a little more time talking to her other than making sure he got the best table and that the drinks flowed.

"Listen, Kathryn, I'm sorry for listening in to your singing."

Kathryn's cheeks flushed. "It's forgotten, don't worry."

"But your singing is fucking fantastic."

"And you'd know, Cathal?"

"I never pretended to be a great musician, but I know a great one when I hear one. Really, why don't you come in and meet Sylvia –"

"No, Cathal! I don't want to be a singer. I play a bit of music for my own entertainment. Now, please, just leave it." She turned and walked out of the house.

* * *

Cathal pulled up outside the run-down flats and handed an envelope over to Stephen.

"Thanks, Cathal!" Stephen put the envelope inside his blazer pocket. "I'll start looking for a new place to live tomorrow. Thanks for everything."

"Just don't fuck up, and let's stay out of each other's way. As I said, I'll be avoiding Exclusive in future, but my cousin James might be in there occasionally and he'll probably recognise you and come screaming at me that you're working there. So if he should ever talk to you, I know nothing about you being in the club or anything else about you? Understand? I don't want to cause stress to my family."

"And what if he asks Kathryn Foy?"

"He won't ask her; they aren't that familiar. And even if he did, she gives nothing away."

Stephen looked admiringly at Cathal. "I remember you couldn't plan or organise anything. When did you become so cunning?"

"The night you tried to fuck up the rest of my life."

Stephen nodded and put out his hand. "No hard feelings?"

Cathal paused and then shook Stephen's hand quickly and briefly. "No, none at all."

* * *

Sylvia walked through the recording studio and came face to face with Cathal.

"Where are you off to in a hurry?" Cathal asked.

"Tina, sorry, *Martina* Cawley has arrived back from India a new woman. She's in recording a song, and the producer phoned me and said I'd better get down and listen to it."

"I might come along for the ride," smirked Cathal. He always found Tina an amusing character.

They stepped into the studio and stayed discreetly at the back. Tina was seated at a piano, singing a ballad. Cathal did a double-take at Tina's Indian-inspired clothes and image. They listened intently for a few minutes.

"She's singing a love song!" Cathal whispered, incredulous.

"C'mon." Sylvia opened the door and they crept out.

"I haven't heard anything as syrupy sweet as that since The Carpenters!" Sylvia said, shocked.

"What happened to her?" said Cathal. "Where's all the mad make-up and persecuted lyrics?"

"I don't know. But I need to get on to MPI's Marketing Department immediately and see what they make of this." She looked at Cathal. "You all right? You look very tired."

"No, everything's fine, thanks. We completed the photo shoot for *Hi Life*."

"Ralph Conway was on. He's delighted with the shots of Lana and you – he says they'll take centre piece of the feature."

"Great!" Cathal raised his eyes to heaven.

"Fair play to you, Cathal. I know you hate that kind of thing."

"It should please the fans, and MPI . . . I know this album has been going really slow and there's been a lot of problems with it. And I'd really like to thank you and MPI for your patience, Sylvia."

Sylvia looked unsettled, which was out of character. "There's no need."

"There is a need. You and MPI have been great, not putting pressure on us and being understanding. Thanks, Sylvia."

"Cathal, I don't think I can take you being like this –"

"You've been great over the years – and . . ." he looked tired and emotional, "well, you're a lot more than a manager to me."

Sylvia blinked her eyes, and smiled. "I'll talk to you later, Cathal." She turned around and began to walk away, the smile quickly leaving her face.

* * *

Nicole nodded as Lana continued talking about her *Hi Life* photo shoot.

"By the end of the day, we were exhausted so we invited two of the guys who worked at the magazine back to my house, Tony and Clive. We just had something to eat and drank some wine. I mean I didn't drink much. It's funny. A few months ago I would have been plastered on the floor, but I'm doing really well now. For the first time in my life, I know my limits and am staying within them."

"And are you having cravings for drink, or drugs?"

"Occasionally I want to throw a bottle of vodka into me. But with Cathal's support I realise that's just hiding, isn't it?"

"Were – were the others drinking much?" ventured Nicole.

"Clive was exhausted after the day, so he left and I went off to bed. Cathal and Tony stayed up for hours talking."

Nicole nodded. "They get on?"

"Yeah. Cathal really likes him, thinks he's sound. They've become quite friendly, actually."

Great, thought Nicole. More pie in the sky to distract Tony from his real life.

"And do you get on with him?" Stop it, Nicole! she screamed at herself.

"With Tony? Well, I had a few suspicions confirmed to me when we were alone."

Nicole sat forward. "Suspicions?" Her heart was racing quickly. Was there another woman? She felt herself become sick.

"Yes, he's always been polite to me but he doesn't think I'm up to the job."

"Oh!" Nicole sat back. "How did you find that out?"

"He told me!"

He was always loose-lipped when he had drink on him, thought Nicole.

"Tony said that I hadn't achieved much since I had become marketing manager."

Nicole was surprised Tony had been so brave as to say it. Maybe there was a little bit of the old Tony left in him after all.

"Did you argue with him?"

"No, I think he regretted saying it and then he backed down."

"I see." Nicole nodded. Definitely the drink talking.

"So I'm going to prove myself. " Lana spoke confidently. "I'm going to show them all. I'm going to be in that office before everyone else, and leave after everyone else."

Nicole felt agitated. If Tony saw Lana working her ass off, he would start putting in even longer hours to compete. "Do you think you're going to manage to do that?"

"Sure, I'm just going to apply myself with the same determination as I used to apply myself to drink and partying. I've already got some interesting ideas I want to run past Ralph."

"Do you not think that may alienate your work colleagues even more?"

"At least they will respect me."

CHAPTER 36

Lana was writing furiously. She really would have to start learning to type properly. Their weekly meeting with Ralph was due any minute and the rest of the management team were sitting in reception, ready to go in. They were all talking amongst themselves, but aware of Lana's presence.

"Were you anywhere interesting this week?" Diana asked Ruth.

Ruth looked through her notes. "Lillie's on Monday, Renard's Tuesday – the cast from that new Gabriel Byrne movie were in. Exclusive Wednesday. David Shorely was there with his new girlfriend!" She pulled a horrified face.

Diana looked concerned. "Weight problem?"

"Let's put it this way: she wasn't so much eye candy, as the whole goddamned candy store!"

Diana tutted. "She needs to read my column a bit more."

The phone rang on Tony's desk and he answered it. "Yeah, everyone's here. He stood up and said, "In we go!"

Ralph was smiling as they entered. "The photos of the Affidavit special are fantastic! The Hartons are thrilled.

They think it's going to be our biggest seller of the year. Well, done, Lana, on getting us those fantastic locations!"

"My pleasure," nodded Lana.

"How we doing on production?" demanded Ralph, directing the question at Gavin.

"Going to print tomorrow morning. This has been very tight deadline, with the extension of the Affidavit feature –"

"I didn't realise the time limit," interrupted Lana. "I'd better quickly come out and say something. I contacted the CEO of Mercedes –", who happens to be a close friend of my father, she thought, "and he wants to sponsor the whole Affidavit feature."

Everyone looked at Lana in shock.

"Now I haven't discussed figures with him –"

"I'm sorry, the advertising deadline is gone on that issue," stated Gavin. "In future, when you come up with marketing ideas like that, you need to give us at least a month's notice, not the day before we go to press."

"What do you mean sponsor?" asked Ralph.

"Well, not take adverts, but to have the name Mercedes at the top of the article and in a kind of logo at the bottom of each page. I mean, let's face it, there were enough Mercedes in all the photos with all the different guys driving one. I thought it was perfect niche marketing –"

"We don't really do sponsored articles, just advertisements," interrupted Gavin firmly.

"But it is a good idea for a one-off big feature like this one," Ralph was becoming excited, "and if the deal is already set up by Lana, we only have to agree on the price."

"I'm sorry," Susan looked incredulous, "the whole layout of the magazine is done. I can't start interfering with it at this stage –"

Ralph slammed his hand on the table. "You can, if I say so! Delay the printing of that magazine till tomorrow afternoon. If the production and advertising team can't insert a couple of logos then they're not up to the job!" He glared at Susan and Gavin.

There was a strange feeling in *Hi Life* for the rest of the day. The deal with Mercedes was put together in an hour, the logos quickly inserted into the feature. Everyone knew it was a massive money-spinner and a great idea. Everyone was shocked that Lana had come up with the deal. Everyone was furious with the way she had clumsily railroaded over all procedures. And nobody was in a position to say anything to her.

*   *   *

Cathal and Lana sat side by side on the sofa in his apartment, looking at the front cover of *Hi Life*, with the members of Affidavit smiling out. The caption underneath read: "Exclusive: *As Affidavit record their new album, they invite* Hi Life *into the studio and their homes to discuss their music, life and loves.*" Cathal skimmed through the magazine and was surprised to see most of the magazine was devoted to Affidavit. He was even more surprised to see that the photos of him and Lana dominated the home photo shoots.

"Well, Sylvia and MPI certainly can't complain I didn't do enough personal publicity this time," he said.

"Do I look okay in the photos?" Lana was excited but very nervous about the scale of the feature.

"You look great," he said and kissed her.

"It's really weird, seeing myself like that all over the magazine."

"I know, it still is for me after all these years."

"You're not mad that I supplied all the home shots?"

"No, I was delighted I didn't have to take them at my gaff. But Sylvia can fuck off now. I'm not doing anything with this level of intimacy again for a long time."

"Do you see the Mercedes logos all over the features?" she asked excitedly.

"I do!" He was amused by her excitement. "You're a clever little marketing executive. You're really getting mileage out of me, aren't you? If you're not having me publicise your father's election, you're selling me to Mercedes."

"Oh, I don't mean to –" She pulled back, concerned.

"I'm joking!" He put an arm about her and kissed her again. But was he, he wondered. He couldn't help adding ironically, "I'm sure the Conways were even more excited with the cash it brought in."

"Cathal," she looked at him seriously, "is everything all right? It's just you haven't been yourself recently."

"There was a bit of bother at work, but I've sorted it all out now."

*   *   *

Kathryn scooped the last bit of casserole on her plate up, ate it and glanced at Simeon across the kitchen table from her. She had to tell him about *Hi Life* that night. She couldn't put the Conways off any longer. Margaux had called her that day herself, and in the sweetest possible way demanded a date to do the feature. She was so nervous of telling Simeon. He was on an even keel at the moment, but after his last decline it had been real hard work to get him back to where he was now.

"Simeon, I don't know if I mentioned before to you

about that award I won for *Hi Life* magazine?"

"Yeah, something for dressing well or something, wasn't it?"

"Something like that. Yeah. It's just they want to do an interview and a photo shoot at home with . . . well, with us"

"With us?" His eyes bored into her.

She was suddenly very afraid. "Yeah, look, Simeon, it's a stupid idea – forget I said anything. It doesn't have to involve you at all. They can interview me at Exclusive, and take the photos of me there – there's no reason to bother you with it."

"Do they know who I am?"

"Well, eh, I told them I had a partner . . . they want to find out about me and my home life."

Simeon had that look of excitement in his eyes that he got occasionally. He stood up and looked animated. "They remember me from my music and are using you to get to me!"

She opened her mouth to protest but stopped herself in time. He was looking excited by the whole thing and maybe he would agree to it. "Well, I mean, they obviously will be asking you about your profession as a musician."

"It's a cheap shot trying to use you, though. I don't like it when people do that to you, baby."

She felt her heart began to soar. He hadn't spoken to her with that affection for a couple of months.

"How do you feel about it?" He was pacing up and down.

"I agreed to do it, so I kind of have to."

He came over to her, took her by the hands and raised her up. "I'm only going to talk about certain things with them, baby. I don't want to talk about any recent music

I've done, only the stuff people are familiar with, okay?"
He started to kiss her.

*　　　*　　　*

Cathal answered his mobile as he pulled into the
carpark at Sylvia's office. It was Lana.

"Hiya, babe!" he said.

"I'm just letting you know that the latest edition of *Hi
Life*, the Affidavit special, is the biggest seller of the year,
and that's after only being on the shelves for three days!"

"You're joking!" Cathal was amused as he got out and
locked the Jeep behind him.

"Everyone is delighted with it," she went on excitedly.
"The sales are through the roof, and that's the Irish *and* UK
markets!"

"Well, that should make everyone at MPI happy."

"Ralph is over the moon – and he thinks it's down to
the interest in the two of us."

"Could have something to do with it. Listen, I'm
running late for this meeting with Sylvia and the band. I'll
call you later."

Cathal knocked on Sylvia's door and entered. Seán,
Rob and James were already there with Sylvia.

"Sorry I'm late, everybody!" He sat down in the only
free seat. He looked around and smiled at everyone. "Why
is everyone looking so serious?"

Sylvia leaned forward and looked at him directly.
"Cathal, there's been a few changes."

She looked at the other three guys. Rob and James were
looking down at the floor, while Seán was sitting back,
smiling, and looking straight at Cathal.

Cathal shrugged. "Changes?"

Nobody spoke.

"Thanks, guys," said Sylvia, looking at the others. "I'll say it then, will I? Cathal," her voice was smooth and soft, "Seán has been offered a contract with Channel 4 in the UK to present a music show."

"Oh!" Cathal was genuinely shocked.

"Myself and Joanne have been offered the show together as co-presenters," said Seán.

"Well, I can't say I'm not pissed off," said Cathal. "I mean, how are we supposed to finish the album without you? I take it you're not staying to finish it?"

"Myself and Joanne are outta here for London."

"Okay." Cathal looked at James and Rob. "Our main concern is to finish the album and so we need to really get our heads down –"

"Cathal," Sylvia interrupted, "when MPI learned of Seán's decision, they took the opportunity to review the situation."

"What do you mean?" Cathal sat forward.

"Well . . ." Sylvia looked at James and Rob, but their stares were fixed on the floor.

"Ah, for fuck's sake, somebody tell him!" snapped Seán. "The band's over, Cathal."

Cathal's forehead creased in a frown. "What are you talking about?"

Sylvia sighed. "Cathal, when Seán announced he was leaving, MPI felt the group couldn't go on as a three-piece. To be honest, they've been worried about projected sales figures, and there have been such problems recording this album – I mean, it's going nowhere –"

"So they're just dumping the rest of us?" Cathal was furious.

"Not quite!" Seán said, smirking.

"Shut up, Seán!" James almost shouted. He looked at Cathal, his eyes full of anguish. "Cathal, MPI offered me a solo contract and I've accepted it."

"What!" Cathal felt like he had been struck. He visibly paled. "And when did this all happen?"

"Just over the past few days," said James sheepishly.

"And nobody thought to tell me till now?" Cathal looked at Rob and his voice filled with concern. "Are you all right, Rob?"

"Yeah, I'm fine." Rob forced himself to look at Cathal. "But . . ."

"What is it, Rob?" said Cathal.

"You might as well get it over with," Seán advised, his voice light.

Cathal looked at the stressed expressions of Rob, James and Sylvia. "Well?" he almost shouted.

Sylvia took a deep breath. "Well, the truth is –"

"Yeah, some *truth* would be nice!" spat Cathal.

"James has been contracted by MPI to record a new solo album. He will be recording Rob's music."

Cathal leaned forward, buried his face into his hands and stayed like that for a while.

"Cathal?" James eventually asked.

Cathal sat up abruptly, his face red but his eyes alert. "The whole thing is perfectly clear – you don't have to say any more. Seán, you're off for television success. James and Rob, you got an offer you couldn't refuse. Cathal, thanks for the memories – now fuck off!"

"It's not like that –" said James.

"Well, how is it then . . . cousin?"

"C'mon, Cathal," said Rob. "You're the only person who hasn't been seeing what's been going on. Seán's been unhappy with the band for a long time. I hated the musical direction we were being pushed to go in. I need to be true to myself, and as a songwriter with this contract I can produce the music I want."

"With James singing it." Cathal looked at James.

"Look, James wasn't developing as an artist in Affidavit," said Sylvia. "We all know his talent and ability, and it was becoming stifled under the constraints MPI were imposing."

"Okay. So everyone is to be looked after except me. That's the story, isn't it?" Suddenly he was beside himself with fury. "The amount of work I've put into this band over the years and for you all to treat me like this!"

"Cathal, will you calm down!" said Sylvia.

"Look, Cathal, we all know you didn't take the music as seriously as we did," said Rob. "I'm not saying you didn't take the band seriously, nobody can take away what you did over the years, but you didn't have the same soul for music that we did. And we tolerated your little press stories over the years, even though they hindered us from being taken seriously, but I mean now you're playing politics with that girlfriend of yours and her father. I mean – Barry Curtis! I don't want my musical credibility affected by you campaigning for him."

"I'm not campaigning for him! I didn't want to do that stupid *Hi Life* photo shoot – it was MPI that forced me to do it!" Cathal nearly shouted.

"And I've been talking with my charities – I told you before, some of his policies are directly opposed to what I'm promoting," said James.

"Don't use that as an excuse. If you wanted away from me just come out and say it, as Seán has, and don't hide behind fucking excuses!" Cathal jumped up. "Thanks for the good times, everybody, and the best of luck with your new lives!" With that, he stormed out.

* * *

Tony and the rest of the senior staff sat looking at Lana's pile of notes sitting in front of her during the weekly meeting in Ralph's office. None of them looked happy, except for Ralph who looked very happy indeed.

"Amazing!" declared Ralph. "The sales figures for the Affidavit edition and the advertising revenue were amazing. Well done, everybody!"

It was such a rare occurrence that Ralph paid a compliment that everyone smiled fleetingly.

"Especially well done to Lana, for all the great locations and pulling in the Mercedes sponsorship deal. That's what we need – great innovation like that!" Ralph slammed his hand on the table.

Tony studied Lana, who seemed to take the praise in her stride. An anger was burning up inside him. It was he who had worked every hour God sent on the Affidavit special. He had compiled and written the whole thing. And next thing, Lana had come waltzing in, hardly put any work in, come up with a few locations, courtesy of her father, and a sponsorship deal, again no doubt courtesy of her father, and she was being given all the credit.

"Now, we are at last making progress for a date for Kathryn Foy's feature. Thanks to Margaux's intervention, as nobody here could come up with anything concrete." Ralph shot Tony a dirty look. "Are we all set for that?"

"All set," said Clive, who looked bored and inattentive as usual.

"Right, now I want everyone to –"

"Could I just say a couple of things?" Lana interrupted.

"Eh – sure, g-g-go-ahead," stammered Ralph, completely thrown at being interrupted in mid-flow.

Everyone turned and looked at Lana apprehensively.

"It's just I've been working on a couple of ideas and wondered what everyone thought. Firstly, I've been in contact with the marketing manager of the Holden Travel Agency and they seem very interested in an idea I had to give a part-payment holiday voucher out with every edition next month. What do you think of that?"

Everyone was silent, but surprise registered on their faces.

"That is a huge expenditure of money on the part of Holden's," said Ralph cautiously.

"They've done their budget on it," said Lana, "and they believe, as I do, that the readers of *Hi Life* are their market and well worth the investment. Ralph, I was thinking of setting up a meeting between us and their marketing manager this week?"

Ralph looked shocked. "Fine"

"Good." Barry was one of Holden's biggest business partners. It was easy to get the doors opened. "The second thing I was thinking – now this is a little bit of a departure for *Hi Life* – what about a whole edition dedicated to the appreciation of food?" She smiled brightly at her colleagues.

"Food?" Ralph was confused.

"What?" Diana looked horrified.

"Yes – food. Let's give our readers a break from all those fad diets and tough regimental exercise routines we are always endorsing and give them a whole edition concentrating on food. We could entitle it *'Food – Have You Forgotten How Good It Tastes?'*"

"Go on." Ralph looked concerned.

"What I was thinking was that we could tell our readers we are forgetting about calorie-counting and stomach-crunching for one edition, and concentrate on features and articles about the best restaurants to eat in, and At Home features with Ireland's most famous chefs. Recipes from these chefs –"

"Lana, I don't think you quite get the picture about what we are trying to achieve here at *Hi Life*," said Diana, whose cheeks were flushed. "We are trying to raise our readers up to the best they can be by giving them the best role models, the best interior design, the best diets. We carry our readers from month to month, pushing them forward, pushing them to be better than they thought they could be. If we suddenly tell them they can eat whatever they want for a month, then all the good dietary encouragement I've giving them would be lost and I don't think I could ever get them back on track again!" Diana looked on the verge of tears.

"Well, I think everyone deserves a break," said Lana, "and I think *Hi Life's* readers deserve a break from being made to feel inferior because of their weight or fitness level. Besides," she passed Ralph a load of papers, "I did some research, and all these restaurants and hotels were very interested in advertising in such an edition. We are appealing to a whole new market of advertisers with it." She paused before delivering the pièce de résistance. "And when I contacted these businesses I quoted them twenty-five per cent more than our usual rate card for advertising fees."

*　　*　　*

"Who would have thought she would be so good?"

Ralph said to Tony after the others had left. "When I offered her the job, I did it because of who her father was – I thought she might be handy with a few contacts. They say the acorn doesn't fall far from the tree – she's obviously got her father's business brain."

"Hmmm . . ." Tony tried to smile.

*   *   *

The evening was dark when Sylvia came out of the office and started walking over to her car. She felt exhausted and low. The last couple of days, sorting everything out with James and Rob and Seán, had drained her. But nothing had prepared herself for the scene with Cathal. She felt very bad.

She spotted Cathal's Jeep parked on its own in the far corner of the carpark. She slowly walked over and saw he was sitting in the driver's seat staring ahead. She steadied herself, tapped on the passenger's window, opened the door and climbed in.

"You look terrible," she said softly as she closed the door behind her.

"How else do you expect me to look?" His voice was bitter, and he continued to stare out in front.

"Cathal, I know it looked as if everything was sorted behind your back, but it wasn't like that."

He turned to her and stared at her. "How exactly was it then?"

"Everything just happened so quickly over the past few days –"

"That everyone just forgot about me?"

"That album was going to flop, Cathal. We knew it, and we had to cut our losses and move on quickly."

"But after all these years?"

"You know how the music industry works – it's ruthless."

"And so are Rob and Seán and James . . . and you. Tell me, Sylvia, when I spoke to you at the studio and started saying how grateful I was to you, did you know about all this by then?"

"I knew about Seán leaving, but not about James and Rob. Look at the bigger picture. You were given an amazing chance a few years ago that brought you around the world, gave you money and respect and set you up for life. You've always admitted to me that you're not a great musician. Just be grateful you had a great run."

"I thought we'd go on for much longer."

"You were never going to have the longevity of U2. You were never in their league."

"But what'll I do now, Sylvia?" He looked lost.

"As I said, you've made some good investments. You're set up. Just sit back and enjoy life for a while." She placed a hand on his arm and squeezed it. "Go home, Cathal, and I'll give you a call tomorrow."

* * *

Lana let herself into Cathal's apartment carrying a big box of shopping.

"I had such a good day!" she declared, walking through the lounge and past Cathal who was seated on the couch. "I really came up with some brilliant ideas for the magazine and everyone loved them." She went into the kitchen and started to unpack the box onto the island. "Everyone except for Diana, who looked very upset because I dared to say that people might not want to be on a permanent diet. They didn't have Heineken, only Carlsberg." She opened a can for him and walked into the lounge with it. "And I've come up with a great new logo for the magazine *'Hi Life – Your Best Friend' –*" She stopped when she saw Cathal's face, white as a sheet, as he stared blankly out the patio doors. "Cathal?" She put the can on the table and sat beside him. "Cathal?" she asked again, feeling scared at his expression.

"It's over," he said quietly. "Affidavit is over."

"What do you mean?"

"Sylvia and the guys brought me into the office today and said the band was finished. Seán and Joanne are going off to London to present a new TV show. James and Rob have been offered new contracts with MPI."

"But why did this happen?"

"Seán wanted out and MPI weren't confident we could go on without him. You know what a disaster the whole album was turning into – they took the opportunity to bin us."

"And what about you. What have they offered you?" she demanded.

Cathal shrugged and then he smiled. "Just memories."

"Oh, Cathal!" Lana felt her eyes fill with tears.

* * *

Cathal could hear the city sounds outside as he lay in the semi-darkness beside Lana. She was a quiet sleeper, and one of her arms was across his chest. He felt numb and vacant most of the time. And when he didn't feel that, he felt terrified. He hadn't expected this. He knew things were going badly with the band but . . . What had he done wrong for this to happen? He needed to know. He reached over and got his watch. It was two o'clock in the morning. He gently moved Lana's arm and got out of the bed.

* * *

One hour later he had driven through the empty Dublin streets across the city and was outside James and Donna's house. He punched the code into the keypad and the electric gates opened. He drove into the gravel drive and got out of his Jeep. He stood outside the front door and took the giant knocker and banged it against the oak wood loudly. There was no response, so he knocked again and again. A light came on upstairs and he could hear a commotion.

A window opened upstairs and James stuck out his head. "Who the fuck is it?" he shouted.

"It's Cathal!"

"What the fuck are you doing here at this time in the morning?" James slammed the window shut and Cathal could hear a lot of talking upstairs.

Lights came on in the hallway and through the glass on either side of the door he could see James coming down the stairs, in a silk dressing-gown.

James unbolted the door and opened it. "Cathal, couldn't this wait until the morning?" he said wearily.

"No."

Donna came down the stairs, tying a knot in the belt of her dressing-gown which was identical to James'. "What the hell is going on?" she demanded.

"I've just come over to celebrate James' new contract'," said Cathal, managing to smile and look angry at the same time.

"Have you been drinking?" Donna accused, walking

into the lounge.

"Not a drop," said Cathal, following her in.

James rubbed his face and back of his neck with the palms of his hands before following them in.

"How could you do this to me, James?" demanded Cathal. "For fuck's sake, after everything we've been through over the years, not to even discuss it with me first!"

"I didn't have time. They produced the contract there and then. It was too good an opportunity for me to miss."

"Too much money, you mean."

"Not just that. They're allowing me to produce the music I want to."

"You and Rob."

"Yeah."

"Nothing there for me."

"Come on, Cathal!" Donna said, sitting down. "Rob and James can work together to produce some really great music."

"Come off it. You're not interested in his music, only the great glory of the James and Donna Show – you're probably already negotiating a deal with *Hello*."

"There's no talking to you when you're like this," snapped Donna.

"And Seán's off to produce a TV show in London!" Cathal's voice was sarcastic. "We all know how he loves presenting."

"You should have stuck with Joanne Bailey, Cathal – it could have been you landing that TV contract now," said Donna.

"How could I stick with somebody I couldn't stand just for a job? James, I know you. There's more to all this than just solo contracts. C'mon, tell me!"

"Cathal . . . I just feel you're going down the wrong road again . . . with Lana."

"Now we're getting somewhere," Cathal said loudly and threw his hands into the air.

"We tried to warn you enough times that she's bad news, and," James looked at Donna, "we don't want to be associated with someone like her."

"Someone like her. She's a beautiful, intelligent, gentle and unique woman – what's wrong with that?"

"Ha!" Donna called out loudly, and shook her head in disbelief.

"She's had some problems, and made a few mistakes." Cathal's voice was pleading. "For God's sake, haven't we all?"

"No, actually!" snapped James. "We haven't – but you have. You'll always make mistakes. Like you are now with Lana."

"And we're not going down with you," Donna said with a determined air.

"You love reminding me of how I fucked up years ago, don't you? You love reminding me of how your father rescued me from that drug deal – how I was going nowhere until you brought me into Affidavit – how I owe everything to you. Just subtly letting me know that under the surface I'm a loser."

"James did give you a chance, Cathal. You've had a great run, and now it's time to bow out."

"As everyone keeps telling me!" snapped Cathal.

Nobody said anything for a couple of minutes.

"Things don't have to change between us," said Donna. "We can still be the best of friends."

Cathal got up. "I'll phone you tomorrow. I hope everything works out for you with your contract and everything."

CHAPTER 37

Cathal was exhausted from lack of sleep, but he still couldn't rest. He went down to the shop to get some milk. He saw the *The Sun* and picked up a copy. The headline read: *"Affidavit call it a day – James goes solo, and Seán heads for TV."* Cathal read the article quickly. It was all about James and Rob's deal with MPI and Seán's contract with Channel 4. How quickly the MPI public relations team took over, he thought. He saw Sylvia's handiwork all over the article. There was no mention of Cathal.

* * *

Stephen drove along the coast road from Sandymount, from the new apartment he had just rented, in his new convertible, deposits courtesy of Cathal. It was a beautiful sunny day, and he had the roof down on the car, with "Everyone Wants To Rule The World" blaring from the radio as he inhaled the sea breeze, trying to forget the stuffy lingering smell of the inside of the prison. He was en route to meet Kathryn at Exclusive, and he congratulated himself on how he had handled everything.

Kathryn looked at the CCTV when the bell rang and saw Stephen standing there. She picked up the phone on the wall.

"Come on up," she said, and pressed the buzzer. She got up and walked out of her small office, locking it behind her, and made her way into the main club.

"What's the weather like outside?" she asked as she made her way over to the bar.

"Scorching. Nice and cool in here though."

"Yeah. Come over here and I'll start with showing you the bar system,"

Stephen picked things up very quickly, Kathryn admitted as she went through all aspects of the club management. It was obvious he was very experienced in nightclub management. He also seemed extremely diligent and enthusiastic. And most importantly, she couldn't pick up any attitude from him.

"Right," she said, "that's really all the bare essentials you need to know for now anyway. Just two major rules I have. This is a cash business, so the temptation for staff to steal is always there. Now the team I have is trustworthy and honest, but if I ever catch anyone with their fingers in the till, it's instant dismissal and I hand them over to the guards. If I'm not here, I expect you to do the same."

"I'm totally in agreement with that." Stephen nodded.

"The second thing is drugs. I can't express how tough I am on drugs. I will not allow my customers to use drugs on these premises. And if I ever catch anyone, they are banned immediately, regardless of who they are. If I catch a member of staff with drugs, or on drugs, it's instant dismissal, and again the guards are informed. I expect you to enforce this house rule."

"I couldn't agree with you more."

That night, Kathryn discreetly watched Stephen. He worked like a Trojan all night long, was tough but fair with the staff, and charming but removed from the customers. Maybe Cathal Fitzgerald had done her a favour after all.

*   *   *

Declan, Affidavit's accountant, looked at Cathal sitting across from him in his office, and felt worried. Cathal, who usually looked so healthy, in control and quick-witted, seemed worn out, exhausted and finding it hard to focus.

"Well, Cathal, it's like this, you haven't anything to worry about in the future, that is unless you plan to dramatically alter your lifestyle and start spending big time. I mean, since you didn't write any songs in your career, you obviously missed out on huge royalties that way. But you've earned a lot, didn't squander it, made some shrewd investments, and got the apartment in Dublin, the house in London. You just have to be careful not to be extravagant. Because the investments you have will have to sustain you the rest of your life."

Cathal nodded. "Thanks, Declan." He got up and left.

Declan was surprised. He was used to being put through his paces with Cathal.

*   *   *

Nicole fidgeted with her pen at her desk, and looked at her watch. Five to three. Lana would be along shortly.

She and Tony were like strangers sharing the same house now. She thought what a bizarre set-up she was in.

She found out more about what was happening in Tony's life through her sessions with Lana than from Tony. It made her very uncomfortable. She tried to be professional and steer the conversation with Lana away from Tony. But sometimes, when Lana talked about him, she couldn't restrain herself. She was only human, after all. Besides, if she and Tony were as happy as they once had been, there would be no temptation to prompt Lana into further revelations. As it was, she needed all the information she could get to gain some insight into what Tony was going through – and hopefully save their marriage.

The door opened and in walked Lana. She looked upset. She sat down opposite Nicole. "I'm a bit stressed today. Cathal's band has disbanded."

"Really?"

"I've never seen him like this. He's really shook up. I think of him as so strong. I'm worried about him."

"Have you spoken to him about it?"

"He's kind of closed up about it . . ."

As Lana continued to speak, Nicole tried to concentrate but found it hard. She glanced at her watch. The session had been going on for nearly fifteen minutes, and Lana was still going on about Cathal.

"I guess it's the rejection he feels. Seeing the other guys, particularly James, going off and doing great things and him being left behind. They are a shower of bastards! And just when things were going great for me. I'm enjoying work so much. I'm buzzing on coming up with lots of new ideas all the time. And I love seeing all their expressions when I do."

"What do you mean? Do they resent you?"

"A little bit, I guess. Tony resents me. It's so obvious. I know he goes out with Clive and the others for drinks after work – they haven't invited me along, though – that's when he isn't out jogging with that idiot Diana!"

"Is she an idiot?" Be careful, Nicole!

"I just can't understand somebody living their life as such a health freak. She has Tony totally under her thumb."

Nicole became anxious. "Do you suspect that something is going on between them?

"An affair?" Lana laughed out loud. "No. Sure, she's about fifteen years older than him. No, she kind of mothers him all the time."

Hmmm, thought Nicole sitting back, Tony always loves being mothered.

* * *

Cathal was surprised to hear a knock on the apartment door. When he opened it, he was taken back to see Joanne Bailey there, dressed in a fur coat that swept down to the ground.

"Hi there!" she said brightly, before walking past him into the apartment.

"What are you doing here?" he asked as he closed the door over.

"I remembered the password at the main door, so I thought I'd just come on up. I suppose I just came over to say so sorry about Affidavit splitting up. You must be devastated!" She pulled a sympathetic face.

"Congratulations on your new show," he said, wondering what her game was.

"Thanks. We're heading to London this evening, me and Seán. I'm so excited. It's everything I ever wanted."

"What do you want, Joanne?" he sighed.

"Nothing from you, because what could you give me? I'm here to give you something." She reached into her purse, took out a ticket and handed him it.

"What's this?"

"I took the opportunity to buy you a bus ticket. It's a one-way ticket back to Ballydull, or wherever the fuck you come from!"

He stared at her in amazement.

"Because that's the only place you can go now. How dare you treat me like you did? Nobody dumps me. You didn't know what you were messing with. I wasn't one of your little slappers. And I'm enjoying every minute of this. What does it feel like, Cathal? The press have stopped ringing you, haven't they? I mean, don't get me wrong, you'll still be invited to lots of events for a while, and you'll still be known. But gradually that will dry up, and you'll just become a distant memory. You've no talent, so you can't go anywhere from here. That's why I bought you that bus ticket. There's no point in prolonging the agony. Sail off into the sunset now. Because Lana isn't going to be around for long. She was only with you because of who you were. She'll quickly fall back into that vacuous rich set she grew up with now. Anyway, I'd better go, I've a plane to catch. First show going out live on Friday night. Tune in – I'm sure you won't be doing anything else!"

He felt anger burn inside him. And he knew if it was under normal circumstance, what had been normal before, he would have dealt with her in a few seconds flat. But the fight had gone out of him. And even worse, what she was saying was only what had been repeatedly going through his head over the past few days. What she was saying was true.

She walked past him to the door and opened it. She turned and said, "Oh, and Cathal, you look like shit, incidentally."

Cathal sat in the semi-darkness, feeling a mixture of

fear and anxiety. He remembered James and Donna saying they didn't want to go down with him. He was angry with himself for falling for Lana, if that had cost him Affidavit. Then he was angry with Lana. But he realised that was stupid. It was because of his past that they didn't trust his judgement now.

Lana let herself into the apartment. "Cathal!" she called, turning on the full lights. The room lit up and she saw Cathal sitting there.

"Cathal, you don't look well!" She went and sat beside him. There were loads of photos scattered about on the coffee table, photos from different parties with him and the band. They all looked as if they were having the time of their life.

"I was nobody before Affidavit, and I'm going back to being nobody again."

"That's not true!" she said.

"It is! I just can't believe the ending came so quickly . . . I feel as if I've lost my identity. I was so confident in being who I was, but now I feel the rug has been pulled from under me."

She hugged him quickly. "Cathal, I know what's happened has affected you, but you're just going to have to accept it. Listen – come over and stay at mine. Pack whatever you need and come on over. I think getting out of your apartment will be good for you."

Cathal nodded.

*   *   *

Sylvia hung up the phone. She had spent thirty minutes trying to placate Jack Better. He was very uncomfortable with Tina Cawley's reinvention and the sound of her new music. He thought, as Sylvia did, the public wouldn't take to this new Tina. MPI's marketing department had done their research and the results were that MPI were not prepared to start recording this new album of Tina's without full proof it would be as successful as her previous ones. Sylvia had come up with the suggestion that Tina do a series of interviews on Irish and British TV and also sing some of her new music on them. This would give MPI significant feedback about how successful an album would be. They could judge the public mood correctly. Sylvia understood Jack's concerns. The music industry was unforgiving and they had already lost money and time recording those songs for the Affidavit album that never was. She sat back in her chair and crossed her legs. They had done the right thing with Affidavit. They had cut their losses while they could. She could now concentrate on James with Rob's songs. She thought of Cathal and genuinely felt very sorry for him. She had seen it had hit him badly, but then she'd known it would. He had given everything he had to the band. She hoped he'd be okay. She was tempted to ring him to ask how he was, but decided against it. There was no point in being a reminder of a life that was now closed to him.

* * *

"We're up two per cent in the polls" Gloria declared happily to Barry in his office.

"That's brilliant!" he said.

"It certainly is. I put this rise down totally to my idea of bringing Lana and Cathal into the equation. It's giving us extra publicity and giving you a glamorous edge as well as showing your personal side. The *Hi Life* interview was a real vote-catcher. That's what the public want." Then she frowned. "Okay, that's the good news. The bad news is that you are still not assured victory in the election."

Barry sat back in his chair. "Any ideas of how we can up the tempo?"

Gloria nodded. "First of all, we continue to use Lana and Cathal at every opportunity. Try and make sure they attend any events we are doing. We have a short shelf-life on this, now that band Cathal was in is over. The press will still be interested in him but they'll move on. But hopefully that will be after the election."

Barry felt uncomfortable about the way Gloria was speaking. He had hoped getting Lana involved in the campaign would help her self-esteem as much as it helped his election hopes. And he was genuinely fond of Cathal and didn't want to use him for his own ends like that.

Gloria saw his frown. "Anything the matter?"

Barry looked serious. "I just want you be aware that I'm happy for Lana and Cathal to be involved but only if they want to. I don't want us to manipulate them."

"Of course." Gloria tried to adopt an honest look. "But I don't think Lana or Cathal would be very happy if you lost the election, would they? And if I can remind you, that is very much a possibility. Anyway, I'll leave these poll results for you to study." She handed them to Barry, and he went to take them. Her hand brushed against his and there was a little spark of electricity between them.

"Sorry, Barry," she said in a whisper and smiled at him, while allowing herself to blush and look as demure as possible. Not an easy feat for Gloria.

*   *   *

Cathal put the key Lana had given him into her front

door and opened it.

"Hello!" he called as he pulled his suitcases in after him. There was no answer. The housekeeper must have already left, he thought, closing the door behind him. He walked into the lounge and sat down, looking around at the stylish antiques. It was good to be away from his apartment. It was as everyone had said to him. He'd had a good run, and was now comfortable for the rest of his life. He would now just get on with it and live the rest of his life with Lana.

He picked up his mobile and dialled James' number.

"Hiya, just me, checking in to see how you are." Cathal forced himself to sound upbeat.

"Full of hassles," said James. " We're in the studio at the moment recording my new album. Rob's new songs are fantastic. Wait till you hear them!"

"I'd love to come down and listen –"

"Shit, listen. The producer's giving out to me here for having my mobile on. Better go. Talk later." James hung up.

Cathal was taken aback by James' abruptness. He had been hoping for an invitation down to the studio to listen to the new music. Obviously he wasn't wanted. He suddenly felt James being out of his life was like the rug being pulled from under him. James had always been this role model who had done everything right and had always been a great friend to him. It was unfair if he allowed himself to feel bitter over his solo career. James was a talent, a nice guy and deserved the best. He just had a feeling he had lost James and Donna now. Time to move on, he reminded himself.

He picked up the phone and dialled Lana.

"Hiya!" he said, forcing himself to sound cheery.

"Hi! You sound a bit better."

"Just letting you know I'm in your house now. Just

wondering what you wanted for tonight's dinner."

"I've a meeting with Carlsberg at three, so I should be home early enough. Whatever you feel like, we'll have. Surprise me."

"Okay. And thanks, Lana."

*   *   *

Lana hung up the phone and thought for a second. Maybe he was coming round. She had been seriously worried about him. He meant everything to her.

Her phone rang on her desk and she answered it. It was the sales manager from Easons. "Hi – I have all the new promotion stands for the magazines for Easons . . . sure . . ."

Tony tried to concentrate on editing an article but it was hard to with Lana talking loudly on the phone all the time. And if she wasn't doing that, she was typing in the loudest and strangest way he had ever heard. Very distracting. He wished she was given her own office. She really annoyed him. Little did everyone think that she would be so good at this job. Ralph and Margaux worshipped her. And he was now just an afterthought to everyone. He really wished he could speak to Nicole about it, but they just nodded to each other now as they passed each other in the house. It would only be a matter of time before they separated properly and one of them would move out. He wondered how things had come to this.

*   *   *

Nicole had moved out of the main bedroom and into the small second bedroom in the cottage. There was no point in sharing a bed, when they shared nothing else.

There had been no discussion about it. She had just moved
her stuff from the main bedroom and that was it. They
were even buying separate groceries now. Which suited
her fine. She could get whatever she wanted, instead of all
that organic stuff Diana had recommended Tony to get all
the time. She was at home working on her notes on Lana.
Lana in herself was interesting. It was obvious she had a
completely addictive personality and she had simply
swapped her addiction for drink and socialising for an
addiction for Cathal and work. She also realised, when she
perked up so attentively whenever Lana mentioned Tony,
that she still loved Tony totally.

*   *   *

Kathryn was really impressed by Stephen. He was a
natural when it came to running a club. She had made sure
to watch his every move at the beginning. She had laid
little traps for him with money, stock take and customers
to see how he would react. But he seemed completely
honest and trustworthy. And he had that knack of making
customers feel special, but taking no nonsense. She could
at last take two nights a week off and know the club was in
safe hands. She could spend some time with Simeon, who
was in great form. Since she told him about *Hi Life,* he had
taken on a new lease of life. He was really looking forward
to it. And when he was like that, there was nobody better to
be around. He made her feel completely special. She had
become a bit paranoid after Cathal Fitzgerald had listened
in to the singing. She double-checked the club now any
night she stayed behind to compose. Cathal Fitzgerald.
Now there was a surprise. Affidavit had been such a fixture
for so long, she had half-expected them to go on forever.

Cathal never came into the Club any more, and she assumed it was because the group was over. She saw it time in and time out. A star one year, unheard of the next, no matter how big they were. And the bigger the ego, the bigger the fall. Although Cathal never had a big ego. Part of her felt sorry for him, despite their recent run-in. He was an interesting guy, and it was a pity he would no longer be around. They had started off in the social scene around the same time. She had heard he'd moved in with Lana Curtis, who by the sounds of it was becoming businesswoman of the year. Well, if she applied herself to work with the same rigour as she did to partying, drinking and drugs, she was bound to be a success. She picked up a paper and saw yet another photo of Cathal and Lana at a première. Kathryn wondered what Cathal did all day.

*   *   *

Cathal grabbed a shopping basket as he entered the Tesco on Baggot Street.

The days went slowly since Affidavit broke up.

He walked around the aisles, choosing carefully what they would have for dinner that night. His routine was pretty much the same every morning. He would get up late, purposefully missing the housekeeper. Then he would watch a bit of music television for a while. Then he would often meet Lana for lunch. Or he would meet up with a friend from his Affidavit days, a PR or a producer, for something to eat or a lunchtime drink. But as time went by, he realised he didn't have much to say to them, and all he did was listen to their stories from the industry which made him miss the Affidavit days. Then he would just wander around town, going into shops. In the evenings,

Lana and he would go out to one of Barry's do's or to one of the openings or launches they were always being invited to. Often they would meet up with Lana's friends, Patricia and the rest of them, in the evenings, and either go out for dinner with them or around to each other's houses. They weren't really his cup of tea. He didn't understand their sense of humour at all.

He would have a game of golf with Barry once a week. And talk to his family on the phone every day. Life was good, he reminded himself. He never heard anything from James or the others from Affidavit. Occasionally he thought about Stephen Rourke and wondered how he was getting on at Exclusive before quickly banishing the thought.

*   *   *

Cathal poured more wine in everyone's glass. Lana had invited Patricia and the gang over for dinner and there was great merriment around the table as everyone laughed and talked. He listened into their conversation as they talked about their weekends in Marbella and London and really could find no common ground with them.

Lana reached over and grabbed his hand. "Are you all right?"

"Yeah, sure," he answered, smiling.

*   *   *

Cathal got out of bed, went downstairs and sat in the semi-darkness in the lounge. He began remembering all the times over the years with Affidavit. And he had no illusions about being a great musical talent. But he *did* have other talents. How he used to deal with the record companies, make sure everyone was doing what they should do. Dealing with the Press. Deciding what songs would work and what images would work for the band. What he had was management skills. And he became excited as he knew what he wanted to do. After all, he couldn't just do nothing for the rest of his life.

*　　*　　*

Sylvia braced herself as the receptionist announced Cathal was here to see her. She hoped he wasn't going to be all bitter and upset. That was usually the way it was. The stars would head off and only when they started panicking about their futures did they turn up on her doorstep full of accusations.

Cathal knocked lightly and came in. To her relief he looked well and seemed in good form.

"How's it going, Sylvia?" he asked brightly, taking a seat opposite her.

"Same shit, different day, Cathal. You know how it is!" She had to admit it was nice seeing him again. "You look well."

"Been taking it nice and easy over the past while."

"Good, you deserve to after all the hard work you put in on the road." Experience told her not to relax. He was still a dropped artist.

"How's James doing?" he asked.

Sylvia was surprised that James hadn't been in contact with him. "He's very busy recording. But the album is going to be unbelievable. A whole new direction for him. We're very excited about it."

You're talking to me in the professional terms you use for outsiders, thought Cathal.

"So, what can I do for you?" She sat back and crossed

her legs.

Cathal pretended to look surprised and smiled "We're good friends, Sylvia, or at least we were. Can't I drop by for a chat?"

Sylvia shrugged. "Of course, any time. How're things going with Lana?" She wasn't sure where this was going.

"Good. She's over at *Hi Life* now. So she's busy . . . you know . . ." Just come out and say it, Cathal shouted at himself. "Sylvia, I was just wondering about something, to be honest." He gave a little laugh. "Like financially I'm fine, but I'm a bit bored."

Here we go, thought Sylvia.

"My life seems to be filled with dinner parties and smiling for photographers at political events."

You are practically a Curtis now, thought Sylvia.

"And you know me, Sylvia. Dinner parties were never really my kind of thing. I like to be at the cut and thrust of things. I love the music industry and the whole buzz of it, and to be honest with you, I'm missing it. So with all the experience I have over the years, I was thinking of maybe going into the management side of things. I was wondering if there were any jobs going here with you?"

"Highly unlikely," Sylvia said without missing a beat.

Cathal felt his pride crushed.

"Cathal, today's music industry is cut-throat and very technical and legal. Do you know how many CVs I get in every day from people with MBAs? They're queuing up to get into this industry, all wanting to be the next Simon Cowell or Louis Walsh."

Or Sylvia Henderson, thought Cathal.

"Cathal, I'm not being funny, but you don't even have the Leaving Cert. You just don't have the qualifications that I would need from somebody working for me."

"You started as a receptionist and worked your way up!" Cathal shot back.

"That was a long time ago. Things have changed. Can I be honest with you, Cathal, as well? You pissed Jack Better and a lot of the record executives off over the years with your attitude."

"What attitude?" Cathal was getting annoyed. "I just didn't let them walk all over us. Good management skills, I would have said."

"I'm sorry, Cathal, there's nothing here for you."

* * *

"Come on. You lazy thing!" Simeon boomed, coming into the bedroom.

"Oh, Simeon!" complained Kathryn, as he swept back the curtains.

"Come on, it's a beautiful day, and we're going out for a walk through Stephen's Green and some shopping on Grafton Street!"

Kathryn was smiling as she pulled herself up and looked at Simeon's happy face.

"Life is beautiful and we need to get out there today and enjoy it!" Simeon said, putting his arms around her.

* * *

Cathal felt like digging a huge hole and jumping into it as he walked into town from Sylvia's office. She had so quickly dismissed him. It was strange for someone he had been so close to, just to disregard him like that. How clever James had been! Leaving it to Cathal to fight their battles, so that it was he who had the reputation for being difficult in the industry.

They were going over to Patricia's for another dinner party that night, and he felt claustrophobic at the thought of it.

He was walking through Stephen's Green when he was surprised to come face to face with Kathryn Foy. He was even more surprised to see her holding hands with a man.

"Hi, Cathal, we haven't seen you in Exclusive for a while," Kathryn said, feeling embarrassed and exposed at being seen holding Simeon's hand like that.

"No, been busy. You know how it is," said Cathal.

She thought he looked agitated and had lost weight. He looked lost and she felt sorry for him. Maybe she had been a bit too unforgiving about the time she caught him listening to her music. "Eh, this is Simeon, my partner."

Cathal smiled and nodded at Simeon. He wasn't sure what kind of man he saw Kathryn Foy with, but he had never imagined her with someone like Simeon.

"Listen, thanks for recommending Stephen for the job," said Kathryn. "He's working out really well."

"Oh, eh, that's good. I'd better run," Cathal nodded and took off, leaving Kathryn feeling perplexed.

*   *   *

Cathal sat in Lana's lounge, wondering how he could get out of that night's dinner party. He looked at the piano for a long time. He moved over to it and opened the lid. Putting his fingers on the keys, he started to play old Affidavit songs. Listening to the music he was playing made him feel nostalgic and sad. He started playing a few different types of songs. And then, while he was thinking of what had been going on in his life over the past while, he allowed himself to express how he was feeling through the keys.

526

CHAPTER 38

Kathryn laughed till her sides hurt. Simeon was doing impressions of different people, including her family, and she couldn't help but find them funny.

"Oh, Simeon, stop it! You're being cruel!" she pleaded.

Simeon went on to do an excellent impression of Kelly. 'Do you have three hours, please? I would like to bore you with my latest acquisitions of diamonds.' Simeon's voice quickly changed to an impression of Kelly's husband, Jim. 'Only if *you* will spare me *six* hours – I have a need to bore you about my thirty-eight carpet shops!'"

Kathryn felt guilty laughing at her family, but couldn't help herself. "That's enough!" She wiped away the tears from laughter. "You know that feature for *Hi Life* I was telling you about? I've kind of fixed a date for them to come and take our photos in a couple of weeks. Are you sure you're okay with that?"

"Of course I am. In fact I'm looking forward to it. Here, I'll open another bottle of wine!" He was full of energy and practically ran into the kitchen to get a bottle.

He came back out and went to fill Kathryn's glass.

"No more for me. I have to go into work soon," she said.

"Ah, don't bother going in tonight! You have a new assistant, don't you? You're owed weeks of holidays, aren't you? Start taking some of that time you're owed!"

Kathryn thought hard. It was true what he was saying and Stephen was more than capable of minding the club. And she was enjoying herself so much.

Simeon reached over and kissed her lips. Her mind was made up as she reached for her phone to call Stephen.

"Hi, Stephen, I'm not going in tonight. Can you manage on your own?"

Stephen was quick to assure her. "Don't even worry about it – I'll take care of everything."

"I'll have my phone beside me at all times. If there are any problems, I can be in Exclusive within ten minutes."

"There will be no problems. What good am I, if you can't start taking some of those holidays you're owed?"

"Thanks, Stephen."

* * *

It was after midnight, and Exclusive was packed as Stephen made his way though the crowd into the members' lounge.

"Deirdre, there's a table over there needs clearing, and a customer over there waiting to give their order," he instructed a hostess.

He surveyed the members' lounge, and recognised a few celebrities and well-known names. He had used every bit of charm he had to ingratiate himself with as many well-known people as possible. Already people greeted him by name when they came into the club or had started asking for him at the door.

He spotted a talented young actor, who had just got a

break in the States. Success had gone to his head and he was experimenting big time. Stephen could smell them a mile away, knew what to look for and knew the gestures and expressions to reel them in.

"Hi there, Roger. You okay for everything?" Stephen asked.

"Just getting some more champagne in. Got a bit of entertainment to do!" He nodded over to the three girls he was with. They were in their early twenties and good-looking and were laughing continuously over everything, delighted to be in Roger's company even if it was just for the night.

"It looks like you've got your work cut out for you for the night," Stephen joked.

"I can handle them."

"It's going to be a long night of partying for you, then?"

"Sure is."

"I have a friend who partied last weekend for forty-eight hours without any sleep."

"He must have been shattered."

"He got a little help to see him through."

Roger's eyes glinted. "I could do with some help like that. Is your friend here tonight?"

"Yes, but it's better you go through me, if you want anything."

"What's on offer?"

"Anything you like."

Ten minutes later, Stephen was in Kathryn's office, measuring out cocaine and counting the cash Roger had given him.

*   *   *

Kathryn sat in her office, looking through the books. Profits were up, the staff roster was under control, and even stock-control was on schedule. She felt relieved Stephen had worked out so well. And it was great that she didn't have to worry constantly on her nights off any more. She had been stupid trying to run the place without an assistant for so long. As she thought about Stephen her thoughts drifted to Cathal, and seeing him looking unhappy in the park. Things were so good at home and at the club at the moment, she didn't want any negativity between her and a customer of such long standing as Cathal. Besides, she owed him one for recommending Stephen.

She grabbed her mobile and dialled his number.

*   *   *

Cathal stopped playing the piano and made some amendments on the music sheets beside him. He then tried the piece again. He was happier with it as it ran much more smoothly. He wasn't sure what he was doing. But he had been going to the piano or taking up his guitar every day and writing music. He had started writing nervously, utterly unconfident and unsure of himself. But then he reminded himself that the music was for nobody but himself, to express how he felt in the way he knew best. And as he nervously proceeded, suddenly loads of stuff was coming tumbling out. Suddenly he was putting music to his years with Affidavit, and then the break-up. Then he was writing about the feeling of rejection from James and Sylvia and the others. Then about Lana. Then he was going way back and writing about what it was like for him with Michelle, and then what happened with Stephen. He wasn't actually writing the words of what had happened to him. But he was writing the music of how it made him feel. And suddenly all the barriers were coming down.

His mobile rang beside him.

"Yeah?" he answered.

"Cathal, hi. Kathryn Foy here."

He was surprised to hear from her, and immediately thought it was something to do with Stephen. "Yeah, Kathryn?"

"Cathal, just bumping into you the other day, I realised we hadn't seen you in Exclusive for a while. I'm just checking everything is all right with you?"

"It's fine," he said abruptly.

"Cathal, I probably overreacted a little about you listening in to me singing."

"Are you missing me coming into the club?" His voice was cold. "Profits down because Cathal's Visa card isn't permanently behind the members' bar?"

"No, Cathal, I was just concerned –"

"Save it, Kathryn – the only reason you're phoning is because you're missing the huge amount of money I throw into the club all the time –"

"No, Cathal, that's not true, actually –"

He hung up on her. People. He had been right about them all along. They had been only interested in who he was. He could take it from all the Kathryn Foys and journalists. It was Sylvia and James he couldn't take it from.

He started playing his music again.

*   *   *

Cathal sat at the dining-room table, looking at Lana

and her friends. He sighed to himself. They were boring.
He looked at Lana as she described in detail all the events
they had gone to as part of her father's election campaign.
She was totally animated from it. She had really
blossomed and her confidence was huge now. Going to
work at *Hi Life* had been amazing for her, and she had
really come into her own.

The plates were left in their places untouched after
everyone had finished eating, as the wine and the laughter
kept flowing. Not one of these would have even thought
about taking the plates downstairs to the kitchen, let alone
stacking the dishwasher. They would leave it until the
housekeeper arrived in the morning. When he first started
attending dinner parties with Lana's friends, he had
started clearing away the dishes, but Lana had quickly
grabbed his arm and insisted he leave it. She looked
almost embarrassed by his actions.

Patricia was telling the story of a friend of hers who ran
an organic hotel in the west of Ireland. She was going into
minute detail about the food and drink on offer there. He
had heard her tell the story eight times before, as had
everyone else at the table, but nobody seemed to register
that. He allowed his mind to drift to the music he had
written that day. A new tune was running through his
mind and he couldn't wait to practise it the next day.

*   *   *

Cathal Fitzgerald was playing on Kathryn's mind. She
usually didn't care less what people thought about her.
But this was bugging her. He seemed to think that she had
phoned him because she missed the money he used to
throw into Exclusive. She couldn't blame him for thinking

that, as that was the reason she had phoned and grovelled when the photo of him and Joanne Bailey appeared. He had totally disarmed her when they met that time, and she had been amazed by his honesty and no-bullshit approach. She had assumed that he wasn't coming to the club due to the break-up of Affidavit, but maybe it was because she had been so cold to him after he heard her singing. Anyway, she wanted to resolve the issue. She dialled his number.

"Cathal, it's Kathryn Foy again."

"Look –"

"Just hear me out. I really would like to meet up for a coffee. We've known each other a long time and I feel there has been agitation between us since you heard me singing"

"I'd rather not"

"Look, if for no other reason than the fact I gave Stephen a job. I could have objected strongly to Barry and he would have noted what I had to say."

Cathal thought for a second. The last thing he needed was to upset the apple-cart with Stephen Rourke at the moment. He knew what Kathryn was like. If he didn't go into the club, she would keep at him to see why.

"Okay. Let's meet up," he said.

"Where?"

He looked down at the song he was working on. He didn't want to bother going into town that day. "I'm over at Lana's. Take down her address and come on over."

* * *

Kathryn got out of her car, took in the house and couldn't help but be impressed. A three-storey-over-basement in the heart of Dublin 4. She climbed the steps and rang the doorbell.

The door opened and there stood Cathal, dressed casually in jeans and sweater.

"Come on in!" he invited.

She stepped in and closed the door behind her, then followed him through to the lounge.

"Do you want anything to drink?" he asked.

"I'm fine." She threw off her cashmere coat and sat down. "As I told you on the phone, Cathal, I overreacted when I realised you were listening to my singing. You just caught me unawares. Believe me, I don't care if you never come into Exclusive again – I'm not here because I want you back as a customer. But I'm fearful that you aren't coming because of the way I've been behaving to you and that would be a stupid reason to stop coming to your favourite place. "

What would you say if you knew the real reason, he thought. He was suddenly curious "What were you doing singing in the club on your own at that late hour?"

"Does it matter?" she said coolly.

"You've a brilliant voice and a fantastic understanding of music."

She blushed.

"Why don't you do something about it?" he pursued.

"I can't."

"I don't understand."

"I can't emphasise how much I love music. I adore it. It's my biggest passion. I used to sing years ago."

"You're not making sense, Kathryn."

"I don't know you well enough to talk about this."

"We've known each other for years."

"On a superficial basis."

534

"I heard you sing your heart out that night. You have the ability to make it very big."

"Oh, Cathal!" She put her face into her hands before looking up at him. "But I don't want that!"

"Will you sing something for me again?" he asked.

She shook her head. "I'd better go. You're welcome at Exclusive any time." She stood up.

"Wait. I want your opinion on something!" He stood up. "Just come over here." He beckoned her over to the piano.

"What's all this?" she asked, looking at his music notes.

"It's songs I've been working on."

She was intrigued and picked one sheet up. "I didn't realise you were a songwriter?"

"I'm not. There's just been so much going through my head since the band split up, I've been trying to express it in some way."

"Have you shown these to anyone?"

"No."

Whenever she saw music, Kathryn's passion took over. "Will you play some of it for me?"

"You know, my voice isn't great," he smiled. "You sing it!"

"No!"

"I've already heard you sing for two hours, remember?"

She sat down nervously and started sifting through the music sheets. Cathal began to play and sing and eventually Kathryn took over at the piano while he joined her on the guitar.

"That line doesn't fit in at all," she said, stopping. "You're expressing all this pure emotion, and then the barriers come up here and the whole song falls down."

Cathal nodded, taking in her advice. He watched her as she slowly sang a song called "What Will I Do?".

Eventually, she sighed and said, "I'd better go. It's nearly six." She got up.

Cathal nodded, realising Lana would be home soon, and it might be hard to explain Kathryn's presence at her piano.

Kathryn closed over the piano. "Cathal –" she turned to him and smiled, "you have talent. You really do. These songs are good. In my opinion, there are parts that need improving or changing, but that's only a small thing. Why ever did you never try to write before?"

"I never thought I had any musical talent. I just thought I was a freeloader. James and Rob were so gifted that I didn't ever try to write anything."

Kathryn felt exhilarated having spent the afternoon singing. It was amazing to be the first to sing new songs, and to give her opinion. As she looked at Cathal's nervous face, she couldn't help smiling that this party-boy image had been hiding a real talent all these years.

She went and got her coat, then he walked her to the door.

"The best of luck with it, Cathal. With your contacts, it shouldn't be too hard to get the music heard by the right people once you are completely happy with it." She opened the door.

"And what about you, Kathryn? Going back to singing by yourself after hours in Exclusive?"

"I'll see you in the club." She walked down the steps and towards her car.

"Kathryn! Do you want to come by tomorrow for another session?"

Her face looked confused as she thought hard. Then

she smiled and nodded.

* * *

"I've been thinking," said Gloria. "The *Hi Life* exclusive was so successful, why don't we invite them in again to cover the election night?"

"What had you in mind?" Barry sat back and surveyed her as she paced his office at Kildara.

"An election-night party here at Kildara. Invitation only. What we need to give them is showbiz. Lots of balloons, famous acts singing during the night, lots of designer clothes on famous people. Nothing tacky but everything larger than life. Show the people that Irish politics is moving into a new era with your election. A stunning star-filled party here would mean all the media attention would be firmly fixed on you on election night. At the same time, it would act as a carrot rewarding your supporters and campaigners, making them feel they have truly "arrived" –"

"And, more importantly, would curry favour with those whose support I might need in the future," said Barry shrewdly.

"And who knows from there? The top job here and then on to Europe . . ."

They spoke with the easy confidence of people who seldom failed in life, but believed what they wanted was just waiting for them to reach out and grasp.

"I'm going to get Kathryn Foy on the case," said Barry. "She's a great organiser and will make sure everything runs smoothly on the night. And Lana can arrange it with the Conways."

Gloria came and sat on the desk beside him.

"It's going okay so far, isn't it?" He looked up at her as

he picked up the phone.

She smiled and nodded. Leaning towards him, she put an arm around him. "Barry, it's going *just* as I planned."

* * *

"It's good but it could be better." Kathryn delivered her verdict as Cathal finished playing the chorus of a song.

"Really?" He looked disappointed.

"Look, if I heard you play that two or three weeks ago I would have thought it amazing. But now I'm aware of what you're capable of, I say scrap it and start again."

"I don't know how to make it better," he frowned.

"Trust yourself. You're a good songwriter. Play it from the start again."

Cathal started strumming the guitar and she listened for a minute.

"Stop!" she cut in. "There! That bit there. It's not right. It doesn't fit in."

Cathal scribbled down the notes. "I'll work on it." She really impressed him. Her ear for music was amazing. She had been coming over to Lana's every second afternoon for a couple of weeks, just listening to what he had written and giving her opinion. He wasn't sure he would have kept on writing if it hadn't been for her encouragement.

"Time to go." She stood up.

"Listen, I really want to thank you again for giving me your time like this," he said. "I really feel alive again since I've started songwriting."

"That's no problem," she smiled.

"But I'm being really selfish. I'm taking up your time. You're working at nights and you need your rest during the day, or to spend time with your boyfriend. I can't let you continue doing this."

Her face clouded over. "Cathal, I wouldn't do it if I didn't enjoy it. It's only two or three hours every other day. It's no big deal." She almost felt panicky at the thought of not being able to come there and listen to his music, and sing. In a strange kind of way, it reminded her so much of when she had met Simeon first and had hung around studios and sessions, just delighted to be able to listen to his music.

"If you're sure?"

"I'm sure." She walked to the door.

He felt it was weird that despite all the time they were spending time together he still didn't know anything about her. "Your boyfriend doesn't mind either?" he ventured.

"No, he's fine." She opened the door.

"What's his name, incidentally?"

"Simeon. I'll see you tomorrow." She left quickly.

*   *   *

Lana was excited about the election night party to be held at Kildara. Ralph had been thrilled at another exclusive for *Hi Life*, especially when he was told about the stars that Barry would have there on the night. Lana had spent the day working on the project.

"This party exclusive is going to be massive!" she told Cathal as they sat on the couch that night. "I think it's going to be even bigger than the Affidavit Special. Since Dad's so well known in the UK and because of the calibre of the guest list, it's going into the UK edition as well!"

"That's cool!" Cathal tried to sound interested. But the idea of the party bored him. He studied Lana's face, so animated as she discussed the different publicity angles. She had changed so much, he thought.

"Dad's getting Kathryn Foy in to organise the night smoothly."

"Really?" Cathal's was thrown by this information.

"Listen, another idea I had was another exclusive with *Hi Life* just about the two of us. You know the kind of thing – life after Affidavit and stuff. I've heard that James and Donna are negotiating a deal with *Hello* at the moment, so we should get in first, don't you think?"

*   *   *

Cathal got up in the middle of the night and went downstairs into the basement. He had been going over the piece in the song that Kathryn had recommended he changed. He took up his guitar and, playing it softly, tried to perfect it. He had a Eureka moment and quickly jotted down the new chorus. He played it again and again, becoming increasingly excited about it. He looked at his watch. It was nearly two-thirty. He picked up his phone and dialled Kathryn's mobile.

"Hey, Kathryn, it's Cathal. Are you at Exclusive?"

"Yes, I'm just throwing the last of the customers out. Something wrong?"

"Nothing. Well, I know I sound mad, but the song I was having trouble with, I think I've clinched it. Would it be ridiculous for me to come over to the club and let you listen to it?"

"What, now?" She couldn't help laughing.

"I'm sorry. I'll play it to you tomorrow. Got a bit carried away. You're probably exhausted –"

"No. I was going to stay back tonight to play a bit

540

anyway. Call me when you're outside and I'll let you in."

Cathal hesitated. "Will Stephen and everyone be gone?"

"Give me thirty minutes and I'll have the place cleared."

*   *   *

"It's perfect now!" Kathryn face was lit up with excitement.

"Really?" Cathal was sitting at the piano in the members' lounge.

"You have a world-class song there," she nodded.

"I want to hear you sing it," he said, moving over on the long piano stool.

"All right." She sat down beside him.

He was amazed to see her get so excited about his music. For years the only expression he'd ever seen on her face was one of professional coolness. And now here she was with different expressions crossing her face every second. He knew her singing would suit the song perfectly. Because he had her voice in mind when he was working on the song. He watched intently as she sang. After she finished, they sat in silence for a while, both feeling moved.

"And that's the title of it: 'What Will I Do?'?" Kathryn asked, breaking the silence.

"Yeah."

"It's brilliant . . . "

"Will I see you later today?"

"Oh . . . I won't be around the rest of the week."

"Oh?" Cathal felt disappointed.

"I've got to do this feature for *Hi Life*, after winning the award for Social Personality of the Year." She pulled a face.

"You're not looking forward to it?"

"I'm dreading it. I've done everything I could to avoid doing the fucking thing, but they won't give up. So I have to try and make the apartment look amazing and me look amazing and Simeon look amazing. It's such a load of bullshit."

"I know. I've been forced to do photo shoots for them myself. How's Simeon about it?"

"He's looking forward to it, strangely enough. I thought he wouldn't like it."

"What does he do?"

"He's a musician," she smiled. "Simeon Loftus."

Cathal searched his mind and vaguely remembered the name from years ago as one of the many also-rans in the Irish music industry. "He doesn't play any more?" he asked.

"He's been on a break." Kathryn smiled as her eyes became distant. "Nobody could write music as well as him. Nobody could perform with the same depth as him. I used to go to all his gigs and just be taken over by his music."

"Is he writing at the moment?"

Kathryn looked down at her watch. "It's very late. We'd better go home." They stood up.

"Kathryn, I've been thinking a lot and I'm going to be bringing this song and some others I've written over to Sylvia Henderson soon to listen to them."

"The best of luck with them. She should have a variety of artists queuing up to sing them."

"I don't just want any artist . . . I want you."

"What?" Kathryn half-smiled and half-frowned.

"Kathryn, your voice is exceptional. You could have a

big future ahead of you as a singer. Singing my songs. I don't think anyone could sing them as well as you. You really understand them."

"No, Cathal. It's not on the agenda. I don't want to sing publicly."

"If you let this opportunity go, you'll never forgive yourself."

She felt herself get excited about the prospect. And then she was overcome with nerves. Then she thought of Simeon. How could she even contemplate doing it? It would have a terrible effect on him. He was the great musical talent, not her. It would destroy him if he even heard she was singing. God, it totally humiliated him when people recognised her as a nightclub manager, let alone as a singer or song writer.

"Cathal, the answer is no." Kathryn's voice was firm, "Good luck with whoever MPI selects to sing your songs, but it won't be me."

CHAPTER 39

Kathryn checked herself in the bedroom mirror. God, she wished the day were over. The idea of all those *Hi Life* people being in the apartment really freaked her. She had gone over to Kildara the previous day for a meeting with Barry. They had discussed the election party and her role on the night. She made it clear she wanted to be in charge. No mess-ups like what happened at the launch party. With the amount of event management and PR companies out there, she did take it as a compliment that Barry had asked her.

Then she had dropped into Exclusive to meet Stephen. As she was taking the next four nights off, she went through the roster with him to make sure they would be fully covered with staff.

"Any problems –"

"And I'll be on the phone to you in an instant," Stephen had finished.

She had opted for a cream trouser suit to start the photos off with. Ralph had said that firstly they would take a few casual photos around the apartment, and then they would break the day up between photos and interviews. Simeon came bounding into the bedroom, dressed in an Armani suit, a new Rolex glistening on his wrist. Don't think of the Visa bill today, she willed herself.

"You look gorgeous!" He enveloped her in a hug and kissed her.

"Are you feeling all right?" She had been terrified he would go into a depression that morning and they would have to call the whole thing off.

"I'm feeling on top of the world!" He smiled broadly at her.

She held him tight. "Thanks for doing this," she whispered.

* * *

"I'm really looking forward to the party at election night," said Lana to Tony as he drove them over to Kathryn's apartment for the photo shoot. "Ralph was saying he wants to do a lot of photos of me and Cathal on the night."

"Did you ever hear of overkill, Lana?"

"What do you mean?"

"You were plastered all over *Hi Life* with that Affidavit exclusive."

"I have become quite the little celebrity," she giggled.

She was annoying him today and he couldn't hold back. "You're typical of what being famous today is all about. Nothing in your own right, but famous for being someone's girlfriend/daughter. Just showing up at fancy do's wearing posh frocks."

"Jesus, Tony, you're bitter!"

As he pulled the car into Kathryn's apartment block, he was annoyed with himself for being so honest. It did make him look bitter. Maybe he was bitter. No, he had come a long way, he told himself. He'd gone from being the nobody Kathryn Foy threw out of Exclusive to interviewing her for an exclusive.

And they still don't respect you, he told himself.

*   *   *

Kathryn took a quick look around the apartment as the doorbell rang.

"Come on up," she said. She opened the front door and waited.

Two minutes later her home was being invaded by a troop, led by Ralph and Margaux, followed by Lana, Tony and Clive.

"Kathryn! At last!" declared Margaux, smiling broadly and approaching her with her arms opened. "I thought this day would never come!"

Kathryn cringed as Margaux enveloped her in a hug and kissed both cheeks. She had never liked all that luvvie kissy-kissy stuff.

"I know. I apologise again. Things were very busy at work." Kathryn pulled back. "Margaux, Ralph, this is my partner Simeon Loftus." She steeled herself for how Simeon was going to react. To her surprise he opened his arms to Margaux, smiling.

"So good to meet you," he said warmly as she kissed him on both cheeks.

So far so good, thought Kathryn.

*   *   *

"Okay," said Clive looking through his camera at

Kathryn and Simeon stretched out on the couch, "Let's try and look comfortable, everyone!"

Kathryn tried to smile, but she knew it looked fake.

"Come on, Kathryn. What are you trying to do to me here? Lighten up a little!" said Clive good-naturedly.

"I'm sorry. It's just hard to look comfortable when everyone is staring at you"

Margaux turned to Tony and Lana. "Do you two want to go into the kitchen for a while?"

"Sure," said Lana as she and Tony got up.

"I just love your apartment" enthused Margaux. "I think it's amazing what they did with these old warehouses – the ceilings are so high!"

"Thanks," said Kathryn, grateful to Margaux for trying to make her feel at ease.

"That's more like it!" said Clive happily as he began to snap. "Hey, Simeon, that's the pose of a natural there!"

"I've been doing this kind of thing for years, mate," said Simeon.

"Have you?" Clive was surprised.

"Of course, don't you remember the photos I did for *Hot Press* a while back?"

Clive continued to snap while he spoke. "No, when was that?"

1990, thought Kathryn.

* * *

"Well, she was the last person I ever thought would be nervous for a photo shoot," said Lana as she and Tony sat down at the island in Kathryn's kitchen and he poured them both a cup of coffee. "The way she stands at the door of Exclusive, you'd think a bomb could go off under her and she'd still look cool. I don't know why I'm here anyway. Ralph suggested I came along in case I'm inspired with any great marketing ideas."

"Well, he thinks you are just a fountain of ideas." Tony didn't bother to hide his sarcasm.

Lana saw red. "What is your fucking problem? You've been hostile to me since I started at *Hi Life* – in the subtlest way of course. I'm working my ass off in there every day."

Tony couldn't hold back "The only reason you're getting all those great marketing deals is because of who you are. If you weren't Barry Curtis's daughter, see how many doors would slam in your face."

"Okay, who I am is opening the doors, but if I didn't have the ability then I wouldn't be following it up with all the marketing strategies that follow."

"You'll just never know, Lana. This job is still just a hobby to you."

"It is not!"

"Hear me out. To me it's everything. I worked so hard for so many years for this break. Can't you see how resentful I'd be that you came in without even knowing how to switch on a computer? I've sacrificed so much to get what you were just born with. I want what you have, and Cathal has, and what the Conways have. I want to be somebody."

They sat in silence for a while. Tony felt a bit guilty as he looked at Lana glumly stirring her coffee. "Listen, Lana. I'm sorry about my comments. You didn't deserve them."

She was a little surprised by his apology. "It's okay. You seem as if you have a lot on your mind."

"I guess I do, with one thing and another."

She didn't know how far to push him. "Look, Tony, we're probably going to be working with each other for a long while. I would like us to be some sort of friends, even though I know we're very different. I can be a good listener, when I'm not talking about myself continuously." She laughed.

"It's nothing, really. I'm just trying to get over the fact that my relationship is over."

"I'm sorry. Were you seeing each other for long?"

"We've lived together for years. We were so close we didn't buy toothpaste without consulting each other."

"And now?"

"We pass each other in the house like strangers."

"I'm sorry . . . what exactly went wrong?"

"Like I was saying to you, I see this job as my one chance at success. I guess I put it before her."

"That's hard."

"The thing is, I love her more than anything. I really do. I'd gladly walk away from this job or any other one, if we could go back to the way we were. I don't know what happened between us – but it's over. And I just want her back."

Lana's face was filled with sympathy.

"I'm sorry for giving you digs all the time. I guess I am a little bitter at the moment."

*　　*　　*

Kathryn had changed into an evening gown and Simeon into a Gucci suit.

"Okay, where do you want us now?" asked Simeon, who looked to be enjoying every second.

"I want to take advantage of that massive window you have," said Clive. "Actually, Simeon, if you could step out of the way – the readers are going to want a good few shots of Kathryn on her own. After all, she is the star of our show. Kathryn, could I have you up by the window? Just rest your hand on the curtain as if you're drawing it."

Kathryn did as Clive asked.

Simeon stood unmoving in front of the window, staring at Clive.

"Sorry, mate," said Clive. "If you could just move left or right. I can't take a photo through you!" Clive laughed, but was unnerved by Simeon's stare. "Simeon?"

Simeon moved abruptly and went to sit beside Margaux and Ralph.

Kathryn felt on edge.

"That's it, love. You look fantastic there. How about that elusive smile again?" Clive coaxed. He had been on enough photo shoots to recognise a difficult one.

A little later they were in the kitchen, with Kathryn and Simeon pretending to cook on the range.

"Okay, what's going on here?" laughed Clive. To his consternation, Simeon was now scowling and refusing to smile, and Kathryn was now overcompensating and grinning falsely. "Simeon, come on. Lighten up a little. Remember that photo session you did for *Hot Press*! Relax!"

Simeon attempted to smile as they pretended to stir a stew.

"Okay, just give me a couple of minutes," said Clive.

He turned and went into the lounge to Margaux and Ralph.

"Okay, this just is not working at all. Kathryn is now pretending to look happy, and she's just looking stupid, whereas Simeon just glares angrily at me all the time."

"There does appear to be some agitation in the air," Margaux said, concerned.

"We'll break on the photos for a while. Everyone go and have a break and come back and start the interview," said Ralph.

* * *

Kathryn sat on the edge of the bath, and ran her fingers through her hair. Why had she agreed to this at all? Her home was sacred, not for these people to walk around as if they owned it. Simeon's mood was changing and she didn't know what to do. She got up and went into the bedroom where she found him lying out on the bed. She feared the worse.

"Are you all right, Simeon?"

He jumped up, smiling. "Not a worry in the world, babe. Come on, let's get this show rocking!"

Clive had needed some air and had headed off a while. Everyone else assembled in the living room to start the interview.

"Now, Tony will be conducting the interview, but myself and Margaux will be asking questions occasionally as they occur to us," explained Ralph. "Lana is just here observing."

"There's no reason to feel tense," smiled Margaux. "We're all friends here, and we just want to show you in the best possible light."

"I'm just going to tape this interview, if you don't mind, as well as take notes," said Tony.

Kathryn felt reassured by their words and relaxed as Simeon put his arm around her.

"Kathryn, was it a surprise for you when you won this award?" asked Tony.

"Yes, it was. I really didn't expect to win and was

delighted when I did."

"You're often seen as the protector of the stars at Exclusive – do you enjoy your job?"

"I love it. Of course, the hours are mad, and it would be nice to just relax at home with Simeon more, but I still get a buzz from it."

"No thoughts of retiring just yet then?"

"No," Kathryn laughed, "not for a long time."

"Simeon," Tony smiled at him, "you must be very proud of Kathryn."

"Proud? Not exactly."

"Eh . . . " Tony was totally thrown. "Er, I mean proud of her achievements."

"What achievements?"

"Well, the award for a start-off?" Tony glanced over at Ralph and Margaux who looked as perplexed as him.

"That tacky thing? We don't even know where it is any more!"

Kathryn bit on her lower lip.

"Eh, Kathryn," said Tony, "your face is very well known on the social pages over the years – how do you manage to fit a hectic social life into such a busy work schedule?"

"It's just about management, really. Often I pop into an opening or a launch in the evening before going on to work. That way I can have a bit of a social life as well."

"Who are your favourite designers?"

"Ah, for fuck's sake, when are you going to ask some decent questions?" snapped Simeon. "Nobody is interested in what she likes to wear, mate! And if they do, they want their heads testing!"

Ralph, Margaux and Lana stared at him, eyes wide.

They're leaving it all to me this time, thought Tony. He

tried to change tack on the interviewing. "Simeon, do you attend a lot of functions with Kathryn?"

"I couldn't be arsed to go to any of those things. I'm invited to a lot of things as a musician myself, but when you're in demand as much as me, you have to be choosy."

Tony remembered something about Simeon being a musician in the briefing Kathryn had supplied them. "Yes, what kind of music do you play?" he asked brightly.

"Are you for real?" Simeon glowered. "I think everyone knows what my music is like! Don't you remember my hit 'Roadway'?"

Please let this be over soon, thought Kathryn.

"Roadway" – what's he talking about? Just play along, thought Tony. "What year was that released again?"

"Eh, 1994." Simeon looked agitated.

"And what have you been working on recently?"

"I've . . . er . . . been . . ."

Kathryn jumped in with "Simeon is one of the most respected musicians of his generation –"

"I can *speak* for myself, you silly bitch!" Simeon almost shouted.

Everyone sat in shock.

Kathryn raised her hand to her mouth and rubbed her lips for a second. "Simeon, would you kindly relax and show a bit of respect," she demanded, as the tears threatened to overcome her. She looked at Tony and smiled. "Continue, please."

Tony glanced over at Ralph, who looked shocked but nodded at him.

"Kathryn, you've had such a long and successful career – what do you think are the qualities needed for that in your profession?"

"I would say integrity, good observation skills." Tears

started rolling down Kathryn's face but she continued to smile. "You have to be strong on the inside. It's all about respect. Giving the customers respect and being respected back. You see, people might think I'm being cold at times, but I'm not. It's just such a tough job to do. And if you don't come across as being capable, then people will walk all over you."

"Sorry, did you use the word 'profession'?" Simeon interrupted, looking at Tony, "Since when did standing at a door of a nightclub constitute a profession?"

Kathryn quickly wiped the tears off her cheeks.

"Listen, you must understand it's very hard for Kathryn to live in my shadow, so I suppose these little awards help her ego. I actually didn't want to do this interview today. But she begged me to, you know. And I thought, okay, maybe the public would like to see where I live and who I live with. Maybe I owe them that. They've been supporting me long enough."

Kathryn stood up abruptly and looked at Simeon. "Since I'm clearly unnecessary for this interview, I might as well go and have a lie-down." She walked quickly to the bedroom.

The others stared after her as she closed the bedroom door and then looked blankly at each other.

Margaux visibly pulled herself together. "Well, I suppose we have enough material to go on for now," she said with a huge fake smile. "Maybe we should just call it a day."

"Okay, so I suppose you'll take the rest of the photos tomorrow," Simeon said as the *Hi Life* crew started packing away their stuff.

"I think we might have enough photos," said Ralph.

"But you hardly took any!" objected Simeon.

"Well, maybe I'll get Kathryn to organise something," said Ralph.

"I'll tell you what – don't bother phoning her –" Simeon scribbled his mobile number on a piece of paper, "call me directly."

Ralph smiled and nodded at Kathryn who had come back out of her bedroom to say goodbye.

"Okay, Kathryn, we'll see you at some stage." Margaux was smiling but she actually looked horrified.

"Sure," Kathryn nodded.

She closed the door after them and leant against it, closing her eyes.

"Relax, babe!" said Simeon. "It wasn't so bad! Not as bad as I thought it would be, anyway. They're all so phoney though!" He bent over and kissed her cheek. "Maybe we should go out for something to eat tonight?"

Kathryn bit her lower lip and shook her head. "Eat? I wouldn't be able to keep the food down after that."

"What?" he looked perplexed.

"Your behaviour to me was completely unacceptable, Simeon. How could you talk to me in front of those strangers like that?"

"I was only pointing out the truth. They were stupid questions he was asking." He went to hold her.

"Get away from me!" she snapped and ran into the bedroom, locking the door after her.

* * *

Cathal tidied his music sheets away as he heard Lana come in the front door.

"Where are you?" she called.

"Just in here."

556

She came in and kissed him.

"You look a little flushed," he observed.

"You would too if you had the day I had!"

"What happened?"

"I was at Kathryn's Foy's photo shoot."

Cathal became interested. "Yeah?"

She sat down beside him. "I've never seen anything like it. Her partner, this guy called Simeon, is a total loon!"

"In what way?"

"He seems to have it in his head he's some kind of star, but none of us had ever heard of him. He kept talking like we were there to interview him and Kathryn was just an afterthought. But it was the way he treated Kathryn which was most shocking."

"How?"

"He treated her like a piece of shit. He shouted at her, called her a bitch in front of us all. He seemed really aggressive."

"And Kathryn Foy took it?" Cathal was shocked.

"It was obvious she was really upset, nearly in tears. Let's face it, the Kathryn we thought we knew is the one we see at Exclusive. I mean she's a real tough ice-queen there, isn't she?"

"Yeah, I suppose."

"Nobody says boo to her without being fucked over and fucked out. And yet this man treated her like she was nothing. We hardly did any photos but we really had to abandon the whole thing halfway and get out of there. She was supposed to be on the front cover, but that's cancelled now. We're just going to use a couple of the photos of her taken today and a couple of quotes and leave it at that."

*   *   *

Stephen was thrilled Kathryn was off for a few nights. He could move some serious quantity of drugs through to the customers while she wasn't here. Not that her being there hindered him too much. He just had to be extra vigilant.

The great Kathryn Foy that everyone quaked over hadn't been too hard to fool at all. He had been wasting his time down the country before prison. It was in the capital that serious money could be made. All these stars and rich kids were just looking for a discreet source. And they didn't come more discreet than him. His contacts had been very impressed when he had acquired his position at Exclusive as they knew the market he would be gaining access to through it.

He was never going back now.

CHAPTER 40

They were at a dinner party of one of Lana's friend's in Dalkey. Cathal felt like an outsider. He got up after the dinner and wandered into the huge garden, to get some air. He sat down on a garden seat and stared into the night sky. The French windows were open and he heard laughter as two men came out onto the patio and lit up cigarettes. He was out of view in the darkened garden, and could observe them without being seen. One of the men was Patricia's fiancé Henry, the other a guy called Keith.

"Are we going on to a club later?" asked Henry.

"I'm up for it!" said Keith.

"You're up for anything!" joked Henry. "Hey, what do you make of our new friend?"

"Cathal? What's the expression? He's as country as dirt!" Both men burst out laughing.

"No – I've got a better one!" Henry said between laughs. "Cathal and Lana –" He started to sing *"He's a little bit country and she's a little bit rock and roll!"*

"She's gas, isn't she? Where does she find them?"

"You know what it's all about, don't you?" Henry adopted a child's voice. "Daddy! Daddy! Please pay me some attention! Look, now I've got a rock-star boyfriend and he can help you win your election!"

"I feel a bit sorry for him. He'll be eaten up by the Curtis machine. Buried into a life of functions and charity coffee mornings!"

"At least he'll never be short of a few bob." Henry stamped out his cigarette "Come on. We'd better head back in."

*   *   *

The next day Cathal walked around town for hours. It was a sunny day and he just wanted to walk in no particular direction. He thought back through his life. And the main thing that struck him was that he had never been independent. Yes, he was a strong character and well able to stand up for himself. But he always had operated within a group that was bigger than him. When he was a teenager, he'd fallen in with a bad crowd because he wanted to belong. He'd been just a cog in the machine of that gang and gone along with things that he didn't agree with because he wanted to belong. Then when he had left that gang and started working for Rourke, he had thrown himself into Rourke's gang even though he knew deep down that Rourke was wrong. On both of these counts he'd had lucky escapes. Then he'd joined Affidavit and for years he was a member of that strong unit surrounded by MPI and Sylvia. And now that Affidavit was over, he was drifting into the Curtis empire where he would again be surrounded and protected. In all these instances he had never had a central role. He was almost just a passenger, going along for the ride. Yes, he worked hard and gave his best, but he was never the one on whom everything depended. He had always been useful when he was around but easily dispensed with when push came to shove. When Affidavit had broken up that had been glaringly obvious. The question now was, did he want to spend the rest of his life doing what was now on offer with Lana and her world? Writing music recently was the only thing he had ever really done for himself and by himself. If he never sold a single record from it, he wouldn't care less because he was finally doing something for himself.

His thoughts drifted to Lana. He cared deeply for her. When he had met her, she had reminded him so much of himself years ago, wild and lost. And they had enjoyed each other. He had closed himself off from wanting any long-term relationship ever since Michelle. And now, thanks to Lana, he had opened up and realised he wanted more from life. A relationship with somebody who had been so open and exposed about herself as Lana had meant there was no need for him to throw up any barriers himself. They had grown together. And she had developed into an amazing person.

But he didn't love her. He hated the lifestyle he was having with her and that had made him look deep inside and examine his feelings for her. He cared deeply, but he didn't love her.

*　　*　　*

"I was just amazed that this highly independent in-control woman had chosen such a fuck-up as a partner," explained Lana to Nicole. "I mean, this man was so rude to her. And he didn't care who was listening."

"Who did the interview?" asked Nicole.

"Tony did it all. To be honest, nobody else wanted to get involved under the circumstances."

"Did he make a good job of it?" Be careful, she warned herself.

"He made an excellent job of it considering what he was dealing with. Actually we were left alone in the kitchen for a long while and we called a bit of a truce."

"You and Tony?" Nicole was intrigued.

"Hmmm. Well, first of all I confronted him about all the little snide gestures and comments he makes. And he admitted that he does resent me because of who I am. But you know, I never realised how much he cared about the job. It means so much to him. He's just really ambitious and wants success. And then he opened up a good bit to me and he admitted he's been having relationship problems."

Nicole felt herself go completely tense.

"The poor guy, I feel sorry for him."

"What exactly appears to be the problem?" Nicole gave a little cough.

"He and his girlfriend are breaking up."

"Are they?" She felt deflated.

"And he's really unhappy about the situation."

"He is?" Control yourself, she screamed silently.

"I don't know what went wrong between them, but he's just really upset about losing her. He says he loves her more than anything."

Nicole felt her eyes mist over. "Is there nothing he can do?"

"He thinks it's gone too far to come back now."

*　　　*　　　*

"Darling, we had better hurry, because we have to be over at The Radisson at eight!" said Lana as she rushed through her front door and made her way to the stairs.

"Lana, I want to talk to you," said Cathal.

Lana turned and walked into the lounge. He was sitting down, looking serious.

"What is it?" she asked.

He patted the seat beside him. She sat down and he took her hand. He smiled softly at her. "I'm going home."

"Home? But this is your home now."

He shook his head gently. "Back to my own home."

She knew from his eyes what he was telling her. "You've found someone else?" Her voice was as gentle as his.

Cathal shook his head. "No. I'm doing this because it's right for me." He felt surprised that when she asked this he immediately thought of Kathryn.

"There's nothing I can say to change your mind?"

He shook his head.

"It's the lifestyle we've been leading, isn't it? You didn't want all this celebrity couple thing. Funny thing is, I started to do it just to impress you, to compete with Joanne and Donna."

"If you knew me at all, you'd have known that would never impress me."

She hit him gently on his arm. "But why did I have to fall for you? I don't know what I'll do without you."

"You!" He laughed. "You're totally together and well on your way to being more successful that your father. It's me who needs to go away and decide a few things. I need to spend time doing stuff just for me, not what other people expect of me. I hope you understand."

"I'll always be grateful to you for helping me through to where I am now," she said.

"And you helped me so much too," said Cathal. "You

made me realise that it's not a crime to care."

* * *

Cathal drove up to an exclusive cul-de-sac in Foxrock. He had only been to Sylvia's house once before, to collect something. She liked to keep her private life private.

He braced himself as he went to her front door and rang the bell. It took a minute before the door opened.

"Can I help you?" asked a man in his fifties with a foreign accent. From the look of him Cathal judged him to be Italian. He was wearing a silk dressing-gown.

"I'm sorry, I think I have the wrong address." Cathal was about to turn and leave, when Sylvia came through from the kitchen, also in a silk dressing-gown and holding two cocktail glasses.

"Who is it, Georgio?" she asked. "Cathal! What the fuck are you doing here?"

Cathal stepped inside, somewhat embarrassed but not prepared to back down now.

"I'm sorry, Georgio. Bring these upstairs and I'll be up in a couple of minutes," said Sylvia.

Cathal looked around the house. The whole downstairs was an open-plan lounge, leading into a kitchen and dining room.

Sylvia turned and looked at Cathal. "You didn't answer my question – what the fuck are you doing here?" Her face was angry.

"Who's Georgio?" Cathal couldn't help smiling.

"He's a friend of mine, not that it's any of your business."

"I thought you told me you gave up all that kind of thing when you got divorced."

"I gave up marriage, not my love life."

"Is it serious?" Cathal was grinning from ear to ear.

"No, as a matter of fact it's *not*," she whispered as she became angrier. "Now, what the fuck are you doing here?"

"I just wanted to talk to you about something."

"Then phone my secretary and I'll see you during the day. You know I don't like to mix business into my personal life."

"Well, actually, no, I didn't know that," said Cathal truthfully. "I thought me and the others were part of your personal life, but I was wrong. We were, as your critics are always saying, just fodder for your music industry to chew up and spit out. Now I see you have a completely separate personal life."

Sylvia sighed loudly. "I never thought you'd be like this. I thought you'd have more understanding of how everything works."

"I didn't, but I do now." He took a CD out of his pocket. "I want you to listen to this and give me your honest opinion. I know we're on your own time, but I think you owe me. How many calls and meetings did I allow in my personal time over the years? Was I not always ready, willing and able when you were issuing your schedules?"

"You were paid well."

Cathal gave a low whistle. "I never really knew you, did I? When all the papers criticised you for being a money-hungry capitalist, I was always the first to defend you. You were here for the love of it."

Sylvia tied the belt tighter around her long dressing-gown and sat down. "Cathal," she sighed again, "it is a ruthless business. You really are only a number, at the end of the day. But you know what, I'm only a number, and so is Jack Better, and everyone else. It broke my heart to see you the day Affidavit finished. I just wanted to come over and give you a big hug. Of course, I built up a relationship with you over the years. And I did consider you a very close friend."

Cathal was perplexed. "So, why did you just dismiss me the way you did?"

"For your own sake. I'd have hated you hanging around the studios, doing nothing except looking on. Or trying to bask in other people's limelight all the time. If you went down that road, you would have become an industry joke. People would have said: 'Here's the guy who used to be in Affidavit – quick, hide, or else he'll try and come to lunch with us!' You're worth more than that. Similarly, when I've had my day with the music industry, I want to make a clean break of it. I don't want to be hanging around and people feeling sorry for me."

Cathal sat down and ran his fingers through his hair. "You should have explained that before, Sylvia. I would have understood."

"Now, Cathal, go home to Lana and make a life for yourself, okay?"

"I will if you do me one favour."

"What?"

"Listen to this CD, and give me your honest opinion."

*   *   *

"Kathryn, hi, it's Cathal here." He gripped his mobile tightly.

"Oh, hi, Cathal."

"Sorry for disturbing you, I know you said you wouldn't be around for a few days, but I was wondering if you were free for just an hour today?"

"Cathal, this really isn't a good time –"

"I wouldn't ring if it wasn't important."

"Maybe next week –"

"Please, Kathryn!"

"All right, but I can't stay long. I'm dropping into Exclusive for an hour at three. But literally only for an hour."

"Nobody will be there?" Cathal checked, thinking about Stephen.

"No. I'll see you there."

*   *   *

Kathryn turned off her mobile. It was probably a good thing that she was meeting Cathal. She could tell him she wouldn't be around to meet him for music sessions any more. She picked up the main landline phone and dialled Barry's number.

"Barry, it's Kathryn here. Do you mind if I cancel that meeting tomorrow with you?"

"That's fine. Is everything all right?"

"Yeah, fine. Actually, Barry, I was going to cut back on my nights a little at Exclusive for the next month or so – to catch up on my holidays and try and clear the backlog. Also I can work from home organising things for your ⁻ion party during the day."

*   *   *

"I just wanted you to be the first to know."

Cathal and Kathryn were seated at a table in the members' lounge having a Coke each.

"I took some of the songs over to Sylvia Henderson for her to listen to . . . and she gave them the thumbs up!"

Kathryn's face lit up. "I didn't doubt she would for a second! Congratulations, Cathal!"

"She wouldn't believe that I wrote the songs. She thinks I've hired a ghost-writer or something!"

"You deserve it, Cathal! You're gifted!"

"I still can't take it in. That's not all – she wants to meet you!"

"Me? Why?"

"You're probably going to be pissed off with me. But I recorded some of our sessions and played them to her."

Kathryn's eyes blazed and her cheeks burned suddenly red. "Cathal, you had no right!"

"I know. It's just I knew I would only have Sylvia's attention for five minutes, and my own voice just isn't good enough to do the songs justice." He quickly reached into his pocket, took out the CD and handed it over to her. "There – that's the only recording – I'll give it back to you."

She took the CD and hit it over the table, breaking it in half. "I'm extremely annoyed with you."

"But, Kathryn, I wanted Sylvia to hear your voice as well. And she was impressed as I was."

"Did you tell her it was me?"

"Yes, she says she knows you on a social level and –"

"Everyone knows me on a social level!" Kathryn snapped. "You can ring her and tell her I'm not interested in meeting her. To be honest, I was going to tell you today anyway, I won't be meeting up with you in future for these silly music sessions!"

"Why?" He was aghast.

"I'm too busy to be bothered with them. Anyway, you're sorted now. MPI will take your songs and give them to good acts."

"I don't want other people singing them – I want you."

"Get over it, Cathal, because it's not going to happen!" She stood up to leave.

"Lana told me about what happened at the *Hi Life* photo shoot the other day. She told me about Simeon."

"I'm sure she's told half of Dublin by now!" Kathryn replied angrily.

"She's not like that."

"Well, if she's not, the rest of them are."

"He's the reason why you won't go in this direction, isn't he? I looked him up on the internet last night. Simeon Loftus. There were a couple of articles about him from ten years ago. The articles sang his praises, said he was full of promise and was going to take the world by storm."

"I'm so tired," said Kathryn, rubbing her forehead and sitting down.

"What happened to him?" Cathal leaned forward.

"You tell me. I haven't a clue." She looked in his eyes. "Nobody was like him when he was young, Cathal. He was so impressive. The way he carried himself, the way he spoke, but mostly his music. God, when I think of that music, I just feel elated. And everyone was waiting for him to make the big break, and the record companies were queuing up to sign him up – and then nothing. He stopped going into the studio – stopped composing – stopped singing. And it hasn't come back to him, and we both know it never will."

Cathal reached over, took her hand and clasped it. "I heard how he was putting you down all the time. You can't live your life ignoring your talent, ignoring opportunities because of Simeon's reaction."

Kathryn pulled back her hand. "I have to go – I'm

really glad about your songs, Cathal. See you in Exclusive sometime."

*   *   *

Lana's last therapy session had really affected Nicole. She sat on the sofa at home thinking about it. Lana had really managed to get to the essence of what Tony was about. Tony was desperately trying to make something of his life. All this time and Nicole had been thinking Tony was shallow, and easily influenced and fickle. It began to dawn on her how important the job was to Tony. She had been so used to him drifting in and out of jobs over the years that perhaps she hadn't taken him seriously at *Hi Life*. Had she handled everything wrongly in not supporting him more?

But Lana had told her Tony said he loved her. Wasn't that the most important thing?

Tony came through the front door of the cottage.

"Hi!" he said quickly, before making his way to the stairs.

"Are you –" she cleared her voice, "are you going out tonight?"

He was a little taken aback by her speaking to him. "I might be meeting Clive later." He continued up the stairs, then stopped. "You okay?"

She shrugged. "Do you want to talk for a little while – or are you too busy?"

"No. I haven't that much to do." He came back down, put down his briefcase on the floor and sat on the other end of the couch. They looked at each other for a while.

"What's happened between us?" Nicole asked eventually.

"I really wish I knew," he smiled sadly.

"We're sharing a house and treating each other like strangers. We used to do everything together. I've missed you, Tony."

"I've missed you too. More than I can say."

"It's my fault. I was totally unsupportive of you when you got the job."

"No, Nic, it was me. I pushed you out."

"I was just so used to being the priority in your life – I couldn't bear for you to care about anything else so much."

"You were always my number one priority. I just had been given this chance, and I wanted to make the most of it."

"I realise that now. I was jealous – jealous of a magazine! And I feared that when you were out every night, you were with someone else."

"How could I even look at anybody else when I had you?"

"You still have me . . . if you want me."

He reached over for her. "Of course, I do."

* * *

The music was blaring in Exclusive, The Killers screaming "Somebody Told Me". Lana allowed herself to be consumed by the music as she danced madly on the dance floor. She had been dancing non-stop for two hours. Opening her eyes, she made her way from the dance floor and into the members' lounge.

She went up to the table where Patricia and the rest of her friends were, grabbed a glass of whiskey and knocked it back in one.

"Steady there, you've work in the morning, remember?" laughed Patricia.

"Bring another round of whiskeys," Lana told a passing hostess and sat down "I'd forgotten what it was like to really enjoy myself." She grabbed a glass of vodka.

"Any word from Cathal?" Patricia asked.

"Oh, yes, he rang me today. He's been so nice to me, so I don't even have the luxury of hating him."

* * *

Kathryn brought some pills to Simeon who was lying in the bed.

"I'll leave these here for you," she said, and put them down on the locker.

She left the bedroom, closing the door behind her. She lay down on the couch, pulling her knees up into a foetal position.

He had been like that ever since she attacked him after the *Hi Life* photo shoot. He had quickly gone into a decline and taken to the bed. She still burned with humiliation but she had forgiven him. The others didn't understand it wasn't his fault. He was unwell; he was mentally unwell. And she had been carrying the burden of it for years. Trying to keep everything on an even keel, hoping against hope that one day everything would be fine. When deep inside she knew it never would be. Surviving on memories of what Simeon had been like, with a quick re-emergence of his old self every so often to keep her going. But now she just felt exhausted from it, from him, and wondered how long she could go on. She had been putting a barrier up to the world for so long, and meeting up with Cathal for those music sessions had made her deal with somebody beyond just work, or organising events. She had allowed herself to talk about life and emotions through the words of the songs. She had even allowed herself to sing in front of somebody.

*   *   *

Nicole sat in her office, smiling to herself, as she thought about Tony. It was like it had always been between them. And in a way, she owed it all to Lana.

She looked at her watch. Lana obviously wasn't coming that day. Typical Lana, not to have the good manners to ring up and cancel.

*   *   *

Lana's head thumped as she sat at her desk. She picked up her phone and rang the packagers.

"I haven't got delivery for those display stands. They were supposed to be in yesterday . . . I don't care about your machine problems!" Lana had raised her voice almost to a shout. "When you give me a delivery date, I expect you to keep it! If they're not in by tomorrow, you can cancel the order!" She slammed down the phone.

"Somebody got out of bed the wrong side this morning," Tony said, as he sat back at his desk and looked over at her. She stinks of booze, he thought. "You had a late one last night, I gather?"

"Don't worry, Tony. No matter how late I was out, and no matter how much I drank, I was still at my desk before you this morning, and look at these!" She held up sheets of paper. "These are all retailers who I have been speaking to today who want to increase their orders of *Hi Life*, some by up to fifty per cent. The marketing of this magazine has never been done as well as by me, and everyone knows it!" She spoke triumphantly, but also angrily.

"Okay, Lana, well done!" His voice was soothing. "Just don't push yourself too hard, okay?"

She got up from her desk and grabbed her handbag. "Just going to the ladies. See you in five."

She walked down the stairs and into the toilet. She checked there was nobody there, before opening her handbag, taking out a little bottle of vodka and drinking from it.

* * *

"She doesn't want to know," Cathal explained to Sylvia in her office.

"She what?" Sylvia nearly shouted. "I know Kathryn Foy always held herself as if she was a bit too good for everyone in this town, but who the fuck is she to turn her nose up at the chance of a record contract?"

"She says she only does it for her own entertainment. I think she's having some personal problems at the moment as well."

Sylvia threw her arms up into the air. "I want her voice for some of your tracks, Cathal. I will find other artists no problem. But I think you should try her again."

"Okay, I was looking for an excuse to see her again, anyway."

"Really?" Sylvia looked at him knowingly.

He stood up. "I'll give you a call later."

She smiled to herself. He was completely back to his old self. "Oh, and Cathal," she called, "not sure if you've any plans later, but do you want to grab a drink in that pub around the corner?"

He looked at her seriously. "You're asking me to do something in my personal time, Sylvia."

She held her glare. "I know I am."

"I'll see you there at six."

He left the office and was bounding down the corridor when he came face to face with James.

"I was going to give you a call later," James smiled happily.

"Were you?" said Cathal evenly.

"Yeah, listen, I heard about your songwriting. Sylvia was really impressed. I never knew you wrote songs!"

"I didn't know myself."

"Things have been a bit hectic with recording my album at the moment. But why don't you come on by the studio later for a listen? I'd love to hear your opinion. And then maybe later come by to me and Donna. She'd love to see you."

Cathal stared at James and then shook his head. "No, James." He turned and walked away.

*   *   *

"Are you sure you don't mind?" asked Tony. He was sitting at his desk talking to Nicole on the phone.

"Of course I don't, stupid!"

"It's just I promised Clive I'd go for a few drinks tonight."

"Look – you go out and enjoy yourself. I don't want you thinking you have to check in with me any time you want to go out."

"Nah, I'll tell Clive I can't make it. I'd prefer to be with you."

"Will you stop it?" Nicole was laughing out of

exasperation. "I'm popping home to my parents for a couple of hours, so you go out, enjoy yourself, and I'll see you later on. Okay?"

"Okay. I love you." He hung up the phone as Lana came into the office.

"Are you off out with Clive and the others from advertising?" she asked.

"Just going for a few drinks."

"Eh, Tony, don't you think it would be good manners to invite a work colleague along?" She raised an eyebrow.

"I, er, didn't think you'd be interested."

"Try me! There's drink involved, isn't there?"

*   *   *

"Hey Kathryn!" Cathal called across the street as he saw Kathryn climb the steps up to Exclusive.

Kathryn sighed as she saw him run across the street to her. "Cathal, I'm only popping into the club for five minutes to do the roster, then I have to head on. I've no time to listen to any music, or any more bullshit about Sylvia Henderson."

"If I promise not to mention anything about music or Sylvia Henderson, will you come into the Fitzwilliam for a quick drink with me?"

"I don't have time, Cathal." She had to get over to the doctor's to get a prescription for Simeon.

"Just one drink, Kathryn?"

"OK – you've got five minutes. You know, you're an awful bully!"

The bar in the Fitzwilliam was quiet and he ordered them two sparkling waters.

Curiosity got the better of her. "Have they come up

with any ideas for artists to sing your songs yet?"

"They've come up with about thirty-five so far."

"Anyone standing out yet?"

"There's a new American artist who's had a couple of hits, and they think "What Will I Do?" could be the right vehicle for her to skyrocket her career."

"Well, as long a she's not total crap, that song would skyrocket any career."

"You working in the club tonight?"

"No, I'm owed holidays, and I'm trying to organise this big party for Barry as well. I don't know if you've met this Gloria Reagan woman?"

"I have had the dubious privilege"

"She wanted Kildara filled with silver helium balloons with *'Barry'* written across them. Have you ever heard anything so tacky?"

Cathal laughed. "Did you tell her it was tacky?" He knew the answer.

"Of course, I did. Then we had a bit of an argument. I was in no mood for her, so I was a little rude."

"You, rude, Kathryn? Nah!" he laughed.

"Anyway, now we've compromised on white balloons, not too many of them, and we're having white roses throughout the house to match. I believe Lana backed me up on that idea or so Barry says! I haven't seen her but I passed her car as she drove into Kildara yesterday."

"Yeah? Er, we've actually broken up."

"What?" She was shocked and intrigued. "What happened?"

"Oh, we grew apart. She's completely taken up with this job of hers at *Hi Life* now. In any case, I care deeply about her but it wasn't enough. I think when you've only one life you have to make sure it's right, don't you?"

"I guess," she nodded and looked down at her drink.

They sat in silence for a minute.

"How's Simeon?" he asked.

"He's fine!" She smiled brightly, then seeing his sceptical look, frowned.

"Do you want to talk about it?" he pushed her.

"I don't talk about my private life – to anyone."

They fell silent again.

"Really looking forward to this American artist singing 'What Will I Do?'," said Cathal then. "Her voice is powerful."

Kathryn found herself become annoyed. "Make sure she goes high at the beginning of the chorus."

"Oh, I will do," agreed Cathal.

"And low at the end."

Cathal nodded.

* * *

"What the hell am I doing here?" Kathryn said, sitting outside the studio in Cathal's jeep.

"C'mon, don't think about it. Just come on in."

"Look, at me. I'm shaking. It's funny, I can face any number of thugs at the door at Exclusive every night and it doesn't bother me in the least. But I'm terrified of the thought of going in there and singing."

"There will only be me there, and the technician. Just pretend you're in the members' lounge at Exclusive."

"Look, if I want to leave at any second, I'm outta there."

"I wouldn't try to stop you. I couldn't if I tried anyway. But if you don't come in, that American will get her hands on the song tomorrow, and that will be the end of that!"

*   *   *

Lana was consumed with loneliness. How she had messed everything up! She had forgotten what had drawn Cathal and her to each other was the feeling of being outsiders, despite having everything on the surface. In allowing their lives to become tabloid fodder, she had alienated him and lost him.

It was amazing how she had slipped back into her old lifestyle. But she didn't care. She needed this time to chill out. She needed a period of feeling uncomplicated and free.

*   *   *

They had spent hours in the studio and afterwards went to the Ice Bar for a drink.

"I'm just tingling all over," said Kathryn, unable to stop smiling. "I never thought it would be like that. I mean I watched Simeon from afar for so long in the studio and I could only imagine . . . but the real sensation of singing in a real studio!"

"You're not going to cry, are you?"

"Ha!" she laughed. "Kathryn Foy doesn't cry!"

Not in front of anyone anyway, thought Cathal. "You've set the ball rolling now. Why don't you come and meet Sylvia and talk about her representing you?"

"I really appreciate all this, Cathal. But I just don't think it's me."

"You'll never know until you give it a chance."

"But how could I do it to Simeon? His music is his life, and now he can't play any more he doesn't have a life any more. If he heard I was launching a music career –"

"You only have one life, Kathryn."

*   *   *

It was literally like taking candy from a baby, Stephen thought. He had established a tight and neat circle at Exclusive to supply to. He was being extra careful. He knew exactly who to approach and who not to. Stay away from the sloppy ones who wouldn't know how to keep quiet. Stay away from people who weren't either very well known or very rich. Aim high. These people had much more to lose than from exposure, and would be totally discreet. And these people had friends who were equally famous and rich who also needed a discreet seller. Wasn't pyramid-selling the name for it? But the money they spent was unbelievable. Which was just as well. Because he wasn't small-time any more like he had been in Tuxedo all those years ago. He was now fronting for some very powerful players, new contacts he had made during prison. And they were as anxious to have access to this market as he was. All he had to do was just make sure the staff at Exclusive knew nothing about what was going on. And make sure the club worked like clockwork so that Kathryn Foy continued to give him a free hand.

It was the third night in a row that Lana had been in Exclusive. Stephen didn't have to be a genius to figure out there was trouble in paradise between her and Cathal. As he continued to observe her, he saw her talking to a man for a long while. Suddenly the man reached over and they started kissing. Stephen couldn't help but smile as it was confirmed Cathal was off the scene. Having said that, Stephen wasn't surprised. Cathal always fucked everything up.

*   *   *

Lana had made her way to the dance floor and her head was spinning from the alcohol. She was enjoying herself, but suddenly became aware of somebody looking at her. She looked to the edge of the dance floor and saw a guy staring. A strange feeling came over her, and she couldn't think straight from the drink. She felt claustrophobic and trapped and wanted to get out of there. She quickly left the dance floor, went downstairs and got her coat from the cloakroom.

She ran down the front steps and into a waiting taxi.

CHAPTER 41

Once Lana started going out after work with Tony and the others, she began to make a habit of it. She had nothing better to do.

"You seem a lot happier recently," Lana observed to Tony as they sat in Cocoon.

"Yeah, I am. I got back together with Nic, my partner."

"Ah, that explains it!"

"I was so miserable without her. It's great now, it's like nothing ever happened. We should meet up as a foursome with Cathal and you sometime, and go out for something to eat."

"That's not going to happen. Me and Cathal split up."

"Oh!" Tony was genuinely shocked. "What happened?"

"Me. What else? Trying to be something I wasn't, and losing the one person I've ever cared about in the meantime."

It made sense to Tony now how Lana had been partying so hard recently.

"Anway, I'm going to the bar – what do you want to drink? I'm on for a big night out tonight. We're going on to Exclusive."

"Hi, I'm sorry, I couldn't get out of it," Tony explained to Nicole down the phone in the corridor at Exclusive. "Lana is in a state because she broke up with her boyfriend and insisted we all come out to Exclusive."

Nicole digested the news. "When did they break up?"

"A couple of weeks ago. That's why she's been partying hard."

And missing her therapy sessions, thought Nicole.

"I'll try and get home asap."

"No, don't worry, Tony. Try and be supportive to Lana – she could probably do with a friend."

* * *

Stephen observed Lana. She was with a different crew from normal. She also seemed out of it.

Ben Cannon came up to him. Ben's family owned half a county. He was in his early thirties, a permanent fixture on the social circuit.

"Just checking if your mate Charlie is here tonight?" whispered Ben.

"He's always here for you, Ben."

"I've a big crowd in with me tonight."

"Charlie will look after them."

"Cool. I'll meet you in the usual place upstairs."

"Ben, is that Lana Curtis over there?"

"Yeah, that's her"

"I've seen her in the papers a bit."

"She's been in them a lot since she started going out with the fella from Affidavit all right." He laughed cynically. "She all very respectable now, since her profile was raised."

"Wasn't she always?"

"You kidding me? Anything went with Lana!"

"She liked Charlie?"

"Couldn't get enough of him."

*   *   *

"Hi, there – can I get you a drink?"

She only noticed him after he spoke. The alcohol was clouding her mind, but she vaguely remembered him from the other night. She remembered he had unnerved her.

"I'll have a double vodka straight, please," she said.

He ordered her drink. As he waited, he heard her phone ring and listened in.

"Hi, Teresa, I'm in Exclusive. Are you coming in? Okay, no problem. I'll see you all in Bang tomorrow for dinner as arranged." She walked back to her table, seemingly forgetting about Stephen altogether. Or just knowing he would follow.

Stephen put the drink in front of her and sat down. "You're some dancer," he complimented.

"You were watching me?"

"You're easy to watch."

"Save me from bad one-liners, please." She turned and started to talk to Tony who was seated beside her. There was something slightly unnerving about the strange guy but also interesting, Lana thought.

"I have to head home," said Tony. "C'mon and I'll share a cab with you."

Lana tossed off her drink, got up and left with Tony without even a glance at Stephen.

*   *   *

Kathryn walked down the corridor to Sylvia's office with Cathal.

"Everything's moving so fast!" She looked stressed.

"It does in this business." He reached the door and turned to her. "Don't worry. You'll be fine." He looked her over and decided she looked great, in a black dress. She had star quality written all over her.

Kathryn eyes lingered on Cathal's face. He seemed so sure this was right. And it was his enthusiasm that had got her here. Be honest with yourself, Kathryn. You love being in his company. You're at your happiest when you're with him, messing around with music.

He smiled at her, then knocked on the door and opened it.

"Hi, Cathal!" Sylvia stood up, smiling. "And nice to see you again, Kathryn!" She stretched out her hand.

Kathryn confidently strode across the room and shook Sylvia's hand, before positioning herself in one of the spare chairs.

Cathal was amazed by Kathryn. He had expected her to be full of nerves like she was outside. But she had clicked into the confident in-control persona everyone knew.

"I heard your recordings of Cathal's songs and was quite impressed. What were you doing wasting your time at Exclusive with a voice like that?"

Kathryn smiled. "I wasn't wasting my time. I was earning my living and enjoying every minute of it."

Sylvia studied Kathryn. She came across as very self-assured. Why wouldn't she be? She'd been running Exclusive long enough. She looked great and she would be very easy to market. She preferred her acts starting off to be younger and a little more naïve - in that way they did what they were told. But having said that, silly temper tantrums and egos came as part of the package with that. She guessed that Kathryn Foy was far too much in control to go down that road.

"From a marketing point of view, it would be very easy to launch you here in Ireland. You're a well-known face from Exclusive, and I think the press would be interested in you launching a music career. Abroad, you would appeal to a more mature sophisticated audience. An Irish Norah Jones, maybe?" Different marketing and PR ideas were racing through Sylvia's mind. "It's a lot of work, Kathryn."

"I think anyone who knows me knows I'm not afraid of that."

"If I negotiated a deal for you with MPI or another label, it would be a lot of travel. You'd have to give up your job at Exclusive – that goes without saying. Just ask Cathal and he'll tell you how tough it is."

Kathryn felt herself become excited as she felt Sylvia was going to offer to represent her. She had thought Sylvia was just going to suss her out that day. She remained cool on the exterior.

"Press intrusion is part and package of being a singer these days. Could you cope with that?"

Kathryn nodded. "I understand that."

"Anything in your life that may cause embarrassment, or hinder your career?"

Cathal glanced over at Kathryn quickly, thinking about Simeon.

This action was not lost on Sylvia, who scrutinised Kathryn's face intently for anything.

"No, nothing at all," Kathryn answered smoothly, no flicker of emotion.

Sylvia sat back. "I guess in that case I would like to represent you."

*   *   *

"I could drink sake until the cows come home!" said Lana.

"And you often do!" commented Patricia.

There were eight of them around the restaurant table having dinner. It was early in the night as Patricia and Henry were having a party back at their house later and it promised to be a long night.

"Did you enjoy yourself at Exclusive last night?" said a voice beside Lana.

She turned around to see Stephen. "You again!" she laughed.

"I'm just having dinner over there with a few friends." He nodded to a far corner. She vaguely looked over. She was seated at the end of the table, and he grabbed a chair and sat down beside her.

"You certainly know how to enjoy yourself!" he laughed.

"Well, that's what life is for, isn't it?"

"I couldn't agree more. Can I get you a drink?"

She pointed to all the half-drunk bottles on the table. "I think we have enough. I finally know my own limitations!" She refilled her glass.

It certainly looks that way, he thought sarcastically. "What do you do for a living?"

"I'm a beautician!" she giggled.

"All right, darling, we'll be there shortly!" Patricia

turned off her mobile and stood up. "That was Henry – the party is hotting up so we'd better head back."

Everyone stood up and started gathering their coats.

"Nice talking to you – bye!" said Lana to Stephen. She stood up to go.

It took them ages to pile out of the restaurant.

Stephen sat in his car watching them. The rich were so stupid. Laughing loudly and taking forever to flag down taxis and get in. As Lana and Patricia and a couple of others got into a taxi, he indicated out of his parking space and followed them.

Stephen pulled into the driveway of Patricia and Henry's house which was packed with cars. He took in the size of the ultra-modern house, as he took a bottle of wine from the back of the car and locked the car. He could see the party was in full flight through the windows. He had seen Lana and her friends simply push open the front door so he knew it wasn't locked. He walked up to the door, pushed it open and went in. Nobody even looked at him as he made his way through the revellers.

He spotted Lana out by the pool, talking to some guys. She seemed much drunker than when she was in the restaurant. He started talking to a group of girls positioned by the patio door, who were talking very loudly, as he kept one eye on Lana all the time. He charmed the girls and one of them had a hysterical laugh that caused people to look around. It was only a matter of time, he thought. He felt a tap on his shoulder and turned around to see Lana.

"Hi, there," he said, smiling. "Are you following me?"

"Hardly!" She looked affronted. "I didn't realise you knew Patricia and Henry."

"I don't really. I know their friend Tim. You know Tim?"

She thought for a second, but she didn't know half the people at the party anyway. "You could have given us a lift if we'd known."

He felt she was warming slightly to him. "You'll have to excuse me a second. I'm going to go round the front for a smoke," he said, moving away from her.

"You can smoke here – they won't mind," said Lana.

He looked at her knowingly. "No, I mean a *proper* smoke!" He winked at her.

She watched him go back inside and make his way to the front door. She found herself following him out. She spotted him on his own by some cars. Her high heels crunched on the gravel driveway as she walked over to him.

"Hi, there!" she said, smelling the whiff of marijuana as she approached.

"It's a nice night, isn't it?"

She sat down on the bonnet of a Mercedes. "It depends how you're looking at it. Are you going to be greedy with that?" She nodded to his marijuana.

He blew out the smoke slowly. "Of course not." He passed it to her, and she put it between her lips and inhaled, enjoying every second of it.

"I needed that," she said, closing her eyes.

"Life's been a bit pressurised for you at the moment?"

"Yeah." She took another drag. "Just coming out of a relationship."

"That can be tough. I guess I'm in similar circumstances. I just came out of a long-standing situation as well."

"Thanks for that." She handed back the joint and made her way inside to the party.

*   *   *

"Your hair is really silky," Henry said to Lana, as he stroked a strand of hair from her face in the kitchen.

"Thanks," she said lamely, enjoying the effects of the pot.

"You heard from Cathal at all?" asked Henry.

"No, he's probably just glad to be away from me!" she sighed.

"Don't put yourself down." He placed a hand on her shoulder comfortingly.

Lana was oblivious to the fact they were in Patricia's line of vision. So was Henry. Patricia was glaring angrily at them.

"You're as well off without him," Henry said, stroking her back. "Stick with your own. You know where you are with us."

By three in the morning people were leaving, and Patricia was in furious form after being ignored by Henry all night.

"I suppose I'd better go," said Lana.

"Oh? I'm surprised you don't want to stay!" Patricia spat.

"What do you mean?"

"The way you've been running around after Henry all night, throwing yourself at him!"

"What are you talking about?"

"You've always been the same, Lana! Craving men's attention! At least when you were seeing Cathal you managed to control yourself somehow."

"Patricia, you are out of order!"

"Save it, Lana!" Patricia stormed off.

Lana looked after her in shock.

Stephen sidled up beside her. "Sorry, I couldn't help but hear. Are you all right?"

"Patricia was just such a bitch to me! I can't believe what she said to me! And she knows what a hard time I'm going through!"

She marched out of the house with Stephen close behind.

"Where am I going to get a taxi from?" she said aloud.

"Where are you headed to?"

"Ballsbridge."

"I'm heading back into town, if you want a lift?"

She looked at him dubiously. "All right."

"She really is a cow!" stated Lana, as he drove her back to town. "As if I'd be interested in Henry! She's obviously delusional!"

"People can be funny," Stephen sighed.

"I'm just here on the right," she said.

He pulled the car over.

"Thanks for the lift," she said.

"I was just going to have another smoke, if you're interested?"

Lana thought for a second. She would love another smoke. "Come on in," she said.

"Nice place," commented Stephen as he sat down in the lounge and lit up. He passed the joint to Lana.

"Thanks," she said, accepting it.

"So what about you and this guy you were seeing?" probed Stephen.

"It wasn't his fault. It was mine. You actually couldn't meet a nicer man. He was the best." She felt herself become upset.

"I know." Stephen smiled sympathetically. "Life can be hard, sometimes." But not for spoilt little rich bitches like

592

you. "However, I have a friend who can help out with these situations."

"A friend?" she asked.

"His name is Charlie." He smiled as he took out a plastic bag of cocaine from his inside pocket.

* * *

Lana struggled up on the couch and looked around. It was morning.

"Hello . . . Stephen!" she called, remembering the previous night's event. She felt cold and shivered. She realised he had gone. She quickly got up and began to dust the traces of cocaine away from the coffee table before the housekeeper arrived in.

She rubbed her arms to try and warm up and went upstairs to have a hot shower before heading into work.

She couldn't remember Stephen leaving as the night had become a bit of a blur with all the quantity of coke she had done. She turned on the television in the bedroom. The breakfast time news was on.

The immaculately groomed presenter said: *"With just days to go before the general election, all parties are stepping up the pace in order to secure crucial votes, particularly in marginal constituencies. In Dublin North, Barry Curtis has slowly edged into the lead with a single per cent vote lead over his nearest rival. Last night, Mr Curtis was again on the campaign trail meeting shoppers at Blanchardstown Shopping Centre."*

Footage of Barry walking through the crowd with an entourage came on the screen, with him shaking hands.

Suddenly a smiling Gloria Reagan was being interviewed, with the caption *'Barry Curtis's Campaign Manager"* at the bottom of the screen.

"It's been a pretty exhausting campaign so far. How is Barry holding up?" asked the interviewer.

Gloria smiled earnestly. "Barry feels it's so important to be out here with the people, listening to what they have to say, and listening to what they expect of him if he is elected to Dáil Éireann."

"It must be very encouraging for you to hear the latest opinion polls which put Barry Curtis into the lead?"

"We're not going to be complacent. It's only a slight lead, and so we urge all of Barry's supporters to get out and vote for him on election day!"

The newscaster came back on screen. "That was Gloria Reagan speaking. In Galway, the election campaign —"

Lana turned the television off and sat down on the bed. That Gloria had really taken over. Lana was due to go out to Kildara that day for a meeting about the election-night party. She had been getting on so well with her father, she thought she might broach the subject of her worries about Gloria and how she felt he should draw back from her.

*   *   *

Cathal lay out on the couch in his apartment, chilling out. He felt very good. Better than he had for ages. He was filled with pride whenever he thought of the music he had written. He thought of James trying to be friendly again. But it was too late. Their friendship would never be the same again, after he had discarded him so quickly. And funnily enough, Cathal didn't want it to be the same either. He was sick of living in James' shadow all these years. They had all treated him as a glorified personal assistant over the years, slyly reminding him constantly that he was surplus to requirements. And now that he had been apart from James and Donna, he really didn't miss them with their constant interference and disapproval of his life, while they sat in their model lives. He felt free. Even if everyone rang him up and begged him to come back to Affidavit, he wouldn't go. He thought of Lana. He had really liked her, and they got on great, but again in her exclusive world he was made to feel inferior and a support act. He hoped they could remain friends, because he did care about her a lot. But for the first time in his life, he felt in control of his future, doing something he loved and which was from himself. His thoughts drifted to Kathryn. Sylvia had organised a photo shoot for her later, and he said he would go along with her. The professional photos would be an essential part of Sylvia pitching Kathryn to the record companies. Cathal thought Kathryn was a funny one. Tough one minute and vulnerable the next. They had a lot in common. In fact he couldn't stop thinking about her.

*　　*　　*

Waiting outside the photographer's studio in her car, Kathryn looked at her watch. She picked up her mobile and dialled Cathal's number.

"Where the hell are you, Fitzgerald?" she snapped.

"I'm just walking down the street now," he said.

Seeing him, she got out of her car, and locked it behind her.

"You took your time!" She pretended to look angry.

"Ah, did you miss me?" he teased.

"I'm just concerned about keeping the photographer waiting. Do I look all right?"

He looked her up and down critically. "Hmmm, you'll do, I suppose."

She belted him across the arm. "I'd like to see what your first photo shoot was like!"

His rolled his eyes to heaven. "Let's not even go there! C'mon, you look gorgeous." He put his arm around her and they walked towards the building.

They were totally comfortable with each other. But when they saw the receptionist give them a second look, Cathal quickly took away his arm, and Kathryn adopted an aloof look.

* * *

"So what do you think?" asked Cathal. He was showing Kathryn the piano he'd had delivered to his apartment.

"How much did that set you back?" She was impressed.

"I see it as an investment. " He sat down and started playing "Killing Me Softly". She sat down beside him. "So, Ms Foy, how do you feel now that you're going to be famous?"

"It's doesn't feel real yet."

"Have you told Simeon about it?"

She shook her head and looked down at the ground. He reached over and pushed a lock of her hair back off her face. She looked up into his eyes.

She turned quickly and walked through the apartment. "Your apartment is pristine, all too bright – I don't think it's me."

"No, you prefer dark nightclubs and shady people."

"There is nothing shady about my clientele. They are the crème de la crème. Anyway, I'd better go."

"You around tomorrow? I'm working on a new song,

and I'd like to get your opinion."

"Just you'd 'like'?" She raised an amused eyebrow.

"Sorry – I'd *love* to have your opinion."

*　　*　　*

Lana had just come from a meeting with a perfume company interested in sponsoring next year's Personality of the Year Contest. She turned on her mobile and checked her messages.

"Hi, Lana, this is Nicole. I'm just a little concerned about you, as you've missed our last two sessions, and you haven't returned my calls. I really would appreciate it if you called me back."

Lana raised her eyes to heaven. Where to start if she tried to explain to her therapist now what had been going on in her life.

"Hi, Lana, it's Cathal here. Just checking how you're getting on. Hope everything is fine with you. Give me a call for a chat."

Lana felt herself overcome with sadness on hearing his voice. He had left a few messages on her phone asking her to call him. She hadn't. She knew he was just being nice.

Her phone rang. "Hi, Lana Curtis speaking."

"Hi, it's just me!" sang Patricia's cheery voice.

Patricia chit-chatted about the party and what she had been up to, but made no reference to their falling out. Lana wondered if she should mention the row or the cruel comments Patricia had thrown at her, but decided against it. As Patricia ranted on, Lana's thoughts drifted to Stephen. She wished she hadn't let him into her house and taken his coke. But it had made her feel better.

CHAPTER 42

"I still can't believe it!" Kelly looked across at her sister in shock, as they ate lunch at Fire restaurant after Kathryn had told her the whole story.

"I can't either!"

Kelly scrutinised her sister. "You've signed up with Sylvia Henderson to launch a singing career?"

"Yeah. I don't know whether to laugh or cry."

"Mum and Dad will be thrilled!" Kelly reached over and kissed her sister. Then she frowned. "What does Simeon say?"

Kathryn sighed. "I haven't told him yet"

"It might be an idea to tell him soon. I mean, you don't want him going into a record shop and seeing posters of you everywhere, do you?" She suddenly realised her sister was close to tears. "What's wrong?"

"Everything!" Kathryn wiped away a tear, and suddenly she was blurting it all out about the *Hi Life* photo shoot. "I just can't cope with him any more, Kelly. He's so up and down, and when he's down it can last for months."

Kelly was in shock to see her sister, usually so closed up about everything and putting on a brave face, at last letting go.

"I mean, if he finds out about my music career it might just push him over the edge. Anything I've done, any small degree of success I've had, has a terrible effect on him. The one thing he had was his music – if he finds out about this –"

"Kathryn, you've wasted enough years on him! Just finish with him."

"It's easy for you to say that. I'm all he has. I'm not stupid, Kelly. I know it's wrong for me. And I can't divide my life up into compartments any more, keeping him separate from everything. But what can I do? And in spite of everything I still care a lot about him . . . but , to top it all off . . . I've fallen for someone else."

"Oh, for fuck's sake, Kathryn! You spend years juggling a finely balanced act, and then you throw all of the balls into the air at the same time! Who is it?"

"Cathal Fitzgerald." She was wiping away tears again.

"What?" Kelly nearly shouted, causing people to look.

"It's just we've been spending so much time together, and it just kind of happened. I'd forgotten what it felt like . . . I'm so used to being totally together, and now my life's a mess!"

*   *   *

Lana scanned the crowd looking for him, and felt herself fill with disappointment when she couldn't find him. Finally, tired of searching, she turned and walked through Exclusive back to join the others in the members' lounge. She suddenly felt a hand grip her arm.

"Hey!" She swung around to object.

"Were you looking for me?" Stephen asked.

She looked haughtily at him. "As if!"

Stephen came closer to her and whispered, "I have some cocaine if you want it."

She stared at him. She couldn't move for a minute as her mind thought back to a time in her life when she was off the rails. She had overcome all that with Cathal's help. But she was in danger of going back there.

"No thanks." She began to walk away. She expected Stephen to follow her, but he walked off in the other direction. Oh hell, she was only young once! And her time was running out fast. She turned and went after him. "Where is it?" she asked.

He patted his pocket.

Her eyes searched around the club. "Where can I do it?"

He beckoned and she followed. He led her up a stairs and down a quiet corridor to a unisex toilet. He checked no one was around and then nodded for her to go in. He followed her and locked the door behind them.

He poured some cocaine out on a glass shelf over the sink and chopped it up with his credit card. She waited, anticipating. She had never had stuff as good as his before. She inhaled and felt buzzing straight away. It was only this once, she told herself. Definitely the last time.

"Thanks, that was great! I'll leave first, in case the management sees us."

He laughed. "I *am* the management!"

"You?" She was filled with confusion. "But, Kathryn Foy?"

"I'm her assistant."

"But my father-"

"I know — owns this place." He looked at her meaningfully. "So I'm relying on your discretion here big time, okay?"

She nodded and put her hand on the door to open it. He gripped her wrist.

"My mobile number." He handed her a piece of paper. "Call me any time you feel like some more."

*   *   *

"Lana, it's Gloria Reagan here," said the austere accent on the other side of the phone.

Lana felt herself tense. "What can I do for you?"

Tony glanced curiously across at her at the tone of her voice.

"Just in relation to the election-night party. If yourself and Cathal could arrive in early, I'll show you where I want you to be for the photographs later on in the evening."

"That could be a problem, Gloria."

"And why?"

"Cathal and I have broken up."

"What?" Gloria sounded horrified. "So near the election! Could you not have waited until after? Your relationship has been one of the items that have boosted support for your father!"

Your concern is touching, Lana thought.

"Who knows about this?" demanded Gloria.

"Just ourselves."

"Well, I should think for the sake of your father, you should at least put on an act for the night, don't you?"

Lana hung up, feeling angry at Gloria's cold calculating way. And yet, she had a point. If the press got wind that she and Cathal were broken up it could detract from Barry's election campaign. She turned around to Tony.

"Has Gloria Reagan faxed an itinerary of photos

through for my dad's party?"

"Yeah, there's a copy of it here somewhere." He sifted through the paperwork on his desk, before passing her over a couple of pages.

She started reading through the photo schedule out loud: *"Barry, Gloria and guests by the pool. Barry, Gloria and guests by the stairs. Barry, Gloria with Lana and Cathal. Barry, Gloria –* what the hell is this?" She glanced down through the list. Gloria had put herself into nearly every photo by Barry's side with a variety of famous guests.

*   *   *

They sat side by side at the piano, practising a song.

"No, you're doing that all wrong!" Cathal chided. "Try it this way." He played some keys.

"Hmmm, maybe." She tried what he said and sang a few lines with it.

"See, I always know best!" he joked.

"I should just realise that and never question anything you say again, really, shouldn't I?" she said sarcastically. She turned her head and they stared at one another smiling, their faces close. She rested her hand on the side of the piano and it started to shake slightly.

He reached over and put his hand on hers. "Why is your hand shaking?"

She looked at him. "I don't know."

He moved forward and began to kiss her.

She hadn't been with anyone else but Simeon for years, and she was overcome with guilt, thinking of him at home in bed in a state of depression. "I can't!" She pulled away.

"I'm sorry – I thought – I thought you wanted what I wanted."

"I can't . . . Simeon . . ."

"Why don't you take something for yourself for a change?"

She looked at him for a long while, and then they were kissing again.

*　　*　　*

Lana arrived up at Kildara to meet her father. Gloria really was taking the piss with this photo itinerary and she needed to tell her father in no uncertain terms what it would look like. It would look like they were having an affair. She entered the house and made her way to Barry's office. The door was ajar and, hearing voices, she peeped through the opening.

Barry was sitting back in his chair, while Gloria sat on his desk facing him, her legs crossed. They looked to be talking very intimately. And then Gloria moved closer and brushed something off Barry's shoulder. But the brushing turned into a gently stroking. Then Lana saw Gloria lean forward and let her lips gently brush against his while her fingers slid into his hair. They pulled back slightly and stared into each other's eyes. Then they were kissing again.

The phone ringing on his desk was like a sudden screaming through the silence.

Barry sat back abruptly in his chair, before picking up the phone. "Hi . . . yeah . . . right, Eddie, and when did that happen?"

Lana turned quickly, her heart thumping, and walked out of the house.

Lana was speeding through the country roads after taking the turn off the dual carriageway. A passing car beeped loudly at her, warning her to slow down, but it only made her accelerate. She pulled into her mother's gateway, jumped out of the car and pressed the intercom.

"Hello?" said Eileen.

"Eileen, it's Lana."

"Oh! Lana! What a surprise! I'll open the gates for you."

Lana drove hurriedly up to the house where Eileen stood waiting.

"Is everything all right?" Eileen asked.

"Fine. Just felt like seeing Mum."

"Oh, she'll be delighted to see you," said Eileen but she looked at Lana a bit strangely. Lana never dropped in on a whim. "She's in the drawing-room."

Lana followed her across the huge hallway.

Eileen gently knocked on the door as she opened it. "We have a surprise for you, Ann."

Lana entered the huge drawing-room, and saw her mother sitting at the end, looking out of the long Georgian window down to the river.

"I'll leave you to it." Eileen closed the door after her.

"Hi, Mum." Lana walked across the drawing-room.

Ann was smiling happily. "Oh, it's lovely to see you." She got up and held out her arms. Lana went into her mother's arms and held her tight, inhaling her subtle fragrance.

Ann resumed her seat. "I'll ask Eileen to bring in tea."

"No, I don't want tea," Lana said quickly, sitting down on the chaise longue opposite her mother.

"How is everything with you?" Ann smiled.

Lana ignored her question and gazed at her mother, at her fragile beauty. She had an urge to quickly go away again. What she was contemplating was too cruel, and could destroy her mother's state of mind. You have to do it, she said to herself.

Ann was beginning to look concerned. "Lana?"

"Did Dad visit you last weekend?"

"No, he's very busy at the moment with the election. I've been trying to follow it on the news, but it disturbs –"

"The previous weekend? Was he here?"

"No. I don't expect him at this time to –"

"Oh, Mother! Are you that stupid?"

Ann's face was overcome with shock at Lana's tone and words.

"You've buried yourself here in the country for years, leaving Dad alone up in Dublin and London and all around the world. You've left yourself and your marriage wide open!"

"What are you talking about?" Ann was aghast.

"What kind of a marriage have you made for yourself and Dad? A weekly visit here. He's a man full of energy and life – and you are terrified of life."

"He would never leave me," Ann said with a quiet confidence.

"No. Because he loves you. But there's a woman called Gloria Reagan. Have you heard of her?"

"Your father has talked about her, yes. She's his campaign manager," said Ann.

"Oh, yes, his campaign manager. And this woman, full of confidence and life, has embroiled herself so far into Dad's life that –"

"Why are you saying these things?" Ann interrupted.

"I'm saying it because it's true! You know the big election-night party at Kildara? Do you know it will be Gloria Reagan standing beside Dad all night long. Gloria Reagan who will be beside him when the election results are read and who will be the first to embrace him after. Gloria Reagan who will be the woman beside him talking to the media. Gloria Reagan who will be beside him in every photo that will appear nation wide the next day! While you hide away down here in your own little world!"

There was so much more Lana wanted to say, but the hurt on her mother's face stopped her in her tracks.

"Why are you being so cruel?" Ann asked quietly.

"I'm saying it because I love you, and I love Dad. And I want to make you understand that love alone won't save your marriage."

Ann had paled. "But . . . what can I do?"

"Leave this prison you've created for yourself and start living your life again!"

"I can't . . . I can't leave here. There's too many frightening things out there."

"Yes, and the most frightening thing is Gloria Reagan!"

Lana got up, went to her mother and took her hand. "This might be hurting you to hear, but I had to tell you. It's up to you what you do. But I couldn't live with myself and see what's going on and not let you know."

CHAPTER 43

They lay in Cathal's bed, and the afternoon sun streamed in.

"You know things can't go back to the way they were now. We've changed. Our lives have changed. You'll have to leave Simeon." Cathal spoke quietly.

Kathryn said nothing.

"Kathryn?"

"How can I leave somebody who is at home unable to move from depression, and waiting for me to bring home his prescription pills two hours ago?"

"Are you still in love with him?"

"No," she sighed, "no, I'm not. And that feels like a relief. I've spent years loving somebody in desperate circumstances."

"So, what's the problem then?"

"He's dependent on me. Completely."

"And how do you think you're going to manage your singing career in those desperate circumstances?"

"I'll face that when I come to it. Besides, Cathal . . . this is probably just a one-off for you."

"It is not!"

609

"Cathal Fitzgerald, this is me, Kathryn Foy, remember? I'm not some silly model or TV presenter running after you. I've seen you come and go over the years at Exclusive and I've got your number." She was smiling. "I'm the one who would arrange a discreet taxi for you and your pick-up to leave the club on too many occasions to mention. Or make sure you and your date were left undisturbed in a discreet corner of the members' lounge. In fact, I don't know what the hell I'm doing here!" She started to laugh. "I was more or less your pimp for ten years! I've seen you at your best and worst over the years. Best usually at the beginning of a night, and worst at the end!"

He laughed too. "That's in the past."

"And what about Lana Curtis?"

"I'll always have nothing but the utmost respect and affection for Lana."

His words annoyed her.

"But we're from two different worlds," he went on. "I was completely uncomfortable amongst her set. And they treated me like an amusement to be tolerated. Lana changed too. Her values seemed to change – the things that drew us together in the first place disappeared as she achieved success in her own right. But I owe her a lot. I spent a lot of years frightened before I met her."

"What do you mean? Frightened of what?"

"Frightened of mistakes I made in the past and not really trusting in myself. Frightened that I was really a nobody with no talent and just trying to fool everyone. But I've worked through a lot of issues, and Lana was part of that. As I said I'll always have a love for her, but we're not meant to be together."

"And you are now with Ice Queen Me?" She looked at him suspiciously.

"That's how I feel. We're from the same place and we understand each other."

"I'd better go," she said abruptly. "Duty calls. And I'm working tonight."

"You haven't said anything about us." He looked concerned.

"I need to give this a lot of thought, Cathal. It's not straightforward." She reached over and kissed him. "I'll call you later."

*   *   *

Lana looked at Stephen's mobile number for half an hour before picking up the phone.

"Stephen, hi. It's Lana here."

"Oh, hi. How's everything going?"

"Good – good. I was just checking if you would be in Exclusive tonight?"

"No, night off, I'm afraid."

"Oh!" Her heart sank and she rubbed her lips. She felt so stressed, the only thing that would calm her would be a fix.

"I could come round to your house if you're looking for what I think you're looking for?"

She thought hard for second. He had already been there, so it was no big deal.

"Yeah . . . okay."

"I'll see you at eight. I'll . . . eh," he gave a little laugh, "need some money though."

"That's no problem," she said. "I'll sort you out when you come here."

She hung up the phone. Money was never one of her problems, she thought.

"I left numerous messages on your phone." Nicole looked at Lana, filled with concern.

"I know," Lana said.

"So . . . what's been going on?" Nicole probed. How she now hated all of this! She knew exactly what was wrong with Lana through Tony.

"Myself and Cathal have broken up."

"I see." Nicole tried to look surprised.

"His choice." She began to tell Nicole about the break-up. It was as Nicole had suspected. Cathal had replaced her addiction to drink and drugs. Addictive personalities will find their way to depend on something, she thought.

"So, how have you been coping?" she asked.

"Throwing myself into work and going out with friends," Lana said, deciding to leave out her excesses. "I was down at my mother's today."

"Yes?"

"I suspect Gloria Regan is planning on being the new Mrs Barry Curtis."

Nicole's face creased in concern. "Why do you think this?"

"The way she has completely taken over my father's affairs . . . the way she looks at him all the time . . . lots of things . . . I . . . I saw them kissing. And . . . and I decided to tell my mother." She placed her head in her hands. "I told her that while she's been hiding as a recluse, Gloria has been moving in for the kill . . . I don't know what I've done."

*   *   *

Cathal sat at home watching an old movie. He couldn't wait to see Kathryn again. He thought about her situation with Simeon. He wondered why he didn't feel guilty.

612

Because she's not happy with him, he thought. It's over between them. And yet he didn't know whether she would be prepared to leave Simeon. She must. He and she were made for each other. They matched perfectly. They both had spent their lives hiding behind fronts. Looking after other people.

*   *   *

Kathryn sat in her office. The club was packed outside, but she had hardly been out managing at all. She couldn't get Cathal out of her thoughts. She totally trusted him and wanted to see him again. She picked up her phone and dialled him.

"Hi, just me. Did I wake you?"

"No, just sitting here watching TV. How's work?"

"Fine." There was silence for a long while. "I want to see you again . . . tonight."

*   *   *

Stephen's talent in life was to reel people in. He had always known just the right buttons to press to bring people into his power, under his influence. He had used it to magical effect before prison. And even in prison, he had not just survived but prospered because of his talent. In fact, if anything his talent had been perfected and sharpened in prison. And now he was using it to dazzling effect in Dublin's exclusive social scene. But as he climbed the steps to Lana's house, even he was amazed to have this opportunity. He had done a lot of discreet research on Lana and now totally had the measure of her.

And he had Cathal to thank for leading him to her.

He rang the bell. She opened it a minute later.

"Hi, come on in."

He smiled brightly, and followed her into the lounge.

"Drink?" she asked.

"Yeah, a whiskey please." He sat down.

She went and poured two whiskeys.

"Look, I'm really sorry about the other night – after Patricia's party," she said, looking embarrassed as she handed him a whiskey. She sat down. "I'm really sorry about the state I was in. Thanks for the lift back and everything. Sorry for falling asleep on the couch like that." She gave a little laugh. "I was pissed – I wonder about myself sometimes."

"You were fine. Just enjoying yourself, that's all."

She was thinking of something to say.

"You were working today?" he asked.

"Just a half day. I had this meeting with a plastic-surgery company who want to do a feature on stars that have had work done. I explained to them the stars mightn't be too pleased being exposed."

Stephen laughed loudly. "I would say that's true!"

"I – I didn't realise you worked at Exclusive."

"Sure, been there a while now."

"Do you," she looked at him cautiously, "meet my father much?"

"No," he shook his head, "only the once for the interview. It's Kathryn Foy who meets him all the time." He gave a laugh. "I'm just the boy!" For now, thought Stephen.

She felt relieved

An hour later, Lana had consumed a few whiskeys.

"Do you like living alone?" asked Stephen.

"I much preferred it when Cathal was here. It's strange – you're happy with life, think you've met the man of your dreams and everything is hunky-dory for the rest of your lives – and then everything falls apart."

Stephen looked full of concern. "You thought a lot of him, didn't you?"

She nodded and wiped away a tear. "Yes, I did. But if I'm honest with myself, I always knew it wouldn't last."

"Why?" Stephen took out a bag of cocaine and poured a little out on the glass coffee table. She looked at it expectantly.

"I just knew." She stared at the coke. "He was never really mine. You just know that. I knew he was far too normal to ever really force himself to fit into my life for too long. I guess I'm just trying to see it for what it was now. Two people who needed each other at the time." She gestured to the coke. "I'll, eh, I'll go and get some money."

"No," he insisted, "don't worry about it tonight – it's on me."

"Are you sure?"

"Of course." You have to speculate to accumulate, thought Stephen. He passed her a rolled-up note. "Ladies first."

She bent over, inhaled and sat back, allowing the familiar feeling to overcome her. "You know, I'm mad to be doing this shit again – I swore I never would – I had terrible problems with it before."

"How so?"

"I just got into a certain lifestyle and it messed up my head. And here I am back doing it again. But it's only temporary." She leaned over again.

"Same for me. It just helps you through bad times."

*   *   *

"I can't promise you anything," said Kathryn as she lay in bed with Cathal. "You can't do just what you want in

615

this life, Cathal. Not when you've got responsibilities."

"Look, I spent years looking after people. Making sure James and the others and Sylvia and MPI were okay. It's just like being an accessory in your own life. And I was going the same route with Lana, just becoming an emotional crutch for somebody, and nobody is going to be happy with that in the end. You have to think of what makes you happy."

*　　*　　*

"Come on, I think you need to go to your proper bed," said Stephen, looking down at Lana, asleep on the couch.

"No . . . I'm fine," she grumbled.

He reached down, hauled her up and forced her to put an arm around him. He led her upstairs.

"I'm very tired," she muttered.

"Yeah, that's why you're going to bed, sweetheart."

He went into the main bedroom and threw her down on the bed. Then he walked around the room, opening drawers and looking through them. He found a key and tried it against all the jewellery boxes. It opened the largest. It was filled with necklaces, earrings and rings. He examined them all, then took one of the smallest rings and popped it in his pocket, before locking the box up and putting the key back.

He went over and looked at her sleeping form, then bent over and slapped her face a couple of times lightly.

"What?" She struggled awake.

"I'm going now. Give me a call tomorrow."

"Okay," she yawned, turned over on her side and fell fast asleep again.

He bent over and licked her face before leaving.

CHAPTER 44

Ann Curtis sat in the library of her home, and replaced the receiver of the antique phone, having just spoken to her husband. He had just explained to her that he wouldn't be visiting her this weekend as it was so close to the general election day. She had accepted this politely and without discussion. She looked down at the copy of *The Irish Times* on the desk in front of her, with a photo of Barry and a smiling Gloria Reagan under the heading *"Curtis Moves Closer To Victory"*. She never got the papers, but since Lana's visit a few days before she had asked Eileen to send out for the press every day. True for Lana, Gloria seemed to feature heavily in all the photos and features. Ann had felt frightened of different things for so long that she almost took it as the norm. But this was a totally new fear. And it was worse.

She got up and walked over to the long antique mirror and looked at herself. She had aged very well, she thought, not that she ever gave much thought to her looks. But her life here hardly gave her reason to age. She had a small appetite and really just ate what she needed. She wasn't one for the sun, so she had no sun damage. Never drank or smoked. As she peered closer at her skin, it hardly had a line. If you live in a bubble, that's what happens, she thought. She crossed the room, opened a drawer and took out some photos. She looked at photos often. They were from the past. She looked at photos of her and Barry at a funfair when they had just got married. They were laughing and looked very happy. When did she laugh last? She couldn't remember. She looked at other photos of her and Barry and Lana as a little girl. They were crouched down either side of Lana, hugging her tightly. How they adored her! She had never wanted all this money that Barry had made. She never thought he would make so much. Of course she knew he was extremely ambitious and bright, and she knew he would do well in life. She thought they would end up in a nice upper middle-class suburb, with nothing really standing out about them from their neighbours. When he became so successful, she really couldn't handle it. And there was such a threat of kidnap in Ireland at the time. She couldn't cope. As she looked back at the photos of herself when she was young, she wished she felt like that again. Carefree. She had always been confident of Barry's love for her. But from what Lana had said, it was now under threat. And really, listening to Lana, she was right. How could a man of Barry's energy be content with a recluse for a wife? She had always privately thought that Barry had been selfish in his pursuit of money. That he never had asked her what kind of a future she wanted, which maybe didn't factor in being one of the weathiest families in Ireland. He had just assumed that she had wanted that, because, well, didn't everybody? But now as she thought about it, she realised that she had been selfish too. Leaving her husband alone and unsupported. It was a testament to him that his eye hadn't wandered years ago. But now with his pending election, they were entering a whole new ball-game. She knew with this new life, she would lose him. She knew he loved her still, but he didn't know she loved him. She took up the paper and looked at the photo of Gloria Reagan. It was true for Lana, this woman was a threat. And did she have enough fire to fight her? She would have to find the fire, because she would not let Barry go.

* * *

Kathryn sat in Cathal's Jeep outside Sylvia's offices. Jack Better was in Dublin, and was now waiting inside to meet her.

"What if doesn't like me?" she said, shivering slightly.

"He will."

"I'll come across as a nervous wreck."

"Will you stop it! You always come across as totally impressive."

"I wish you were coming in with me."

"Believe me, you're better off without me. He doesn't like me and it's better he doesn't realise how close we are until he offers you a contract."

She looked at him and smiled. He seemed so confident they would be together for the long haul. How could she explain to him that was very uncertain in her circumstances? She thought back to the morning, and spending an hour and a half trying to convince Simeon to get up and have something to eat and have a shower. He had eventually hauled himself out of bed, eaten a few cornflakes, had a one-minute shower and taken to the bed again. How could she leave a man so dependent on her? And yet as she looked at Cathal . . . he was the only thing that made her happy.

"Best of luck!" He reached over and kissed her, before she got out of the car and strode into the building confidently.

Cathal took out his phone and dialled the *Hi Life* office. He had left lots of messages on Lana's phone but she hadn't responded. Now, he was being plagued by Gloria Reagan, insisting he turn up at some big election-night party at Kildara and pose with Lana, pretending they were still an item. Gloria had, in minute detail, explained the seriousness of negative publicity, and Cathal certainly didn't want to cause either Barry or Lana any hassle. He mightn't agree with Barry's policies, but he cared too much about Lana to let her or her father down. And he also felt guilty about foisting Stephen on them, and so this was a small price to pay.

"Hi, there, it's me!" Cathal was surprised when Lana answered the phone directly.

"Oh . . . hi!" She also sounded surprised.

"I've been worried about . . . did you get my messages?"

She had felt her heart jump at the sound of his voice. "I did."

"You could have responded."

"I've been busy." She felt upset, but hid it.

"I'd really like to meet up with you and talk," said Cathal.

"Things are a bit hectic at the moment," she said, thinking how she had met Stephen nearly every night that week, and got off her face on drugs. If she met Cathal, he would detect it immediately.

"Gloria Reagan has been on to me, wanting me to go to your dad's election-night party."

"I know. She's been saying the same to me."

"I'd like to go to support you and your dad," he said honestly.

"It would mean us being photographed together. You know how you hate all that." She couldn't hide the bitterness in her voice.

"As Gloria said, if the press find out we're not seeing each other, it might overshadow your father's election."

"I know. We'd both be grateful if you could come."

"I'll collect you at seven on the night then."

*   *   *

"She's coming in late every morning and it's obvious she's burning the candle at both ends," Tony told Nicole over dinner. They had gone to a local Italian bistro around the corner from their home.

"Does Ralph say anything to her?" asked Nicole.

"You kidding me? Lana Curtis can do anything in there and nobody would say boo to her."

"Is her work suffering?"

"Funnily enough, no. She came in for just three hours yesterday, but managed to pull off some sponsorship deal." He looked thoughtful. "I guess she is talented."

"Well, tell her then!" urged Nicole.

"No way, she's needs to be brought down a peg or two, not praised!"

"She sounds like a very insecure girl to me." Nicole was seriously concerned. "And I think you should support her in any way you can." She reached over and took his hand. "Be nice to her, Tony . . . sounds like she's taking the break-up of her relationship very badly. It could have been us."

He nodded and squeezed her hand tightly.

* * *

Cathal popped open a bottle of champagne and filled two glasses. They were out on the balcony of his apartment. Sylvia had just phoned them to inform them that MPI was offering Kathryn a recording contract, singing Cathal's songs.

"I can't believe it!" Kathryn said, taking a sip.

Cathal sat down beside her and cast his mind back to when Affidavit were offered their first recording contract. "Savour this moment. You'll never have another feeling like it the rest of your life."

"They really liked me!" she said.

"Sylvia said they expected you to be very big – and with her and MPI behind you, you will be."

"And your songs," she said and clinked his glass.

"Yes, and my songs," he offered cautiously.

She sighed and looked down. "I'd better get back."

"I hoped you'd be staying tonight."

"I can't . . . I've been so busy arranging the Curtis party, I haven't seen Simeon all day."

"And is that so bad?"

"It is for him." She stood up, bent over and kissed him. "I'm sorry." She turned to leave.

"Kathryn," he grabbed her hand, "you're going to have to make a decision soon – this isn't fair to any of us."

"I know," she nodded.

* * *

The Sunday Independent social page read: "*Word is*

quickly spreading that the place to be on election night is Kildara, home of Barry Curtis. The guest list has become the hottest in town, as a host of national and international celebrities will be there to celebrate the expected election of the magnate. The party is being held in conjunction with Hi Life, where Barry's socialite daughter Lana, girlfriend of Cathal Fitzgerald, works. Phones are already buzzing with people trying to pull favours to get invited. For those who can't manage to secure invitations, and to save face, sudden flights are being arranged to be out of town in Marbella. Don't forget to cast your votes before take-off!"

* * *

"Your father's party is the talk of the city," said Stephen. He was at Lana's house.

"I know. I'm probably going to need something before it." She looked at him expectantly.

"Anything you want. Your requirements are becoming a little pricey though. Your father doesn't pay me that much!" He laughed with fake embarrassment.

"Of course, I'm sorry. I've told you before – whatever it costs, let me know."

"I could do with a little advance." He looked sheepish.

"Wait a second." She went upstairs for a few minutes, then came back down. She threw a roll of money at him. "Is it enough?" she asked.

"Plenty." He put the money into his pocket and took out the cocaine.

* * *

"I'm flying here!" Lana said.

They were in the living-room.

"Just enjoy the effect, baby!" Stephen was sitting opposite her, watching her as her eyes opened and closed from the effects of the cocaine.

"Got a little something for you next week for that big party."

His voice came at her in waves.

"What?" she asked.

"A special . . . heroin . . . going to make you feel really good at that party . . ."

*   *   *

Lana looked through the guest list, which had been compiled by Ralph, Barry and Gloria and which was impressive. She saw James Fitzgerald and Donna McCarthy down on the list and felt annoyed. She felt like crossing them off but realised that would be petty. They were a celebrity couple who attended most high-profile events and this would be no different. Another *Hi Life* big success, she thought wryly. The usual rent-a-crowd turning up and guzzling back free drink all night.

"That's all this country needs – another exclusive, commenting on the vacuous lives of B-list celebrities," she said quietly.

"Aren't you looking forward to the party?" Tony asked her.

She looked over to him. "Not really. It's going to be hard seeing Cathal again. The whole world still thinks we're an item. It's just going to be difficult play-acting for the night."

"I understand." He nodded in sympathy. He remembered Nicole's words. "Clive and I are going to the

624

pub tonight, if you want to come along?"

She nodded. "That would be nice, thanks"

*   *   *

Cathal handed Kathryn back the contract from MPI over coffee in the Westbury. He had got his lawyer to look it over for her. "It's standard," he said. "Nobody's trying to pull a fast one on you or anything. It's more or less the same as the one Affidavit had."

She nodded. "I was almost hoping there would be something wrong with it."

He looked at her. "So you wouldn't have to make a decision?"

"Something like that." Thinking of Simeon, she put the contract into her handbag. "I'll take another look through it before I sign it and give it back to Sylvia."

"If I told you I loved you . . . would it help you make up your mind?" he asked.

She stood up and bent to kiss his cheek. "If you're talking to Sylvia, tell her I'll have the contract over to her within a couple of days."

*   *   *

Clive and the others had gone home, leaving Tony and Lana alone in Cocoon.

"Tell me, Tony, when does it begin to feel better?" she sighed, as she took another swig of vodka.

"Breaking up? I don't know – I don't know what I'd have done if me and Nic hadn't got back together."

She took out her mobile and saw that she had four missed calls. They were all from Stephen.

"Fuck!" she muttered.

"What's wrong?"

"I was supposed to meet someone tonight but I forgot – oh, well, it's too late now. I'll give them a call tomorrow."

A doorman came over to them. "If you could finish your drinks and make your way out, please."

"I didn't realise it was so late," said Tony, "Just going to phone home."

He went outside and phoned Nic.

"Hey, just me. Sorry I'm not home. I'm out having a few drinks with Lana,"

"How is she?"

"Still bad," Tony sighed.

"Don't rush home, love. If she needs a shoulder to cry on, I understand."

"I'm kind of tired myself."

Nicole thought of Lana's distraught face the other day. "It's up to yourself – I just would have hoped. if we hadn't got back together, I'd have had some friends rallying around me, that's all."

"I'll see what she wants to do. Love you."

He went back to the table.

"She was cool about me staying out. Do you fancy going to Exclusive for an hour?"

She thought of Stephen there – she didn't want him seeing her out socialising after she had stood him up. Then she thought of the stash of cocaine at home she had bought from him. "I'm on your route home. Let's call a cab and you can drop off at mine for a nightcap – I'll order you another cab from there. You're over the limit to drive yourself."

*   *   *

626

"Are we friends now?" Lana asked as they sipped Bacardi back at hers.

"Firm friends," he nodded and smiled. "Sorry for judging you along the way. And I want to tell you something – you're bloody good at your job."

"You're just saying that!" She swigged back her drink.

"No, I have to hand it to you – the way you put those sponsorship deals together and the way you come up with marketing ideas and execute them, I'm totally impressed."

"Really?"

He nodded. "I wouldn't say it if I didn't mean it."

"Thanks – that really means a lot to me."

"I'll just use your toilet before I call a cab." He got up and went upstairs.

She felt pride at his words. She went and reached behind the clock. She took out her cocaine and measured out a small line. She bent over to snort.

"Do you have the number – what the hell are you doing?" Tony was staring at her, appalled.

"I'm just . . . er . . ." She quickly wiped away the powder. "I didn't hear you come downstairs."

"You're taking coke?"

"Yeah. So what? Look, don't give me a hard time about it, I'm going through hell at the moment, and it's getting me through."

"It's all making sense now. The way you've been recently. Are you fucking mad?"

"No, I'm just fed up!"

"And that shit is going to make you feel better?" He was incredulous.

"Look, just call your taxi cab and go!" She was furious with herself for not being more discreet.

Tony came over, sat beside her and softened his voice.

"Look, I know what you're going through. But this isn't the answer."

"Well, what is then? The only man I've ever fallen in love with and he doesn't want to know!"

He put a comforting arm around her. "Well, then, he's mad – but that shit isn't going to make you feel better."

"But it does!"

He started to stroke her back to comfort her, and she rested her head on his shoulder.

They stayed that way for a long time. When she moved her head and looked up at him and they started to slowly kiss, it seemed the most natural thing in the world to do.

* * *

Tony opened his eyes and blinked a few times at the unfamiliar surroundings. He quickly looked to his right and saw Lana's sleeping form, then started rubbing his temples as he remembered everything that had happened. He sat up quickly and looked at his watch. It was nearly ten in the morning.

"Lana – Lana!" He nudged her urgently.

"What?" she mumbled.

"We're late for work!"

"Tell them I'll be in at lunchtime," she said and turned over to sleep.

He jumped out of bed, looked around for his clothes and started to get dressed. He raced downstairs and grabbed his jacket from the drawing-room. Looking at his mobile he saw he had ten missed calls from Nicole. He ran out the front door and down the street towards work. He felt shaky and nervous after what had happened. Terrified Nicole would find out. Where would he say he was? How would he explain himself?

*   *   *

"Where the hell were you?" Nicole almost shouted down the phone at Tony, when he rang her from his office. "I was worried sick. I was about to call the police!"

"I know. Everything's fine. I'm sorry. I'll explain everything this evening."

He hung up the phone and thought about his encounter with Lana. He was completely shocked that it had happened. He had never thought of her like that before. And yet there was a part of him that was completely flattered about it. Lana Curtis, daughter of a multi-millionaire, had chosen to go to bed with him. Cathal Fitzgerald's ex had been interested in him. He had a strange mix of emotions, ranging from pure guilt to pure pride. He thought about the Curtis name and how famous it was. And suddenly, he was thinking of himself as part of their lives. Of being photographed with Lana in the papers and in the social pages. If she was interested in him like she had been last night, then why not?

*   *   *

Lana braced herself as she went into the office. What a stupid thing to do! The last thing she needed was a fling with the guy she shared an office with.

"Hi!" she said briskly as she sat down at her desk and switched on the computer.

"Afternoon!" He smiled over at her. "How do you feel today?"

She glanced over at him and realised the situation

could not be ignored. She would have to address it. "Tony. Thanks for your company last night. I really needed someone to be there . . . but that's as far as it goes. What happened shouldn't have . . . and it won't be happening again . . . I hope you understand?"

Her words were like a slap across the face. "Of course – that's exactly how I felt about it too." He started typing furiously, feeling humiliated. She hadn't been interested in him in the least. Just lonely.

He walked home from the office that evening feeling dejected and depressed. He felt so angry and upset at his betrayal of Nicole and the love he had with her. He had been taken in by Lana's money and connections and always had been, if he was honest with himself. Just like he had been with Ralph and Margaux and Cathal and the rest. What Nicole had said all along was true, and he had committed the ultimate betrayal of her the previous night. The fact that he had deluded himself to think that he could have accessed the life he craved through Lana falling for him made the whole thing worse.

He put his key in the door and walked in.

Nicole was waiting for him anxiously. She put her arms out to him and he enveloped her in a hug.

"I was so worried when you didn't answer your phone all night!" The tears rolled down her face.

"I know. I'm sorry. I'm so sorry for everything!" He was suddenly crying too.

"Tony! What is it? What's happened?"

He knew what he would say to excuse his absence. He pulled away from her. "It's Lana – she has a drug problem"

"What?"

"She was very lonely and so I went back to her house

630

for a nightcap, as you suggested. I came into the room and found her snorting coke."

"For fuck's sake!" Nicole was genuinely upset and saddened for Lana. You've lost her, she told herself.

"I stayed at her house for the night because she was in an awful state. What could I do?"

"Of course!" She hugged him tightly. "You were very good to stay with her. She's obviously in a vulnerable position." Nicole thought hard about what to do. "Tony, you need to tell somebody in her life who cares enough to do something about it."

"Like who? Just ring up Barry Curtis or something?"

"I don't know. She's pressing the self-destruct button big-time . . . Cathal Fitzgerald!"

"What?" Tony was aghast.

"From what I know, she'll listen to Cathal. And he'll listen to you."

"No, I can't!"

"You have to, Tony. If anything happens to her, it'll be on your conscience."

*   *   *

Cathal was sitting out on the balcony looking at the red sky over the city, thinking about Kathryn. He hadn't heard from her all day. He was filled with fear that she would stay with Simeon. In his head he had his whole future mapped out with her, and he couldn't imagine life without her.

His mobile phone rang and he saw Tony's number on it. "Tony! Haven't heard from you for a long while. How's tricks?"

"Good. Cathal . . . I'll get to the point. I'm very worried

about Lana, and I think you should know why."

* * *

"I'm not going until you let me in!" Cathal shouted through Lana's letterbox, after ringing the doorbell and banging the door for fifteen minutes.

He heard the door open and Lana stood there. He looked at her. She looked exhausted and as if she had been crying.

"Can I come in?" he asked.

She shrugged and he followed her in.

"You sounded odd on the phone when we spoke. I'm very concerned about you," he said earnestly.

"Don't be. I'm not your responsibility." She sat down and took a swig from her glass of vodka.

"I'm concerned about you because I care about you."

"I've had a really bad, bad day, Cathal, so I really don't need you standing there and pontificating at me, okay?"

"Not okay!" He grabbed the glass of vodka from her.

"Hey!"

"What the hell is happening to you? For fuck's sake, Lana, you were on top of the world. You had your life sorted, you were enjoying being a media darling, you had a great job, you had –"

"*You*! I had you. All I cared about was having you! I only did the other things because I thought they'd impress you!"

He sighed and sat down. "Then you didn't know me at all, Lana. Because they didn't impress me. What impressed me was you. Your personality, your sense of fun, maybe your vulnerability."

"I've fallen apart since you left." She rubbed her

temples.

"I'm sorry – but I had to leave – it wasn't right for me."

"You hated my life and didn't want to fit into it."

"Yes, that's true in a way. I was sick of being paraded out as your boyfriend at election campaigns and at dinner parties and all your friends just tolerating me, but looking down their noses at me. That made me think deeply about our relationship and I realised that, though I care a great deal about you, I didn't love you enough to stay. Lana, after you became successful, we weren't compatible any more."

They sat silently for a while.

Finally, Lana spoke. "So, what have you been doing since you went – fading into obscurity?"

"I've been writing a lot of music," he sighed.

She looked surprised. "You always said you couldn't."

"I know – but I just started writing one day for myself."

"That's good. Look, Cathal, I understand why you left, and I'm grateful for the time we had together. But now you just have to let me get back to my life."

"On drink and drugs? You're taking drugs again, aren't you?"

"My therapist says I have an addictive personality, so just let me get on with it!"

Her phone rang and she saw Stephen's number come up. She took the call. "Hi . . . sorry about last night . . . Yeah, you can come over now." She hung up.

"Who's that?"

"It's really none of your business."

"You're seeing someone new?"

"No!" She wished he would just go. She couldn't stand this. "It's my supplier actually – so unless you want to join us in a cosy session, I suggest you leave."

Cathal got up. "If that's what you want, Lana. At the end of the day nobody can help you but yourself. No therapist, no rehab, no counselling, no parent, no boyfriend – only you. Give me a call if you need a friend – a real friend."

He got up and walked out of the house, slamming the door behind him. Shaking his head he went down the steps, got into his car and pulled out of the driveway. He pulled out down the street and as he drove off, he saw another car indicate and drive into Lana's. Cathal stopped the Jeep abruptly and parked. He sprinted back along the street and looked over the hedge. His heart started beating fast as he saw Stephen Rourke climb the steps of Lana's house and ring the doorbell. A second later, Lana opened the door and Stephen walked in.

Cathal was shocked. He quickly made his way back to his car and sped off.

*   *   *

"Thanks for coming over," said Lana. "Sorry about last night. I was out and forgot about our arrangement."

He closed the door after him and followed her into the lounge.

"Drink?"

"Whiskey," he said.

"Where were you?" he asked.

"Just out with some work friends." She handed him the drink and was struck by his icy stare.

"People don't stand me up, Lana!" His voice was menacing and she felt a shiver.

"I'm sorry," she said.

"You know, if you want to play silly games with me, I'll

leave right now, and we'll not have to see each other again." He put down the drink, turned and went to leave.

She thought of her supply of coke. "No – wait – it was a truly unforgivable way to carry on – I'm truly sorry."

He walked up close to her and stared into her eyes. "You wouldn't stand Cathal Fitzgerald up, would you?"

She blinked a few times, then quickly turned and went to the mantelpiece. She took a wad of money from it and handed it to him. "Take this. I owe you for what you've brought tonight, and it can also cover the stuff before the election party tomorrow."

"It's not a case of the money, Lana," he said, putting the money in his pocket.

"I know."

He sat down. "As I said, I've something special planned for you tomorrow night. It's going to make all your previous trips seem like just the appetisers."

CHAPTER 45

ELECTION DAY

The television presenter on the morning news smiled at the camera. "Voting got off to an early start across the country with polls predicting a large turnout in all constituencies. In the Dublin North constituency, Barry Curtis was one of the first to cast his vote."

Footage of Barry Curtis entering a polling station came on screen. Barry stopped and smiled for the cameras. Gloria Reagan smiled beside him.

Ann Curtis got up, crossed over the room and turned off the television.

*   *   *

Nicole anxiously waited for Lana to show up. Considering what Tony had said, she half-expected her to skip the session, and felt relieved when Lana walked in. She looked tired and drawn.

"So, how have you been since last time?"

"I'm fine, I guess. I'm throwing myself into my social life – isn't that what you're supposed to do when you break up?"

"I don't think there's any text-book theory of what's the right thing to do."

"Pity. Maybe I'll write it some day."

"It's election day. That must be exciting for you?"

"There's this stupid party on tonight, and I'm just looking forward to having it over. Let's just elect the great Barry Curtis and get on with it!"

"You're feeling cynical?" Drugs tend to do that, thought Nicole, wishing she could just confront her about it and trying to think of ways to manipulate her into trusting her enough to confess. "You've been drinking a lot?" she ventured.

"I guess." Lana shrugged.

"Does that not worry you?"

"It should do, I suppose."

"Maybe you should take it a little easy for a while?"

"Maybe." Lana rubbed her temples.

"Just concentrate on work and have a few early nights."

Lana looked up and smiled. "I can't even keep out of trouble at work!"

"Something happened there?"

"I did a stupid thing the other night. I slept with Tony – you know, the guy I share an office with."

Nicole felt as if all the breath had been knocked out of her body. "Tony?" she gasped.

"Yeah! Imagine!" Lana laughed lightly. "I guess we finally worked out our differences – in bed!"

The room started to swirl in front of Nicole. She clutched at the arms of her chair.

"Stupid really, he just came back to my house for a nightcap – and one thing led to another – as it does."

"You actually had sex with him?" Her own voice

seemed come from a distance.

"Unfortunately. I told him the next day to forget about it and move on."

Nicole was afraid she was about to throw up. She forced herself to say, "He's involved with somebody, isn't he?"

"Yeah. He has a partner."

"How could you do that to another woman?" Her voice had risen despite her efforts to control it.

"Oh, I know!" Lana raised her eyes to heaven. "Don't get all puritanical on me! I feel guilty enough as it is!"

Nicole slammed her hand on the table. "I don't think you do!" Her voice rose further.

"Steady on!" Lana said, surprised. "I thought these sessions were supposed to be non-judgemental?"

"They are until you interfere in my life!" Nicole almost shouted the words and tears were suddenly streaming down her face.

Lana looked at her, horrified. "What is wrong with you?"

"*You!* I'm Tony's partner!"

"What?" Lana's mouth dropped open. "Since when?"

"Since years ago!"

"I really don't understand – what's going on here?"

"You never do!" Nicole stood up and accused her. "You're Lana Curtis, and you've been brought up to do whatever the hell you want to. To take what you want whenever you want it, including Tony! And then you wallow in self-pity because you don't have any fucking purpose in life!"

"I didn't know – this isn't fair!"

"I've felt nothing but compassion for you since I met you. All I wanted to do was help you and to set you on the right track – and you've ruined my life!"

Lana was suddenly crying as well. "I'm s-s-sorry!"

"No, you're not! You never cared a toss about Tony. You just wanted some company for the night, and good old dependable Tony would do. It never crossed your mind about his girlfriend. I hate you!"

Lana stood up, her heart palpitating. "I'd better go."

She raced out of the office and down the corridor and out on to the street. She raced all the way down the block and then into a small alleyway and leaned against the wall panting.

* * *

Kathryn walked through the main hallway at Kildara, watching the designers set up the house for the party. She had a few words with the caterers to make sure everything was all right and then spotted Gloria Reagan talking to a security guard.

"Under no circumstances can anyone gain entry to the party unless they are on the guest list," Gloria was saying, "regardless of whether they have invitations or not. I've heard a rumour that fake invitations have been put into circulation."

"Yes, ma'am," said the guard.

Kathryn raised her eyes and continued on to see how the flower arrangements were coming along.

* * *

Tony was sitting opposite Ralph who looked much stressed.

"This party is one of the biggest we've ever covered so

I want no fuck-ups from anybody!" said Ralph. "I want you standing at the main entrance checking in guests as they come through the door. "

Tony looked at Ralph, confused. "But, will I not be wasting time there, when I should be going around interviewing the guests?"

"Don't contradict me! There are going to be some seriously important people there and myself and Margaux will handle the interviews – you can write them up later."

Tony felt himself becoming angry. He was being dismissed to the background and expected to do all the hard work later. "I think it would be better if I did some of the interviews myself," he pushed.

"I said no!" Ralph almost shouted, causing Tony to jump. "Just stay out of the way tonight. Make sure everyone signs in. I've been hearing some stories back about you!"

"Stories?"

"Yes – that you are getting too familiar with the people we cover in *Hi Life*."

"I don't understand."

"That you've been out socialising with Cathal Fitzgerald and his gang a few times, and hanging out in Exclusive, talking to people you only know through your job here."

"What's wrong with that?"

"Everything. Don't get above your station, Tony. You're just an employee here, who writes up some of the articles. These people aren't your friends. You're not one of them and you'll never be one of them. Lana works here, but she's a Curtis, so you should stay away from socialising with her as well. Know your place."

* * *

Lana sat in her lounge with the curtains drawn, feeling utterly miserable. She was still in shock over Nicole's revelation. And it was true what she had said. She was a truly selfish woman, with no consideration for others. She couldn't face going to the party that night and sent Cathal a text saying not to call for her because she wouldn't be going. Then she turned her phone off.

Stephen was coming over that evening and she felt the need for a fix like never before.

* * *

Cathal sat opposite Sylvia in her office.

"Jack Better was totally impressed by Kathryn," said Sylvia.

"I thought he would be."

"Is she delighted?"

"Nervous."

"I can't imagine Kathryn being nervous of anything."

"You'd be surprised. She's quite different underneath that cool exterior."

Sylvia looked at him. "You're together, aren't you?"

"We've been together, if that's what you mean."

"You're not interested in continuing it?"

"Oh, I am – but I don't think she is. It's very complicated."

Cathal's text bleeped and he read it. *"Not going to party tonight, talk later, Lana."* He frowned. That was worrying.

* * *

Leaving Sylvia's office, Cathal came face to face with James.

"Hiya," James said smiling.

"Hi." Cathal was cold.

"I've been hearing all about Kathryn Foy from Sylvia. I believe you're behind it all."

Cathal shrugged.

"I'm not surprised. You were the one behind Affidavit's success."

"Sure!" Cathal said sarcastically.

"I really would like to meet up for a few beers."

"Yeah, give me a call."

"We're going to the Curtis party tonight, so maybe we can catch up there?"

"Come on, James. I hate bullshit, always have and always will. You haven't wanted to know me for ages, so don't start all this buddy-buddy stuff now."

"That's not true!"

"It is! You and the others pushed me out of the picture without a second thought for me. I went through a really bad time, and you never checked to see how I was."

"I'm sorry, Cathal." James looked upset.

"I'll see you around." Cathal walked past him.

CHAPTER 46

ELECTION NIGHT

The young female reporter smiled into the camera. She was standing beside the entrance of Kildara as a procession of luxury cars drove past her into the driveway.

"Well, the much talked-about party at Kildara, Barry Curtis's home, has already kicked off here and it's only seven in the evening! The party is expected to be attended later by the Taoiseach and senior government members. The latest news on the Curtis vote is that it's running very close. And since this is a victory party going on here tonight, let's hope they'll have something to celebrate!"

*   *   *

Tony thought of Ralph's remarks all the way home. He was furious that he was being delegated to the signing-in table at the party. After all the hard work he had done! He wasn't being treated with any respect! He hurried into the house.

"Have to rush!" he said as he raced to the stairs. "I'm late for this party and need to change quickly. You won't believe what Ralph has done now –" He stopped abruptly.

Nicole was standing at the fireplace. He never seen her like this before. She looked furious and distraught.

"Nic?"

"How could you do this to me? Do it to us?"

"Do what?" He went over to her.

"Stay away from me!" she almost shouted. "You slept with her! You slept with Lana Curtis!"

Tony paled as his mouth dropped open.

"How could you," she was crying now, "betray me? Betray everything we were and were working for?"

"How do you know?" he managed.

"I'm her therapist. I know everything about her."

"Her therapist! For how long?"

"Since before you knew she even existed."

"Nic!" He went to put his arms around her.

"Don't!" she screamed. "I never want to see you again!" And she crumpled to the floor, crying.

*   *   *

Donna came down the stairs fixing her earrings and gave herself the once-over in the mirror before going into the sitting-room.

James was sitting there, playing with a bottle of beer.

"We'd better hurry or we'll be late for this party," said Donna. "You know that photo shoot I did for *Image* magazine? They're going to do a piece on us and want the wedding date – so we have to fix it soon, all right?"

James looked at her nervously. "Donna, I have something to tell you."

"Well, why don't you tell me on the way to the party?" she said, tossing back her mane.

"Donna, I don't want to get married." He looked up at

her sheepishly.

"Poor taste, James. Now get a move on!"

"I'm not joking. I'm not marrying you. I don't want to."

Donna stared at James in shock. "Have you gone crazy? What are you talking about?"

"I'm sorry to be so abrupt. I'm really sorry. But it was the only way I could do it, the only way I could tell you."

Donna was still standing staring at him, her hands clasped to her face.

"I've given it a lot of thought," he went on. "I want to make some big life-style changes and –"

"But you have to get married to me! Everything is arranged! Even the dress! I've a meringue upstairs going stale!"

"I'm s-s-sorry."

"But you love me, James! And I love you! And together everybody loves *us*. We're the Donna and James Show!"

"But that's it, Donna – behind all those photo shoots and magazines spreads, I don't really love you and I don't like the life we're leading."

*   *   *.

The doorbell rang and Lana switched off the television.

"Hi," she said, opening the door and letting Stephen in. He followed her into the lounge and studied her. She looked unkempt and out of it. She obviously had already finished off what he had left her last night.

"I'm honoured you're choosing to be with me, instead of at your father's big party," he said, sitting down on the couch.

She shrugged. "They won't miss me."

"Get me some vodka," he instructed.

She got up, shuffled over to the drinks cabinet and poured a drink. Then she brought it over to him and handed it to him clumsily, spilling some on him.

"Watch it!" he snapped.

She turned away.

He patted the seat beside him. "Sit here."

She did as he instructed.

"Are you ready for your special present tonight? Congratulations, you're just about to move up the ladder and try the big boys' stuff. This will make what you had in the past look like child's play." He took out the bag and put it on the coffee table.

She licked her lips and reached over for it.

He gripped her wrist tightly. "Not just yet, baby. I want a favour first."

"The money is on the mantelpiece."

"Not just the money." He smiled at her.

*   *   *

"You're late!" snapped Ralph as Tony came into the hallway at Kildara.

"I'm sorry. I got held up at home." Tony felt shaky. He had gone upstairs and changed into his suit and then left the house, Nicole still sobbing.

"Come over here!" snapped Ralph. Tony followed him to a desk that was inside the front door of the house. "Just stand here for the night, and as people come in, get them to sign in." He turned around to Gloria who was resplendent in an evening gown.

"Gloria," Ralph was all sweetness and light, "Tony is finally here."

"Oh, all right." She looked seriously at Tony. "Now, I'm

very worried about any gate-crashers. We do not want a repeat of what happened at the Exclusive party. So take the invitation, check their name on the list, get them to sign in and only then allow them entry, do you understand?"

Tony nodded.

"Do exactly what Gloria says all night," warned Ralph before walking off.

Gloria nodded at Tony triumphantly, remembering how he had crossed her during the Affidavit photo shoot.

Tony looked around and there seemed to be a lot of guests already arrived, mingling and drinking champagne as a band played. He felt numb from his confrontation with Nicole.

*   *   *

"Will you be all right from here?" Eileen asked as she pulled up outside Kildara.

Ann nodded and clasped Eileen's hand. "Thank you for everything," she said. "In fact, thank you for everything over the years. What would I have done without you?"

Eileen smiled. "You make it sound as if you're saying goodbye! Sure I'll be on call in case you need me. I won't go far – so just ring my mobile if you need me, my dear. Off you go now – and enjoy yourself!"

Ann got out of the car, took a deep trembling breath and faced the house.

The smile faded from Eileen's face as soon as Ann's back was turned. She hoped and prayed that this was a good idea and would not lead to disaster.

Kildara looked exactly the same to Ann though it had been years since she had last seen it. People were walking past her. Glamorous people, all dressed up to the nines and laughing as they made their way into the party. She nervously followed them up the steps and through the main doors.

"Welcome. Please avail of whatever drink you want." Gloria smiled as people signed in and walked past her.

Ann immediately recognised Gloria and stood still for a second taking her in. She gazed around the hall to see if she could see Barry or Lana, but she couldn't.

She walked past the reception desk.

"I'm sorry, can I see your invitation please?" Tony said to Ann.

"Oh . . . I'm sorry. I don't have one." She looked at the young man and smiled.

"I'm afraid it's invitation only," said Tony.

"Oh, I didn't realise . . . I'm Barry's wife."

Gloria immediately turned around on hearing this and stared at the graceful woman.

"Barry Curtis's wife?" Tony asked, bemused.

"Yes. I've just come up from the country and –"

"I'm sorry – Ann, isn't it?" Gloria moved over, smiling brightly.

"Yes, it is," Ann smiled back at her.

"I'm sorry, but there is a strict rule here tonight. No invitation, no admittance."

"Oh, but I'm sure –"

"I'm really sorry but we have been instructed to make no exceptions to the rule."

Ann's smile fell.

Tony stared at Gloria in disbelief.

"I really wish there was something I could do, but I can't. You're not on the guest list. Now, I'm sorry, but I'm afraid I'm going to have to ask you to step out of the way and leave. There are people trying to get in."

Ann nodded, turned and walked out of the house and down the steps into the night.

*　　*　　*

"If you don't want money, then what do you want?" Lana asked, through bleary eyes.

"Just a little word in your father's ear," said Stephen.

"About what?"

"Exclusive. Kathryn Foy has been spending a lot of time away from the club what with one thing and another. I've been running that place better than she ever did. Maybe a new position could be found for Kathryn elsewhere."

"You want to be the manager of Exclusive?"

"Yep," he nodded.

She looked down at the drugs laid invitingly out on the table. "I'll see what I can do."

"You're a good girl!" He stroked her back. "I've been waiting a long time for someone like you."

She reached out for the drugs.

He put his foot up on the coffee table and pushed them out of her reach. "What's your hurry, baby. We've got all night. Don't want the party over before it starts, do we?" He gripped her shoulder and pulled her back on the couch. "Lighten up and relax," he said, "and give me a smile."

She forced herself to smile at him.

"That's more like it. Bet you didn't need any encouragement to smile at Cathal Fitzgerald, did you?"

She shook her head lamely. She was shivering slightly.

"You know, we used to date the same girl years ago."

"Did you?" She licked her lips and her eyes moved to the drugs again.

"Yeah, girl called Michelle...Of course everyone has a story like that, don't they? You know the kind of thing – my boyfriend's sister's uncle once went out with President Bush's secretary. Our own little claim to fame."

"I guess so," she nodded.

"So that's my claim to fame. I went out with a girl who went out with Cathal Fitzgerald – but I want to raise the stakes – do you hear me?" He grabbed her chin roughly and held it firm. "You're a mess tonight, do you know that?" he whispered. "And you want those drugs, don't you?"

She nodded.

He moved closer to her and put his lips on hers.

She brought a finger up and pressed it against his mouth. "I don't think so," she said crisply, smiling and pushing his mouth back with her finger.

He pulled back from her in astonishment.

She stood up and said quickly, "Thanks for the offer, and I know I've been a little low recently, but I'm never going to be that low."

He saw the bleariness was gone from her eyes, as they shone brightly. She pushed back her hair, and she wasn't shivering any more.

"What the hell is going on here?" he said, confused.

"And thanks for the offer of all this heroin, but I'll take a raincheck," she said brightly, "You might have been waiting all your life for someone like me, but I sure as hell haven't been waiting for you!"

He stood abruptly. "You think you're being very clever with whatever games you're playing, but you'll be sorry when you're coming on bended knees begging me for a fix in a couple of days' time!"

"I don't think so. I'm not going near that shit again, and I don't care what I have to do to stay away from it. It makes me into someone else, someone I don't want to be. Somebody I'm ashamed of. Oh, and I don't think I can recommend you for the manager's role at Exclusive under the circumstances – in fact I don't want you in my father's club any more peddling your shit. I'm firing you."

"You're in no position to fire anybody," he sneered.

"I think you'll find I am and I just have."

He moved towards her aggressively and went to grab her.

"Think about that very carefully before you do it!" said Cathal, coming into the room, "We already have drug-pushing charges against you – do you want assault as well?"

Stephen stared at Cathal as everything began to make sense. "I thought we agreed to stay out of each other's way!"

"Then you should have stayed away from Lana. I actually believed you wouldn't risk prison again by doing drugs. I admit, I was terrified you would go to the Press about me, but I honestly thought you deserved a break. Everyone deserves a second chance."

"I want you to clear that shit off my table and get out of my house. If you go near Exclusive again, I'll tell the police you were dealing drugs," said Lana evenly and confidently.

"And it would be straight back into prison for you," said Cathal.

Stephen turned quickly, grabbed the bags and put them into his jacket. "I wouldn't lose too much sleep over him, love," he said to Lana, "He's a loser. And a bit of fame and money could never change that." He walked out of the house and slammed the door after him.

Lana sighed deeply, then moved over to Cathal and embraced him. "Thank you so much. I honestly hadn't a clue what danger I was in."

"I couldn't believe it when I saw him coming to your house last night."

"If I had taken those drugs today, who knows where I would have ended up with him?"

"Lana, when you don't take control of your life, there's always going to be another Stephen around to destroy you."

"I know. The ironic thing is, my mother has spent all her life hiding behind walls because of fear of people like him. And then I just go and invite him into my home, into my life. I think I have grown up today."

"Come on," he said, smiling. "I think there's a party we have to get to."

*   *   *

"Clive, over here, quickly, take a photo of these people here!" Ralph was nearly hysterical. Most of the guests had arrived at this stage, and the Conways were almost in frenzy at the numbers of celebrities on offer.

Tony looked on from behind his table, feeling like an outsider.

"Hi, Tony!" said a voice and he turned to see Cathal and Lana come through the front door.

"Oh, hi!" Tony looked at Lana, who quickly nodded at him and walked into the party.

"Thanks for the tip off about Lana," Cathal whispered. "You've helped her more than you'll ever know."

"I'm sure," said Tony watching Lana as she was being greeted and kissed by Ralph and Margaux.

"Tell you what – join me for a beer later on. It would be good to catch up, okay?"

Tony nodded. Cathal smiled at him and went to join the party.

*   *   *

Ann Curtis stood at the side of the road, terrified at the noise and speed of the traffic. She looked an unusual sight to the passing motorists, dressed in a flowing gown and diamonds, and a few cars beeped their horns at her as they drove by. She felt convulsed with fear but struggled to fight against her panic. She knew if she gave in to it, it might overwhelm her. And here, far away from her quiet country haven, this time it might destroy her.

*   *   *

Kathryn strode through the crowd speaking into her walkie-talkie. "There are a lot of used glasses piling up near the band. Get them removed immediately!" She looked around the crowd. How she loved being in the thick of organising a good event! You'll have to kiss that goodbye soon when you start singing, she told herself.

There was a tap on her shoulder.

"Hi!" It was Cathal.

"You here with your date?" She raised an eyebrow and smiled cynically.

"I'm here with Lana, if that's what you mean!"

"You make a beautiful couple – the Press will be devastated when they find out it's all over," she said sarcastically.

He stepped a little closer. "I'm more interested in finding out if it's all over with us."

She sighed. "I know . . . Simeon was in a deep depression this morning."

"It's not right, Kathryn, leaving everything in limbo. You're going to have to make up your mind soon." He reached forward and touched her cheek.

"Sorry, Cathal – I need time. This is not an easy decision. I'd better go – there's some crisis at the front door." She moved away.

"Can I have a word, Cathal?" asked James.

"I guess. It's a free country."

"Well, at least until your man is elected!" James nodded over to Barry.

"Let's try to be nice, hey? We're all here courtesy of the man, so let's be good guests and wish him luck!" Cathal frowned. "Where's Donna?"

"She's not here. I broke the engagement off this evening."

"What?" Cathal was amazed. "What happened?"

"I didn't love her. We were the beautiful couple around town who everyone loved, and I thought that was enough for me."

"I thought you were made for each other!"

"It was all an act on my part. I really am sorry about what happened between us. I'm sorry if I ever upset you. I'll be totally honest with you – I couldn't take you going out with Lana."

"Why did that matter to you so much?" Cathal asked. "It seemed so – personal!"

"It was. We hated her because of who she was. We – me and Donna – we couldn't take it. When you became an item, everyone started focusing in on you two. We knew we could never match her father's wealth and I guess we were consumed with jealousy. If the truth be known, that *Hi Life* feature was the final straw – it completely focused on you two. We thought if we kept putting her down to you, you'd dump her."

"For fuck's sake, James!" Cathal looked disgusted.

"If the truth be told, I've always been jealous of you."

"Of me? Why? My life was always a fuck-up. You were the golden boy!"

"Who nobody ever paid much attention to. You were always the one who stood out, and wasn't afraid to stand out. I always wanted to be that. I loved when things went bad for you, because it made me feel better."

"James . . . I'd like to say it doesn't matter. But it does."

"Will you at least meet for a few drinks and we can talk properly?"

"I have to think about it."

"Ladies and gentlemen, if I could have your attention please?" said Gloria Reagan from a stage that had been constructed in the hallway.

Silence fell over the crowd. Barry was on the stage, as was Lana and some key personnel from the election.

"The election result for Barry's constituency is about to be called. On the screen above me, we will be going live to the constituency hall for the result. Please be aware there is an RTÉ camera crew present and they will be filming us for the news bulletins – so if I could ask you all to refrain from swearing too loudly!"

Laughter spread through the crowd.

Kathryn was on the side of the stage. She spoke into her walkie-talkie. "Turn the screen on now!" she commanded.

The television screen, a live link-up to the constituency

hall, came on. A dead silence fell on the crowd.

Then, when a portly sincere-looking man at the microphone on screen announced "I duly declare Barry Curtis elected!" there was an explosion of cheering at Kildara. The RTÉ camera began to move around the crowd, filming the scene.

Cathal grabbed Lana and hugged her. Lana hugged her father.

Gloria waited until the camera was directly focused on the stage. Then she stepped forward towards Barry and stretched out her arms to embrace him.

An elegant figure stepped in her way, blocking her from reaching Barry.

"I think you'll find this is my place," said Ann Curtis to Gloria. "And I never need an invitation to see my husband."

"Ann! What are you doing here?" said Barry, his face full of delight.

"I'm here for you," she said smiling, and they hugged tightly.

Lana, tears in her eyes, hugged both her parents. "Thanks, Mum, for coming. You'll never know what it means to me!"

"How long will you be staying at Kildara?" Barry asked, gazing down at his wife.

"For good," Ann said firmly.

CHAPTER 47

As instructed, Tony hadn't moved from reception all night and now he stared out at the crowd as they danced around to slow music, the excitement of the election result having died down. He looked at Barry and Ann dancing together like love's young dream, Lana dancing with Cathal and laughing loudly. Gloria Reagan nowhere to be seen. Kathryn Foy was marching around making sure the party was running smoothly. Ralph and Margaux had managed to attach themselves to a big Hollywood movie star and were not letting him go for dear life. And he was looking in on them all. Not a part of them. And never to be a part of them. Know your place – that's what Ralph had said to him. He was to be these people's servant forever. And he thought of Nicole at home, lost for good because he had tried to become one of them, and they had laughed in his face.

He walked from behind the reception table and out of the building.

* * *

"Thanks for making the party run so smoothly," Lana

said to Kathryn.

Kathryn nodded and went to move on.

"Cathal told me about you two," said Lana.

Kathryn looked worried again.

"He's mad about you. And if you don't go for it, you'll always regret it." Lana smiled at her, before going back to join the party.

*   *   *

There wasn't any sound in the house when Tony let himself in. There was only a light on in the kitchen. He guessed Nicole would be sleeping from exhaustion. He quietly walked across the sitting-room to Nicole's handbag, and reached in to get her office keys. Carefully he left the house, closing the door gently behind him. He drove through the city streets to her workplace where he opened the front door with the keys and walked upstairs to her office. He had broken out into a light sweat. He turned the key in her door and let himself in. He turned on the light and locked the door behind him. He crossed over to her filing cabinet and unlocked it with another key. Carefully he went through all the files until he came across Lana Curtis's. He took the file out and went and sat at Nicole's desk. He opened the folder and began to read.

*   *   *

The Channel 4 audience in the studio in London broke out in applause as Tina Cawley came on waving and smiling and sat down opposite Joanne Bailey and Seán on their music show.

Their show, *Music Movements*, had proved to be very

popular, a late-night show that mixed interviews with performances and some showbiz gossip.

Tina was dressed in a long white cotton dress, her hair long and braided..

"Welcome to *Music Movements*, Tina!" smiled Joanne.

"Martina," she corrected.

"Martina. You know, myself and Seán have been watching you on a couple of other shows recently and we're just taken aback by the new you."

"I know!" Tina smiled happily. "I'm just so much happier these days, and I think that's coming across."

"It's been quite a radical change of image," said Seán.

Tina sighed happily. "I'm just being true to myself. I went to India and really got in to the core of who I was and in a special ceremony at the bottom of Mount Salid I released all my negative energy."

"And have been the fans been supportive?" asked Seán.

Tina wiped away a tear. "They say my change has been an inspiration."

"Well, Martina," smiled Joanne, "I know you've been working on some new songs –maybe you could play us out with one?"

"I'm going to sing 'My Heart Is Mended'." She got up and walked to a piano.

Joanne looked into the camera. "Thanks for joining us tonight. See you next week on *Music Movements*!" And she winked at the camera.

Tina started playing and the camera zoomed in on her.

Seán, after listening to 'My Heart Is Mended', pulled a face. "What drivel!" he whispered to Joanne.

"Haven't seen you writing much good music recently either," Joanne said back.

A researcher ran up to her. "Your car will be here in ten minutes to take you to that party at Click."

"They'll have to wait – I need to freshen up." Joanne got up and walked backstage and through a maze of corridors to her dressing-room. She sat down in front of the mirror, remembering the conversation she had with the programme producer the previous night. He was planning on moving to New York and trying his luck there. He had some good ideas for programmes. He had invited her to go with him and said she would be perfect to front a programme for him there.

But Seán wasn't part of the deal. She thought about America. She would love to make it there. She was becoming very well known in the UK. She and Seán were on every guest list in London. Going to New York would mean becoming just another pretty face trying to make it again. But if she did make it . . . if she did . . .

CHAPTER 48

Nicole knew she looked terrible when she got into work. But she didn't care. She was all cried out at this stage and didn't know what to do. When she went into her office, she immediately knew somebody had been in there. She went to the filing cabinet. The person had been very careful replacing Lana's file. But not careful enough for somebody who kept things as immaculately as Nicole did at work.

*   *   *

Tony didn't turn up for work at *Hi Life* the next day. But he did meet the editor of the *News Of The World*. It took one hour to do the deal. He was to become a new show-business correspondent for the paper. He then immediately changed his mobile phone number. He went home and packed all his belongings. He sat for a while looking around the house, remembering all the good times they'd had together. But he knew their relationship was irretrievable. It was time to move on. There was nothing even to be said. He felt incredibly sad about how things had worked out. He thought back on his time at *Hi Life*, and how it had shown him a new world, but wouldn't let him in. In the end he would find his way into that world using a different route, and regardless of the havoc he would leave behind him.

He got up and took a last look around the house. Then he closed the front door behind him and dropped his keys through the letter box.

*   *   *

The front page of *News of The World* read:

'Exclusive – Newly-Elected Barry Curtis's Socialite Daughter's Drug Habit and Credit-Card Fraud. Unstable Wife's Reclusive Life – by Tony O'Brien'

*   *   *

Lana stretched out in bed, smiling to herself and feeling great. She had been out for dinner with her parents the night before and couldn't remember enjoying herself more. Ann seemed better than she had for years and Barry seemed delighted to have her up at Kildara permanently. And Lana felt like a little girl sitting between them, talking non-stop about nothing in particular.

Her phone rang, and she reached over to answer it.

"Lana," said Patricia's concerned voice, "have you seen the front page of *News Of The World*?"

*   *   *

Gloria Reagan swept into Barry's office with such force that the door slammed against the wall with a bang.

"Have you seen this?" she almost shouted, hurling the

newspaper on the table.

Barry took it up and slowly paled.

"I told you that daughter of yours was a liability. She's dragged the whole election down. After all my hard work! After I masterminded your election with such precision! She and her stupid antics have ruined everything!"

Barry stood up. "Shut up!" he shouted.

Gloria was shocked into silence.

"Don't ever talk about my daughter like that! Now the election is over, so I don't require your services any more. Goodbye, Gloria!"

Gloria blinked a couple of times. "But –"

"Forward your bill and I'll see you're paid promptly."

Gloria stared at him as he sat down, throwing the paper in the bin, and continued with his paperwork. She then turned and walked quickly from the room.

* * *

"I know – I know. I'm as angry as you are about this," Ralph said excitedly down the phone to Victoria Harton. Margaux sat opposite him.

"How could you allow something like this to happen?" Victoria swung around in her chair in her office at the European headquarters of *Hi Life* in London. "To allow an undercover reporter from a paper to come into *Hi life* and use us to expose such a prominent member of society."

"He wasn't undercover! He was just a kid on the make!"

"Well, he's made it!" Victoria snapped. "Our reputation has been severely affected. How can the rich and famous – our friends – trust us again, when an insider betrays them in such a vicious way?"

"I've been trying to contact the bastard but he's changed his mobile number!" said Ralph.

"I've already had three exclusives cancelled because of this!"

"I can't believe it! In here pretending to be so diligent and he was working away on his own agenda all along!"

"I really have no option after this but to ask you to step down as the franchise owner of *Hi Life* in Ireland."

"You can't take away *Hi Life*!" Ralph said pleadingly down the phone.

"I just did."

"Give me the phone!" ordered Margaux. She reached over and took it from him. She smiled and her voice was smooth as velvet as she purred down the phone. "Hello, Victoria, it's Margaux here. It's very unfortunate what has happened, but I'm sure if we all work together we can pull through it . . . Victoria? Victoria?" Margaux's face turned sour as she slammed down the phone and her accent reverted to her original Dublin working-class one. "The bitch hung up on me!"

*   *   *

Lana's first reaction when she saw the paper was to run away and hide. Either hole up in her house and don't answer the phone or the door, or take a flight abroad for a long while. But she didn't. She got ready, went down to her car and immediately drove over to Kildara, where she found her parents in the lounge.

"We were just going to come over to you," said Barry.

"All I can say is sorry," she said. "I've let you down very badly."

"How did they find all this out?" asked Ann.

666

"The guy who wrote the story was a colleague of mine at *Hi Life*. He was obviously spying on me." She thought about Nicole. "He had a few connections to people who knew some intimate details about me – and exploited me"

Ann got up and hugged her. "We're here for you, Lana, darling," she said.

"I'm sorry for everything I've done. But I'm not going to run away from it all. I'm going to stay here and put my head in the air and say I've made a few mistakes, but I'm moving on."

"That's my girl!" said Barry, coming over, and then the three of them were hugging.

* * *

A press release was distributed to the media from Barry Curtis's media office.

"Due to recent unwelcome publicity revolving around his family, Barry Curtis has decided not to take the parliamentary seat to which he was recently elected. He wishes to express gratitude to all his supporters during the campaign and regrets not being able to fulfil his role. But it is a case of priorities, and for Barry his family and their privacy come first."

* * *

Tina Cawley sat in Sylvia's office with Cathal and Sylvia.

"You were a disaster!" Sylvia declared. "The feedback from your recent blitz of British programmes was terrible. The fans have deserted you in droves."

"I just can't understand it" wailed Tina. "What's wrong with all the fuckers? Why do they want to see me miserable?"

"This new image of yours just isn't working," Sylvia sighed.

Tina gulped. "Is my career – over?"

"Tina, you are a talented musician and singer and neither I nor MPI are ready to write you off. Okay, so the angry Tina Cawley has had her day, but nobody wants that new act you've been pulling either."

"It isn't an act!" Tina objected.

"Save it. You've heard those two songs that Cathal wrote. I think they would be perfect for you, and I have a definite image I want you to take. We might just be able to salvage your career. But, for once in your life, you have to do exactly what I say!"

Tina stood up. "I'll talk to you later." And she left the room.

"What do you think?" Sylvia asked Cathal.

"You've devised a great image for her, a more sophisticated image. It should work with those songs you've selected."

"You don't mind working with Tina Cawley?"

"Hey – I'm glad to be working with anybody!"

"Incidentally, have you spoken to Kathryn?"

"Not for a few days."

"I've left a few messages on her machine and she hasn't returned them. Could you tell her to get those signed contracts into me asap? Jack Better is screaming at me for them."

*   *   *

Lana moved back into Kildara for the time being. Despite everything that was going on, she had never felt happier. It was wonderful being there with her parents, at last a happy family unit. There was so much to sort out between them all, and they were managing to do it, carefully, slowly, sometimes painfully.

Lana didn't bother going back into *Hi Life*. She didn't even phone to give in her notice. She was taking this time out to decide what to do with the rest of her life. Often her thoughts would drift to Cathal. She enjoyed the happy memories and she felt gratitude to him for helping her to believe in herself. Not only had Cathal saved her from herself, but more dangerously from Stephen Rourke. Sometimes her thoughts would drift to Tony, the guy she had never given too much thought to. She supposed she had taken him for granted and never really bothered to get to know him well. And it wasn't who she was or how wealthy she was that he resented – it was this knowledge that she considered him an afterthought. Even when they had slept together, she had considered him irrelevant. And she had paid the ultimate price. There was stuff in the newspaper that could only have been got from her file. And she knew he had stolen that information from Nicole. When she thought back to that moment when Nicole confronted her with the truth, she was engulfed with shame. She guessed Tony and Nicole had split up. When she thought of Nicole, she thought of the woman with whom she had spent hours giving away the most intimate details of her life to, but about whom she knew nothing in return. She would have liked the opportunity to apologise, and out of curiosity had rung up the practice once but had been told that Nicole had left. She would have liked the opportunity to get to know her as a friend. She had been living life too close to the edge and had finally been found out and now had to live with the consequences.

It was evening time and her parents had gone out for dinner. She went around the house, double-checking that all the doors and windows were locked and the alarm system on. Funnily, since the escape she had from the dangerous life Stephen Rourke was leading her to, she had almost become paranoid about security. Nearly as bad as her mother had been, she thought.

Her mobile rang.

"Hi, Lana, this is Victoria Harton. Just over in Dublin for a couple of days, and wondered if we could meet up?"

CHAPTER 49

Nicole sat in her office, looking at all the packed boxes around her. She thought about how chaotic everything had been. Going home and seeing Tony had left. Contacting the landlord and saying she was moving from the house. Telling the partners in the practice that she was leaving. Handing over her clients to her colleagues. And now here she was, clearing out her office. She had spent a lot of time with friends and family deciding what she wanted to do. She had eventually decided that she would go to Australia for a while. Australia seemed as good a place as any. Who knows, she might decide to stay there if she liked it. She was just waiting for her visa to come through. She needed a break from her profession. She had always thought she was so in control and was such a professional at work. But after the whole Lana episode, she wanted to get away from therapy. She was dismayed when she thought about Tony and how he had betrayed her, not only by sleeping with Lana but by then stealing her files to negotiate a new life for himself. She tried to piece together how her perfect relationship, her perfect life had come to this. Now she wouldn't have other people's problems to deal with all the time, she might be able to think about her own life and figure out what went wrong.

*   *   *

Kathryn looked down at the contract sitting in front of her on the kitchen table. Still unsigned. She started counting out the pills for Simeon's afternoon take.

Why couldn't she bring herself to sign the contract? The choice was simple. Sign the contract and go to live with Cathal and follow her dreams and her heart. Or stay here, continue working at Exclusive and nursing Simeon, the safe option.

He mobile rang and she saw Cathal's number on the ID. She got up and closed the kitchen door over. "Hi!" She kept her voice low.

"Hiya!" Cathal sounded cheerful. "Just in town and wondered if you were around for a coffee."

"I can't . . . I've some stuff to do."

"Where are you?"

"At home."

"Oh, all right. I was in with Sylvia and she said to get those contracts over to her immediately."

"Oh, sure. I'll get on to it straight away."

"Haven't seen you for a while."

"I know – I'd better go, Cathal. I'll talk to you later." She felt bad hanging up the phone. Simeon came bleary-eyed into the kitchen.

"Who was that?" he sighed.

"Just Kelly."

*   *   *

It felt weird walking through reception at *Hi Life* and

seeing Tony's empty desk. As she looked at her own desk, she felt she was missing the place. She walked down the corridor and into the main office to find Victoria Harton seated at Ralph's desk.

"Lana, my dear!" She stood up, held out her arms and kissed both Lana's cheeks, "What can I say? I'm simply destroyed with what that Tony O'Brien did. Such a betrayal! Not only did he betray one of our regulars, but also a work colleague and somebody I hope I may consider a good friend!" She smiled warmly.

Yep, Ralph and Margaux might be gone from here, but the bullshit still remains, thought Lana.

Both women sat down.

"How have you been keeping?" asked Victoria.

"Fine, you know, just getting on with things."

"I'm not going to waste time, Lana, as I have a flight to catch today. I have been very impressed by you since you came to work at *Hi Life* in Dublin. The exclusives you've managed to get for us. The sponsorship deals you put together. Advertising revenue up twenty-five per cent. And it's all because of your hard work and vision!" And connections, Victoria added mentally. "You've been like a whirlwind in this place. What I would like you to do is step in here and take over from the Conways now that they've gone."

"Me?" Lana was incredulous. "But I don't think I have the experience!"

"All you need is a good editor to take care of that side of things, and you get on with the business side as the publisher."

"You've really taken me by surprise. I'll need to think about it."

Victoria was more than impressed with the girl's

ability, but there had been a terrible backlash from Tony's exposure. What better way to mend *Hi Life's* reputation than Lana's appointment, showing she, the victim, still had total confidence in *Hi Life*.

"What would the Conways say?" Lana asked.

"They're history now, darling. They'll lie low for a while and I'm sure come up with some other magazine idea in a year or two. But they won't be coming back to *Hi Life*. Why don't you take it on as a trial? See how it goes. If you like it – stay. If you don't – nothing lost?"

Lana thought. "Okay!" she said, laughing. "All right, I'll do it!"

"I'll tell you one thing, you won't be bored. Isn't that what you want?"

Lana smiled and said, "All my life"

674